George A.  Lawrence

**Anteros**

a novel

George A. Lawrence

**Anteros**
*a novel*

ISBN/EAN: 9783337349561

Printed in Europe, USA, Canada, Australia, Japan

Cover: Foto ©Andreas Hilbeck / pixelio.de

More available books at **www.hansebooks.com**

# ANTEROS.

A Novel.

BY

THE AUTHOR OF "GUY LIVINGSTONE."

*NEW EDITION, IN ONE VOLUME.*

LONDON:

TINSLEY BROTHERS, 18, CATHERINE STREET, STRAND.

1873.

# ANTEROS.

## CHAPTER I.

'A GRAND old place.'

Under this formula, all Loamshiremen bred and born spoke of Templestowe; and if any stranger sojourning within their gates, on the occasion of his first visit, expressed dissent or disappointment, the same was set down to the natural captiousness or envy of the alien. And yet—excepting, perhaps, the ruined tower of a dovecot, and two or three brasses in the church, which had been altered and restored till above the foundation scarcely a stone remained as the builders set it—the place can boast of nothing so old as the elms flanking the main avenue.

The ground slopes gently upwards from the park gates to the portico; and, seen from the furthermost end of the vista—the avenue is hard on a mile in length—the house does look rather imposing; but the nearer you approach, the more clearly you recognise that it has no real claim to grandeur, beyond that which attaches to all things solid and vast. It is, indeed, one of the ponderous edifices in whose sadness of aspect there is no solemnity; bearing the stamp of the early Georgian era, when disciples, less artistic than their master, followed in the track of

B

the respectable architect, to whom even his coevals allotted no kinder epitaph than—

> Lie heavy on him, earth ; for he
> Laid many a heavy load on thee.

Where there is wealth of flowers and greenery, it is not possible beyond a certain point to trammel Nature ; but formalism has done nearly its worst in the planning of the gardens ; and in the square methodical parterres there is no more rest or refreshment for the eye than in any other piece of gorgeous patchwork.

Within doors things are not much better. There are some fair family-portraits, marked, for the most part, both male and female, by a certain hardness of feature that even Lely could only partially tone down. Amongst the other pictures lining the state-rooms and galleries, there is scarcely one that would tempt an amateur to linger before it, or a dealer to loosen his purse-strings : however useful otherwise in their several generations, it is abundantly clear that Art has never been largely patronised by the Ashleighs of Templestowe. Nevertheless, at the time whereof I speak, the Loamshire people stood by their show-place with commendable fidelity, and would hear nought in its disparagement. This was somewhat remarkable, considering their relations with its tenant.

Ralph, Baron Atherstone, had singularly little honour in his own county, and few men had better earned unpopularity. In early youth he had sown the seeds of enmity far and wide, amongst high and low, not only by a haughty, overbearing demeanour, but also by frequent outbreaks of a violent temper, in which he showed scant respect to the age or station of such as thwarted him. People grew shy of inviting him to their houses, when they found by experience that it was always an even chance that, before the night was out, Ralph Ashleigh would make the place too hot to hold some one or more of their guests; and though his tall figure, and clear-cut face, and gloomy eyes were picturesque enough when seen for the first time, they rather marred than heightened the conviviality of the county gatherings.

Neither was he one of those who contrive to balance, by favour with the other sex, disfavour with their own. For awhile the Loamshire matrons were disposed to condone the eccentricities of the heir of Templestowe; but there are limits even to diplomatic indulgence, and ere long there were frowns and significant waggings of the head at the mention of his name, and from the list of eligibles it was virtually erased. Surely it was better to watch humbler fruit, red-ripe for plucking, than to waste time in trying to find a passage through the briers and thorns encompassing the rich grape-cluster which, if more attainable, would still have seemed hard and sour. As for the maidens, after a few experiments, they, so to speak, shook off the chalk-dust from their sandals—such things were in fashion then—in testimony against Ralph Ashleigh. His bearing towards womankind was not boorish or rude, and in their presence his unruly temper was invariably curbed; but shyness, or positive aversion, would have been far easier to deal with than that hopelessly unsympathetic reserve. The most wily coquette could not boast of having drawn from him any greater encouragement than the indulgent, half-contemptuous smile that grown men bestow on the gambols of tricksy childhood.

Lord Atherstone—a sober, stolid widower, entirely wrapped up in agricultural pursuits when he was not embroiled in politics—looked upon his heir with mingled fear and dislike, much as a placid old spaniel may regard a wolf-cub by some accident, or freak of nature, mixed up with her long-eared litter. He was shrewd enough to guess that even if Ralph's misdemeanours were not openly cast in his teeth at the next contested election, the weight of his son's unpopularity would in more than one case turn a wavering scale for the Yellows.  And this—when for generations past the heir of Templestowe, if he did not personally seek to sit for the county, had always headed the Blue canvassers.  That the sins of the children should be visited on the fathers, was a conversion of terms by no means squaring with the baron's creed.  Altogether, it was no wonder if he rose freely at the first hint of his son's predilection for soldiering, and forwarded that purpose with alacrity.  Before he attained his majority, Ralph Ashleigh was gazetted to a cavalry regiment which, soon after, was very suddenly ordered to India.

According to the regular roster, their turn ought not to have come for three years at least; and there was much grumbling at the caprice of the War Office —unaccountable to such as did not happen to know that the great House to which the chief of that famous corps belonged, was more liberal of its influence than of its purse towards its cadets; and that he himself, being proud as he was poor, preferred economising on double *batta* to exchange or retrenchment at home. But the news excited little consternation or regret in Loamshire; and, when Ralph came down for a hurried farewell visit, though many were charitable enough to wish him "God speed," few were hypocrites enough to wish him " quick return."  At his departure no tears were shed; unless it were by his old nurse, a fat and foolish person, much given to strong waters, and by one other—" a strange, flighty girl," the neighbours called her—daughter to the tenant of the Home-farm at Templestowe.  Mary Gilbert never held up her head thenceforth, but pined and dwined away till a fever, somewhat prevalent in those parts, took her off within the year.  Whatsoever her secret was, she held it fast—fast as she held a ring—not a wedding-ring—round which her fingers were locked as they grew stiff and chill.

Time passed on, and only by hearsay was the link

maintained between Ralph and the folks at home; for his father and his agent were the sole recipients of his rare, formal letters, and they contained nothing interesting to the world at large. But his name ere long became familiar to many who had not so much as heard of Templestowe. Though no great war just then was a-waging, there were troubles and fierce flashes of revolt all along the Beloochee and Afghan frontiers, and in gazette after gazette he was mentioned with still increasing honour. Indeed, Ashleigh owed his rapid promotion much less to powerful influence than to his real deserts. He had thrown himself, from the first, heart and soul into his profession; and if Fortune chose to befriend him, she found him neither slothful nor self-indulgent. The vulgar vices to which so many subalterns on foreign service, endowed with few counteracting resources of their own, have succumbed, seemed to have no hold upon him; and the violence of temper, which was still his besetting fault, was subjugated by a sense of duty. He could show his teeth, and use them, too, savagely enough on occasion; but in all matters of discipline he was as thoroughly and unconditionally submissive as a trained bloodhound. In the exploits by which his renown was won and sustained, there was evidence not only of valour verging on recklessness, but of cool foresight and a certain strategic skill; and before he got his troop, those who were rarely wrong in such predictions averred that this man would assuredly set his mark upon his time.

Considering how often by necessity, oftener by choice, he was in the forefront of danger, Ralph had rather exceptional luck in keeping out of serious harm's way. He had had plenty of flesh-wounds; but he esteemed these as lightly as a sempstress does a needle-prick, even if not as conducive to his general health; however, in a certain skirmish, he got separated from his men, and before they dragged him out of the *mêlée*, the tulwars had cut deeper than usual—so deep that they almost reached the life. As soon as he could safely be removed, Captain Ashleigh was invalided to the hills, under positive orders not to attempt to return to his duty till convalescence was complete. He had the option of going home on sick-leave, but would not hear of it.

Though his brother-officers were certainly proud of him, and though he had never quarrelled with any one of them, he was anything but a favourite. This, added to his inveterate dislike to putting pen to paper even in rude health, made it unlikely that he would keep up much correspondence with the regiment. Some six months later, an eminent civilian travelling down country lodged for the night in their cantonment, and was naturally questioned as to the last scandals afloat in the hills.

"There's nothing worth speaking of," the Collector said ; "there has been rather a stagnation in gambling since that General Order came out, and all the immorality goes on in a humdrum, domestic way. I think, when I came away, people were talking about a legitimate engagement as much as anything else ; and that will be stale news here, for the man is Ashleigh of yours."

The Colonel was a thorough disciple of the *nil admirari* school, and had many imitators in the corps, especially, it is needless to state, amongst the subalterns ; but a murmur of surprise ran round the mess-table at this intelligence, and the Chief himself, opening his sleepy eyes wide, sat upright in his chair as he said—

"Ashleigh engaged ? Impossible—unless some Begum has drugged him. Surely none of those sabre-cuts could have touched his brain."

"There's no Begum in the case," the other replied ; " and no foul practice either that I've heard of, unless sick-nursing comes under that head. She's the daughter of Bertram of our service—the Busy Bee they call him, because he's always at everything in

the Ring; but clever as he is, the young lady—
they're all young ladies till they are married, you
know—has hung rather long on hand, and I didn't
think he would have placed her so well. She's safe
for a coronet, I believe ? "

"Yes; and a well-gilt one, too," the Chief said,
with a slight sigh of envy—his own possible peerage
was a very empty honour. "It's one of the best
estates in the shire, and improving every year. The
girl's a beauty, I suppose, or a genius, or a wonder
of some sort ? "

"Not a bit of it—a pale piece of affectation, with
no voice, even if she knew how to sing, and has a
temper, unless she is belied. But some of these
affinities would beat the devil to explain."

Whether these last words were literally true does
not much signify; but assuredly, both then and thereafter, human speculation utterly failed to unravel the
process of Ralph Ashleigh's entanglement. Probably his somewhat fantastic notions of honour had
been cleverly worked upon; but this is the merest
conjecture, for he took no man or woman into his
counsel. Even Lord Atherstone did not hear of the
marriage till long after it was an accomplished fact.

It was not, strictly speaking, a happy match, though
it was troubled by no domestic broils. Indeed, an
occasional storm would have been rather a relief to
the dead monotony of that couple's existence; but
Mrs. Ashleigh, like many spiteful people, was exceedingly timorous, and stood in too great awe of her
husband to favour him with any displays of the
temper hinted at above; she vented it freely, though,
on her native household, and occasionally got up a
very pretty quarrel on a small scale with some one
or other of her military or civil compeers. In Ralph's
own demeanour there was but little change, except
that he had grown, if anything, rather more *brusque*
and stern; yet he seemed more inclined to frequent
the company of his comrades, and sat later in the

ante-room than had been his wont in bachelor days
Certainly, when on active service, his new responsibilities made him not a whit more careful of life or limb.

He was husband and father within the same year.
No living child was born to him besides this one ;
and the boy, weakly from his birth, throve so ill that,
before he was five years old, it was deemed expedient
to try what an English climate could do towards
rearing the heir-presumptive of Templestowe. Colonel
Ashleigh—he had got a second brevet-step by this
time—supported the separation from his family with
singular equanimity ; indeed, it was noticed that after
their departure he brightened up till he became
almost companionable. Would he have been as well
content if he had known that he would never look
on that pale peaked face of his wife again ? Perhaps
he never cared to ask himself that question, much less
to answer it.

Mrs. Ashleigh's first impressions of Templestowe
were not rose-coloured ; nor did her after-experience
of the place greatly tend to alter them. When the
news of his son's marriage first reached him, Lord
Atherstone fell into a fury quite foreign to his stolid
nature. The mere fact of his not having been consulted was in itself a grave offence ; and when afterwards he was certified that the bride's father was an
impoverished civilian of rather shady repute and
obscure, not to say ignoble, descent, it is not to be
wondered at if many suns went down on the old
baron's wrath, and if to the end of his days he never
doubted whether he did well to be angry. Though
anything but a polished person at the best of times,
he was old-fashioned enough to be incapable of rudeness towards any woman who had not broken the
social law ; but his courtesy towards his daughter-in-
law was of the cast-steel order ; and upon the rare
occasions when they were alone together, it was, if
possible, stiffer than when the world's eye was upon
them.

Querulous almost from her birth, that poor woman never before had such real cause for bemoaning herself. How often, and with what regretful longing, her dull weary eyes turned back towards that far East, is not to be told. Life in the dullest cantonment, the most desolate station to which either as maid or matron she had been condemned, seemed enviable compared with vegetation in the dreary mansion wherein, during the height of summer, a chronic chillness seemed to prevail; and where, after a year's sojourn, she felt more of a stranger than on the first day when she set foot in its great echoing hall. The wives and daughters of the neighbouring squirearchy, when they paid their rare formal visits, seemed to take their cue from Lord Atherstone, and were so inflexibly civil, that a quarrel with any one of the set, had she been that way inclined, would have been as impossible as intimacy: even the mild excitement of bullying her dependants was denied her; for she was almost as much afraid of the pampered menials of Templestowe as of their lord; and her own *ayah*, after a brief residence on free soil, acquired unholy ideas of independence, and did not submit so passively to persecution as in aforetime. She was fond of her boy in her weak, superficial way; but he was not a child that even a doting mother could have been proud of, and, even at that early age, showed signs of having inherited no small portion of her own fractious temper and incapacity for disinterested attachment.

All things considered, during her residence at Templestowe, Louisa Ashleigh must have laid up no small store of expiation of her divers offences —they were not grave ones, be sure—against written and unwritten codes; and when the wan Apparitor, with scant notice given, knocked at her chamber-door, he found her, if not so fit as could be wished, not very loath to follow him.

Independently of the suddenness of the catas-

trophe, Lord Atherstone was much shocked and
disconcerted by his daughter-in-law's demise; but,
if the truth must be spoken, with the regret that he
had not shown her more kindness whilst it was in his
power, there mingled a vague sense of injury. He
considered there was a want of *savoir vivre*, in more
senses than one, in her having thus precipitately
shifted on to his shoulders all the responsibilities
attaching to the education of a weakly, wilful child.
However, his letter of condolence to his son was
couched in much more cordial language than he was
wont to employ; and he was a good deal disappointed at the formal reply, wherein he was entreated
to manage the little Philip in all ways as should
seem to him good. Colonel Ashleigh offered no suggestion on the subject, except that the boy should
be sent to school whenever he became troublesome
at Templestowe.

Though he grumbled not a little at first, Lord
Atherstone never found the charge so troublesome
as to be tempted so to relieve himself thereof; and
after awhile, even if the boy's health had not given
fair excuse for not exposing him to the small
hardships of public-school life, the grandsire would
probably have found some other pretext for keeping
him under his own roof and eye. The two got on
well enough together in a queer way. No one could
call Philip troublesome: he had not spirit enough
to be insubordinate; his fits of temper were the
veriest crackle of fire among thorns; and his acts
of disobedience were committed in such a cautious,
unobtrusive fashion that a less complaisant tutor
might have afforded to ignore them. It was not
in Lord Atherstone's nature to pet or spoil any living
creature; but he certainly was more indulgent to
his grandson than he had been to his own children;
and the boy probably felt as much grief as his nature
was capable of, when the old man's death left him for
the nonce entirely destitute of natural guardians.

The new Lord Atherstone had never been troubled with home-sickness since he sailed from the Downs; yet, under ordinary circumstances, he would probably have considered that the urgency of private affairs demanded his immediate return. However, the circumstances in India were anything but ordinary. The embers of revolt, strewn all along the frontier of the Suliman range, no longer smouldered; and few, who had watched the progress of events there, doubted that ere long there would be a blaze not to be quenched without much blood-shedding. Lord Atherstone was no politician; but from long frontier experience he was less likely to err than many of more sagacious foresight; and besides, natures like his are not often misled by their instinct when they scent battle from afar. He had now for some time been in command of his regiment, and had brought it to a state of efficiency remarkable even at that epoch, when more than one famous cavalry-corps chanced to be stationed in India. He assuredly did not rule by love; and, though his sense of justice was seldom swayed either by temper or prejudice, it was utterly merciless. He was unsparing both of his tongue and of the lash—the triangles were an honoured institution in those days, you will remember — yet officers and troopers, though they grumbled without ceasing, were wonderfully proud of their chief, and would scarcely have had him exchanged.

Now, when the results of his labour were to be put to sharp practical proof, was it likely that Ralph Atherstone would let another reap, and mayhap spoil in the reaping, all that he had sown, only that he might go and tend at home a puling child and a fair inheritance—ay, though the child was his sole heir, and the inheritance was his family's before the Great Charter was signed? Was it likely that he would sit still in his place and listen to sedate deliberations, diatribes against radicalism, and exhortations to rally round the constitutional standard — were these couched in eloquence more sonorous than often echoes through the upper House of St. Stephen's—knowing all the while that at that very moment, through the clear air of Eastern dawn, his own trumpets might be ringing, and that before the hour was out his own guidon might be rocking in the fray, whilst the troopers, whom he loved perhaps better than they wist of, were approving the skill taught on so many patient parades?

Of the many passions that possess a man, there is probably not one so engrossing, when it has thoroughly gained the mastery, as the lust of war. During all the fifteen years of Italian campaigning, I doubt if Hannibal, when he was at his weariest, ever looked longingly back on the palace towering above the gardens of Megara, or on the fertile domains that called him master, beyond the Punic Sea : more grateful to his eyes, be sure, was the marsh by Trasimene, or the plain watered by Aufidus —the burying-ground of Æmilius the Consul and forty thousand more.

Lord Atherstone never hesitated as to the course he should pursue. He sent a packet home by the next mail, containing his will duly attested, and certain necessary instructions and powers, expressed at greater length and in more business-like form than might have been expected from one of his habits. In the event of his own death, there were named as his son's guardians the family lawyer and a cousin—Hubert Ashleigh by name—who held a family-living not far from Templestowe. He wished the sole charge of the boy, for the present, to be offered to the said cousin, annexing to the offer such a liberal maintenance as a poor parson would be very unlikely to refuse. There were probably many other documents of like nature, though scarcely of like importance, penned that night ; for on the

morrow the march to the front was to begin, that
ended on the banks of the Sutlej.  Some, had they
been so minded, or had they had heart for the jest,
might have imitated the quaint testament ascribed
to Rabelais: "I owe much; I possess nothing;
the rest I leave to the poor." Yet none of these
lay down on his camp-bed with a lighter sense of
responsibility than did the twelfth Baron Atherstone
when all was signed and sealed.

Throughout the stirring times that ensued Ralph
did his duty—it may be not a whit more thoroughly
than many who did not achieve one tithe of his
renown.  He had always had exceptional luck in this
way, and it clave to him still.  His daring was
proverbial in an army whose besetting fault of rashness was encouraged by its Chief's example; and
he seemed to have a knack of always being in the
right place at the right time; but this would not
altogether account for it.  Certain figures in some
*tableaux* always stand out prominently, howsoever
the grouping may be changed.  In the lull that, as
all men know, happened after Sobraon, whilst the
Sikh leopard lay licking his wounds, and preparing
for a last struggle that was to end in his taming,
Lord Atherstone's regiment was ordered home.  He
himself, travelling overland, reached England some
weeks before his men; and spent the interval, as
might have been expected, almost entirely in setting
his house in order.

There is no reason to doubt that, had he so willed
it, he might at this time have become exceedingly
popular in the neighbourhood.  Graver offences than
the rudeness or violence of youth are forgotten or
annulled in sixteen years; and it was some time
since Loamshire had been able to boast of a real
native hero.  So olive-branches from all parts of the
county were strewn before the gates of Templestowe,
and its master needed only to stoop and gather them.
Active conciliation was needless; if he had met con-

gratulations with the merest form of acknowledgment, or even submitted to them passively, the result might have been different; but this was precisely what Lord Atherstone would not or could not do. He declined to receive all addresses except one from his own immediate tenantry; and when upon the first occasion of their meeting at Quarter Sessions, the Duke of Devorgoil, as the mouth-piece of his brother-magistrates, began a set complimentary speech, Ralph cut him short at the third sentence with the remark,—"That he was infinitely obliged; but that he could not admit that a soldier deserved any thanks for carrying out his orders." The shock of an irreverence to which he had not been accustomed since he left Eton, interfered for a week at least with the mighty magnate's digestion; and, though he did not deem it advisable absolutely to put Ralph under ban, he thenceforth considered him as a most pernicious person, more likely to lower than to elevate the credit of the peerage.

It is hardly to be supposed that any sane man would deliberately set himself to alienate the good-will of his fellows; and it may be that Lord Atherstone himself saw and even regretted his mistake when it was too late; nevertheless, up to the time of which we are speaking, he had not exerted himself to amend it.

For some three years after his return from India they saw little of him in Loamshire; for he was always with his regiment. But a difficulty with one of his officers brought Lord Atherstone into collision with the War Office; and the authorities, for once espousing the weaker side, appended to their decision something very like a reprimand. Ralph made no remonstrance at the time, and never was heard to allude to the subject again; but within that same week his papers went in for exchange to half-pay. Thenceforth he resided almost constantly at home.

# CHAPTER II.

TEMPLESTOWE was not much cheerier than it had been in the old lord's time. Philip Ashleigh of course had been brought back, so soon as a permanent establishment was again organised there; but he did not get on nearly so well with his father as he had done with his grandsire. The two differed, physically and morally, as widely as any two created beings can differ—having nation, language, and station in common. Setting other dissimilarities aside, Philip was endowed with a constitutional caution verging on timidity; and this unlucky failing was a perpetual exasperation to his father. You may fancy whether it was pleasant to a man who had spent his life in the saddle, and whose cross-country riding up to very late in his life was a standard of hardness in more counties than one, to see his heir clutching nervously at the pommel whenever the quiet beast that bore him increased its pace beyond the steadiest trot or the smoothest canter. Patience and judicious encouragement might have done somewhat—not much perhaps—to amend all this; but Lord Atherstone was by no means equal to the occasion: he chose rather to allow his son to grow up in his own way, and follow his own caprices, furnishing him with ample means to gratify them, had they been much more extravagant.

Philip Ashleigh was neither dull, nor especially weak-minded. Though his intellect was not large or elastic enough to take any wide range, he was possessed of a certain astuteness of observation and

correctness of insight into matters passing immediately around him.  He very soon recognised that
he was no favourite with his father, and never
likely to be : the discovery did not much afflict
him ; but it produced a certain sense of injury not
altogether unpleasant.  He was very like his mother
in some things, and never felt really comfortable
without a grievance.  Considering that he might
have been idle from year's end to year's end, had
he been so disposed, it was rather creditable to
him that he should have made such good use of
his time with his tutor.  He was a great reader
besides on his own account, and by the time he
went up to Oxford, had amassed a larger store of
general information than nine out of ten can boast
of who have not to work for their living.  At
college he made few friends, and not very many
acquaintances.  Though his conduct was perfectly
blameless, even his tutors were fain to allow that
they liked men better who gave them more trouble.
Somehow you could not look at his cold, cunning,
supercilious face without feeling sure that, if he
walked uprightly, it was because it suited his con-
venience and inclination ; and, if by any chance he
did stumble, it was not likely that any kind, or
brave, or genial impulse would set him straight again.
He took a fair though not a brilliant degree ; and,
within a year, was returned for a borough, just without the borders of Loamshire, that happened oppor-
tunely to come into the market.

Lord Atherstone was not a little astonished when
he was made aware of his son's political aspirations ;
but he was pleased to boot.  Ambition, ever so
mildly developed, was a sign of manhood at all
events ; and thenceforth he treated Philip with more
outward consideration.  Ere long a greater surprise
awaited him.  In the autumn next but one ensuing,
he was informed that, subject to his consent, his
son proposed to contract an alliance with Lady

Marian Kerneguy, sole unmarried daughter of the Earl of Dalwhinnie.

The process of Philip's wooing must have been rather curious to witness. Probably some such thought crossed his father's mind as he pondered over the announcement, bending his grizzled brows the while; but he asked no questions on this point, nor indeed on any other, beyond what were absolutely necessary. There were no valid objections to the match : the fact of the bride's being portionless could not be considered as such when the bridegroom was sole heir to Templestowe ; and, in point of descent, the Ashleighs could claim no advantage. Two of the other sisters. had married honourably — one magnificently; and if, judging from her photograph, the Lady Marian's outward charms were not equal to her reputed mental advantages, that was a matter emphatically for Philip's consideration.

So Lord Atherstone's consent was not hard to gain. In the matter of settlements and allowances he behaved with a liberality that almost staggered the canny but conscientious Scotch lawyer acting for the other side ; and before the marriage took place, a wing of Templestowe was newly furnished and arranged for the residence of the young couple, when-ever they should choose to inhabit it. They did choose to do so pretty often ; always indeed out of the parliamentary season, when they were not visiting in Scotland or elsewhere ; for Philip Ashleigh was far too prudent to keep up an establishment of his own when he could live at free quarters, and his wife was not likely to put extravagant ideas into his head, or to grumble at any reasonable economy.

On the whole, things went on much more smoothly under the new arrangement. The household, of course, was entirely maintained by Lord Atherstone ; but Lady Marian managed it precisely as she pleased, and to do her justice, she did not abuse her authority.

She was not prepossessing certainly   At first sight

C

her sharp, eager face produced rather a disagreeable impression ; but she improved on acquaintance ; her keen eyes, if sometimes satirical, were rarely—very rarely—spiteful ; and her off-hand manner, when you got used to it, had a certain piquancy. Not that she did often speak or act off-hand. She had much more cleverness than she got credit for, even with those who were supposed to know her best; and had, thus far, rarely failed carrying out any one of her fixed purposes. For instance, she had set her mind, whilst almost a girl, on being mistress in her father's household so long as she should remain unmarried ; and in this, without the advantage of being either the eldest or the youngest child, she had succeeded. She had also determined to marry in due course of things, and, if possible, to marry a particular class of husband. In the furtherance of this purpose she displayed an infinite tact and patience. She was perfectly aware of her personal disadvantages when placed in daily comparison with her sisters — two of whom were strikingly handsome, whilst the third was almost faultlessly beautiful—and was wont to avow this in their family-circle. The most suspicious of the other three never thought of imputing to Marian anything so absurd as rivalry ; and she strove too earnestly and unaffectedly to help the course of their several wooings to run smooth, to be accused even of envy. But, truly, none of those who carried away brides from Dalwhinnie quite squared with Marian Kerneguy's ideal of a consort. She had no fancy for being a cipher, or even a subordinate power, in any household, however magnificent ; and yet nothing was further from her intentions than to stoop to a needy or plebeian alliance where, by mere virtue of her maiden rank, she might expect to rule.

Altogether, the odds were tolerably heavy against Lady Marian's being soon suited ; nevertheless, these long shots do occasionally come off. In her twenty-second summer the shadow took form and substance

in the shape of Mr. Ashleigh. She never from the
first deluded herself as to his character, or set him up
on a pedestal whence sooner or later he must have
tumbled. She guessed him to be selfish, and cold-
hearted, and fretful; of narrow, though fairly cultivated, intellect; anything but the stuff, in fine, out of
which a woman's or a people's hero is moulded; but,
with judicious management, she felt sure something—
enough at least for *her* purpose—might be made of
him; and, feeling confident in her own nerve and
address, no more thought of rejecting him as a suitor,
than a trainer would of casting a promising though
plain colt for showing temper in his first rough trial.

The thread running through Philip Ashleigh's matrimonial intentions would be much harder to follow.
There was not a grain of passion or romance in his
nature: even when moved to anger, he always delivered himself with a certain reticence and reserve;
and it was scarcely to be presumed that any softer
emotion would tempt him to speak unadvisedly. He
had liked Marian Kerneguy from the earliest days of
their acquaintance; there was similarity in their
literary tastes, and she could talk well on many or
most of the subjects in which Philip was interested;
but he was never absolutely fascinated; and it is not
probable he would ever have offered her his hand, if
he had not, after mature consideration, come to the
conclusion that he might look long and far before he
found any helpmeet so likely to be useful to him in
his future career. Being exceedingly opinionated,
and not specially sagacious, Philip made many mistakes in life: in this instance he assuredly made
none.

The world only saw in Marian a cleverish managing
sort of a woman, with a ready tongue, and a certain
knack for making rough places in conversation
smooth; and her husband himself never acknowledged
her aid except by a few words of careless thanks; but
this did not make it the less valuable. The member

for Heslingford's oratorical displays were still hampered by the pragmatic formalism which had marked
his maiden efforts; but the accuracy of his statistics
was always unimpeachable: if he seldom threw any
new light on a subject, he not seldom brought to
bear upon it one or two facts which had escaped the
notice of abler debaters; and his points, such as they
were, were put with a certain neatness. Thus much
even his depreciators were fain to allow—confessing,
moreover, that they "didn't think he had it in him."
How some of these would have triumphed, if they
could have guessed what infinite pains it had cost
Marian Ashleigh, overnight, to instil into her states-
man the result of her own patient toil and research!
But none ever did guess it. Philip himself, as was
aforesaid, accepted his wife's assistance as a matter
of course, scarcely worth acknowledgment; and the
wife was more than content it should be so. She had
abundance of ambition; but it was vicarious, like that
of myriads of women who have lived before, as well
as after, *Sic vos non vobis* was penned.

When Lady Marian came to reside at Templestowe,
she determined, if it were possible, to establish the
same supremacy there, so far as household matters
were concerned, that she had maintained at Dalwhinnie; and this intention was carried without the
semblance of a struggle. Furthermore, she earnestly
desired to bring her father-in-law under her dominion;
and it is very probable that here too she would have
succeeded, had it not been for the peculiarity of Lord
Atherstone's habits, which to a great extent rendered
him inaccessible to domestic affinities. The fierce
physical energy had not abated within him when no
more real work was left to do; it was bound to find
vent somehow, and it did so in the commonest of all
ways—indulgence in the rough out-of-door sports that
send a man home weary, if not satisfied. Amongst
these, hunting stood first and foremost with Lord
Atherstone. He was a five-days-a-week man, in the

most literal sense of the word. Very often, hours before Philip Ashleigh had summoned up courage to face a raw, gusty morning, his father would be sending his cover-hack along, right in the teeth of the squall, towards some distant meet in the heart of the great grazing-grounds that lie beyond the Loamshire border. Frequently, if he returned late after a hard day, Lord Atherstone would dine in his own rooms; so that sometimes a week would pass without the other inmates of Templestowe once seeing his face. This was the manner of his life throughout the winter and the early spring; as soon as the weather was open enough to give an outside chance of sport he was off to a salmon-river in Norway, whence he came back straight to his grouse-moor. The autumn was the Ashleighs' visiting-season, so that they were not likely to be at Templestowe when Lord Atherstone returned thither.

Thus perhaps it was more from lack of opportunity than from any other cause that Lady Marian had failed in attaining any substantial influence over her father-in-law. That Lord Atherstone could treat any woman residing under his roof otherwise than courteously was impossible; but his manner towards Marian from the first was marked by a certain deference; and it was evident that he entertained no small respect for her opinion in matters both great and small. On one point only was he utterly inaccessible: he never could be induced to accompany Marian to any one of the ceremonious festivities given in her honour when she came into Loamshire after her marriage; and, when she hinted that Templestowe ought to make some return in kind, she was met by such a hopeless negative that she never ventured to repeat the suggestion. Lord Atherstone was not at all incensed; he was simply impracticable.

"You may fill the house to the roof-tree with county-people if it please you," he said; "only wait till I'm out of it. I shall go to Norway early this year, and

you may have a dinner here every day through the
Whitsuntide recess, you know.  The Loamshire folks
and I understand one another pretty well by this
time.  I can't alter my habits even to suit such an
occasion as this."

Lady Marian was far too wise to argue the question; neither did she avail herself of the permission
to throw open Templestowe in the absence of its
master.  Somehow, it was perfectly understood
throughout the county that the seeming discourtesy
was in nowise to be imputed to the Ashleighs; but
people shook their heads, more disparagingly than
ever, when they spoke of Lord Atherstone.  The
interdict extended only to Loamshire people, and both
Philip and Marian knew that they had perfect liberty
to invite to Templestowe any one of their kinsfolk or
acquaintance; but they used this privilege very sparingly; and, during the three years that elapsed
between their marriage and the opening of this tale,
almost the only guests who sojourned there were certain of Ralph's ancient brethren-in-arms.

# CHAPTER III.

It was set down above that, in the height of the hunting-season, sometimes a whole week would pass without Lord Atherstone and his children meeting face to face. But this is scarcely correct; for there was no exception to the rule of the three breakfasting together on Sunday morning. This was part and parcel of the day's routine; just as much as was attendance afterwards at morning-church, irrespective of the state of the weather. It is to be feared that deep religious feeling had little to do with the baron's exactitude; neither in other respects did he seem specially solicitous to set a good example to his dependants: but he had come to look on the whole performance in the light of a duty; and, this once settled, he would no more have neglected any portion thereof, than when on service he would have omitted to hold church-parade.

It is one of those dark, raw, wintry mornings on which things both animate and inanimate are apt to look their worst, with the exception of the fire, which is imperiously attractive. On Philip Ashleigh's sharp, narrow face there are evident signs of discontent, as he trifles listlessly with his toast and coffee. He is a poor breakfast-eater at the best of times, and now his appetite has entirely failed before the prospect of a chilly drive, followed up by a two-hours' sitting in about the draughtiest church in Loamshire; during the latter half of which he will have the privilege of listening to a divine, with whom he chances to differ on every conceivable point—theological, social, or moral. He is debating in his own mind whether he really does not feel unwell enough to give himself a sick certificate; but somehow, though he is sure the excuse will pass unquestioned, he does not feel equal to encountering the cold, incredulous smile that will be certainly seen on Lord Atherstone's lip when he accepts the evasion.

Lady Marian, though tolerably cheerful, all things considered, is not precisely chirping. She has not the remotest idea of shirking her duties; but they are none the pleasanter for that; and Philip has been unusually tiresome this morning. She has kept her temper admirably, as she always does; but it is uphill work, and the drag will tell sometimes.

Lord Atherstone's face as he sits over against her, though changes of temperature cannot be supposed to affect him, looks unusually set and stern. There is a good deal to study in that same face, though assuredly little to admire. The features are too marked ever to have been handsome, even before the brow was so furrowed, or the hollows under the temples and prominent cheek-bones so deeply sunken. The eyes are very keen and bright; but bright with a hard metallic lustre, and appear smaller than they really are, from being set so far back under overhanging brows. The mouth signifies little, for it is almost entirely hidden under a huge grey moustache of such dimensions as are seldom seen in Western Europe, trailing almost to the shoulder-blades; and this is the more remarkable from the cheeks and chin being closely shaven. Lord Atherstone is not much above middle height; but an extreme erectness of carriage, added to an angular gauntness of outline, rather enhances his stature. The lack of flesh has plainly nothing to do with ill-health; but is partly natural, partly produced by incessant exercise. Whether on foot or in saddle, Ralph carries his years exceedingly lightly; yet, it must be owned, he looks them all.

"I wonder why the post is invariably late on Sundays?" Philip begins. It is rather hard that he is not allowed to finish even his complaint in peace; for, while the words are on his lips, the door opens and the letters are brought in.

If, as many men assert, the inevitable post is amongst the crosses of life, it is one that may be much alleviated or aggravated, according to the time and season of its befalling us.

I remember a certain country-house, attractive in all other respects, that, for not a few, was utterly marred as a place of sojourn by reason of the manner of the postal delivery. With a terrible punctuality, in the very middle of breakfast, the ominous leathern satchel appeared, and its contents were distributed to whomsoever they might concern by the white hands of the *châtelaine* herself. Any one fond of studying the weaker side of human nature, might have gained some useful hints by watching this ordeal—no lighter word is sufficiently expressive. The womankind, as a rule, came out of it jauntily enough. If there was any matter dark or dangerous hidden under those dainty envelopes, they carried it off with the superb placidity of absolute innocence, or of experienced diplomacy; but the men bore themselves far otherwise. Out of many, I can only recall one who seemed exempt from the general embarrassment and discomfort. He was an elderly bachelor of untold wealth, and of such a repellent exterior, that no human creature was likely to address him except on business pure and simple. The miserable subterfuges and attempts at dissimulation practised by the others were painfully comic to witness. The worst perhaps, because it was most transparent of all, was the assumed carelessness of one individual, who, after just glancing at his letters, always laid them aside as if they could contain nothing worth prompt perusal. Now this man was in the bonds of fealty, more or less legitimate, to a despotic beauty who also was num-

bered in that fair company; but, all prohibition notwithstanding, he persisted in keeping up communica-
tion with a favourite cousin, with whom, according
to his own account, he maintained quasi-fraternal
relations. Every letter, however harmless, issuing
from this especial quarter, was considered by the
reigning power as nothing less than treasonable;
and the criminal's condition, whenever the post-bag
brought one of these contraband missives, was a
caution to all conspirators, present and to come.
Without interchanging one glance with the imperial
eyes that watched him from the other side of the
table so scornfully, he knew that his assumed indifference did not for a moment impose upon her, or
even upon other less interested spectators; he probably felt a real curiosity to see what the letter might
contain; and nothing is so provoking as small futile
sacrifices. Yet, day by day, he used to enact the same
dreary farce with a power of self-abasement truly wonderful. And all this took place in a house whose
hospitality is limitless, and where every guest has the
largest license to amuse himself according to his own
good pleasure.

It was only on Sunday that the post-boy reached
Templestowe at such an inconvenient hour, and the
letters were always sorted before they were brought
into the breakfast-room. That morning there was
a huge packet for Philip Ashleigh, a smaller one
for his wife, and one single note for Lord Atherstone.

He opened it hastily, but read it very slowly; for
it only contained about four lines, and it was fully a
couple of minutes before he laid it down. Lady
Marian, after just glancing at the outsides, threw
down her own letters, and looked forth, so to speak,
from her ambushment behind the great silver urn.

Lord Atherstone's face was singularly impassive,
as a rule: even when he was very wroth, its expression seldom altered in the least; the words,
hard, bitter, or cruel as they might be, issued from

lips that moved scarcely more than an automaton's; and his complexion was too deeply tanned and weather-stained to change. Nevertheless, there was one sign whereby a very close observer might guess that emotion of some sort or other was stirring within him : this was a slight darkening of colour round the prominent cheek-bones—you could not call it a flush; it was rather as if the skin had suddenly become strained there, and so checked the free circulation of the blood. The effect never lasted above a second or two, and very few, even of those who had known Ralph most intimately, had ever noticed it ; but of these few Lady Marian was one.

Her eyes rested now on her father-in-law's countenance as long as they could do so unobserved; then they fell on the half-open letter on the table, and rested there yet longer. Lord Atherstone had not followed the direction of her glance, and it was more mechanically than because he had any suspicion of being scrutinised, that he folded up the note and thrust it into his breast-pocket; but, before he did so, Lady Marian had had time to satisfy herself that the handwriting was unmistakably feminine. If she had read the note through, it probably would not have helped her much in her mystification. It was dated from a quiet West-end hotel, and contained only these words :—

"Dear Lord Atherstone,

"You have probably forgotten that I promised to let you know when we were passing through town. It is to clear my own conscience that I write to tell you that we are here for a week on our way to Devonshire.

"Very truly yours,

"Isabella Shafton."

Never in all her life had Marian Ashleigh been

so thoroughly *intriguée.* She was not in the habit
of judging any of her fellow-creatures by a very high
standard, and did not give her father-in-law credit
either for blameless morality or exalted philosophy.
Under the influence of violent or vindictive passion,
she held him capable of committing himself even
to the verge of crime; but from any temptation proceeding from womankind she had till now supposed him safer than most saints that have flourished
since the time of Saint Simon of the Pillar. For
three years she had watched narrowly, though quite
unobtrusively, his goings-out and comings-in, and
had contrived to be furnished with tolerably accurate
accounts of his demeanour and way of life when
he was absent from Templestowe; and neither personal observation, nor report had led her to believe
that Lord Atherstone had ever lingered in female
society a minute longer than was absolutely required
of him by courtesy—much less that he had shown
the faintest predilection for the company or conversation of any individual.

But Lady Marian was too astute not to be aware
that her chain of evidence was not altogether perfect. There were two or three weak places, if not
gaps, that prevented the other links from being
quite trustworthy: she could only argue on probabilities after all; but these made up a strong case—
so strong that, now, with her surprise and apprehension there mingled something of the disgust of
a mathematician who, after working out a long
problem in dynamics, finds the result vary materially from his calculation. She was very careful to
prevent her eyes, when they met Lord Atherstone's,
from betraying either curiosity or vigilance; nevertheless, she was aware that he avoided them, as he
addressed himself to his meal with a haste and
eagerness quite disproportioned to his apparent
appetite. There was a conscious look, too, about
him which provoked Lady Marian intensely. When

she spoke, it was with a peevishness quite foreign to her usual manner.

"I wish I could afford to keep a town correspondent, as the country papers do; then one might have a chance now and then of getting a letter worth reading through. I can guess at the contents of mine without opening them—they are all written to pattern. Philip, I hope you have had some bad news this morning; that would be so much better than none."

Her husband looked up at her rather sulkily. He was so unused to anything like a display of temper on his wife's part that he supposed she was jesting; and, considering the weather and the circumstances, thought the levity ill-timed.

"What nonsense you talk, Marian!" he said. "It would serve you right if you were to be taken at your word. But I've no news—good, bad, or indifferent. My letters are all official or on business. You may look through them if you like."

"And answer them too," she said, shrugging her shoulders. "It's a great proof of confidence, Philip, certainly. I'm hardly so grateful as I ought to be, especially as to-day is popularly supposed to be a day of rest. And *you* haven't a crumb of news for me, Monseigneur?"

There was a gleam of intelligence, if not of mischief, in her bright black eyes; and, for the second time, Lord Atherstone's cheek darkened as he looked up and met them.

"I'm sorry to say—not one," he answered slowly. "Mine was but a scrap of a note, and the writer is no acquaintance of yours."

Marian Ashleigh was a very intrepid person, and stood in much less awe of her father-in-law than did most of those over whom he had authority; nevertheless, she was not bold enough to push questioning further just now.

Breakfast was soon over; and, during the drive

to church, only a few desultory remarks on indifferent
subjects were exchanged betwixt the three.  The
sermon was rather above the dead level of rural
eloquence; but the good seed fell on stony ground,
that was scattered over the manor-pew.  Philip
Ashleigh being, as has been aforesaid, in a state
of chronic antagonism to his rector, invariably made
a point of looking bored from first to last, even if
he refrained from overt movements of impatience;
but his wife, as invariably, tried to counteract this
by a show of attention admirably acted if it were not
sincere.  On this occasion she was quite unequal
to the task; and the rector could not have conscien-
tiously commended the example of any one of these
his chief parishioners.  There was no mistaking the
meaning of Lady Marian's restless, wandering glances;
and the most confident of preachers would scarcely
have supposed that Lord Atherstone, as he sat
motionless, with folded arms and bent head, was
pondering over the discourse then in delivery.

The burthen of the leaden sky had begun to descend
in a sharp sleet-shower as they drove homewards.
The look of injury deepened on Philip's face; and
Lady Marian, by no means so sensitive, could not
repress a shudder as she drew her sables closely
round her.

"I don't envy you your ride to cover to-morrow,
Monseigneur," she said.  "Is the meet very far off?
Don't you almost hope it will freeze?"

Lord Atherstone gazed out of the carriage window
as he answered,—

"I don't think there'll be a frost; at least, not a
lasting one.  But it don't affect me: to-morrow,
I'm going to London for two or three days.  If you
have any commissions for me, Marian, you had
better let me have them to-night."

He did not look round till he had quite finished
speaking.  If he had done so a second sooner, he
would have seen the lady's firm white teeth press her

lower lip somewhat sharply; but she replied in her usual careless off-hand way—

"Thanks; it's very kind of you, especially as I dare say you have quantities to do. It must be real business that takes you up to town just now. I won't be troublesome. If you will bring down two or three tiny parcels, that will be all."

Throughout his life Lord Atherstone had cherished a singular dislike to any form of evasion. He carried this to an extreme, and had been more than once involved in a serious scrape simply because he would blunder on straightforwards, instead of availing himself of a side-door of escape invitingly open. Even now, though evidently disinclined to talk, and though he did not for an instant admit her right of questioning, he did not choose to leave Lady Marian under what he—knowing nothing of her secret thoughts— held to be a false impression.

"It isn't exactly business that takes me up," he said, gravely; "still, I may be a good deal occupied. However, you needn't scruple about your commissions; I shall have time enough for them, and to spare."

She muttered a few words of thanks, and then dropped the subject; neither was it renewed. It was only at dinner that the others saw anything more of Lord Atherstone.

When Marian had any threads of thought to unravel she infinitely preferred being alone; but to-day this could not be. Philip had got into a fashion of doing most of his letter-writing in his wife's morning-room; why, it would be difficult to say, for he rarely consulted her, and still more rarely employed her as his secretary—feeling a sort of satisfaction in getting through his own work in his own way. Perhaps it was pleasant to vent his peevishness on another person, however unsympathetic; for Marian, though she humoured and managed her husband wonderfully well, declined to encourage mere fretfulness. As a

rule she rather encouraged his presence than otherwise; but on this particular afternoon he was decidedly in her way.

With a real anxiety in her mind, it was inexpres-
sibly irritating to see Philip disquieting himself
about such trifles as how best to answer the vague
application of some meek constituent, who "hoped
Mr. Ashleigh wouldn't forget him if anything turned
up in his line." However, she kept silence, and her
temper to boot, till the last epistle was finished, and
Philip, cowering over the fire, indulged in a steady
bout of grumbling.

"If there's one thing I hate more than another,"
he began, "it's being hurried over one's correspondence. What with church-going in the morning, and
the absurdly early hour the post leaves at, it is a
scramble from first to last; and, of course, there are
more things to answer on Sunday than on any other
day  But it's quite of a piece with all the other
arrangements, or disarrangements, of this house. To
get the least possible amount of comfort and con-
venience at the highest possible price, has been the
rule ever since I've known it."

Marian Ashleigh's voice, though generally cheery
enough, was not soft in any of its inflections: there
was an incisiveness in it now which, even to her
husband, sounded strange.

"You have always disliked Templestowe, I think,
Philip. Would you like to make the experiment
of living elsewhere? If you would really be happier,
it might be worth trying."

He glanced askance at her again, much as he had
done that morning at breakfast; but this time it
was quite evident she was not jesting.

"What have my likes or dislikes to say to it?" he
inquired. "Beggars cannot be choosers. You don't
suppose I'm Quixotic enough to think of setting up
house for ourselves, whilst we can live at free
quarters?"

"Scarcely beggars," she said, in the same hard, cold tone; "at least, I have not been brought up in such magnificent notions of penury. When the settlements were drawn, our allowance was considered, by those who ought to know best, as amply sufficient to maintain a separate establishment; and so it would prove, I don't doubt, with fair management. I have never hinted at such a thing, because I'm perfectly content here, and because I see the wisdom of laying by for a rainy day; and we *have* laid by—not a great *magot*, but enough to start us if we chose, or if we were obliged, to walk alone."

"What on earth are you driving at?" he said, more fretfully than ever. "Of course we don't choose; and as for being obliged—what reason have you for supposing we have outstayed our welcome? You are rather a favourite with my lord; and, to do him justice, he would never want to get rid of me unless we quarrelled. I have steered clear of that so far, and I am not likely to begin at this time of day. Is it only a crotchet you have got into your head, or have you taken offence at something?"

She smiled—not quite so pleasantly as was her wont.

"I'm not given to crotchets that I'm aware of, or to take offence either, especially when none can possibly have been meant. Monseigneur and I are, as we have always been, perfectly good friends. But, Philip, with your talent for discovering rocks ahead, I do wonder that it has never occurred to you that our tenure here need not necessarily depend on your father's good-will. Suppose he were to marry again?"

Ashleigh started from his stooping posture as if he had been galvanised; but he so far controlled himself as to mask his astonishment under an angry laugh.

"That *is* a crotchet with a vengeance," he said. "Why, I should just as soon expect to hear of my

D

father's playing the mountebank in Heslingford
market-place, as of his proposing to any woman,
gentle or simple. Look at his age."

Lady Marian's eyes glittered with covert satire.
She could not help realising how many more of
all the essentials of youth were still to be found in
Lord Atherstone than in his son. In a question of
a hard day's work, comparison would have been
absurd; for Philip, from his childhood upwards, had
been something more than an imaginary invalid:
but in point of vitality, and freshness of energy, his
inferiority would have been equally evident. It was
somewhat mortifying to Marian to recognise this fact;
nevertheless, she did recognise it fully; and Philip's
cool way of ignoring it almost provoked her to
retort uncourteous. But she had never yet said a
severe, scarcely ever a sharp, word to him, and she
refrained herself now, only saying quietly,—

"I don't think his age has much to do with it;
his elders marry every day: yet I own that, up to
this morning, I had as few misgivings on the subject
as yourself. I don't feel quite so confident now.
I'm not going to make any mystery about it. You
didn't notice, I dare say, that Monseigneur only got
one letter this morning; indeed, it was not a letter,
it was only a short note; but it brought a change
on his face that I've noticed only twice before. On
both of those occasions he was angry — fearfully
angry; this time the change was more marked than
I have ever seen it; but he was not vexed, I am
certain of that—just as certain as that the note was
in a woman's handwriting. He's going to town
to-morrow—not on business, remember."

Philip was one of those who up to a certain point
are very stocks of dogmatism, but who, directly they
feel the ground giving way under their feet, begin
to flounder about miserably, invoking assistance
from far and near. Though he never by any chance
deferred to it in public, and very seldom in private,

he had an immense respect for his wife's judgment;
and his blank, helpless stare betrayed a conviction
that she had not shot far wide of the mark now.

"Suppose — suppose it is so?" he stammered.
"What can we do?"

Probably some indefinite idea relative to the
statute *De lunatico* was floating in his brain, but it
took no substantial shape. Lady Marian laughed
in her turn. With all her consideration for her husband—she really made the best of him to herself no
less than to others—the sight of his complete discomfiture was too much for her sense of humour.

"Do! Why, absolutely nothing but watch and
wait; and we shall not have long to wait. Monseigneur could not keep the secret if his life depended
on it, unless perhaps it were the secret of his failure.
It may be a false alarm after all. At any rate, as
the Rector observed this morning—I don't believe
you heard it, and I confess I heard little more myself
—'Sufficient unto the day is the evil.' That applies
to wedding-days as well as to others, I suppose. I
don't mean to fret until I know what or whom I have
to fret about; but I've been all this morning puzzling
over this till I've got a headache. I am going to try
to sleep it off after I've sent the letters away; so, if
you mean to stay here, you must ruminate silently."

Ashleigh was very discontented. He would have
liked to have gone on speculating and complaining,
in his purposeless way, indefinitely; but he knew by
experience that, when his wife desired to be left
alone, she became inaccessible as an obstinate oracle.
So, muttering and mumbling, he took himself off to
the library, which, next to the room he had just
quitted, was his favourite place of resort — he was
still a great reader in a desultory fashion—and got
through the afternoon as best he could. He and
Marian did not meet till dinner-time, when the head
and front of the house, and of the presumed offending,
was present.

Philip was remarkably silent throughout the meal; but, when he could do so unobserved, levelled at his father such furtive, suspicious glances as a timid person might cast at a man supposed to carry about him some terrible weapon likely to explode unawares. However, Lord Atherstone seldom troubled himself about his son's good or evil temper; and Lady Marian made as much conversation as he cared for; so the evening passed off smoothly enough on the whole.

# CHAPTER IV.

THIS will be as convenient a time as any to take up, for your benefit, the link wanted in the chain of Lady Marian's reasoning concerning her father-in-law's proclivities or antipathies in the question matrimonial.

On his way southward from Scotland, in the previous autumn, Lord Atherstone had fulfilled a promise of some standing, by turning aside to the shooting-lodge of an ancient comrade who dwelt on the hither-side of the border. General Percy was a bachelor, inveterate and irreclaimable; and one might almost have expected as much to hear under his roof the echo of ghostly footsteps as the rustle of silk or muslin. Indeed, he himself looked somewhat ashamed when he confessed to his friend that their party was not purely masculine.

"They are about the only relations I have left," he said apologetically,—"and blood's thicker than water, especially up here in the north; but I wish they had chosen any other time for their visit. Women never seem to think it possible they can crowd you, either in a house or in a carriage. I couldn't well refuse to receive them either: it would have seemed unkind just now; for Isabel Shafton has had a good deal of trouble lately about that boy of hers, and she's always asking my advice about him. I wish she'd asked for it before she put him into the —— Hussars. They went a fair pace when you and I remember them; and they have made it much hotter since—a great deal too hot for Miles Shafton to live with. I hope my cousins won't bore you ; we haven't found them much in the way so far —indeed, we scarcely see them except at dinner."

Whatever his private prejudices might have been, Lord Atherstone's misgivings—if such a word ever really expressed the state of his feelings — were negative, not positive. Marian Ashleigh was quite right in believing that for many years he had never sought or willingly put himself in the way of feminine society ; but, when it was inevitable, he accepted it with perfect equanimity, and, in spite of a certain taciturnity and reserve, appeared sufficiently at his ease therein.

"I am not quite such a savage as I look, Percy," he said, "or as they make me out in Loamshire. You needn't have taken the trouble to account for your cousins' presence here. It would have been very unlike you, if you had put them off. It'll be rather a relief to hear something talked about at dinner besides shooting ; I've had nearly a surfeit of that lately."

Though when at home Lord Atherstone, as you know, kept most irregular hours, in another man's house he was the pink of punctuality. An echo was still lingering in the dinner-gong as he crossed the stone-paved hall. The other inmates of Kirkfell, it seemed, did not keep quite such military time ; for, passing through the half-open door, he perceived that the drawing-room had only one occupant. He had certainly no eye for artistic effect ; but on the threshold he stopped still, almost holding his breath whilst he stood at gaze.

A woman's figure, thrown out in relief against the dusky red light streaming through the westward window—nothing more ; for the face was averted. It was a remarkable figure to be sure. Too tall even for the heroic standard of female proportion ; yet of such wonderful symmetry that few would have taken an inch from its stature, or wished an outline fuller or finer. The lady's head was bent over some flowers

that she was tying together; but from the curve of
the neck it was easy to guess that, when erect, it would
be carried not less haughtily than gracefully.

This was the picture that Lord Atherstone studied
with more attention, perhaps, than he had yet bestowed
on any masterpiece either of nature or art. His
footsteps had made no sounds on the flags of the
hall; so that his entry was unnoticed, and his contemplation was only disturbed by his host's voice
close to his shoulder.

"You are more than punctual, Atherstone. I am
glad of it; for I needn't make this first introduction
so formal. We are too old comrades for you and any
of my kin to meet quite as strangers. Lena, I rely on
your help to make Lord Atherstone thoroughly at
home at Kirkfell."

The lady had turned with a start; but, as she
came forward slowly, and swept nearer and nearer
—her ample skirts of filmy white seeming to bear
her up like a cloud—her manner was remarkably
self-possessed, and her few words of welcome did not
sound like a mere form of courtesy. The autumn
day was closing in fast, and Lena Shafton's back
was turned towards the fading western light; yet
Ralph Atherstone perused her face not less thoroughly
than if they met under the broad glare of noon.

The first feeling of many men looking on that face,
after they had admired the figure, would have been
disappointment. Except a pair of large brilliant
brown eyes, it hardly contained a feature which a
critic, and not a captious one either, might not have
depreciated. The nose, though not ill-shaped, was
something too broad, and wanted clearness of outline; the cheeks, though soft and smooth, wanted
roundness; the lips, ripe and tempting as they were,
might have been more delicately chiselled; and two
ranges of faultless white teeth did not help to make
the mouth—decidedly too large—look smaller. It
had been matter of wonderment to many of Lena's

fast friends, to say nothing of her rivals, that, from her *débutante* days until now, so few had been found to contest her right to rank amongst reigning beauties. Perhaps it was her imperial way of self-assertion that imposed on people irresistibly; and it was only in her absence—when they were looking at her photograph, for instance—they confessed that they had admired despite their judgment. Ralph's keen glance took in all the defects set down here; only it was not as defects that he noted them, but rather as items harmonising perfectly with the entirety of a type of womanhood differing from, if not excelling, any that he had looked upon yet.

So, and never otherwise — sleeping or waking, whether it were frowning or smiling, passionate or cold, enticing or repellent—that face appeared to him whilst his life endured.

If there be such a thing as love at first sight—I believe that modern science has not eliminated it from morbid pathology—it would be difficult to fix the term of age which insures to either man or woman perfect safety from infection. But it was nothing approaching to this that Ralph experienced now. It was rather such a dazzling and confusion of the senses as might have assailed one of the champions of Scandinavian story, who, after long wandering through a desolate land, where sparse sun-gleams scarcely lit the sullen horizon, and scanty lichens seldom peered above the eternal rime, suddenly found himself over against the gate of a witch-garden, wherein all manner of strange fruits and flowers seemed to blush and blossom under a tropical glow.

Partly by choice, partly from force of circumstances, in former days—wholly by choice of late—Lord Atherstone's life had been very solitary; but if, through all these years, fair faces had been as plenty round him as bluebells in spring-time, it is possible that he might have kept the even tenor of his way,

till he met **Lena Shafton.** If the horoscope of such
men could be read, it would be seen that a singular
—perhaps one single—conjunction of influences is
needed to bring about a certain end : this conjunction may occur only after long delay—it may be,
never ; but when all the conditions are fulfilled, the
result is inevitable.

Whatever Ralph felt, you may believe that he
betrayed it by no sign. Indeed, his manner was so
remarkably formal, that Miss Shafton thought that,
with the best possible intentions, it would be rather
difficult to make such a guest feel himself at home
anywhere. Nevertheless, her first impressions were
not unfavourable. Lord Atherstone's appearance
struck her as being decidedly picturesque in the
*vieux grognard* style ; and her large brown eyes dwelt
on him, with a curiosity rather less languid than they
usually deigned to bestow upon strangers. Before
the three could have begun a conversation, had they
been that way minded, the door opened again, and
Mrs. Shafton came in.

A handsome woman decidedly—handsomer, perhaps, if judged by the rule and canon of beauty,
than her daughter, in spite of her forty-odd summers ;
but that she had known care and trouble was evident ;
and she carried these less lightly than she did her
years. Though her brow was still smooth and her
complexion fresh and clear, her face, when the features
were not in active play, would settle down into an
eager vigilance disagreeably suggestive of a purpose
underlying the outward amenity. For Mrs. Shafton's manner was much more cordial than Lena's ;
and there was a mixture in it of vivacity and *câlinerie*,
wonderfully attractive at first, if the fascination did
not always endure. In spite of prejudice, and—
what is much more to the purpose—in spite of pre-
occupation, Lord Atherstone was fain to acknowledge
this ; and within the next ten minutes he took himself
sharply to task for having, in the privacy of his own

chamber, spoken unholy words concerning feminine intruders.

"There is no order of precedence among cousins," General Percy said when dinner was announced. "Atherstone, will you take in Mrs. Shafton? I mean to keep Lena by me till I finish what I've got to say to her: there's no one here likely to be jealous, I think."

There was a gruff laugh of assent; for it chanced that the speaker and his guests were as nearly as possible of the same standing. But one man did not smile. It was not that he was inclined more than the others to resent his old comrade's jest. What kept him grave was an uneasy doubt, lasting no longer than the flicker of summer lightning, whether, under circumstances different from these, it would be so certain that Ralph Atherstone had utterly outlived jealousy.

Nevertheless, he was rather pleased than otherwise at having to take charge of Mrs. Shafton. He and Lena sat at opposite ends of the table, of course; and, for that first evening, at all events, he preferred studying at his ease, from that safe distance, the picture which, when first seen, had affected him so powerfully. Neither was his contemplation often disturbed; for Mrs. Shafton, when she found him inclined to be taciturn, had the tact to fall in with that humour rather than attempt to force it; and, after a remark or two dropped on her right, turned the current of her conversation almost entirely on her left-hand neighbour—a portly veteran, who, albeit in all points of the matrimonial law blameless, was noted for his admiration of mature beauty, and meant to make the best of his present opportunity.

Amongst other antique customs kept up at Kirkfell was that of sitting late and long after dinner. There was no deep drinking; for every man there was too staunch a sportsman to imperil steadiness of hand, or clearness of eye, on the morrow. But the host and his guests, all of whom,. with one exception, had shot there for many seasons, liked lingering over their wine, recalling old times and old friends and old stories—with .an occasional spice thrown in of modern scandal ; and when they did adjourn, they tarried in the drawing-room only long enough to swallow their coffee upstanding, on their way to the smoking-room beyond. It was perfectly understood that the women-kind were not expected to preside over this refresh-ment unless they fancied it ; and, as the sitting was unusually late that night, nobody but Lord Atherstone was the least surprised to find them gone to their rest. It was something more than surprise that he felt, if the truth must be told. Chafing at his own weakness, he was fain to confess that he was really disappointed when, on entering, he saw that no gleam of snowy drapery relieved the darkness of the half-lighted room.

He saw it gleaming more than once before morning broke in the course of his troubled dreams.

# CHAPTER V.

ALL the next day was spent upon the hill. When the party assembled at dinner the order of arrangement was inverted, and Lord Atherstone sat next to Lena, who took her mother's place at the head of the table. He was not much more talkative than he had been on the previous night, and Miss Shafton seemed by no means anxious to make conversational running. She was perfectly courteous, but decidedly listless. Indeed, during the ten days of Lord Atherstone's stay at Kirkfell she could not be charged with having, either by word or gesture, or with other coquettish device, manifested any wish to attract him.

None the less for that the spell wound itself closer round him, hour by hour, till sometimes the tightening of the coil seemed to check the beating of his heart and the current of his blood. Why he refrained not only from speaking, but from compromising himself notably, would be hard to say. It could scarcely have been diffidence, properly so called, for this was almost as foreign to his temperament as personal fear; though surface-shyness will doubtless affect the most reliant of men who live over-much alone. Possibly a misgiving as to the nature of the fascination to which he was yielding, and a desire to prove whether it would stand the test of distance and absence, may have been among his motives for reserve; certain it is that he maintained it so successfully that neither Lena nor her mother, whose eyes were much the keenest in detecting signs of masculine weakness, ever guessed that his peace of mind was in anywise imperilled.    Mrs. Shafton was honestly surprised —they chanced to be alone at the moment—when on the morning of his departure Lord Atherstone answered her polite regrets thus :—

"I am sorry to go—very sorry—though I've out-stayed my time twice over ; but I should be sorrier yet, if I thought our acquaintance was to begin and end here.    I suppose you pass through town some-times, even if you don't make any very long stay. Will you promise to let me know when next you do so ?    It's more than probable I may be there about the same time, and I shouldn't like to miss seeing you."

Mrs. Shafton gave the promise with much alacrity ; and in the first glow of elation began once more to indulge in an amusement she had almost forgotten of late—the building of an air-castle.    But before the foundations were laid the reaction came, and she left the work unfinished from pure faintness of heart.    You would not have wondered at this, had you known her past history.

Her first false step was made very early in life, when she teased and cajoled her doting father into allowing her to marry Cosmo Shafton, of Blytheswold.    For one of his indolent, easy-going nature, Squire Bellingham stood out surprisingly long; and, setting his wilful daughter aside, no one wondered at his objections to the match.    For a couple of centuries a taint of wildness had attached to this branch of the Shaftons, that in the opinion of many savoured of insanity.    The last of the family acres, transmuted into gold, would long ago have helped to glut the greed of gamblers and wantons, if it had not been for another family peculiarity.    For generations past, the tenant for life of Blytheswold had always been more or less at variance, if not at enmity, with his presumptive heir; and the consequence was that, out of sheer obstinacy or malice, the latter never could be induced to join in any act of alienation that would have lightened his senior's burdens—preferring to stagger on stubbornly under his own, to purchasing temporary relief on such terms.

However, if the actual acreage of the property was not materially minished, each successive possessor had done his share towards encumbering and impoverishing it. To an agricultural enthusiast, that estate would have been worse than the mere abomination of desolation; and only boldness akin to desperation would have tempted any practical farmer to grapple with cold tilths, sour pasture-grounds innocent of drainage, and tumble-down bartons, through which the rain and wind wandered almost at will. Truth to speak, the tenants of Blytheswold were, as a rule, rather like squatters than yeomen : living from hand to mouth, and paying their rent by fits and starts, not often without compulsion, they were generally at open war with their landlords, who, in their turn, whenever they got fair hold, tightened the screw mercilessly.

Cosmo Shafton kept full pace with his forbears in extravagance and in worse vices yet. Before their honeymoon had waned, he had tested his wife's patience sorely, and never ceased to try it up to the hour of his sudden death. Riding home from a drinking bout, he was thrown and killed on the spot. If, during her married years, Isabel Shafton had not shown herself a very Griselda, she had controlled her temper — naturally hasty —wonderfully, and exhibited remarkable powers of endurance. To do her justice, she showed equal courage in facing the difficulties that beset her widowhood. After infinite labour, she succeeded in reducing into something like order the formidable tangle of her late husband's affairs; and showed no mean talent for stewardship in her management of the estate during her son's minority. But it was dreadfully uphill work from first to last; and, if it had not been for the small fortune strictly settled on herself, it would have been impossible to have kept the hearth warm at Blytheswold.

She had short respite from other cares and anxieties; for Miles grew up so ominously like his father, both in person and disposition, that each fresh sign of resemblance woke in Isabel Shafton a fresh flutter of apprehension, and the burden of her fears grew daily. She was not so strong as she had been, or perhaps had waxed weary with the struggle; but, at any rate, she quailed before the boy's outbreaks of temper far more than she had ever done before Cosmo's violence; and when Miles expressed his determination to obtain a cavalry commission, and his predilection for one particular corps, it was from a wish to avoid the contest, rather than from acquiescence in the wisdom of the step, that she set herself to carry out his wishes. The result has been hinted at already. Before Miles Shafton was twenty-three, he had contrived to encumber his patrimony almost to the extent of his tether—he was not the last of the entail, which extended to a whole line of cousins —and had become importunate in his demands for ready cash.

Neither had Mrs. Shafton found Lena a staff of support in time of trouble. In her languid way, she was to the full as hard to guide as her reckless brother: of governing her with the strong hand, Mrs. Shafton had long ago despaired. That it was Lena's bounden duty to prop the tottering fortunes of the family by an advantageous alliance, should such fall in her way, was self-evident; but not a whit the more for that did she exert herself either to make opportunities, or to use them when made to her hand.

A maiden aunt, on the Bellingham side, residing

in a quiet street in Mayfair, considered she could not acquit herself of family obligations better than by giving her niece a chance of establishment. So for two successive seasons, or nearly so, the country mice found free entertainment with their town-bred relative, upon the sole condition that they were to purvey their own amusement out of doors.

Beside any amount of that vague admiration which is as the foam floating round the car of Anadyomene, Lena Shafton, on her first season, had three substantial chances of promotion. None of the trio, perhaps, were brilliant offers, and Mrs. Shafton herself was content to allow her daughter to stray yet a little further through the hymeneal grove in the hope of finding a fairer or straighter wand. Only she wished that Lena would show a little more interest in the matter. It was provoking to see her profoundly indifferent as to which way the momentous question should be answered; for, though each suitor in turn was dismissed of her own free will, it was quite evident that had a little external pressure been applied, she might have said Yes, instead of No. Wooers were little likely to come riding over the bleak fells stretching round Blytheswold; so throughout the autumn and winter, Lena's maiden meditations were not troubled. They returned to town early in the ensuing spring; and before the season was far advanced, Mrs. Shafton had ceased to murmur at her daughter's listlessness or want of purpose. Whether the change was for the better, is quite another question.

There were few names better known in London, about that time, than Caryl Glynne's. Probably not above half the stories told of him were true, and the rest were somewhat exaggerated; but, after sifting grain from chaff, a very sufficient store of wild oats was laid up in his garner. As you will meet him hereafter, it is not worth while to sketch him here. It is enough to say that he had grown famous.

through his unscrupulous plotting against the peace
of better men's households. For divers reasons,
chiefly financial, he had haunted foreign parts during
the past year, and now reappeared with a kind of
fresh *prestige*. His friends—he kept friends in one
sex, at all events, in spite of all—made as much
of him as if he had been travelling for the ad-
vancement of science or for the honour of nis
country, instead of loitering abroad till incensed
creditors could be brought to hear reason. On the
second evening of their acquaintance, there came
such a light into Lena's great brown eyes as had
never shone in them yet; and before the week was
out, Mrs. Shafton, in bitterness of spirit, called
herself fool for having ever murmured at her
daughter's apathy.

Glynne was a detrimental in the broadest sense
of the word. Not only might his expectations
be represented by a blank—on the resources of
the future he had already drawn to the uttermost
—but furthermore, if by any miracle he could have
started again with unclogged wings, there was
little chance of his ever turning out a decent
working bee. All this, and much more to the
same purpose, did Mrs. Shafton set before her
daughter; but, with Lena, to hear was by no means
to obey. Opposition and attempted constraint only
made her more wilful and reckless, till at last people,
not over scrupulous or uncharitable, began to frown;
and evil whispers got abroad concerning clandestine
meetings and the like, such as cannot light on any
reputation, how fair soever, without leaving scath
and stain.

As is usually the case, the person most interested
was the last to hear what was being bruited abroad;
and when, in sheer despair, she determined to re-
move Lena from temptation by carrying her off
suddenly to the north, Mrs. Shafton never guessed
that she went too soon, or too late. Too late—

because the harm, if there was ever real harm, was done already : too soon—because it would have been better far to have faced the gossips than have given them leisure, and probable grounds to boot, for binding up scattered rumours into a substantial faggot of scandal. Though the reading of the Riot Act had been delayed, Mrs. Shafton, having once asserted her authority, had the sense to maintain it so long as there seemed occasion. Neither did Lena seem inclined to persist in rebellion ; but thenceforward, so far as her mother knew, made no attempt either by word or letter to bridge over the gulf dividing her from Caryl Glynne.

Yet the mischief could not be repaired.

Miss Bellingham, though by no means an austere virgin, had a great respect for the proprieties, and had no mind that experiments on the patience of the public should be made under her roof. The ensuing spring brought no invitation from Grey Street to Blytheswold ; and Mrs. Shafton lacked the means, even if she had had the courage, to venture on an independent campaign. From that day forth, the visits of the pair to town were rare and brief. Generally they only rested for a night or so in passing to or from Devonshire, where some relations—less well informed, or less extreme to remark what had been done amiss, than Rachel Bellingham—resided.

After all, if the charge against Lena had been thoroughly investigated, no severer verdict than 'Not Proven' could fairly have been recorded. During the interval betwixt that unlucky year and the opening of this tale, she might doubtless, had she been that way seriously inclined, 'have put away the reproach of her virginity,' and filled a wife's place in more than one honourable home. But she did not seem anxious to change her condition ; and, somehow, contrived

to close the lips of those who would have given
her a choice before they actually committed themselves.   Hints, entreaties, and reproaches—as Mrs.
Shafton's patience waxed threadbare, these last
were not spared—were utterly thrown away.   Sometimes it seemed as if Lena, from malice prepense,
raised her mother's hopes on purpose to dash them.
At last, it came to be understood amongst the
few men who, either in the north or south, were
intimate with the Shaftons, that 'Lena didn't go
in for marrying.'   She was perfectly charming to
talk to, especially if she chanced to be in a listening
humour; but few could flatter themselves that they
had ever tempted her beyond the hither verge
of flirtation; and the sense of security, when it
ceased to be provoking, was not disagreeable.

Both mother and daughter were decidedly popular
—each in her own way—in the contracted circle
of their acquaintance; and Mrs. Shafton amply made
up for Lena's want of vivacity.   Watching her demeanour abroad, and listening to her pleasant chat,
you would never have guessed that Blytheswold held
any skeletons.   It did though, and more than one;
neither were they hidden in corners so dark and remote, but that the mistress of the house had to face
them pretty constantly.   In fact, the poor lady had
almost ceased to believe in there being any silver
lining to the clouds encompassing her path : nor was
it strange if divers misgivings chilled the faint glow
of hope kindled within her by Lord Atherstone's
last words.

As to the meaning of that farewell, or the feelings that prompted it, there was no uncertainty
with the speaker himself.

A long day's journey lay between Kirkfell and
his next halting-place southwards; and before it
was half done, Ralph Atherstone had put the last
flimsy veil of self-delusion aside, and had looked
the truth in the face, whether it were evil or good.

He was not free from doubts here, and this is no wonder. Haughty, proud, and self-reliant, both by training and temperament—he appraised his natural gifts under rather than above their value, and blinked none of his disadvantages; but, had his vanity been overweening, it is possible that an inner voice would still have whispered warningly.

There are times and seasons for weaving of heart-chains, as for all other earthly matters, grave or gay. Surely few of us are so wayworn or battered but that we can remember, distinctly enough for all practical purposes, how, when, and where we first set our hand to that pleasant pastime. If fears beset us, they arose from no doubt as to the wisdom of our choice, or the certainty of future felicity in case our vows were crowned, but only from a dim apprehension, that a few base mechanical difficulties might not be swept away quite so easily or quickly as was desirable. Yet, in the very uncertainty, there was an excitement that would have been lacking had the way lain straight and smooth before us. I am not speaking now of the page-love, which is but a graceful form of boy's play, but of attachments which, however imprudent they may appear, are not on the face of them futile. Can we not remember how, whether hope or dread for the moment prevailed, we were always sensible of a glow of self-satisfaction in the consciousness that, if our chin were still innocent of the barber's shear, we had with the first earnest inspirations of manhood cast away childish things once and for all? Whilst making confession either to ourselves or to the friend of our youth, we, so to speak, draped ourselves in the virile toga. Troubles might be in store for us, of course, for we did not flatter ourselves that even the prospering of our suit would exempt us from the common lot of humanity; we were not prepared to deny that there was a subdued severity in the smile of our mother-in-law elect, or that her prosy and pompous consort might prove in more ways than one a 'stiff customer;' but we should have spurned, as rank blasphemy, the idea that our peace could ever be imperilled by Her towards whom all the current of our being set so strongly.

That complete trustfulness—then—like the reserve of the princess in the story, was 'natural to our age and station,' and could not justly provoke derision. But if, when well stricken in years, being subject to the like influences, we betray the like simplicity, can we expect that, in the congratulations of our acquaintance, there will mingle neither compassion nor scorn? It is a saving clause, to be sure, if betwixt ourselves and the Object there be a certain congruity of age; but somehow behind that same clause very few care to shelter themselves, preferring to run the matrimonial risk without such heavy insurance.

It is hard to debar a man, quite lonely in life, from carrying out his pleasure, provided it consist with virtue and honour; but surely it is wiser to count the possible cost thereof than wilfully to ignore such reckoning. Ralph Atherstone, at all events, was not so far gone in infatuation; and yet, in very truth —howsoever absurdly it may sound—he was then under the dominion of a first love. With the circumstances of his engagement and married life you are acquainted already. It might have been further recorded that, throughout his Indian career, his name was not once connected with any of the *liaisons* which were not less rife then than nowadays: if he was not blameless as to the others, he kept himself singularly void of offence with regard to the Seventh commandment. Since he came to reside in England it had been just the same.

On the other hand, he had assuredly registered no inward vow of celibacy; but, had he done so, he could scarcely have taken himself more sharply to task for having now yielded to temptation. It was but a poor satisfaction to remember that he had not actually compromised himself in words. The delay, in his eyes, savoured of cowardice, when he knew that sooner or later he would speak out. That his present frame of mind was, to a certain extent, morbid, he recognised fully. Would time and absence work a remedy? Ay—and did he care to be cured?

To both questions on that Sabbath morning Ralph Atherstone must have answered, " No."

# CHAPTER VI.

HARD service and long service are, as some have good reason to know, by no means synonyms. Though Lord Atherstone was still in his prime when he went on half-pay, and though a couple of medals, with clasps to match, were the sum of his decorations, he had probably set his life on hazard tenfold oftener than the majority of those who have grown grey in staff-harness, and whose breasts are *plaqués* with ensigns of merit. It is certain that during not one of the enterprises, in which the chances for and against return were about evenly poised, had his pulse beat so irregularly as it did when the train bearing him Londonwards moved off from the Heslingford platform. Perhaps this is a weak parallel after all: for men whose natural hardihood has waxed callous under experience, there are excitements infinitely more intense than that of mere personal peril. But these last had never had any hold on Ralph Atherstone: though no one gave him credit for asceticism, he was perhaps less open to the temptations of drink, gambling, or luxury, than many who are reputed saints. So he was fairly startled, not only at the power, but at the novelty, of the emotions at work within him that morning.

He was alone as it chanced; for, if Lord Atherstone found little favour in his own county, lavish gratuities made him popular on the Great Central Line; and it was seldom indeed that the guards did not discover a vacant compartment somewhere for his special behoof.

For several leagues, the vale stretching away on
either side of the line was as familiar to Ralph as
his own demesne.  He had a wonderfully accurate
eye and memory for a country; and, on ordinary
occasions, could have pointed out quite easily the
very corner where, two years ago, after about the
quickest thing of the season, the hounds were balked
of blood by an open drain; and the special pollard
overhanging the spot where a rotten bank, crumbling
under Fire King's hind hoofs, gave that good horse
his first lesson in swimming.  But to-day he seemed
to be passing through a country utterly strange to
him; and he gazed out of the carriage window
vacantly and mechanically, like a traveller who, in
the tame monotony of the scenery around, forgets
that it is new.  For awhile, one thought chased
another through Lord Atherstone's mind so swiftly
that there was little order in his meditations; but,
ere long, the strength of his nature asserted itself;
and he was able to look his position in the face,
at least as steadily as he had done on his journey
southwards from Kirkfell.

He had done with doubts now, so far as all de-
pending on himself was concerned.  He was going
straight to Lena Shafton, to ask of her the gravest
question that man can ask of woman.  He did not
repent for an instant of this resolve; and he thought
he never would repent of it, whatever her answer
might be.  Nevertheless, it seemed to him that, if
she answered No, there would be laid on him a
burden not only of disappointment, but of intolerable
shame.

This, of course, was thoroughly irrational.  The
difference of age betwixt himself and Lena was
great, no doubt, but not sufficiently so to be grotesque.
That threadbare parallel of January and May would
not stand here; for there was no more on one side the
barrenness of late winter, than there was on the other
the freshness of early spring.  Though he had lived

much out of the world of late, he knew enough of its
ways to be aware that, in all likelihood, haughtier
necks than Lena Shafton's would bow themselves to
take up an ancient coronet—to say nothing of such a
dower as might fairly be laid on Templestowe.
Whatsoever fault either friends or foes might find
in the proposal he was about to make, there was
surely nothing in it to provoke laughter. But it
was not so much the ridicule of others, as his own
self-contempt in after time, that Atherstone dreaded ;
and this to one endowed—or afflicted if you please
—with his peculiar pride, was quite a sufficient bug-
bear. A fantastic one, no doubt. But will the mock-
ing spirits always depart out of the presence of the
wisest of us, when we cry, that they torment us
against reason, or before our time ?

Few amongst the many who had called this man
tyrannical and oppressive, denied to him a certain
sense of equity, though his judgment might often
be questioned, and his sentence impugned ; and, in
his own fashion, he was thoroughly just now. If not
only his hopes but his self-respect were to be wrecked,
he felt that, then and afterwards, he could absolve
Lena from having lured him on by any false signal.
Once or twice he did fancy that her eyes had rested
on him with a kind of interest ; but he had never
read in them encouragement, much less a challenge :
her face had never lighted up when he drew near;
or lowered regretfully when he turned away ; or,
whilst he lingered by her side, ever softened in
its languor. It was best so. If his heart was not
worth her acceptance, she had held it at least of
better worth than the baubles which coquettes toss
to and fro in their light-minded play. And, at the
very worst, if she were to refuse him ever so coldly,
he felt right sure that she would never boast of her
triumph or his discomfiture. And as for himself—
if the old pluck had not quite left him—he would
carry away his bitter secret just as he did the Afghan

bullet, when he sat saddle-fast for a full hour before any wist that he was wounded.

It was odd certainly that, often as the current of his thoughts changed, it never once occurred to him to speculate what would be the effect at Templestowe if his present purpose were divulged there. If only Philip had been concerned this would not have been so remarkable; for, if there was no enmity betwixt the two, there was decided estrangement. When Mr. Ashleigh compared himself with his sire, a sense of intellectual superiority was always ludicrously at variance with that of physical disadvantage. He looked upon him much as a clerk in the middle ages may have looked upon a moss-trooping baron —a personage at once tremendous and contemptible; with whom it was alike impossible to argue, and unsafe to trifle. His father had certainly treated Philip with a little more outward deference since he took parliamentary and matrimonial honours; but, inwardly, he had little more respect for him than heretofore. In the senatorial successes, for instance, he utterly declined to believe, especially since, sorely against his will, he was induced to assist at one of those displays.

"They read better than they sound," he allowed, when Lady Marian afterwards insisted upon his opinion; but, in spite of this, to those same orations in print he never vouchsafed more than a passing glance. If the honest electors of that convenient borough were satisfied with their hire, and with their choice, it was well. But in any moral or social difficulty Lord Atherstone would assuredly have gone out into the highways for counsel, rather than have sought it from the member for Heslingford.

With Marian Ashleigh, however, it was very different. If she had failed, through mere force of circumstances, to gain any absolute ascendency over her father-in-law, she had at least gained so much influence, that he would not lightly have gone counter

to her expressed opinion or implied wishes. For
three years she had virtually been mistress of Templestowe ; and had ruled with so much tact and
moderation, that it was not without certain qualms
that Lord Atherstone first contemplated the possibility
of requiring her to abdicate. Furthermore, he had
a certain respect not only for her shrewd common
sense, but for her power of quiet satire ; and he
was quite conscious of having yesterday morning
rather sought to evade than to encounter her keen
black eyes, though they betrayed no scrutiny. It
was odd that, on the spectrum of those musings by
the way, her figure should never have been reflected.
Perhaps it may be accounted for—thus. Though he
had never read a line of philosophy, Proverbial or
other, Ralph had somehow acquired a few practical
maxims which stood him in good stead. Amongst
these was—' Unto the day, the day.' He probably
thought that it would be quite time enough to
disquiet himself, as to the fashion in which a bride
would be welcomed at Templestowe, when the bride
was won.

At the last halt before reaching town, the guard,
not without contrition, unlocked the door to admit
two other passengers. Atherstone scarcely glanced
at them from under his bent brows ; nevertheless,
the thread of his meditation was broken, and he soon
became aware that the new-comers were grumbling
at the train's being disgracefully behind time. Looking at his watch, he was fain to acknowledge this.
Yet it scarcely seemed to him an hour since he lost
sight of the pinnacles crowning the western tower
of Heslingford Minster; and now they were already
within sight of the grimy fringe of the Great City's
robe.

Late as it was, however, he had spare time on
his hands ; for he was not minded to call upon the
Shaftons till after twilight had set in, when he was
nearly sure of finding them at home. So he sent

his servant with the luggage to his hotel, and betook himself to his club, where he lunched—frugally, after his fashion, but with a very fair appetite.

By far the greatest crisis of his life was impending; but this consciousness rather quieted than excited him, and his pulse now was steady as a time-piece. Though his manner never grew positively amiable, some of Ralph's ancient comrades could have told you that there were seasons when his face looked rather serene than impassible, and when his voice lost its harsh inflections : on these occasions dangerous work was always close at hand.

There had been no frost as yet ; but such hunting men as were not absolutely insatiate of sport, or exceptionally strong in their stable, were well content to give the weather a day or two to settle. So Lord Atherstone encountered more than one acquaintance, both at his club and as he walked towards the hotel where the Shaftons were staying. Assuredly the most suspicious of these never guessed that any graver reason than fancy, or ordinary business, had brought the ' bruising baron' up to town just then.

Mrs. Shafton had hardly reckoned on any reply to her note. Nevertheless, when the morning's post brought none, she had experienced something of the disappointment that affects a skilful fisherman when, after his favourite fly has floated like thistle-down over the nook at the tail of the eddy, where he well knows a heavy trout is lying, there ensues no ruffle of the water. For good and sufficient cause, she had not consulted Lena before the missive was despatched, nor made confession to her afterwards. The being compelled to lock up her misgivings in her own bosom, did not make them the lighter to carry. Neither could she reasonably expect a call that day. And yet, as the evening closed in, the hue of her reflections darkened apace

Waiting and watching in the twilight is dreary work ; and Mrs. Shafton had just made up her mind to ring for candles, when Lord Atherstone was announced. With all her self-command—of this useful commodity she had her full share—she could scarcely repress an exclamation of pleasure; but her greeting was perfect—neither over-eager, nor conscious, nor constrained. Inferior practitioners in this branch of science, if they do not gush out into premature affection, are apt to case themselves in unnecessary dignity. In these delicate shades of colouring the artist-hand is approved : you may quarrel with the design and *morale* of the picture if you will, but you must needs do justice to the execution. This visitor, as you are aware, did not need much management; but a more diffident one would soon have been set at his ease by such graceful welcome.

The manœuvring matron has been rather roughly entreated of late by our essayists; but surely they must allow that she has a wonderful knack of making her friends—and her foes too, for that matter, if it suits her end—feel themselves at home. Do you remember Mrs. Rawdon Crawley's reception of her brother-in-law in Curzon Street, and those fine touches about the coal-scuttle and the *salmis ?* Similarly situated, good Lady Jane would have hoped that her guest found his room comfortable and enjoyed his dinner. That is polite and hospitable enough in its way; but the real tactician carries up the coals herself, and seasons the dainty dish with her own white hands. Neither are these characteristics only of the adventuress. You will find a *châtelaine,* with quarterings enough to satisfy an Austrian herald, just as careful to render *petits soins* to the persons she delights to honour.

How otherwise do you suppose that Lady Hernscliffe has contrived to dispose of daughter after daughter, neither richly dowered nor passing fair, not only creditably, but so brilliantly as to move to hatred and malice all save the most charitable of her compeers ? ˙A man installed under her roof—with a

purpose you will understand—finds himself at once in
an atmosphere of comfort such as mere luxury could
never secure, and which in all probability is new to
him, in howsoever pleasant places his lines may have
fallen.    His favourite tastes are divined and anticipated magically ; and even for his favourite vices there
is tacit indulgence.    There are no black looks from
the hostess, if he chooses to breakfast at unholy
hours ; nor grumbling from the host, if he lounges or
dreams away all the forenoon under the lawn cedars,
instead of 'going a-gunning' with the rest of the
male kind ; neither is it a heinous offence, if the scent
of a last cigarette floats out into the stilly night from
his chamber casement.    Why should not his own
household be managed in a like cheery and convivial
fashion ?    Domestic talents, of such a rare order, must
surely be hereditary.    The nubile virgin, whom he
had begun to admire amidst the glare and glitter and
bustle of the season, appears infinitely more attractive
under the soft home-light.    So, from the potential
mood of marriageable, to the future of marrying, the
transition is very easy ; and, before autumn is far
spent, it is known to all whom it may concern, that
another bud from that luxuriant rose-tree is to be
grafted on a stock quite as stately as any of those on
which her sisters are blooming.

"I kept my promise, you see," Mrs. Shafton said
as she shook hands with her visitor ; "but I certainly
did not expect to see you so soon, if at all.    It was so
very unlikely that you would be in town whilst we
were passing through.    Perhaps I ought to thank the
weather for it.    I suppose hunting is stopped in
Loamshire ?"

"Not that I am aware of," Atherstone replied.    "But
I wonder you did not expect to see me.    Did you
think it was only a civil speech, when I asked you to
let me know when you came to town ?    I have forgotten how to make civil speeches, if I ever knew."

"Then it was business that brought you up," she

persisted. "It is not often that business is so accommodating. You don't want me to believe that you
have travelled all these miles on purpose to improve
our Kirkfell acquaintanceship?"

Clever and courageous as she was, she was only
a woman after all; a woman, too, whose nerves
trouble and disappointment had sorely tried. It was
no wonder if, now that a great prize seemed almost
within her grasp, her voice shook a little, and her
eyes sank under Ralph's steady gaze.

"I want you to believe not only that, Mrs.
Shafton," he said very quietly, "but much more. I
want you to believe every word that I shall speak to
you to-day. If you will only listen patiently, we shall
understand one another, I think, very soon."

She did listen; and neither spoke nor stirred, nor
even looked up, till Lord Atherstone had made it
clear that his single purpose in coming there, was
to ask Lena to be his wife. He was curt and concise
in his proposals : without shirking the obvious objections of shortness of acquaintance and difference in
age, he touched on them so lightly, that he evidently
thought these were rather for the daughter's than the
mother's consideration. And yet a matron, more
disposed to stand on punctilio than this poor lady,
could not have considered herself neglected or
ignored.

There are certain formularies of gesture, no less
than of words, proper to these occasions; yet the
emotion that Mrs. Shafton betrayed was not wholly
stage-play. 'She was surprised, of course; quite
bewildered, indeed. Nevertheless, she was free to
confess that Lord Atherstone's proposals were to
herself most acceptable ; he had her best wishes, and
she promised that he should not lack her support :
but she feared her influence would not go far, even
if it were right to sway Lena's inclinations.' If the
first words of that reply conveyed a conventional
falsehood, the last were bitterly true ; and the sigh

that followed came from the depths of the speaker's heart.

"I thank you heartily," Atherstone answered. "But don't think me ungrateful if I pray you to use no influence whatever. I would rather, much rather, take her decision straight from herself, quite un-biassed. And—it sounds rude, I am afraid—the sooner I hear it the better."

His blunt straightforwardness made affectation impossible ; indeed, the *brusquerie* rather braced than agitated Mrs. Shafton's nerves.

"I can please you so far," she said. "You shall see her alone, before I do. If I am not very much mistaken, that is her step I hear."

Through the closed doors came the rustle of silks trailing slowly ; and, the next minute, Lena entered.

"They told me some one was here," she said, after she had exchanged greetings with Lord Atherstone ; "and I guessed who it was, though they travestied the name. Yet you are nearly the last person I should have expected to find in town in the height of the hunting season. What brought you up?"

Her manner was amicable enough ; but there was never a sign of consciousness or confusion on her face, nor the faintest change of colour ; and that last question sounded as if she had no special interest in the answer. Thus much Ralph recognised instantly : perhaps he had hardly reckoned on any other recep-tion ; yet he was slightly disappointed.

"I had business in town," he said, rather coldly, "as I have been trying to explain to your mother. And besides, it is doubtful hunting weather just now. You will be glad to find yourself in Devonshire. They have a monopoly of sunshine, I hear, down there."

"They don't work it out, then," she returned. "If they fall short in frost, they make it up in sea-fogs. On the whole, where we stay is not a bad place for a dormouse to winter in ; but as I don't happen to be a dormouse——"

The pause was very expressive.

Then they began to talk about Kirkfell, and General Percy, and other subjects of mutual interest, till at last Mrs. Shafton rose.

" I have two letters to write before post-time," she said; " but they will not detain me long. If I find you gone when I come back, I shall know you have been bored."

She kept her promise of non-interference to the very letter; for, instead of exchanging with her daughter one glance either warning or intelligent, she was careful as she passed out to avoid the question of Lena's eyes.

# CHAPTER VII.

INFINITE, no doubt, is the variety of circumstances under which matrimonial overtures have been made. Putting aside the sensational stories where all the powers of earth, air, fire, and water are invoked to strengthen the situation—some very practical and civilised people would be loath, if not ashamed, to relate how and where they were brought to confession.

A soldier of my acquaintance, not long ago, revealed the state of his affections to the person most interested therein, behind the Stand at Ascot, just as the numbers were being hoisted for the Cup. Solitude can be found, they say, in the heart of any crowd by those who seek it aright; and perhaps, while the isolation of this couple endured, the bellow of the Ring, swelling each instant into more furious waves of sound, was to their ears like the soothing murmur of a distant sea; and the scanty branches, waving over the broken meats, seemed like the shade of a primeval forest, where foot of man has never strayed. At any rate, the result was prosperous. Neither will I admit that yonder bold dragoon's chances of domestic peace are much lessened by the incongruities of time and place under which his suit was urged.

The experience of the average of men on this subject must necessarily be limited; but, if notes were compared, many might agree that ordinary difficulties of courtship are less embarrassing than the fatal facility of being left *en champ clos*—under conditions.

Lord Atherstone was neither nervous nor diffident;

nevertheless, it is certain that other feelings, besides
the mere straightforwardness of his nature, made him
willing to shorten the pause which ensued when they
were left alone. However, Lena spoke first.

"Do you stay long in town; or are you only a bird
of passage, like ourselves?"

He glanced down at her keenly from where he stood
leaning his arm on the mantelpiece; for he had risen
when Mrs. Shafton rose.

"That hardly depends on myself. Cannot you
guess what is my business here? Your mother knows
it already."

She let her eyes rest on his face for a single second;
and in that space the secret—if secret there were—
was told. Ralph's countenance was calm enough;
but there was no mistaking its earnestness—the
earnestness of a man speaking with a solemn purpose.
Lena's cheek flushed, as if in vexation; and her eyelids drooped—rather wearily than bashfully.

"I am quite willing to listen," she said; "but I am
too stupid at guessing. Life is not long enough for
riddles."

"Mine is not likely to be, at all events," he said
with a half-smile. "You are quite right too; it is
always best to speak out, even when one shrinks
from the confession. And I do not shrink. Perhaps
you don't know that, when I left Kirkfell, I begged
your mother to let me hear when you were passing
through town. Well: it matters very little. I did
not ask it without an object; and the object was
nearly the same as that which has brought me here.
I thought, then, it was more than likely that my happiness would, one day or other, be in your hands to
make or mar. I am quite sure of it now. I have
been so for weeks past. It is because I am so sure,
that I feel no shame in asking you this question. Is
it quite impossible that you should ever care for me
enough to become my wife?"

The flush faded from her face, leaving it paler than

its wont; but there was none of the surprise or confusion there that might naturally have been provoked by the sudden avowal. If she had not expected the situation, she certainly accepted it with wonderful equanimity.

"Impossible!" she murmured. "Nothing in this world is impossible, they say. If the word had been 'improbable,' the question would have been easier perhaps to answer: certainly I have never asked it of myself yet. Was it likely that I should? Have you forgotten that the length of our acquaintance should be reckoned rather by hours than days?"

"I have forgotten nothing," he said. "I have counted those hours just as accurately as I have the years that make up the difference between your age and mine. I ought to have outgrown rashness long ago; and I have only one excuse for having spoken over-hastily; and that same excuse, though it is true, will sound absurd. It is a wrinkled hand that I offer you to-day; but it has never pressed any woman's more kindly than in friendship. It is not necessary, or even fit, that I should tell you how my marriage was brought about. Only I can say that I did not deceive my wife, either before or after we stood at the altar together. She was content to take my name on certain terms; and I hope, while she lived, I kept my share of the compact. Since she left me in India —it was some years before she died—I have lived utterly alone; and I never thought it could be otherwise with me, till I came to Kirkfell. I could not promise that my nature should be changed. I shall be rough and hard to the end, I fear. Yet I think never so rough, as willingly to speak a bitter word to you; and never so hard as to balk one of your wishes, or carry it out grudgingly. You don't seem inclined to laugh: I thank you for that, at all events."

She put forth her hand, as though to check him; but drew it back again so quickly, that he could not have taken it, had he been so minded.

"Do not speak so. I know, right well, that there are women, a thousand times better worth winning than I ever was, or could be, who would be proud of listening to the words you have just spoken ; and yet I know that for your sake, if not for mine—perhaps for both our sakes—I ought to shut my ears, now and always. Yes, for your sake chiefly"—she went on, before he could interrupt her. "You said, you thought it would be in my power to make or mar your happiness. I might mar it worse by saying Yes, than by saying No, to-day. I have often doubted, whether I am fit to be trusted with any man's happiness; and, of late, I had begun to think—I am not sure if I had not begun to hope—that I should never be tried."

"I am not afraid," he said simply; "and, before you say No, remember this. I do not ask for your love as yet—only for the chance of gaining it ; and, if I fail at last, I will never complain; but I will be content—more than content—with your loyalty. If I have been hasty in asking you this question, you need be in no haste to answer it. I will wait as long as it pleases you."

Her face was strangely troubled now, and her voice low and broken.

"I will not ask you to wait long—not longer than till this time to-morrow. But I must think; I must——" She checked herself, biting her lip sharply.

He took her hand as it hung idly down, but did not clasp it: he only lifted it to his lips, with an honest reverence that, in most women's eyes, would have been worth a hundred courtly graces ; and, at that moment, Lena herself felt anything but ashamed of her suitor.

"So it shall be," he said. " I will not weary you any more to-day. Indeed, special pleading like mine might lose a better cause. Nor will I see your mother again till you have decided."

He pressed her fingers before he let them go, but much more lightly than he had done when he bade her good-bye at Kirkfell; and Lena returned the pressure silently. So they parted.

For some minutes after she was left alone the girl sat quite still : the lashes half veiling her dreamy eyes never moved or stirred; neither were they lifted when the door opened again.

The keen, vigilant look was very strong on Mrs. Shafton's face as she entered; and, if she had affected composure, her voice would have betrayed her.

"He has gone, then—and so soon? Is it possible that you sent him away?"

Lena looked up with the languid defiance in her eyes that her mother saw first when it was ordained that Caryl Glynne's name should no more be mentioned betwixt them, and that she had seen often enough since then, to her cost.

"I did not send Lord Atherstone away, mother. He himself thought it best to go without seeing you. Cannot you guess why?"

Mrs. Shafton started violently, half rising out of the chair into which she had thrown herself; and her fingers were clenched, as though in passion or pain.

"I won't believe it," she cried out; "you can't have refused him. It would be too ungrateful—too cruel."

Lena smiled provokingly.

"What very large words!" she said. "Of course they can only refer to Lord Atherstone. I felt honoured by his offer, and told him so; but I really can't see why I should have been bowed down with gratitude; and—as for cruelty—some people would think it would have been more cruel if I had accepted him."

"You did refuse him, then?" the other said, almost in a whisper.

There was no anger on her face now, but such a sick despondency as stirred even Lena's compassion.

" I couldn't help teasing you," sñe said ; " but there is no occasion for fainting, mother. I did not refuse Lord Atherstone ; I only asked him to give me till to-morrow to decide. Was that very unreasonable, all incompatibilities considered? He did not seem to think so."

For a person who, as a rule, kept her feelings pretty well in hand, Mrs. Shafton felt absurdly inclined to be hysterical. The change from disappointment to hope was rather too much for her; the reactions of her life had been so invariably the other way. She crossed over to where her daughter sat, and kissed her on the cheek and brow. The warmth of the caress was very significant ; for, though indulgent to her children, she was by no means a 'gushing' parent. Lena submitted passively to the embrace, but did not return it.

" Don't give me more credit than I deserve," she said; " I only promised him that I would think it over."

But Mrs. Shafton was not to be discouraged again so easily. It was the first time that she had ever known Lena look seriously, not to say favourably, upon an eligible marriage-offer. That she should have been brought to this point was a great step gained — so great, that she could afford now to temporise.

" You were quite right to take time to consider, darling," she said soothingly; " you could hardly do otherwise, considering the shortness of your acquaintance. Only, be sensible and brave : you must look things in the face sooner or later. If I were to die to-morrow, you would be nearly penniless, and alone in the world—quite alone ; for what kind of a guard or help would your poor brother be ? I feel so tired, sometimes, that I should be almost glad to lie down and sleep once for all, if I only knew you were safe. You would be so very safe—there. In spite of that *sauvagerie* on the surface, no woman could help trusting Lord Atherstone; and very few would not learn to love him in time. Indeed, I would not try to persuade you if I did not feel sure you would be happy  I have never yet tried to force your inclinations, you must own that; and I never crossed them—but once."

Lena drew herself away with a manifest impatience.

"I thought that 'once' was buried long ago," she said coldly; "we need not call it up again, especially not at this time. Now, mother, I will promise you to think over everything—everything. And I will do my very best to be worldly-wise, if you will promise not to say another word on the subject, and to leave me quite alone to my own devices till to-morrow afternoon. You shall hear my answer then; and you may scold or praise me just as much as you please. If I consult any one in the meantime, it will only be Grace Moreland; and you know she is almost certain to take your side of the question."

To all this the other readily agreed.

Lena retreated to her own room immediately after dinner, so Mrs. Shafton was condemned to a solitary evening; but it seemed to her anything but long or weary. As she sat musing alone, there hovered often on her lips the quiet smile of beatitude. The bark that she had steered to the best of her strength and skill, had not yet entered the safe roadstead; and certain shoals were still to be weathered before it should be moored in port. Nevertheless, after the harassment of long sea-turmoil, there was relief inexpressible in floating through stiller waters under the loom of the land.

# CHAPTER VIII.

"IT is too atrocious, Lena. You come here under the pretence of consulting me—just as if you would ever really consult anybody—and then you frighten me into becoming your accomplice. I believe this is what people mean when they talk of adding insult to injury."

Mrs. Moreland was a distant cousin and a very close friend of Miss Shafton's; they had been thrown a good deal together in early days; nor had their intimacy at all cooled since the former's marriage two years ago, though they met more rarely; for it was a long costly journey to Blytheswold, and the toy-house in Blakeney Street contained no guest-chamber. Grace's face, if not precisely pretty, was exceedingly pleasant—so pleasant, that even anger could not materially transform it. When most incensed, her eyes flashed forth only harmless summer lightning; nor could her small rosy mouth achieve anything more menacing than a pout, tempting the offender almost irresistibly to proffer the kiss of peace.

"Don't be childish, Gracie," Lena retorted, with some disdain. "I have been perfectly honest with you. I suppose one may ask an opinion, without binding one's self down to abide by it; and you were not frightened into anything. I simply told you it was necessary I should see Caryl Glynne this morning—or that I meant to see him—it comes to nearly the same thing; and you yourself proposed that he should come here."

"Proposed!" the other went on, still very piteously; "what a way to put it—when you know it was only to prevent an act of simple insanity! *Je ne suis pas bégueule, moi;* but I could call it nothing else, if you had gone to visit that man alone. I have done for the best, though I shall suffer for it as a matter of course; but mind, Lena, you promised he should not stay here more than half-an-hour. Bernard does not come home to lunch above once a month; but I am morally certain this will be one of his days. You have no conception how angry he would be, if he knew of this."

"I had no conception he could be angry at all," Lena observed. "That is quite a novel idea; invented, perhaps, expressly for this occasion. But you needn't be nervous, Gracie. If our talk lasts over that time—it is next to impossible—the excuse will satisfy even Saint Bernard's scruples. Don't let us two quarrel this morning: I am not in spirits for it; I have such a long hard day before me."

Very few could resist the charm of Lena Shafton's manner when it grew caressing. Mrs. Moreland instantly accused herself of unkindness and injustice, and testified her penitence in true feminine fashion; but, before the petting process had lasted long, there came a knock and a ring; and Grace arose and fled away swiftly into an inner sanctuary, just large enough to hold herself and her writing-table; saying, as she shut the door behind her—

"A short half-hour, remember."

Not a few of his numerous acquaintances in the artist-guild had taken for their model that head of Caryl Glynne's; and though in almost every case it was the labour of love, rather than of lucre, not one had succeeded to his own, much less to the sitter's satisfaction. The face in marble, however deftly worked, could find only hard and cold presentment; and by brush or crayon its peculiar tones, if not faintly rendered, were sure to be exaggerated. The

faultless regularity of feature was easy enough to
reproduce; but not sculptors only were baffled by
the mobility of expression, though none of the tran-
sitions were violent, and the whole picture was
pervaded by a mellow repose. The hair and beard
in themselves were a painter's puzzle. It was some
time now, since from an intense black, they had
passed into a deep steel grey; the snow had not
fallen in streaks or patches, but in tiny flakes, so
evenly sprinkled, that there was harmony rather
than contrast of colours; and you could not say how
or where they mingled. Now this change had not
been brought about by age, or sorrow, or pain; for
Glynne's health, though not rudely robust, was exceptionally good; and he was tolerably case-hardened
against fears or regrets: it was simply a freak of
Nature; and her fantasies are often more attractive
than her work which is done by rule. The effect,
though somewhat startling at first, was on the whole
decidedly becoming; and amongst the few who,
after mature consideration, would have wished it
altered, Caryl himself was certainly not included. A
clear, pale complexion—dark eyes, rather soft than
piercing—a slender, graceful figure—hands and feet
such as few of his country-women can boast of—these
may stand for the other accessories of a sketch that
you can fill up according to your fancy.

How Caryl Glynne would have greeted Lena
Shafton, had they met under no kind of constraint,
it is not necessary to inquire. It may be that something in her face, which was not exactly a warning
look, bade him be on his guard; or perhaps he only
obeyed the promptings of his own prudence, when
he took her hand decorously, scarcely holding it so
long as old friendship would warrant.

"You have come quicker than I expected," Lena
said; "but the time is short. Sit down by me here,
and don't interrupt me till I have said my say; and,
when you answer, speak low."

It was almost a whisper; yet each syllable would have been heard as distinctly by one listening ten yards away, as by him whose ear was not a foot from her lips.

"I am not going to reproach you, Caryl," she went on; "it is too late for such folly; and I am not going to be plaintive over the present or the past. Some day, I suppose, I shall wish that I had never seen you. I do not wish that yet—quite yet. You remember our exchange of promises. I don't boast of having kept mine; for I have had no real temptation to break them. I don't ask how you have kept yours. I might have heard stories enough if I had chosen to listen; but I never did choose; and I would not hear your confession now, if you cared to make one. I believe that you meant what you said at the time, and meant it all along, and mean it still. You were to make me your wife, whenever it should be possible, you know. Answer me this question truly—Is there one gleam of hope more for us now, than there was on that dreary morning —ah! so long ago?"

"Poor child!" he said very gently. "So you are weary of waiting. I don't wonder, and I can't complain."

There came a look into Lena's eyes, the like of which none had ever seen, save the man on whom they were resting now.

"Not weary, Caryl," she said—"never weary: but I must have something firmer than reeds and rushes to cling to; the stream sets very strongly just now. I have not troubled you with our home-worries; and I don't think you have any idea how near we are to absolute ruin. The Shaftons of Blytheswold usually come to grief sooner or later; but Miles has gone down hill rather faster than could have been expected; and though my mother has crippled herself to stave off the crash, it cannot be delayed much longer. Can you wonder if she looks to me for help?

And cannot you guess that I can bring help in no
way but one ?"

A hard, evil change came over his face.

"What ? The old stale story—older, I daresay,
than Iphigenia ? It is curious how the angry gods
always hanker after maiden sacrifices. That is a
little too classical, isn't it ? Well then—

How is he ca'ed, your bra' wooer ?

for I presume you are not dealing in politic generalities. He's a landed laird at the least, of course, if
not a belted Earl. Don't be reticent, pray ; you had
better go on improving the occasion."

Her eyelids quivered, and her nostril dilated
slightly ; these were the only signs that the taunt
had stung her.

"I asked you a very simple question," she said ;
" and, when you have answered it, I will tell you
what you please. What do you want me to say ?
That I would rather work for my daily bread as
your wife, than live in state as any other man's ?
That would be waste of words, Caryl—you know it
as well as I do ; but we neither of us know how
to work, I am afraid ; and I would rather bear anything—yes, anything—than feel that I was hampering
you more than you are hampered already. Only
remember, it is not I that blench from the risk, whatever it is. I may have been afraid before ; but I
am not afraid to-day. If you say to me, ' Come,' I
will come, and never repent it afterwards. Dare you
say it ?"

There was brief silence ; and then he spoke under
his breath, his countenance still darkening.

' It would be madness—utter madness. I am worse
than a beggar now ; and, if things don't mend, I
may be an outlaw soon. Anyhow, I am not likely
to keep my head above water much longer. Whenever I do go down, I'll think of the chance I have
had to-day ; but—I'll sink alone."

One quick sob broke from Lena Shafton. The hope still surviving in her had been so weak and drooping, that you would scarcely have thought the uprooting of it would have brought so sharp a pang; nevertheless, only a brave effort kept her voice under control.

"You have answered my question quite honestly, I am sure: now I will answer yours. Yesterday Lord Atherstone asked me to marry him, and gave me till this afternoon to decide."

Possibly certain unselfish impulses had prompted Glynne's last words; but all such vanished under the provocation of the point-blank avowal. Like many better men, he never valued any privilege or possession aright, till he was on the point of losing it; and never estimated the weight of any impending trouble or danger, till he stood within the shadow of the λίθος ἀνάιδης. A cool reasoner, under circumstances where most persons forget to reason—he had long ago admitted to himself that his hold on Lena Shafton was really untenable; and furthermore had recognised the probability of his being called upon at any moment to stand aside to make room for some wealthier and worthier suitor; nevertheless, the consciousness that the vague 'some one' had become a definite unit, chafed him savagely.

"So it was Robin Gray after all," he said, "at least so far as age goes: but there the parallel ends; the 'bruising baron' is by no means 'a douce auld carle.' However, there is something paternal in the arrangement—that's one comfort. One ought to be thankful for mercies ever so small."

Her eyes were no longer timid or tender.

"I sent for you to ask the question that you have just answered; but I had something else to say, and you make it easier for me than I expected. If I marry now—and it is next to certain that I do marry—I will be honest in intention at least: the past must lie where it lies. And I could not be honest even so far, if it were not settled that between you and me all is over from to-day—quite, quite over. I will meet you as a friend always, and I would help you if I could; but I will not admit your right to ask for one iota more. If you do ask, you will find me harder to deal with than you imagine; and, in spite of his fatherly age, Lord Atherstone, I fancy, is well able to take care of his own."

"A superb resolve," he retorted; "but—supposing, for the sake of argument, that you mean all you say —do you think a hold, like mine over you, is slipped off like a worn-out glove? You are bold, *ma mie*; but there's such a thing as being over-bold."

Her gaze was still steadfast, and in her smile there was a touch of scorn.

"Yes: it's lucky I'm not a coward, Caryl. A coward might fare worse at your hands than even I have done. Surely we understand each other. I know that you could stop my marriage, or possibly make it an unhappy one; but you know, too, that if you did this, it would never bring you a step nearer to me. I don't believe that out of simple malice you'd try to hurt me; when, up to this moment, you never could quarrel with a look, or word, or thought of mine. So I have small reason to be afraid, you see."

"I didn't mean to threaten you," he said, sullenly, but not so viciously. "I only meant to warn. The danger that I was thinking of would come from yourself— not from me. You will find it hard to remember, just at the right time, all the texts about wives' duty; and harder, perhaps, to forget old times. But you may go your way in peace, for any hindrance of mine. I'll drop into the amicable position as gracefully as I can, without giving Lord Atherstone occasion to air his valour. If you ever go astray in my company, you will be following not my beck and call; but—your fate. I believe we both mean honestly just now; and yet I fear—that's the right word for it—that all is *not* over between you and me."

Her eyes drooped now; and she shrank a little, like one who, hearing an evil prophecy, thinks that it may prove true, though the lips that have uttered it seldom speak sooth.

"I am not afraid," she repeated; but her voice somewhat belied her words. "And now it is time that we should say good-bye. Say it quickly, Caryl —it is far best so—and say it kindly."

He had risen whilst she was speaking, and grasped both her hands; but he rather held her aloof than drew her towards him.

"Good-bye," he said hoarsely. "If I didn't think it would bring you bad luck, I'd wish you happy. I am glad you were not afraid of my hurting you; you were right enough there. Do you believe, that every scrap you ever wrote to me is burnt long ago? You do believe it. Well—I am glad of that, too. Good-bye, once more."

He flung her hands away with a kind of roughness; but there was no anger in the gesture, only the passion of one putting away from him a fierce temptation : even so a man, parched with thirst, might fling aside some ruddy fruit, the juice of which is deadly. Then he turned, and went hastily out.

Lena made no effort to detain or recall him; but sat quite silent and motionless, her hands lying listlessly where they had fallen.

So Mrs. Moreland found her a few minutes later, when, hearing no more the murmur of voices, she ventured in cautiously. Neither did Lena stir, till the other's lips were pressed upon her forehead : then she started, shivering all over.

"He might have kissed me once—just once," she murmured.

Though she looked up into her friend's face piteously, it was evident that she spoke only to herself, and was scarcely aware of the other's presence. Neither then nor thereafter did Lena Shafton make more moan; and yet she had just passed through one of those crises, that tell more upon a life than lustres or decades.

If you have ever read that sad cynical book of Mürger's, "*La Vie de Bohéme,*" you will scarcely have forgotten the episode of the *Manchon de Francine,* or the burial scene in the cemetery under the November fog. The earth has just been heaped over the small sordid coffin ; and by the side of the low mound, in which the wooden crosslet is to be planted, a mourner is standing, whose face had startled not a few of those who came to celebrate the feast of the dead. Yet the one audible plaint that breaks from his lips is for himself, rather than for his lost love— "*O ma jeunesse ! C'est vous qu'on enterre !*"

At much such a funeral Lena had just assisted. The freshness of girlhood had passed from her long ago ; nevertheless, when she came here to-day, there did survive in her some hope howsoever faint, some trust howsoever insecure, some tenderness howsoever wasted. All these now were cold and in cerement ; and of the pall covering them, it were best never to lift one corner in the after time.

In Caryl Glynne, too, though in lesser degree, there was worked a change. Lena's love had not been hard to win ; he had accepted it as if he were gathering his due ; nevertheless, he prized it, after his fashion. If he had not always, since, kept his fancy in curb, he could not be charged with having created any fresh scandal ; and more than one of his ancient allies had found him strangely negligent and formal. As he walked away that morning, there was a void within him, such as he had never known before ; and, though he was little given to romantic fancies, there was ringing in his ears, like the refrain of a sad old ditty, this one word—

Alone !

Of any purely unselfish emotion he had probably ceased to be capable. If the link, betwixt himself and Lena, had proved more enduring than others

G

which had been snapped or loosened so easily, the excitement of difficulty had much to do with this; but that she had exercised a wonderful fascination over him, is certain. He thought still, as he had thought on the second evening of their acquaintance, that there was no one quite like her in all the world. If any freak of fortune had made him wealthy during these late years, I do not think he would have debated within himself for one instant, whether he should break or perform his promise; and, though the old adage about reformed rakes has recently fallen into much disrepute—*pour cause*—it by no means follows that the marriage would have been a miserable one.

But when Wildair and Millamant saw the errors of their ways, and swore their great oath, 'henceforth to live cleanly,' they always had a competence, if not a fair estate, to retire upon. To the pauper profligate it is allowed, of course, to repent, but rarely to reap the fruits thereof in equal measure with his wealthy brother. As our old acquaintance, Rebecca, remarked:—"It would be easy to be a good woman on five thousand a-year." Rely upon it, some excellent intentions, as well as brilliant inventions, have lain in abeyance purely from want of base capital.

Lena Shafton had many faults—Caryl Glynne vices not a few. The love subsisting betwixt them was a wild bitter gourd, that it would be a sin to compare to the honourable domestic tree, under whose branches so many Christian couples find pleasure and peace; nevertheless, when it was cut down, there was taken away their best, if not their last, chance of thriving.

# CHAPTER IX.

MRS. SHAFTON was by no means a devout lady; her religious observances, it is to be feared, were conventional, if not compulsory. When she 'bouned her to rest,' she knelt down to her orisons, just as regularly as she brushed out her hair; it had been her custom so to do from early childhood, and she could not have omitted either ceremonial without a feeling of incompleteness and discomfort. In like manner, she regarded church-going rather as a social than a sacred duty. But the murmured thanksgiving that escaped her when she heard what answer Lord Atherstone would receive, came straight and fervent from her heart; and the ejaculation was not only sincere, but nearly if not quite disinterested.

In her pleading with Lena yesterday, she had spoken nothing but truth; perhaps not quite all the truth. It was true, that she felt so tired sometimes, that rest in whatsoever shape it came must needs have been grateful; but she had got so used to shifts and straits that they had ceased to vex her keenly; and, if only her own fortunes had been at stake, when the access of depression was over, she would have found strength to struggle on to the end, even if the end seemed not near. It was the uncertainty —or worse than uncertainty—in her children's future, not in her own, that haunted her by night and by day; and it was with scarcely a thought of her own personal comfort or profit, that she had pressed upon Lena, as far as she dared, the expediency of accepting the marriage-offer. It is possible that she nourished a vague hope, that from such a powerful alliance some sort of advantage might accrue to Miles; but she had had no time as yet to put this into shape or substance; and, indeed, was more than content that the unlucky prodigal for the present should be kept discreetly in the background.

Just one more word in favour of the match-makers. They have long been fair game for every pen, male, female, and epicene; and it is a wonder that under the shower of missiles their ranks have not been perceptibly thinned, or their energy abated. Nevertheless, if these matters were sifted thoroughly, their machinations might be found more free from the leaven of selfishness than are most human plottings. The instances where they can reckon on any profit, private or personal, are surely rare, and with the advance of civilisation must become rarer. You might as well compare the Derby Dilly with the Scotch Express, as poor Clarissa's coevals with their modern antitypes; but on no one point perhaps would the difference be more marked, than in their filial relations. Is it possible that scarce a century has slipped away, since the well-nurtured damsel curtsied lowly on entering the presence of her parents, and, in saluting them, always remembered to temper affection with reverence? If the daughter of our Period does not practically emancipate herself during her maidenhood, she generally assumes independence before the fashion of her trousseau is changed; and, if she were slack in such self-assertion, there is always the chance of a husband ready and willing to take up the daggers; for, remember, the more eligible the *parti*, the less tractable in all likelihood will be the son-in-law. The meekest of men, after being courted and adulated for a certain time, will be apt to carry his head somewhat high —too high at all events to bow it readily to a pseudo-maternal yoke. The Old Soldier will always be a stock-personage in domestic drama. There, up

to the last retributive scene, she may make the pair of
innocent turtle-doves flutter at her frown, and fly in
obedience to her nod; but in real society she is a
very minor power. So, when patience, science, and
endurance such as, whilst depreciating the object, we
needs must admire, have achieved their end, there
will remain—the consciousness of having done her
duty in the state of life to which she was called—the
fulfilment of the maternal instinct that she shares
with all others of the like who exist amongst God's
creatures—the vanity of emulation—and the hope that
each conquest may be a stepping-stone to others, till
no more are left to aspire to. Beyond this, the selfish
reward is scarcely more substantial than the grey
olive wreath of Olympia; neither does the wearer
of this chaplet gain much honour in her own country.

The hunting of the nubile youth is not a very
noble or elevating pursuit; let us hope that this
accounts for man's lack of success therein. If you
have any doubts of our disability, you have only to
watch the widower trying his hand at *chaperonage.*
He may be foolishly fond in his indulgence; he may
allow his girls to crowd his dinner-table with their
admirers to the exclusion of his own familiars; he
may occasionally await their pleasure—this is a rare
instance—far into the small hours, rubberless, sup-
perless, yet uncomplaining; and so things may go
on promisingly for a while. But in the finer professional touches he will fail none the less lamentably;
and, very soon recognising this, will be only too glad
to transfer his charge to some discreet kinswoman—
retiring himself into the background, till the question
of settlements shall arise.

Our weapons are a great improvement on the
Nemæan club; but, since Hercules failed in spin-
ning, we have never learnt to wield the distaff.
Ought we not, therefore, to assign some credit to
the slender fingers that reel off, so deftly, the thread
that sooner or later binds most of our fellows?

Having relieved herself by her brief thanksgiving, Mrs. Shafton was very temperate in triumph.

"You have made me so happy, darling," she
said; and a kiss followed as a matter of course.
But she was far too wise to lavish praises or
caresses, more likely to irritate than to soothe.
Indeed, something in Lena's face prevented her
mother from being quite comfortable or confident
as yet: it was neither angry nor sorrowful; but
the restless, uneasy look would have been better
away, and in all her movements subdued impatience was observable.  She made no pretence
at touching the luncheon that had been kept
waiting for her; and, after a second glass of wine,
her cheeks remained so perfectly colourless that
Mrs. Shafton was constrained to remark thereon,
and even to suggest that this might be artistically amended.  But Lena would not hear of such
a thing.

"I am sorry if I look like a victim," she said,
—"especially as I don't feel the least like one.
I dare say Lord Atherstone will be satisfied; and
I don't think he would approve of a make-up, even
for such a special occasion.  At any rate, I shall
risk it."

Her mother did not press the point, and soon
afterwards retreated to her own chamber; whence
she did not emerge till the important interview
was over.

Twilight was closing in again when Lord Atherstone was ushered into Lena's presence; but the
room was not dark yet, and it was lighted up
besides by a cheerful fire.

Very keenly Ralph's eyes rested on the girl's
face, as she rose up to meet him; and they read
nothing of encouragement there.  When he took
her hand, he felt as if his fate was still swaying
in the balance.  He had been patient—strangely
patient for him—during the hours of suspense;

but he was too eager now to know the best or the worst, to go through any form of greeting.

" Well ?"

That was all he said; and it would be difficult to represent, in type, the intense question of that one syllable.

Letting her hand rest in his, she smiled upon him—coldly, it is true, but still she smiled.

" I can't tell whether it will turn out well or ill; but I can say 'Yes' to the question you asked me yesterday."

His fingers closed round hers—less tenderly than with the quick muscular contraction of one shaken by sudden emotion; and she felt, rather than saw, that his whole frame trembled. There was nothing 'superior' about Miss Shafton; she had, indeed, more than her share of her sex's weaknesses; and certainly she did, just then, savour thoroughly the womanly triumph of controlling a nature stronger than her own.

" Do you—can you mean it?" Ralph said in a whisper. " I can hardly believe it yet."

Lena disengaged herself gently; and sank back into the place she had quitted, motioning him towards another chair close beside her.

" I do mean it. You remember what you asked me for, and what you promised to be satisfied with. At present, I dare not offer more; but I will try my very best to be happy, and to make you so. Now, would it have been easier to believe all this if I had answered you on the instant?"

Was it the remembrance — almost too late—of a resolve formed before he came; or the promptings of his better angel; or the paleness of her cheek and the chilliness of her smile, that caused Ralph Atherstone to refrain, yet an instant, before he set the cup to his thirsty lips? I cannot tell. This much is certain : he made no effort to detain Lena, and did not take the chair she indicated;

but, passing round her where she sat, stood in just the same posture as yesterday; and, as he made answer, he looked down on her with the same earnest gaze.

"It would have been harder—infinitely harder. I remember my words quite well, and I mean every letter of them still. Don't misjudge me if you can help it; but I have thought a good deal in these last hours, and there is something I must say. It is more for your sake than mine, I swear. Your mother promised me that she would not try to influence you, and she has kept her promise, I am sure. That is well; but it is not quite enough. I will accept your faith—how gladly you never can guess; and wait, more patiently, perhaps, than you think possible, for your affection, if I am only assured —I want no other assurance than your own, mind —that you are now heart-whole and heart-free. Ah! I see you are angry."—Indeed, her cheek did flush stormily.—"I don't wonder at it. Yet I must speak out in my own rough way. Being what you are, it would have been a miracle, if no one more lover-like than a battered old soldier had sought your love. I want to know nothing of the past, and I have not a fear for the future, if you can only tell me that, at this moment of our speaking, no other man's shadow falls between us. It can only be a shadow at the worst; or I should have had another kind of answer."

Lena was constitutionally very fearless—indeed, a Shafton of Blytheswold seldom stumbled through blenching at danger — and no mercenary motive swayed her; for this match was none of her contriving, and the marring of it would have cost her not one selfish regret; but a cowardly schemer—not wholly sordid and treacherous—looking up into the face of that true, loyal gentleman, might have found it hard to lie.

"I am not angry."—Her voice and colour were

quite steady now.—"You have a perfect right to speak as you have spoken; and I think I am glad you have done so. No; I have never yet been forced to answer the question you asked me yesterday; but, perhaps, that is because I always wished to avoid it, except—except once. In my life I have only cared for one person; I did care for him very much—more than I shall ever care again. If you wish to hear who that was, and how it ended, and how long ago, I won't refuse; but it is all over— as much over, as if he were dead. If it had been otherwise, you should not have held my hand to-day. If you choose to take me as I am, you will not need to be jealous even of a shadow."

Her eyes met his unshrinkingly; and, as they met, a light came out on his face, mellowing its rugged outline.

"I don't wish to hear one other word," he said; "I am satisfied, once and for all—so satisfied that, when I doubt again, it will be because you yourself have told me, it is time. When I listen to any other witness, I hope that God in my greatest need will forget to listen to me."

Bowing his head, he kissed her on the brow— not passionately, but with a fond reverence, and a certain solemnity withal; like one setting his seal to a compact whereon hang interests of life and death.

Thus these two were affianced.

In this her half-confession—that it was incomplete was not her fault, remember — was Lena Shafton quite honest and sincere? For the moment, beyond a doubt, she held herself so to be. Only a few hours ago, the sudden mention of a certain name would have set her pulses throbbing; but, now, that name had been very close to her own lips without causing them to tremble, and without waking within her a single pang of longing or regret. There was much strength in her nature, though perhaps not an abiding strength. When she said 'good-bye,' it was no form of words. Then and there she crushed, or meant to crush, her luckless love so effectually that it never should trouble her more. That she had done this, she did then implicitly believe. If Caryl's warning, that 'all was not over betwixt them,' had crossed her mind, she would have set it at nought boldly, even scornfully. Utter folly, you will say. But is the case so rare, that we should wonder at or discredit it?

Have not some of us, in our time, beguiled ourselves in like fashion, and suffered for it, too? In our wisdom and valiance we set our foot upon the snake's head; and keep it there till the venomous beast has ceased to writhe, and lies quite helpless, and harmless, and still; and so wend on our way rejoicing. And it is well with us for a while. By-and-by, in the midst of our late-found innocence and integrity, a smile meant for another, that we catch in passing, brings fierce, jealous pangs; or a look meant for ourself — only for ourself — brings back a thrill of guilty pleasure; and, before the pain or the pleasure has passed, a tightening round our heart stops its healthy beating. No need to tell us what that means: we have felt it often enough before. We know at once, of a surety, that the creature was stunned, not slain: perhaps it only mimicked death till we were at a safe distance; and then, coming to its evil life again, lay in wait till it could creep back unawares to its old coiling-place—there to abide, till some charmer shall be found powerful enough to cast it forth for ever and aye.

The parallel is not very novel or original, I own; but I fancy it will be needed, some few times yet, before romances cease to be written and read. Perhaps the iteration is excusable, considering how often through over-true tales winds the trail of The Serpent.

# CHAPTER X.

THOUGH about his philosophy there is always a savour of fresh flowers and old Falernian, and though his saws are set to lightsome music, our friend Flaccus uttered words of wisdom now and then; and dealt stricter justice to himself than Cæsar or Mæcenas. Thus he wrote, when his tenth lustre was waning :—

> Jam nec spes animi credula mutui,
> Nec certare juvat mero,
> Nec vincire novis tempora floribus.

The lines are not hard to construe; and certain elders, under certain circumstances, might with advantage lay them to heart. We cannot wonder at the jubilation of Lycus when the *dissimilis Chloe* consents to smile upon his suit; but, if he would moderate the first exuberance of his transports, it might be better not only for his dignity but for his interests. Chloe, at least, would be little likely to quarrel with such reserve in her adorer.

Under Ralph Atherstone's rugged exterior, there was hidden a shrewd tact that not inaptly supplied the place of innate delicacy. His manner that afternoon might have appeared to some rather formal and cold; but in her present frame of mind it exactly suited Lena. She had no aversion for her affianced, and already it was pleasant to feel herself under thoroughly safe protectorate; nevertheless, it was an intense relief to find that she was not expected to be even passively amative.

Ten minutes after the words of their betrothal had

been spoken, the pair were sitting side by side—at a fairly decorous distance—discussing their future as placidly as if months had passed by. Lord Atherstone was quite frank and explicit about the state of affairs at Templestowe.

"There must be a change, of course," he said; "sooner or later—perhaps the sooner the better; but it takes some time to make a new home, and I should be loath to hurry Philip and Marian in their arrangements. She has been a good daughter to me. I fancy you'll get on well together. At any rate, you won't mind sheltering them till they're settled?"

"How could I mind it?" Lena interrupted; "it is the very thing I should have suggested. I wish I could be sure that Lady Marian would like me; she might give me so many hints about housekeeping. You know I shall make all sorts of mistakes; for our *ménage* at Blytheswold is on the most limited scale, and I have had no practice even there; and, besides, I shall feel so fearfully like an interloper at first."

"Never *that*, I hope," he said, gravely. "Marian's a very good manager, I believe; and I'm much mistaken in her if she doesn't help you to feel yourself at home at once. I shall write to her—not to Philip—by to-night's post, and I have not much time to spare. I must see your mother, of course, before I go."

He leant forward as he rose and kissed her—this time upon the cheek; but still with the same formal courtesy that had marked his first salute.

Five minutes later Lena sat in her own room alone, rather dazed and bewildered; but with an impression, nevertheless, that everything had gone more smoothly than she had expected. At any rate this much is certain; if by speaking a word she could have undone the evening's work—ay, and the morning's to boot—that word would not now have been spoken.

Over Mrs. Shafton's interview with her intended son-in-law it is not necessary to linger: though brief, it was very much to the purpose; and, when it was ended, she had every right to indulge in the luxury of a long blissful reverie. For the shoals were weathered now, and betwixt her fair ship and anchorage lay nothing but the common chances of life and death.

If Ralph Lord Atherstone had been asked, whether from infancy upwards he had ever stood in awe of any human being, he might very safely have answered 'No.' For his homely old father he had entertained but little reverence—not a particle of fear; and, if in his early soldiering days he held his Chief in some inward as well as outward respect, it was to the authority, not to the man, that he deferred. Of late years, wheresoever he abode, he had had the right to command; and had naturally waxed more and more independent of others' opinion. Notwithstanding this, it was not without a kind of awkwardness and reluctance that he began the letter, wherein his affianced was to be presented to her future relatives; indeed two or three sheets were torn up before one was filled. Thus the note ran at last:—

"MY DEAR MARIAN,

"By all rule and precedent, this letter ought to be addressed to Philip. I address it thus, simply because I think that the news it brings concerns you more nearly than him. If I have not misjudged you both, he has always rather disliked Templestowe than otherwise; whilst you have grown fond of the place, and therefore would be more interested in any change. There will be a great change, and very soon; for I hope, within a few weeks, to bring a wife home. Her name is Lena Shafton; and she comes of as good a stock as any in the North-country, though the Blytheswold branch is the younger one. In all other respects

I suppose the world will call my choice unwise; but
the world and I have had so little to do with each
other of late, that this does not trouble me. I believe
that the future Lady Atherstone would become a higher
station than I can offer her. And she believes that
there is nothing to hinder our happiness, though I
am more than twice her age. This ought surely to
be sufficient. I do not expect any congratulations
from you; but I do expect that you will help to make
Lena's way smooth at first; how, your own sense and
tact will tell you better than I could suggest. If I am
wrong in this reliance, it will be unlucky for us all.
You know enough of our family arrangements, to be
aware that I could not, if I would, materially affect
Philip's future interests. And I should be sorry
indeed, if I thought that you could possibly interpret
a word I have written into a notice to quit Templestowe. I hope—and Lena thoroughly sympathizes
with me here—that you will make it your home, till
you have found another quite to your mind; and you
will be welcome there, at any and all times, till my
death brings you back to your own. You need not
answer this, as I shall be home by the end of the
week. When we meet I do not wish my intended
marriage to be a forbidden subject; I only wish it to
be considered as practically an accomplished fact.
About such things perhaps, the least said is the
soonest mended. You will show this to Philip, of
course, so that I need send him no separate message.
I am, now and always,

"Affectionately yours,

"ATHERSTONE."

A simple, straightforward letter enough, and though
a trifle imperious, kindly, not less than honestly,
meant; yet it did not altogether satisfy the writer.
He imagined Marian's keen satirical eyes gleaming
and her lip curling as she read; and this fancy might
account for the half-defiant term of more than one

sentence. However, it was finished, such as it was.
As he rose from his writing-table, Lord Atherstone
shook himself, like a man who has been working hard
in a constrained posture ; and he did not feel quite
at ease till he had dropped the letter into a pillar-box,
on his way down to St. James's Street.

You remember the brightening of Ralph's face,
when Lena gave him the last assurance he required.
In despite of his late occupation, this could not have
altogether vanished ; for he had not been long in his
club when a man, who had watched him curiously for
a minute or so, came up and accosted him. The two
had been intimate, and friends, so far as the temperament of one allowed, since they first served together,
and still called each other by their Christian names.

"What's happened to you, Ralph ?" Sir Charles
Wroughton said. " You look positively benevolent.
If you hadn't more money than you could spend, I
should have thought you had come into a fortune ;
or, if you were a score of years younger, that you
were going to be married."

Atherstone smiled rather grimly.

"Considering it was a snap-shot, and made in a
bad light, that second barrel does you credit. It has
an odd sound, I daresay ; but—I *am* going to be
married."

In the distant corner where they stood their talk
could not be overheard, and the room was nearly
empty ; but the long shrill whistle, with which the
other greeted this intelligence, caused more than one
reader of the evening papers to look up.

"It does sound odd," he assented, after a pause of
several seconds. " But what does sound matter after
all ? I believe we're both of us in the very bloom of
our age, if the world would only think so ; and you're
the wiriest of the two. At any rate, we can give
weight away yet to most of the cigarette-and-absinthe
lot. No! it isn't the age that staggers me ; but I
thought you were more set as a widower than I am

as a bachelor. Is it indiscreet to ask the lady's name? Or, at all events, do I know her?"

"There's no mystery in the matter; and you knew her about a week before I did. It is Percy's niece, Lena."

Wroughton's eyes ceased to twinkle, and his jovial countenance fell.

"Percy's niece?" he muttered; "wild Cosmo Shafton's daughter? The——"

He was not a recluse like his friend, you see, and was pretty well posted in all the scandals of the last ten years. If the sentence had been completed, it might have run—"the girl they talked of with Caryl Glynne?"—but he gulped the words back, and went on—"How we should have laughed, when we were all up at Kirkfell, if any one had prophesied what would come to pass! You most of all, Ralph, I do believe."

"Not unlikely—just at first; but, before I got south, I knew my own mind, though *she* never knew it till yesterday. You've my free leave to laugh as much as you like now—not that you would ask it. You haven't congratulated me yet."

In much going to and fro in the world, Sir Charles Wroughton had not rubbed off all his honesty, and still had a fair amount of conscience left at the service of his friends: he would not be trapped into a conventionalism now.

"Compliments would be rather out of place between you and me," he grumbled. "You don't want to be told, at this time of day, that I wish well to you and —and—yours." It was a tough monosyllable; but he mastered it at last. "There will be plenty to congratulate, and not a few to envy you. She's handsomer than any picture I've seen."

Atherstone's face brightened again. It was very evident how even that acknowledgment gratified him. And then their converse turned on safer ground.

Years after, with the regret of a man who has in

his obstinacy set at nought a clear evil omen, Ralph remembered the strangeness of his old comrade's manner, and how, in the meagre expression of sympathy, his tongue had halted. When the end had come to pass, Charles Wroughton called himself coward for not having spoken out bluntly; though, after all, he had nothing surer to rest upon than report or surmise. But, in truth, no plainness of speech would have much availed. If proof positive had been set before Ralph Atherstone just then, he would probably have refused to listen or to read; and vague hints or warnings would no more have turned him from his purpose, than floating flecks of thistledown would check or change the course of the north wind.

# CHAPTER XI.

THERE is this advantage about a multiplicity of grievances—that the sufferer seldom frets long over any single one. In the earlier part of that week, Philip Ashleigh had several small worries; and these gradually thrust into the background the danger that had appeared so formidable on Sunday, till he began to consider it rather an imaginary one. Indeed, he said as much to Marian; and, when she declined to agree that her suspicions might have been groundless, was exceedingly peevish, giving vent to some sharp strictures on women's fancies and the like.

Marian had scarcely been in her wonted spirits since that incident at the breakfast-table, and she did not feel up to futile argument; otherwise, perhaps, her reply would not have been so meek.

"I daresay you are right, Philip," she said. "I am sure I hope so."

The which submission her husband accepted with a sniff of superiority.

Wednesday's post arrived in due course; and Lady Marian's letters were brought to her, as usual, before she rose. There were several, as it chanced, that morning; but her eye lighted at once on the one in Lord Atherstone's handwriting, and she snatched it up, casting the others aside. However, in despite of this apparent eagerness, she held it in her hand for a brief space before, with a kind of effort, she tore open the envelope.

A more useless faculty can hardly be imagined,

for it profits little to guess at the truth a few seconds before we are certified thereof; but it is odd how often even obtuse people are *clairvoyant* in this especial line. Lady Marian had received perhaps a score of letters bearing the same superscription, and there was no sort of reason why this one should not, like the rest, have related merely to ordinary domestic arrangements; but that such was not its character, she felt as sure before she broke the seal as when she had perused it to the last word.

As she read it through very slowly, her countenance betrayed neither anger nor surprise; but there came over it a certain malign look, of which before you would not have deemed it capable; and this abode there after she had laid the letter softly down, and whilst she leant back musing with eyes half closed. The news were not unexpected, of course: indeed, for three days past, she had almost reckoned on receiving some such a missive; yet the blow came home none the lighter. Perhaps you have not realised, why it stung her so keenly.

Though Marian had little personal ambition, she was intensely fond of power: it was not for ostentation's sake, or even with a view to any substantial profit, that she sought it; in the mere consciousness and exercise of authority lay her delight. The mistress of such a household as the Ashleighs might prudently maintain, would be a very different personage from the *châtelaine*—in fact, if not in title—of Templestowe.

Only very weak or well-disciplined natures can adapt themselves to those rapid descents, even where there is no degradation, without a murmur. When it was noised abroad in Elba, that the dethroned Emperor was already so reconciled to the change as to begin to busy himself with the economy of his island, those who had him in ward ought to have doubled their precautions; for that placability, if not a feint, must surely have sprung from the certain knowledge that the bark was even now hovering in the offing that would bear him away to make another rally for dominion. Since the days of Walworth, has the civic chair been filled by one so stout or so humble of heart as to have met, without one pang of regret, the uprising of the ninth sun of November?

But, howsoever Marian Ashleigh may have chafed at the thought that her reign at Templestowe was nearly ended, this was not the darkest element in her present discontent. Philip, as you know, always had a grievance on hand, with which his wife—in outward seeming, at least—generally contrived to sympathise; but there was a grief, a common grief, concerning which the lips of both were sealed—the grief of a childless marriage. Though most of her husband's maladies were as imaginary as his other troubles, Marian knew very well that the father's surviving the son was scarcely an improbability; and in such a case—supposing further that another heir to Templestowe should be born from Lord Atherstone's second marriage—what chance would there be of her ever being 'brought back to her own?' Pondering over these things, it is no wonder if her countenance lowered. After a few minutes, she arose, without so much as glancing at the rest of her correspondence; and, throwing on a wrapper, went into her husband's dressing-room hard by.

In that brief passage her face had nearly regained its usual composure; nevertheless Philip, who was not particularly sharp-sighted, guessed what had happened before she put the letter into his hand. He took it and read it through, as it were, mechanically, his jaw dropping lower and lower; and, when it was finished, looked up at his wife with a blank helplessness that was almost pitiable. Perhaps she so interpreted it; or perhaps she thought a triumph, under the circumstances, too trivial: at all events, she refrained from the feminine formula of—" I told you how it would be,"—and spoke very gently.

"It sounds hard now that it has come, doesn't it, Philip, even though we were half prepared?"

As Ashleigh set his teeth together, there was a look of his father about the lower part of his face—weak and inane enough as a rule—and his answer was almost inaudible; it would have been better had it been quite so, for the syllables that caught her ear made Marian shrink a pace backward.

"Hush!" she said; "such words would be too wicked, even if there were cause. Lord Atherstone has done no more than he has a perfect right to do; no more, perhaps, than we had a right to calculate upon. You cannot deny that he writes kindly and generously, and even considerately—for him."

"Generously!"

The word came out like the spit of an angry cat. Marian saw that argument with her husband, in his present temper, would be purely wasted.

"I am sorry you take it so," she said; "it won't mend matters. Perhaps by breakfast-time you will be in a more rational frame of mind; and then you can help me to think how we can make the best of it. Now, I am going to read my other letters: I hope some of them may tell pleasanter news."

Indeed, though he brought small appetite to his morning meal, Ashleigh had so far recovered from the shock as to be able to discuss, in his own fretful fashion, their own prospects, and the probable character of the future Lady Atherstone; with whom, as it chanced, neither he nor his wife was acquainted.

But with such vague speculation, it was not likely that one of Marian's character would rest content. Before noon—unknown to Philip—she had despatched a note to a certain cousin in town; praying him to furnish her with all the reliable information that he could gather, bearing on Lena Shafton's family and personal history.

She could hardly have applied to a likelier source. By dint of long service, Archibald Kerneguy had risen

high in the Foreign Office ; perhaps he would have
risen higher by dint of merit, if he had devoted as
much time, and trouble, and talent, to the practice of
his profession as he had bestowed on domestic
diplomacy.   There were very few stories of late years,
written in cipher, to which he had not sooner or later
gained the key.   He was not a mischievous person,
for he was too cautious to be a gossip, and too humane
to be a tale-bearer ; nevertheless, people were afraid
of him, simply because he was supposed to know so
much, and would liefer have offended many loud-
voiced and bitter-tongued satirists than this placid
philosopher.   As he read his cousin's missive, a quiet,
cunning smile wrinkled his lips; but he seemed to
ponder somewhat gravely after he laid it down, and
paused more than once whilst inditing this reply :—

"MY DEAR MARIAN,
       "You know you may always command me
and my resources, such as they are ; and if one cannot
speak freely to one's cousin, there is an end of confidences ; nevertheless, I doubt—rather more than
doubt—whether I am justified in answering your
questions.   Their object, of course, is very plain ;
for Miss Shafton's engagement was discussed last
night at several tobacco-parliaments, I fancy, besides
the one at which I assisted.
       "There will be slaying of oxen, and broaching of
barrels, and lighting of deal-fires, I suppose, when
that same bride is brought home to Templestowe ;
but I do *not* suppose that her reception within doors
will be absolutely enthusiastic.   But then, again, to
find a house—castle, cot, mansion, or villa—where
a stepmother—particularly a young stepmother, and
handsome *par-dessus le marché*—might count on being
honestly welcome, you would have to travel as far
as the Undiscovered Islands, if any such remain.
Now, in my humble judgment, when a bitter draught
is inevitable, it is infinitely more sensible to open

your mouth and shut your eyes, and swallow it like Margery Goodchild, than to submit the potion to all possible tests of taste, sight, and smell. You will see the application of this elegant allegory at once; but that it should for one moment influence you, would be far too much to expect. So, having tried to satisfy my own conscience, I will try and satisfy your curiosity—always under protest.

"We will take the lady's family first. In point of descent, it would puzzle the Herald's Office to pick a hole in the coat of the Shaftons of Blytheswold; but, in a social point of view, their garments, for some generations past, have needed much mending. It is of the males I speak, remember; for concerning the females history is comparatively silent. Ill-natured people have said that, by the side of such *diables déchaînés* as their husbands and brothers, the womankind must needs have seemed quasi-angelical; for myself I prefer to believe that there was no evil to be told, rather than that it was smothered in comparison. At any rate, against Miss Shafton's next ancestress—this is our diplomatic way of putting mother—there is not a word to be said. She has had very difficult cards to play with her late husband and with one, at least, of her two children; and has played them, I have always heard, with great patience, honesty, and skill. The child I refer to is a prodigal, a very prodigal son, presently a lieutenant in the —— Hussars; who is wasting his substance in the good old family fashion, rather more rapidly than his sire and grandsire did before him.

"Next, as to the *physique.* I should have guessed you would be curious on this point, even if you had not put it beyond a doubt by blinking that question altogether. Well: if the figure is not perfect on an imperial scale, I, speaking as a humble amateur, do not quite know where it is to be matched. In the face there are half-a-dozen faults, I daresay; but she has taken beauty-rank ever since I can remember

her, and it is too late—or too soon—-now to try to
disqualify her.

"As to the *morale*,"—Kerneguy came fairly to a
check here, and walking to the window looked out
over the Mall; seeking, perhaps, as cleverer men
have done before him, to gather inspiration from
the thin brown trees soughing and swaying in the
sullen wind. He came back after a while, and wrote
on again, but more slowly than before.

"As to the *morale*. We are on much more delicate
ground here; and, pray remember, the few hints
that I can furnish are founded entirely on hearsay
and guesswork, not on any personal knowledge of
the subject. If my poor skill in physiognomy does
not mislead me, I think I may fairly attribute to the
lady a certain strength of will and passion, and a
temper less violent than intractable. I can conceive
her wilful or reckless to any degree; but scarcely,
under any provocation, cowardly, malicious, or mean.
On the whole, very nearly a grand character; but
of the kind which is wrecked oftener than more
ignoble ones. Now—don't stretch or distort my
meaning—I do not pretend to insinuate that she
has come to any serious grief as yet; but, that
she was much talked about at one time, I cannot
deny. This is no more than any handsome woman,
who lives up to the pace of the Period, ought to
expect; but Miss Shafton had exceptionally bad luck
in the name which was coupled with hers. You
were very little in town before your marriage, and
these matters belong to the Pre-Marianite era;
nevertheless you must have heard more than once
of Caryl Glynne. Perhaps the man is not a whit
worse than many of his fellows; but he has an unlucky *spécialité* for compromising his female acquaintance. And 'acquaintance' is rather a mild way
of putting the intimacy of these two, while it lasted.
I never heard anything worse than imprudences
alleged against Miss Shafton; such as open-air

meetings held at uncanonical hours in the forenoon, and the like; but people made as much fuss about it as if the whole Decalogue had been broken. I daresay Glynne would willingly have married her; but, as his marrying any one but an heiress was and is a notorious impossibility, his good intentions did not count for much in extenuation. To do the mother justice, when the rumours flying abroad came to her ears, she acted promptly and decisively; and, if the meshes entangling the fair Lena were not broken then and there, it was no fault of hers. That they were so broken I am inclined to believe; indeed I should feel absolutely confident of it, if a certain change in Glynne's manner of life had not led me to think that up till now, at all events, he must have had some hope or object of which the world was not aware. He is still very far from sanctity, no doubt; but since then he has contrived to steer clear of open scandals. Don't you admire the charity, that cannot confess improvement in one's neighbour without imputing to him covert, if not evil, motives? At any rate, of late years the Shaftons have lived so very quietly and blamelessly that Society may well afford to bury the hatchet; and, if I cannot congratulate you on your connection, I will not allow that you are greatly to be condoled with.

" I have answered your queries with thoroughly unprofessional candour; and, though I am sure that you will make no ill use of my weakness, I look at what I have written not without self-reproach. Doubtless you would have heard these *cancans* sooner or later, and perhaps in a more garbled fashion than I have set them down; nevertheless it might have been better if I had chanced this.

" My acquaintance with the future Lady Atherstone is very slight; so you may believe it is not in *her* interest that I close this long letter with a short scrap of advice, which you may leave unread if you will.

"Does not the text run thus : 'Agree with thine adversary quickly, whiles thou art in the way with him ?'

"My dear Marian, it was not to men only that these words were spoken ; and there is more of wisdom in them—ay, even of worldly wisdom—than in most saws or proverbs.  I pray you, now if ever, to lay them to heart.  I feel certain that it will be easy for you soon to gain a fast friend and useful ally ; also, it may not be hard to make a dangerous enemy. Either way, my good wishes follow you.  But, in the latter case, with all possible respect for your science and courage, I fear that some day you will have to call a truce, and that if granted, it will be not on your own terms.

"I hope, the next service you require at my hands will be less distasteful to me than that which I have just performed ; though I do not begrudge you even this.

"Always yours,

"A."

It was characteristic, both of the writer and of the person to whom this document was addressed, that it never alluded to the possibility of Philip's sharing in its confidences.  In truth, you would have thought such a caution thoroughly needless, if you had watched Marian during the perusal.  She did not attempt to open the Foreign Office despatch when it came with the other letters ; but locked it away in a casket, and there let it lie till her husband had departed to the Petty Sessions at Heslingford. Then she shut herself up in her boudoir with the precious packet ; and whilst she studied it to the last syllable, weighing the last grain of its meaning, the great bell overhead might have rung out alarums, and she would never have stirred.  After a while—a long while—she dropped the letter, envelope and all, into the heart of the fierce fire that burned close to her feet. Her eyes followed the light grey flakes, as they vanished up the chimney, with a kind of regret. Yet, a more useless paper than that just annihilated can hardly be conceived; for every line, by this time, was re-written in characters more abiding than pen ever traced on scroll; and, before Marian Ashleigh will forget the lightest syllable therein, she will forget the prayers they taught her when she was a little child.

# CHAPTER XII.

ONE forenoon, some twenty centuries ago, Cambyses, son of Cyrus, sitting in his summer-garden, under the shadow of the planes, overheard one of his courtiers extolling the wondrous prowess of a certain Bactrian bowman. Now, the King himself was a matchless archer, and his heart as he listened grew hot with envy. After a while, lifting up his head, he pointed to a single tree that stood afar off in the green sward. "Thou seest yonder palm, Prexaspes," quoth he; "thinkest thou that this Bactrian of thine could aim at such distance at a hand's breadth, and not miss?" And Prexaspes made answer—"Nay, my lord; for I spake only of feats that may be compassed by mortal skill; and such an one is not of these." Said the King—"And if I myself were to make essay, thinkest thou that I should likewise fail?" Prexaspes answered — "I needs must think so, especially as yestereven my lord tarried somewhat long over the beakers." The great black eyes that, even when wrath, or drink, or lust inflamed them not, gleamed ever savagely, roved round the circle till they lighted on a boy, beautiful above his page-fellows—the firstborn of Prexaspes. Then said Cambyses—"Go, bind my cup-bearer fast to yonder palm, so that he stir not a finger, and fetch hither the Macrobian bow." It was the self-same weapon that the spies had brought back from Ethiopia, with the challenge to any Persian to bend it; and, in truth, to that task none had been found equal, save only the Great King.

He strained it now till the horns nearly met; and, as he drew the long arrow to the head, he glanced askance at the satrap, saying, "I aim at the heart." Then came a sharp twang, a shrill whistle, and the dull echo of a bolt smiting its mark; and those who were keenest of sight saw the fair child fall forward over his bonds, with all his limbs a-quivering. "Go now, Prexaspes," quoth the King, "and mark how my shaft hath sped." The father did as he was bidden. When he returned, his face was white and writhen, as the face of a slain man; but, as he made obeisance, he smiled meekly and piteously. "What am I," he said, "that I should have questioned my lord's strength and skill? His arrows are like the arrows of the god Horus, whom these Egyptians adore. The child's heart must needs be cloven in twain." And the Great King laughed loud as he made answer—"Thou art forgiven, Prexaspes. Only, when the Persians call Cambyses drunkard, forget not to tell to what purpose, on the morning after a revel, he bent the Macrobian bow."

A courtly satrap — was it not? Nevertheless, courtiership was in its infancy then: now-a-days, when a skilful archer has stricken down the hope or the object nearest and dearest to our heart, we do not even change colour whilst we acknowledge his prowess; and scarcely grimace whilst the bugles strike up in his honour.

Marian Ashleigh was no special dissembler; but you may guess that, during the next two days, she prepared herself to play her part decorously. It was much more trouble to tutor her husband: characters like his, from their very weakness and instability, are difficult to deal with. I remember a drill-sergeant saying, years ago,—"I don't care how rough the stuff is, so long as there's enough of it," —and the sentiment appears no less morally than physically just. There was no fear of Philip's kicking over the traces, or giving any overt signs of rebellion; but as to keeping him up to the collar, and making him do his work pleasantly, that was quite another affair. However, by dint of much coaxing, a little urging, and just a shade of intimidation, his wife got him pretty well into her hand at last; and when Lord Atherstone arrived he could scarcely have complained of his reception, even if he had been disposed to be captious. Marian's first embrace was more than sufficiently cordial; and so was her first speech, though it was low and brief.

"I do hope you will be happy."

Philip's remarks 'were quite inaudible in the gallery,' but 'he was understood to second the address.'

Perhaps Lord Atherstone did not expect more; at any rate he seemed perfectly content; and not only throughout that evening, but for some days afterwards, his manner towards both the Ashleighs was unusually gentle and kindly. Though he spoke very little about future arrangements, he contrived to make them both thoroughly understand that he neither contemplated nor desired their immediate removal from Templestowe. So things went on smoothly enough throughout the following week. The baron hunted his five days as usual, bruising along just as determinedly as before he incurred fresh responsibilities. He accepted the congratulations and surprise of his friends and acquaintance —for by this time the engagement was fully noised abroad—with a wonderful composure, as if both were matters of course; and had for all nearly the same formula of acknowledgment.

On the ensuing Sunday it chanced that he breakfasted alone with his daughter-in-law; for Philip either was, or affected to be, too unwell to put in an appearance. You have not forgotten perhaps the peculiarity of the Sabbath-post. When the letters were brought in, there was certainly something very odd in Marian Ashleigh's expression. It was like

—yet not altogether like—that which her face had worn on the morning when she first began to doubt the stability of her tenure of Templestowe. Once more she watched Lord Atherstone narrowly, as he took up his letters; but besides vigilance you might have detected a certain expectation in her eyes, not altogether devoid of dread. You might fancy just such a look on the countenance of a conspirator who, having lighted the slow match, lurks in a nook almost too close for safety, to mark the effect of the train.

No need to ask from whom the first letter Lord Atherstone opened came. The smile—almost genial, for a wonder—hovering under his heavy grey moustache as he read, answered that question. The two or three that followed were evidently of no moment; but as he took up the last, Marian, who all this time, whilst apparently deep in her own correspondence, had never once relaxed her watch, could not repress a slight, a very slight, start; and she drew back yet further behind the cover of the great silver urn.

Lord Atherstone's glance was exceptionally swift and keen; nevertheless, he could not possibly have read half down the first page, when he crushed the letter into a ball and flung it on the floor; and on his face there was less of anger than contemptuous loathing. Marian Ashleigh's countenance fell, and she bit her nether lip sharply. She had never studied Greek; yet perhaps much the same thoughts crossed her mind just then, as were in Teucer's when he muttered—

Ὦ πόποι, ἦ δὴ πάγχυ μάχης ἐπὶ μήδεα κείρει
Δαίμων ἡμετέρης, ὅ τέ μοι βιὸν ἔκβαλε χειρός,
Νευρὴν δ' ἐξέρρηξε νεόστροφον, ἥν ἐνέδησα
Πρώϊον, ὄφρ' ανέχοιτο θαμὰ θρώσκοντας ὀϊστούς.*

---

\* O Heav'n, some god our best-laid schemes ot war
Confounds, who from my hands hath wrench'd the bow,
And snapp'd the newly-twisted string, which I
But late attach'd, my swift-wing'd shafts to bear.

After a minute or two Lord Atherstone broke silence.

"Marian, did it ever happen to you to receive an anonymous letter?"

She started—quite palpably now; but being disturbed in her correspondence might well account for this; and her voice was perfectly steady, though a very delicate ear might perhaps have detected in it some slight constraint.

"Never anything worse than a valentine. I was rather fond of them when I was a girl; but when I became a matron I put away such vanities. You don't mean to say that you have been so favoured this morning? Is it indiscreet to ask its purport?"

"I don't know it myself," he replied. "The first two lines avowed the letter to be anonymous; in the third was Lena Shafton's name. After that I would no more have read further, unless she bade me, than I would have gone on drinking poison after fair warning. Perhaps it ought not to be burnt, though, without her leave. What do you think? No man is a fit judge in such a case—I less than most men. You are a woman—wise and kind, as well as good; think how you would have liked Philip to act, and answer me honestly."

She seemed to ponder; and, during that pause, she was once perhaps moved to say—"Burn it instantly, and so let it pass away"—but that weakness endured scarcely for a second's space; and, when she answered, it was with a purpose set and planned.

"I think, if Philip had received such a letter as this seems likely to turn out, and had kept it a secret from me, I should have found it hard to forgive him —harder still to trust him thoroughly any more. However hateful it may be to you, you are bound to show it to Miss Shafton, and let her dispose of it at her pleasure. I am not as wise as you give me credit for; but I do believe I advise now what is best for you both."

"I suppose you are right," he said, discontentedly, whilst he picked up the letter. But he scarcely looked at it as he smoothed out the creases before replacing it in its envelope; and his face expressed the aversion of one who, for reasons good, forces himself to handle tenderly some noisome reptile, that he would fain have trampled under heel. That his appetite was spoiled was very evident; for, after one or two fruitless attempts to settle down again to his meal, he arose and began to pace to and fro, coming to a halt at last just behind Marian's chair. He paused there a little, as if considering; and then, leaning forward, laid his hand on her shoulder softly,—

"My dear," he said, "I so hope you will try and be kind to Lena."

There was something strangely pathetic, not only in the earnestness but in the humility of that inter-cession, coming as it did from one who perhaps never in his life had craved favour or indulgence from any fellow-creature. Many men thus tested, if not abso-lutely moved to compunction, would have been so far embarrassed as to blunder or stumble in their reply; but in these delicate touches of betrayal the feminine superiority is manifest. In falsehood, cruelty, or cunning we are perhaps more than their match; but in doing their cozening gently, they teach us lessons that we shall never learn. When a man is weaving a net to catch his neighbour's soul, if he looks not guilty or shame-stricken, he will at the best brazen it out in Mephistopheles' vein. But—take a woman under the same circumstances—by Saint Iago, she might be Gretchen at her spinning-wheel; and, even whilst she looks up innocently into your face, her lithesome fingers cease not to ply the shuttle.

There was nothing fiendish about Marian Ashleigh. Her Christianity perhaps went beyond formalism, and her morality was something more than surface-

I

deep. But neither restrained her from using all lawful means towards a given end, or from interpreting 'lawfulness' somewhat liberally. Howsoever she might choose to gloss the matter to her husband, she did in her heart consider that Lord Atherstone's present purpose was a manifest injustice, if not injury, to his family, and therefore to be thwarted, if that were possible, by all stratagems not absolutely sinful or shameful. She was not free to admit that either of these epithets could justly attach to the laying of an information which might possibly be true, or to the promise that she would essay a manifest impossibility. When she answered her father-in-law's appeal with a confidential smile, and a whisper— "Can you doubt me?"—she knew it was more likely that oil would mingle with the running stream, than that kindliness would ever subsist betwixt herself and Lena Shafton. Nevertheless, of course she might 'try.'

So, if my sweet cousin Alice, now in her fifth summer, were to set her affections on some bright particular star, I might promise to do my very best to fetch it down from its place in the firmament; but whether I should be justified in thus temporising with this imperious young person, subtler casuists may decide. If all devotees were to make full and free confession, I fancy such a question would not unfrequently be set before their conscience-keepers.

You have probably already attributed to the right source the authorship of the anonymous note. Marian, and no other, indited it, and caused it to be posted in town by a sure hand. She ran a very slight risk here, for she could thoroughly trust her agent; and it was the only one she incurred. The handwriting was so cunningly distorted, as almost to defy detection. Besides this, she knew Lord Atherstone well enough to be certain that he would never allow any other eye than Lena's and his own to rest on those characters. Still she did think that he would have read the letter through, even if he had chosen to discredit every syllable of its contents; and her first feeling was one of sharp disappointment. Nevertheless, that it would be shown to Lena was a great point gained. Then, at least, Lord Atherstone must be made acquainted with the contents; and, if he should decline to credit or discuss them, the seed would still be sown, and sooner or later might fructify. Altogether it was not such a very bad morning's work.

An hour later Marian Ashleigh, kneeling in her place, besought of heaven "to forgive her enemies, persecutors, and slanderers, and to turn their hearts." And, whilst she murmured this petition, stretching forth her hand, she might have touched the man against whose peace she had already begun to contrive—a man who, however harshly and sternly he may have borne himself toward others, had ever kept a kindly word, and look, and thought for her, and whose bread she had eaten ever since she came forth from her father's home.

Once more, I see nothing improbable in all this: there are vices and basenesses peculiar to either sex, of which the other is seldom guilty, simply from lack of temptation thereto. On the point of anonymous letter-writing, womankind seem to be affected with some strange cecity or obliquity of moral vision. For, if the experts are to be trusted, we needs must believe that nine-tenths of these darkling stabs are dealt either by female or by androgynic hands; and that more than a fair proportion may be traced to persons, esteemed good by themselves not less than by the world, who hold their heads high in oratory as well as in church, and who perchance are in all other points of the law blameless. If by a rare chance such criminals be caught in the fact, do not expect to find them specially contrite or humble; they will probably bridle up, brace their lips, and say that they have done what they deemed to be their duty, and are content to be misunderstood. But, my brethren, for our comfort, let us believe that our pious benefactresses may be brought to account concerning these matters yet once again; and that, in such a day, it will be less tolerable for them than for some who, when their guilt was revealed, grovelled before the accuser in an agony of abasement.

# CHAPTER XIII.

"BELIEVE that this is kindly meant, though it bears no signature. It is your purpose, I hear, to make Lena Shafton your wife; and probably you care little whether your choice seems to the world wise or unwise; but has it occurred to you, that there might be other obstacles to your future happiness besides the inequality of age? You are too brave and honest to play the complaisant husband; and, stout as your heart is, it would scarcely bear up under dishonour, or even the suspicion of dishonour. I bring no direct accusation against your affianced; it may be she is innocent in intent as well as in deed; but a woman who will not speak truth before marriage, is seldom to be trusted after. I advise you at least to test her so far—ask her two simple questions. What was the cause of her sudden departure from town, in the season that she wots of; and of her having lived in retirement ever since? Next—How long is it since she saw or heard from Caryl Glynne? If she can answer these questions quite frankly, it will be the better for you both: if she cannot or will not, other channels of information are open to you; even the gossip of the clubs might throw some light upon the matter. You can slight this counsel if you choose; only never in after-time complain that you were not warned."

This letter, on the day after it reached him, Lord Atherstone had placed in the hands of his betrothed, without a word of comment; and he stood watching her now, whilst she read it through, earnestly, not suspiciously.

It would have been somewhat difficult to guess, from Lena's countenance, at the nature of her emotion. Her cheek flushed at first—plainly rather in anger, than in confusion or fear; but, as she read on, she waxed pale again; and a weary, resigned look came over her face, like that of one on whom some old annoyance returns not unexpectedly. When she had quite finished, she dropped the letter on her knees, and looked up at her lover, saying,—

"I am ready—quite ready—to answer."

"To answer—what?"

Her brows contracted at once. She thought beating about the bush singularly ill-timed here, and rather unworthy of the speaker.

"The questions suggested here, of course. What else could I refer to?"

"I am in the dark still," he said quietly; "I read as far as the line in which your name appears—no further. I flung the letter aside then, and I would have burnt it on the instant, if Marian Ashleigh— she was the only person present—had not insisted that it ought to be shown to you."

With much of self-reliance, Ralph had little self-conceit; and he would have been surprised, as well as proud, if he had guessed how much nearer these few words brought him to the one object of his heart. Lena's head had been raised haughtily enough till now; but it sank almost to her breast, as she murmured—

"Is it possible? Could you trust me so?"

He drew close to her side, and stood silent for some seconds; smoothing, so lightly that she scarcely felt the touch, the folds of her braided hair.

"My dear," he said at last, "did you think it was a pretty speech, when I told you that I would never doubt till you bade me do so? You may have your fill of compliments wherever you go; but you will have to be content with plain truths at home, I'm afraid—this was one of them. Will you believe, if I repeat it over again in sober seriousness?"

Her hand stole upwards, and, for the very first time since their betrothal, sought his of its own accord; but her head was bowed still.

"Yes, I believe; only I wish I were worthier. But I can be frank now, at all events; and you must listen, even if you dislike it."

Then, taking up the letter from where it lay on her lap, she read it out aloud, from the first to the last word, in a low even tone. Whilst she did this she felt his grasp tighten round her fingers; and, when it was done, looking up into his face she saw that it was dark with passion—so dark, that the heart of many women would have sunk within them, even had they felt assured that the menace was not levelled at themselves. But Miss Shafton felt neither fear nor misgiving : her smile, though somewhat deprecating, was meant rather to bespeak patience than forbearance; and the next instant her lip was curling scornfully.

"I am not quite clear about the kindly meaning," she said; "but there is truth enough to make a fair libel; and the questions are only such as you might have pressed — not ungenerously or unjustly—ten days ago. I almost wish you had pressed them : however, it is not quite too late now. You have just heard the name of the one person for whom I ever cared. It was because I cared so much, that my mother carried me away to the North at a minute's warning. She utterly disapproved of our intimacy, and thought that it was broken off then and there. Indeed, there never was any real engagement; but, whilst it was possible that I could marry Caryl Glynne, I was not free to listen to any other man; and I never wished to be free. I have believed it impossible for a long, long time; but I never knew it absolutely, till a few hours before I accepted you. I saw him that morning, and said 'good-bye.' There is no mystery about our quiet life for these few years past. My mother will tell you that we have been too poor —much too poor—to afford a house or lodgings of our own in town; and my aunt, with whom we used to stay in those days, has never seen fit to invite us since. She was very angry with me for my folly, I believe; and took this way of showing that she did not mean to abet it. I would have told you all this before if you had asked me—indeed I would; but if, after having heard it, you choose that we should henceforth be no more than friends, I shall always think of you gratefully. And you will think kindly of me?"

She would have drawn her hand away; but he held it fast; and, before he opened his lips, Lena knew how he had decided—knew that, whether for weal or woe, her destiny remained unchanged.

"Friends!" Ralph answered, rather hoarsely— "always that, I trust; such friends as husband and wife should be. Providence works with queer instruments, they say; but a better deed has not often been wrought by base hands, than has been done here. If I could get over the insolence, I could almost thank the informer. My dear, I felt very proud and happy when I took your troth; but you have made me prouder and happier to-day. So proud and so happy, that I can't even wonder that you should have looked on my face without dislike, with that other one fresh in your memory. I know that face well—well enough, to fancy its haunting women to whom Caryl Glynne's name is strange."

Her colour had been less steady than her voice throughout; but it flickered painfully just then; and her countenance lighted up withal, like that of one who, possessing some rare and precious thing, hears it valued at its worth.

"One does not easily forget a good picture," she said after a minute's pause, with a very fair composure; "and there is no sort of reason why this one should be turned to the wall. You might have been amused, if you had watched our adieus that morning; they were so thoroughly cool and business-like. It is bad policy, I think, as a rule, to drop one's old acquaintances without strong reasons; but, if you wish this name removed from my visiting-list, you have only to say so. I shall make no objection; and I am very sure Mr. Glynne will not complain."

There was a tinge of bitterness, perhaps, in the last words; but Lord Atherstone did not notice this.

"One never knows what will happen," he said, with his short, deep laugh; "but I feel pretty safe against jealous fits, just now. I am not likely to meddle with your visiting-list, my dear; in this, and in most other things, if you please yourself it is next to certain that you please me. Now, don't you think you had better make ashes of that well-meaning letter at once?"

"No, I don't think so," Lena answered, deliberately. "It is worth keeping, if it is only to remind me—supposing I am ungrateful enough to forget it—how you would have trusted me blindfold. You'll let me have my way?"

Of course, he let her have it. The rest of their interview was comfortably commonplace; and it lasted till Lord Atherstone had only just time to send off this note to Templestowe:—

"MY DEAR MARIAN,

"You will be glad to hear that I followed your advice religiously; and more glad still to hear that Lena, after reading the letter out to me, insisted —for I should never have pressed her—on answering certain questions it contained. What those questions were, or how she answered them, concerns no one but ourselves. But I should like you —you only—to know that, if it were possible, I have better reason to-day than yesterday to rest on her truth and honour. She does not know that I am writing; otherwise she would thank you, perhaps not less heartily than I do, for your sound counsel.

"Affectionately yours,
"ATHERSTONE."

Not one of those simple words had a second intention or shade of sarcasm; nevertheless, judging from the expression of Marian Ashleigh's countenance as she read, you would have guessed that in every one there was a sting. Yet she had acted from the best of motives, of course; and verily she had her reward.

Ay—so had that traitor of old time, down whose throat the full price of treason was poured, in the guise of molten gold.

# CHAPTER XIV.

THE head of her family had in due course been made aware of Lena's engagement; and, though he had not been consulted beforehand, had been good enough to signify his approval thereof. In this same week, Miles came up to town for the express purpose of being presented to his future brother-in-law. It seemed to Mrs. Shafton that the meeting could not decorously be deferred; and yet, from the bottom of her heart, she wished it well over. Lord Atherstone was by no means a polished diamond; but he was thorough-bred, even in his *sauvagerie*, and was about the last man living to appreciate or overlook slang or swagger. That Miles inclined towards both these weaknesses, his mother could not deny. However, her fears for the nonce, at least, proved groundless. Certain instincts of race still survived in this unlucky spendthrift; and, in spite of his inveterate horsiness —Lacon, the steeplechase crack, was his model of manner, as well as his glass of fashion—he did occasionally contrive to remember that he had been born, if not bred, a gentleman. Furthermore, however much the British subaltern may ignore his own duties, or sneer at the service, he has a tendency, you will find, as a rule, to speak with somewhat 'bated breath in the presence of any famous veteran. Travelling in company with the Archbishop of Heligoland, Lieutenant Famish will select his hugest *puro*, and smile serenely through the smoke-wreaths at the wrathful protest of the Right Rev. Father in God; but, if Sir Hector McMurdo be his fellow-passenger, the same ingenuous youth will certainly consult that truculent warrior, before he presumes to dally with a delicate cigarette.

On the present occasion, Miles Shafton bore himself with a singular modesty, savouring indeed of shyness. His brief speech of congratulation, though evidently prepared beforehand, was barely intelligible ; and he was very silent after that, till just at last, when he warmed up into something like eloquence to acknowledge Lord Atherstone's offer of mounts later in the season, if Miles would be their guest at Templestowe. On the whole, the interview was satisfactory to all parties concerned ; and to this effect Shafton expressed himself on the following night, whilst consuming a succession of 'last pipes ' in his barrack-room, with a special confidant.

"He's the right sort, I can tell you, Frank : as hard as nails and as tough as pin-wire ; with an eye like a gamecock's ; and he rides the right sort of cattle too, I'll lay odds—none of the snaffle-bridle lumber that want kicking and hoisting at every fence, and do a brook at twice; but stuff that go bang up to their bit, and catch hold of it, too, sometimes, and go at a bullfinch as if they would eat it, and jump just as far as they can, and gallop all they know. And his are bound to be two stone over my weight; that's one comfort. See if I don't take the change out of some of 'em, before March."

"I should have thought you'd got pretty well enough of your own," the other remarked, "without wanting the run of another stable."

"Well, I've got eight besides the chasers, which don't count; but there's always something amiss with more than half of 'em. Do you think Paston poisons them ? I shouldn't wonder : he crabs every animal he's not had the buying of directly it comes in ; he's clever enough for anything, and robber too, for the matter of that."

"Why the devil don't you shunt him, and have

done with him, instead of always blackguarding
him behind his back? You're a bit afraid of him,
I do believe."

"No, I ain't afraid," Miles said simply; "but I
can't afford to quarrel just yet. I couldn't well shunt
him without paying him, you know. I keep on stop-
ping his mouth with tenners on account; but I haven't
had the pluck to look at his book these three months.
If it wasn't for 'backin' 'osses' like the rest of us,
what a pot of money he'd be worth! I don't believe
I often make a deal, without some stuff sticking to
his fingers. Now, if I went to stop at Templestowe,
I'd send up a good big draft to the Corner; and I'd
get enough ready that way to settle with Paston, and
leave something in hand; and I'd stick in, below the
advertisement, that 'the gentleman can thoroughly
recommend his stud-groom;' and so make a clean
sweep of the lot. That would be a *coup*, wouldn't it?"

"Well, it would," Frank Dacre assented; "and,
looking at it in that light, I don't think Templestowe would be half a bad put-up for you. I
believe you do occasionally get on grass in those
parts, if you don't mind long meets; and some of
those clay countries carry a rare scent. It's natural
that you should be pretty full on your brother-
in-law. But—but I wonder how Miss Shafton likes
it. The baron's a long way past mark of mouth,
isn't he?"

Though late hours, and drink, and devilry of
all kinds, had worked havoc with Miles Shafton's
big brown eyes, they were still sometimes very like
Lena's; especially when, as now, they opened wide
in wonderment or anger.

"Like it?" he said rather sulkily. "Likes it
of all things, of course. Why the —— shouldn't
she? To hear you talk, one would think in these
matches there was weight for age; besides, she
ought to know her own mind by this time. What
makes you doubt it?"

"Nothing in particular," Dacre answered, sending out a long trail of smoke; "only it's just possible, she might have liked someone else. She must have had plenty of chances anyhow, with that figure and face. You'd have to go among the plain-headed ones, I reckon, if you want to find them 'fancy free,' as the poet has it."

Shafton scowled at the speaker. He could knit his brows, felly enough sometimes—this careless, shiftless prodigal.

"Poets be d——d," he muttered. "Why can't you speak out like a man? You've heard some of those cursed stories about her and Caryl Glynne, I suppose—as if there ever *could* have been anything in it! Is it likely, that we'd have ever let her think seriously of such a duffer as that?"

The dignity of the 'We' was superb; considering that Miles, at the time alluded to, was a tailless 'infant,' with rather less voice in the family councils than his mother's waiting-maid. Dacre saw and relished the absurdity: though passably illiterate, he was gifted with a brisk mother-wit and a tenacious memory; and, albeit his troop-accounts were to him a burden and a snare, he could under certain circumstances put two and two together as well as his neighbours. There having been 'anything in it,' did not strike him as so wildly improbable. Moreover he was aware that Miles had certain small social ambitions independent of the stable, and would have given half his yearly pay to be allowed to stroll thrice through the Row, arm in arm with the 'duffer' in question—the other half for the privilege of calling Glynne in public by his Christian name. But all things go by comparison: by the side of Shafton, hampered and encumbered as he was, Dacre was still virtually a pauper; and, though he never plundered his comrade directly or indirectly, the other was useful to him in various ways. In his turn, Frank felt that he could not

' afford to quarrel ; ' especially about a matter in which he had no personal concern. Lastly—though an outsider would hardly think so—there *are* limits, even to mess-chaff.

"You did quite right, Buster," he said, with perfect gravity. (This had been the other's *sobriquet* ever since he joined.) "Such a thing couldn't be stood at any price. Mine was only a shot at random ; and—here's wishing all luck to you and yours. You'll get a week's extra leave out of this business anyhow; and that's something to the good in these hard times. You know that there's an early field-day in orders for to-morrow? Our old man's gone cracked about this new squadron-drill. He'll never rest till he's lamed half the troopers, and worn the flesh off our bones. Now I'm off to roost—good night."

Miles returned the salutation very ungraciously. Wilful and impatient of contradiction to a degree, and occasionally liable to violent outbreaks of passion, he was seldom sullen, still more seldom suspicious ; but, when once fairly roused, neither his discontent nor his misgivings were speedily appeased. It was quite true that he counted his sister's fancy for Glynne amongst the things utterly past and gone; nevertheless, Dacre's hint dovetailed so accurately with certain other doubts lurking in his own mind, that he fell a-thinking now— sorely against his will.

He remembered that when he saw Lena alone, before his meeting with Lord Atherstone, if she did not look like a martyr, she looked still less like a triumphant bride elect; and that once only she had smiled—this was when he told her how pleased he was with the match, and she answered—

"You ought to be."

What did she mean by that? Was it possible that by selling herself she hoped to help him out

of his scrapes? Not a very new way of paying
old debts; but he felt — at all events, for the
moment — as if he would a hundred times rather
face duns, and difficulty, and disaster in his own
way, than evade them in this fashion. Great and
good men have consented — reluctantly, but still
they have consented—to escape out of prison by a
feminine stratagem; leaving wife, or sister, or mistress behind them in ward, to abide the consequence. In a like strait, prayers and tears would
have been wasted on Miles Shafton: he would have
cast off the pleader somewhat roughly, grumbling
out 'good-bye' as he thrust her from the cell; and
then, taking no sort of credit for self-sacrifice, would
have waited doggedly, if not serenely, the coming of
the doomster.

"Not a bad devil at bottom"—said his few apolo-
gists. Did it ever strike any of them, that if in earlier
days he had fallen under guidance strong, wise, and
gentle, he need not necessarily have turned out a
'devil?' When in the pursuit of his fancy, he
recked no more of the interests he imperilled, than
the Wild Huntsman did of the corn he trampled
under hoof; but, in his sober moments, he was not
wholly selfish, and could be lavish of things more
precious than coin; and in his ill-regulated, irrational
fashion, he certainly loved his sister. The possibility
floated before him now, of sending all his live and
dead stock into the market—of exchange into a
sedate, beetle-crushing corps—of detachment-duty in
some wilderness where foxes are shot down as vermin,
and shilling whist considered a dissipation—of foreign
service on some station, with no game bigger than
a jackal to shoot or spear; and these visions were
very dreary: yet the worst of them was pleasanter
than that of Lena, standing before the altar with
her face white and set. It was not too late yet:
he would go up to town again to-morrow, and have
it out with her—he would—by G—d.

At this point in his reverie, the ill-used pipe-clay crumbled betwixt his strong, sharp teeth; and the *brûle-gueule* pitched forward against the fender, snapping short off at the bowl. It was an old favourite, and not a light loss, as we all know; nevertheless, Miles felt rather glad of an excuse for giving vent to his spleen and breaking off his meditations, as he leaped up with a curse, and ground the fragments to dust under his spurred heel. Then after driving another 'nail'—a long and heavy-headed one—he betook himself to bed, and in five minutes had growled himself to sleep.

But things looked much rosier on the morrow. The field-day was short and brilliant; and the Chief, albeit in fault-finding humour, was fain to admit that Lieutenant Shafton, in his captain's absence, had led his troop very creditably. Directly after stables, a dealer—long-suffering in point of payment—brought over a five-year-old, that even the captious Paston allowed 'had rare bones, and looked very promisin'' The trial and subsequent purchase took up all the afternoon; and that same evening brought Miles an invitation to a country-house famed for its covers and its claret; and so the time of grace—if there ever was such time—passed by, and any chance of explanation with his sister was lost. Had he carried out his first intention, he might have earned the barren satisfaction, of reflecting that he had done his duty—nothing more.

If the journey on which Lena was embarking was fraught with danger, she started at least with open eyes, after duly counting all the cost. Nor would she have paused or turned aside now for any omen or warning. Was it likely that the woman who, if she could not quell, had so smothered the beating of her own heart, that Caryl Glynne had gone forth from her presence never witting thereof, would, now that the chords were fairly stilled, wake them again at the bidding of Miles Shafton?

K

# CHAPTER XV.

ALBEIT his philosophy was rather practical than proverbial, and he knew nought of the Cabala, the Singer of Israel sometimes approved himself wiser than the Sage who sprang from his loins. Take the episode of Bathsheba's child. It was the first-fruits of the sinful love sealed with the blood of betrayed Uriah; yet nevertheless—alas! perchance *therefore*—more precious in the father's sight than the fairest son born to him in Salem. For six weary days and nights he lay prone and fasting; wrestling with the Avenger in prayer, if the decree gone forth against the frail life might yet be annulled; but when the servants, in fear and quaking, told him that the end was come, the King 'arose from the earth, and washed, and anointed himself, and changed his apparel, and came into the house of 'the Lord, and worshipped; then he came to his own house; and when he required, they set bread before him, and he did eat.'

Many centuries have passed since David set us that brave example; and still they be few who seem to realise, that over what may not be redeemed repentance befits us—not repining; ay!—and that it is as vain to make moan over our ruined hopes as over our buried darlings.

The rule holds good in trivial matters not less than in grave; therefore Marian Ashleigh deserves some credit for the manner in which she bore herself during the brief interval, betwixt the incidents

chronicled above and Lord Atherstone's marriage.
She 'had drawn a good bow at Hastings;' and, if
her shafts had hitherto spent themselves to little
purpose, she was not therefore tempted to break up
her artillery; but rather set about to replenish her
quiver, waiting till the convenient season should
come for voiding it once more. In plain words, she
made no further effort to check or change the course
of events; but stood watching it as placidly, if not
complacently, as the miller watches the brook that
sooner or later will turn his wheel. Moreover, she
tried, not unsuccessfully, to make her husband decently amenable—amiability in Philip being out of
the question. About this time, they removed the
most of their belongings from Templestowe; and
it was understood that they would return thither only
as guests.

Even when the match is entirely to the mind, not
only of the contracting parties, but of all ever so
remotely concerned therein, the making acquaintance
with new relatives is rather a trial of temper and
nerve. If the trotting-out be performed ever so unobtrusively, it is difficult to get rid of the impression
that stock is being taken of our moral and physical
soundness; and, whilst this lasts, the most simple
and benevolent people appear disagreeable, judicial,
and inquisitive. There is a good deal of fancy about
it, of course; but, as the same applies to most mortal
pains and pleasures, this does not help the patient
materially.

You have heard of the tyrannical schoolmistress
who, on each of her birthdays, used to be endowed
with a gift more or less costly, which, by a fearful
fiction, was supposed to be a voluntary testimonial
from her grateful pupils? If you can imagine the
feelings and demeanour of the scholar who, by
virtue of seniority, was compelled to pronounce the
presentation-address, you will form a tolerable idea
of Mr. Ashleigh's, on the occasion of his first in-

terview with Lena Shafton. Lord Atherstone was present; and this in itself would have prevented any overt demonstration of dislike or discourtesy; but the tone of Philip's jerky common-places—to say nothing of the fidgetiness of his manner— showed plainly how the position galled and irked him. Marian's talent, before alluded to, of making rough places smooth, came in conveniently here; without attempting to hold the thread of the conversation, she continued to fill up the gaps before they became awkwardly apparent; and, without forcing familiarity, was as genial as even Lord Atherstone could desire.

Herein she was ably seconded by Mrs. Shafton. This good lady's discourse was not especially wise or witty; after chatting with her for an hour or so people went away with a vague impression of her cleverness; yet probably not a single sentence that she had uttered dwelt upon their memory. However, her small talk made very fair 'padding,' and on this, as on many other occasions, answered its purpose admirably.

Lena was perfectly cordial, but not at all fluttered or eager; indeed, it was not to her a very terrible ordeal. She had not felt particularly anxious before the interview, and the result neither elated nor disappointed her. She thought it would be pleasant for all parties, if the Ashleighs took her marriage in good part; and was willing to conciliate, but not to sue for their favour: if it was granted, she would be reasonably grateful; if it was withheld, she would not be rancorous  Philip Ashleigh she fathomed at once; she was just as likely to make friends with a barrel-organ, as ever to sympathise with his set speeches and querulous egotism; but her nerves were not very irritable, and if he would confine himself to being passively obnoxious she would be satisfied. With his wife she was decidedly prepossessed. Marian's brisk downright ways contrasted agreeably with Philip's prim mannerisms. It looked natural at all events, if it was not absolutely sincere; and Lena, though she had been somewhat of a recluse of late, was no country-bred simpleton. She was well content to accept any amicable advances in the shape of fair currency, without insisting on their being paid in standard gold. Somehow, it did not seem likely that she would ever find herself exchanging confidences with Marian Ashleigh; but that they might be very good friends was by no means improbable; and she desired to do her own part towards bringing about such a state of things.

Of all who assisted at that interview, Lord Atherstone was infinitely the most gratified. To Philip's good or bad behaviour he was utterly indifferent —for years past, he had treated his son's tempers with the contemptuous indulgence that most men extend to feeble, fractious children—but with Marian he was more than pleased. When he put her into his carriage, he simply said, 'Thank you,' and kissed her; but the kiss was warmer than he had ever yet bestowed on her, and the thanks came from the depth of his heart.

And Marian received both with the meek consciousness of one who has well performed a not unpleasant duty. But you would have been edified, if you could have followed the current of her thoughts as she drove away alone, after setting down Philip at his club.

She frowned more than once, rather thoughtfully than angrily; and in her eyes there was an anxious, far-seeing look, like that of a pilot who, peering into the night, finds no rift in the blackness ahead, save such as ever and anon are cloven by the lightning. She had mused so, for many minutes, before her lips parted; and then only this murmur escaped them—

"It will be harder—much harder—than I thought."

A short and simple word, that—IT: yet sometimes

scarcely to be expounded by long pages of commentary, and the turning-point of intricate stories.

Thenceforward the needful preparations went on apace. In the settlements there could be no hitch or difficulty, as they were all on one side; and the tradesfolk, who would have taken their time in executing orders issuing from Blytheswold, even if they had not looked at them doubtfully, worked with a will for the future *châtelaine* of Templestowe. Mrs. Shafton's frame of mind during these days was naturally jubilant; and, to complete her contentment, there was a lull in Miles's demands for ready money. Curiously enough, some of the dew of good luck which had lately descended on his family, moistened the fleece of this wandering bell-wether. For a wonder, one of his steeple-chase 'crocks' did actually win when he had backed it—at a remunerative price too; and the successful plunge, though it was the merest sop to the ban-dogs, checked their baying for a while, and gave their quarry breathing-space.

But, on the very day before the wedding, a change came over Mrs. Shafton, and her spirits seemed to droop unaccountably. Her energies had been sharply taxed of late, it is true; but this did not explain it. Work—work much more wearisome and thankless than this—had become a second nature to her; till now, in the bread of absolute idleness, she found little savour. Assuredly a season like the present, when a few hours more must change a daughter from maid to matron, to most women, who are not social machines, brings certain spasms of anxiety; but, if you had watched Mrs. Shafton narrowly, you would scarcely have imputed the distraction of her manner to mere maternal instinct: it looked much more as if she had a burden on her mind, of which she would fain be relieved.

Throughout that day, she had not a single chance of speaking alone to Lena; and Miles, who came to dinner, did not leave them till close on midnight.

Then—always with that same restlessness in her eyes—Mrs. Shafton followed her daughter to her sleeping chamber.

"Julie will have hard work to-morrow, darling," she observed; "won't you send her to bed? I will be your maid to-night. Don't you remember, when you were little, you used to make a great treat of my brushing out your hair? Let us see if I have forgotten the art."

Lena had let others have their way in all things of late, and she acquiesced now at once, though not over-eagerly. It seemed as though she would rather have avoided than invited a confidential chat just then; however, when she had made ready for the ceremony, she came and sat down dutifully on a stool, leaning back against her mother's knee; and so for several minutes there was silence, whilst the slender white hands waved, deftly and tenderly, over the shining brown tresses that sometimes well-nigh buried them. At last, Mrs. Shafton spoke low and tremulously.

"My darling, are you sure—quite sure—that you are happy? I can't sleep to-night unless I hear you say so; yet, do not say it, if it is not true. If I could only hear you laugh just once again, in the old merry way! Shall I ever?"

Lena started slightly; but she never turned her head, and her pensive eyes gazed always steadfastly into the heart of the fire.

"It tires one to laugh, I think," she answered, "when one has become sage and staid; and yet those laugh who win, they say; so we ought to be merry just now. Oh, yes! I am happy — happy enough for all practical purposes. But, mother dear, if it were otherwise, don't you think it is rather late to put such trying questions?"

The white hands ceased waving; and Isabel Shafton's head bent lower and lower, till her brow almost touched that other head resting on her knee.

"Late—too late," she murmured; "why, for three days past, these words have been haunting me like a rhyme. I thwarted your inclinations once, and perhaps I have half forced them now. Ah! yes—it is easy to force without commanding. If I have done wrong, I think God will forgive me, for He knows I meant to do right; but—but will you?" And then she fairly broke down.

They may lie very close together, and their bitter waters flow often in the same channel; yet in most human hearts the fount of sorrow and the fount of tears are twain, not one. Be sure, that some of the mourners of old time found it easier to cast dust upon their heads, and to rend their garments, and to cut themselves with knives and lancets, than to evince those other outward signs of woe. During that awful vigil when, sitting in sackcloth on the hill of Gibeon, she watched her dead till the harvest moon waned, it is not written that Rizpah, the daughter of Aiah, wept.

As a girl, Isabel Shafton had to struggle hard before she could wed according to her will; as a wife, she had to suffer, as only a proud passionate nature can suffer—seeing others win smiles and soft whispers when she could only win frowns, and words harsh sometimes even to cruelty; as a widow, she had seen the husband whom, in spite of all his faults, she loved very dearly, brought home a corpse stiff and thrawn; but pleading, jealousy, terror, or desolation, had almost always left this woman dry-eyed.

So this outbreak startled quite as much as it pained Lena.

"Don't fret, dear," she said; and, as she spoke, she wound her arm close round her mother's neck. "Indeed, I didn't mean it as a taunt: I would not go back if I could. You did quite right—then and now. Whatever happens, I shall always think so; and do you think so too. And nothing will happen but good, I do believe. Every day I feel safer with Lord Atherstone; and it is so pleasant to feel safe—at last.

Now, I'm going to send you off to your beauty-sleep; I mean you to look your very brightest to-morrow."

As may be imagined, Mrs. Shafton was not hard to convince and console.

It was a very sober wedding; only a few kin-folk and near friends being present, including Philip and Marian Ashleigh; and—as Lord Lothaire observed when, *semiambustus*, he escaped from the confines of the Divorce Court—'everybody behaved beautifully.' There was little more fuss, when the new-married couple departed, than if they had been starting on an ordinary journey; nor, though a sufficiency of good wishes followed them, was there anything tragic in the farewells. By Lena's own wish her brief season of seclusion was to be spent at Templestowe.

To the general good conduct of all parties concerned, the weather did certainly form an exception. The discourteous sun did not vouchsafe the palest apology for a ray; and the day's humour waxed worse as it grew older, till towards evening the air was laden with storm. The strong spirited cattle, that were to carry the new mistress of Templestowe to her home, drooped their heads and shivered, as they waited under the lee of the station for the laggard train; and, more than once during the brief journey, hand and spur were both needed to keep the leaders straight against the blinding rain-swirls. There was threat rather than welcome in the voice of the swaying elms, as the carriage swept up the avenue; and the bride had scarce set her foot over the threshold, when the great door crashed to behind her, with a clang that echoed through the hall from pavement to roof-tree.

Lena was not very superstitious; but she had been bred too far north, wholly to make a mock at auguries. Whilst she sat at dinner, fatigue and excitement could not quite account for her paleness; and she paused and started more than once, as there came a fiercer rally in the turmoil without.

Do you wonder at her weakness? So did not Ralph Atherstone, when, an hour later, he looked forth into the night and remembered that those livid gleams—more grewsome than the horror of great darkness, that came before and after—were shed by his honeymoon.

# CHAPTER XVI.

HESLINGFORD could hardly pretend to the dignity of a manufacturing town; yet a fair stroke of trade was done there, chiefly in the coarser cloth and linen stuffs; and, if the air for leagues around was not poisoned with the reek of her furnaces, even on a breezy summer-day her brows were seldom clear of smoke; whilst an utilitarian's ears would have been gladdened by the concert of her steam-mills. It was a big straggling place; closely packed in the centre, but opening towards the outskirts into many rows, and terraces of 'desirable tenements;' and beyond these, again, scores of detached or semidetached villas encroached on the green fields year by year.

The grey minster had more than a local renown; and besides this, immediately around and near the market-place, there were a few gables and porches that stray archæologists had thought worth photographing; but even in this quarter the aspect of things was rather old-fashioned than ancient, and the most imposing of the private dwellings were only primly respectable.

Unless special business or pleasure had brought you there, you would perhaps have passed on a hundred times, without pausing before a certain tall, square mansion—built of red, or rather russet brick, with stone casings to the narrow windows—that filled up a goodly portion of a short street leading out of a principal thoroughfare. There was no pretence of an approach or court-yard before it. The house stood out bluffly in the same line with its humbler fellows,

dwarfing them by contrast, like a grenadier shifted
into the ranks of a light company ; a row of iron
railings, enclosing about a fathom's-width of gravel,
was all that divided the walls from the pavement.
If you had bestowed a second glance on this building,
you would probably have guessed that, though brick
and stone were scrupulously neat and clean, and the
minutest breaches of time or weather had been carefully repaired, many years had passed since its first
courses were laid ; and furthermore, that the tenant
was a person influential by wealth or otherwise.
No graven door-plate was needed to tell you, that it
must needs belong to the chief banker or lawyer of
the place : if by any absurd incongruity an utterly
idle man came to dwell there, one might fancy him,
by the pure force of circumstances, impelled to dabble
with paper or parchment.

But, like other eminent respectabilities, the staid
old mansion kept for its intimates a very different
face from that which it turned towards the profane ;
not that, even to these, it could ever seem rollicking
or jovial ; but under this second aspect decorum was
tempered with cheerfulness, and dignity ceased to be
austere.   It was a grateful surprise to a stranger
when, after passing through the formal door-way, he
caught a glimpse of greenery at the further end of the
long, cool corridor paved with black and white marble,
that ran through the house from east to west ; and,
traversing this, found himself in a fair garden, the
boundary walls whereof were scarcely to be discerned
for ivy and embowering trees.   A few flower-beds,
richly rather than gaudily coloured, glistened in the
midst of sward fresher and smoother than the show-
lawn at Templestowe ; and no manor-house in Loamshire, which boasted not a few of such, could show
anything to compare with those twin cedars—so lowly
with their trailing branches, so haughty with their
soaring spires.   Moreover, the dull uniformity of the
street façade was broken by bow windows on the

ground-floor, deep as oriels, and by casements above of diverse shapes and sizes.

Building-land in the heart of such a thriving town as Heslingford, was a very mine of profit; and, if the value of property is to be estimated by the capital lying dormant there, the maintaining of that modest plaisance was a costlier whim than the preserving of a deer-park farther afield. Since a Corbett came to dwell here, four generations ago, the family—prospering steadily as a rule—had known, like their neighbours, seasons of trouble and strait; but they had never once been tempted to diminish, by a cubit's breadth, this plot kept for their delight.

They were rather notable people these Corbetts. The founder of the line appeared in Heslingford, as chief clerk in a bank already of some standing there. He was London-bred, and of his antecedents little or nothing was known; but his aptitude for business and industry were such that none were surprised when, after twenty years' hard work, he was received as a partner. Before John Corbett died in a good old age, he had managed, in his placid, pertinacious way, to engross a large proportion of the authority, if not of the profits, of the concern; and his descendants had followed in his footsteps, gradually extruding the original elements; so that for some time past, the ' Co.' following their name had become a polite fiction. The cautious, methodical spirit of their ancestor had long survived him. There is no doubt that the Corbetts might have waxed much wealthier, if they would have embarked in thoroughly justifiable speculation; but they had preferred to increase their pile slowly and surely, avoiding all risks not necessarily incidental to the finance-trade. And those cadets who, in default of finding room in the bank, sought fortune in the law, the army, or the church, showed themselves not less careful than their seniors, in nowise to impair the family credit. Yet, though ' safe,' they were not hard men; and cases might have been quoted where,

to assist an honest farmer or deserving tradesman,
the banker had furnished from his own private resources the aid which he was bound professionally to
deny.

Precise they might be, but scarcely precisians;
their religion was of the steady, church-going order,
with no tinge of fanaticism; and there was nothing
of the maw-worm or money-grubber in their blood;
they entered into sport and pleasure at proper seasons,
not a whit more sadly than their fellows, subscribing
to the Loamshire hounds just as regularly as to the
Heslingford charities; furthermore, they had always
shown a proneness to intermarry with the squirearchy;
and, at the present time of speaking, their personal
interests were certainly more closely allied with the
county than with the town.

Arthur Corbett's grandfather had purchased a
moderate estate, with a good house upon it, a dozen
miles or so from Heslingford; and here resided Jacob
his father, still nominally the head of the firm. But,
enjoying weak health, he meddled very little with the
management; only occasionally sitting in the bank-
parlour to satisfy his own conscience or the fancy of
certain ancient customers who liked maundering over
their business, and usually made it an excuse for a
heavy luncheon and a lengthened prose. So, on the
said Arthur's shoulders rested all the real burden of
responsibility; and they carried it exceeding lightly.

In business-hours the junior partner showed himself to the full as shrewd and painstaking as his predecessors; but when he closed his desk, he seemed
to lock up all his cares in it, and came forth the most
convivial of creatures. It was quite wonderful, what
a large cantle of his time he contrived to allot to
amusements, without in anywise neglecting duty.
He was a good second-rate shot, and a fair, though
by no means bruising rider to hounds; in any scheme
of public or private diversion, from a festival down
to a picnic, Arthur Corbett's name was safe to be

prominent; and his little dinners were renowned throughout Loamshire.

He was a benedict of some ten years' standing now; and around his table there had grown up a very bower of olive-branches; but there was much of the schoolboy about him still; and, with his round musical laugh ringing in your ears, you would have found it hard to believe in either his family or his financial dignities. He had never given his wife a single grave uneasiness, or society a single occasion for scandal; but—sooth to speak—he was an incorrigible philanderer, and was as variable in his devotion as in the fashion of his garments; the which is a wide expression, for he was choice and costly in his attire, erring rather on the side of gorgeousness. Also he affected, not unsuccessfully, the dragoon-swagger, and was far prouder of his commission in the yeomanry than of his deputy-lieutenancy: could he have had his will, he would have invented for that corps such a uniform as would have cast into shade the splendours of the Chevalier Guard.

"The sweetest temper in the world," said his numerous admirers; and so perhaps it was, though it had very seldom been tried. Not only had he passed through no furnace of adversity, but the flame of a taper burning awry had never scorched the wings he fluttered so gaily. His mother—dead now some years —his sisters, and his wife, had all in their turn worshipped and petted him, and his father, in masculine fashion, had spoiled him no less consistently. That their Prince could do no wrong was the prime article of the family creed; and, had he been more faulty and negligent in his domestic relations, he would still have remained their sole standard of excellence. However, no shortcomings in this respect could fairly be charged against Arthur Corbett: the inner fount of his affections seemed always brimming over; and he was content that his kinsfolk, no less than his friends, should drink freely of the abundance thereof.

Endowed with such a character, and ample means withal for developing his genial tendencies, he could not be otherwise than popular—amazingly popular. Perhaps, though they liked him well, men hardly believed in him as implicitly as women did. But, if *le bel Arthur* had been aware of this, it would not have greatly troubled him : he would have been content that things should be so.

Look narrowly at him, and you will see that the *physique* is a very fair reflex of the *morale* of the man.

An undeniably handsome face, if something soft and sensuous, and becomingly framed in crisp waves of pale golden hair—a figure almost commanding in its proportions, with only a promise of portliness as yet ; though the outlines are already rounded. You would say, perhaps, that the figure wants setting up, and the face wants fining down ; and both would certainly remind you of the Bacchic ideal—the presentment not of the Indian god, bearded, grave, and serene ; but of the Theban reveller, made twice immortal by Praxiteles.

His air and manner are pervaded by a self-satisfaction bordering on self-sufficiency ; and to this, at the present moment, is added the beatitude of one who has thoroughly enjoyed a savoury meal. It is only a conjugal *tête-à-tête ;* but his evening attire is elaborate, and jewels sparkle on his breast and wrists, and on the plump, white fingers toying with the curls of the pretty child nestling at his knee.

Emma Corbett by no means emulates her husband's splendour: her dress is plain almost to homeliness, and not adapted to set off even the modest *uxoriam pulchritudinem* of which she can boast. The cares of maternity and of house-keeping have told on her face not a little already ; but she has a pleasant, honest smile, and a pleasant voice withal, though not a musical one.

"So you have actually seen this famous bride. And how were you so lucky ?"

Arthur stretches out his length of limb, yawning luxuriously.

"I saw her, very much; and this is how it happened. Lord Atherstone came to see me at the bank this afternoon; and, when we had finished our business, he asked me if I would like to be presented to my lady, who was sitting in the carriage. Of course I was only too happy."

"And what did you think of her?"

"I—decidedly admire her."

Mark the importance of his manner. It is as though he said—"I am aware that my verdict is too valuable to be lightly given; *cependant je me risque.*"

Emma Corbett smiles good-naturedly.

"How very glad she would be, if she knew that! But it don't exactly describe her, you see."

"Well: she's tall—very tall, so far as I could judge, as she leant back half-buried in furs; and rather dark than fair; with plenty of colouring, though not in the least coarse—colouring all in the right places, too, in spite of the north wind; and her eyes—brown, I think they are—are simply superb."

"And does she seem pleasant?"

Arthur pauses a second or two, as if trying to recollect.

"I fancy she might be—very pleasant, if she chose to take the trouble; but there's a cool, languid way about her; and perhaps she would not always choose. I don't dislike that; it's rather good style than otherwise."

"And does Lord Atherstone seem very fond of her?"

"What a thoroughly wifely question! Yes: he appears very fond of her, and proud into the bargain. If she had been a pearl of great price, he could not have wrapped her up more tenderly. I never thought, till to-day, that it was possible his face could thaw."

"There's an end to most frosts, I suppose," Mrs. Corbett replies. "You make me more curious than

L

ever, to see the last new thing in brides.    I don't
implicitly believe in all your swans, you know."

Corbett laughs lazily.

" Well : you needn't pine much longer.    Next week
won't be a bit too soon to call.    I'll drive you over
myself, if you like.    And now, Meta shall have the
story I promised her if she was good."

# CHAPTER XVII.

FROM very old time it has been proverbial, how ill they fare who, trusting in their own strength, presume to walk in independence, if not in defiance of the deities. They need not fall as fell Capaneus; nor need any wind from the wilderness smite the four corners of the house where the criminals are feasting; but the punishment, we are bound to believe, sooner or later is sure. And why should not the same hold good with those who, either by choice or heedlessness, wander on aloof from their fellow-men, till at length they find themselves out in the desert, standing quite alone? The frail hand that, before it stiffened, was strong to indite many wise and tender words, was seldom better used than when it wrote of—

> The bond which is not loosed by any:
>   And thou and I this law must keep.
> If not in love, in sorrow then,—
> Though smiling not like other men,
>   Still, like them we must weep.

It was in the first bitterness of enmity against his kind that Timon

> Made his everlasting mansion
> Upon the beachèd verge of the salt flood;
> Which once a day with his embossed froth
> The turbulent surge did cover.

If he had lived longer—long enough for Apemantus's curse to take effect—it may be he would have grown aweary of his cave, and have hankered for the fair city whose very hum and bustle sounded sociable, though in the crowd mingled so many

harlots, traitors, and parasites.  Without being senti-
mental or sensitive, a man may find it somewhat
galling, to realize that the great joy or the great
sorrow that has befallen him, does not appear to
interest his neighbours in the faintest degree ; and
the lack of sympathy in the first case, is almost as
vexatious as in the last.

The causes of Lord Atherstone's unpopularity in
his county have been noted above, and how, if not
actually sought, it was thoroughly earned.  Possibly,
since then he had seen the error of his ways ; but it
is not probable that till now he had ever repented of
them.  It happened to him, as it has happened to
many other stark soldiers : whilst they had only their
own safety to think of, their harness was well able to
protect them ; but, in striving to buckler another,
they perforce left their side unguarded, and the
quarrel came home.  Soon after her marriage, he
had said to Marian Ashleigh, " The Loamshire folks
and I understand one another pretty well by this
time.  I can't alter my habits, even to suit such
an occasion as this."  Soon after his own, he would
have altered some of those same habits very readily,
and began to wish that the said ' understanding ' was
not so perfect.  Amongst his bitterest enemies of
either sex, social, political, or personal, not one had
been found bold enough to put any overt slight,
much less insult, on Ralph Atherstone ; but somehow, by tacit consent, he had been edged gradually
aside, till the place, that by all rights he ought to
have filled, knew him no more.  He was seldom
solicited now to add his name to the stewards' list
on the occasion of any public festival ; private invitations were just as rare ; and all the visiting-
cards left at Templestowe were intended for the
Ashleighs.  The few men with whom Ralph was
on familiar speaking terms were hunting acquaintances ; and their conversation was usually confined
to the interchange of ideas on the subject of weather,

crops, and scent, that forms the staple of covert-side talk. The baron hitherto had been perfectly content to be allowed to 'gang his ain gate;' but it was different now.

The bridal *retraite* was past: yet the Loamshire matronhood seemed by no means eager to welcome, or even to recognise, the last recruit to their ranks.

The Rev. Hubert Ashleigh—the same who had acted as Philip's guardian—called as soon as he decorously could, bringing his wife with him. He was a very correct and sensible divine—a trifle time-serving, some people thought, and rather too apt to 'be all things to all men;' but, even where the course was badly buoyed, he had a rare knack of so steering and trimming his sails as to strike that middle one that is generally the shortest as well as the safest in the end. He was chatty and cordial enough when "he just dropped in to lunch without ceremony, because he was sure to catch his cousins at home at that hour;" but, dining that same evening at his archdeacon's with a clerical party, he contrived to make it fully understood that a sense of family duty rather than personal inclination had brought him thus early to Templestowe; neither did he intimate that it was incumbent on his brethren to follow his example.

Besides the Corbetts, some half-dozen squires and rectors dwelling in the immediate neighbourhood, called or left cards; but none of these last carried great weight in the county; and their civilities only brought out in stronger relief the general remissness—a remissness that could not be quite accounted for by weather, wild and wet enough to make a merciful man loath to take his horses far from their stable.

It was not the weather, you may be well assured, that induced Lord Atherstone to give his hunters a holiday; for since his marriage he had not shown at the covert-side. It was his fancy not to go out, till

Lena could decorously accompany him. She had
not had much cross-country practice; but Ralph
soon discovered that she had exceptionally good
hands, a firm seat, and wonderful nerve; so, during
their retirement, whenever there was a lull in the
wind and rain, he gave her an hour's schooling on
a couple of his horses, that, for a wonder, had mouths
and manners, and only required a little steadying
to make them safe conveyances.

They did not pass irksomely, those quiet days.
Lena was not a bit of a philosopher, and not a bit
too proud or too wise to relish keenly the good
things of this world, whereof she had as yet had but
scanty share. It was pleasant enough, to open her
eyes on tapestry still rich and warm in colour, though
a century had passed since it left the loom, and on
soft silken hangings merging into cloudy lace, instead of on white draperies, bare grey walls, and a
scantly carpeted floor. Pleasant—to be tended by the
most skilful of *caméristes*, instead of being dependent
on the second services of Mrs. Shafton's ancient
maid, sometimes grudgingly if not grumblingly rendered; for the good Julie's temper, naturally sub-
acid, had been nipped and soured on the northern
fells, and she deemed, in *ce sacré pays*, a Parisian
fully worthy of her hire, without working double
tides. Pleasant—within doors, to be surrounded by
manifold devices of comfort and luxury, after being
used to faded, meagre furniture and all the small
domestic shifts of 'poor gentility.' Pleasant—to
look forth on a wide rolling park, studded with
timber majestic even in leaflessness, instead of on a
miserable strip of yellow pasture-ground, fringed
with stunted firs that would scarcely shelter a highland steer. Pleasant—when the weather was too
wild to go farther afield, to stroll through the stables,
where the worth of a fair estate was represented by
the tenants of the deep boxes and wide stalls, and to
watch the light of the swinging lamps, reflected on

hides glistening with the last polish of the 'rubber;' and to contrast all this with the ruinous, drafty out-buildings where, since Miles ceased to reside at Blytheswold, stood only a couple of hill-ponies with their shaggy coats all staring. Pleasantest of all— to feel that she had only to speak a wish to find it carried out to the letter, quickly and cheerfully; for both the Upper and Lower Chamber in the household at Templestowe had passed a vote of confidence in their new mistress, and were, in truth, disposed to rejoice in their emancipation from the somewhat strict rule of Marian Ashleigh.

Of the infinite tenderness towards his wife, under-lying Ralph's *brusquerie*, she, at least, never doubted; but he was none of the foolish, fond old men who cloy their pets with sugar-plums, and wax querulous if the darling at last turns her head away. After all, the *reality* in the rare softening and lightening of his stern face, was worth a dozen 'demonstra-tions.' Before she had been a week at Templestowe, Lena discovered that the household, in so far as their master was concerned, were ruled by fear much more than by love. Lord Atherstone never rated his servants; but that they stood in awe of his glance, to say nothing of his frown, was very perceptible. Seeing all this—Lena felt a satisfac-tion in the consciousness, that *she* was never likely to be afraid of him.

Nevertheless, not once since their marriage, had it ever entered into her head to call her husband by his Christian name. The address affected by Marian Ashleigh, seemed to Lena just the right compromise; and so Ralph was 'Monseigneur' still.

Watching the pair, you would perhaps have de-cided that the change in their estate had affected the bridegroom less than the bride: yet the truth was far otherwise. Of the fierce delights of battle, and of 'the hunter's sullen joy,' the baron had had his fill; but the fruits, that men gather only under their own vine and their own fig-tree, were as new and strange to him as cates would be to a Polynesian. Albeit little prone to misgivings, there were moments when he felt almost afraid of his great happiness; and yet he did not fully realise it then, nor ever—till it stood out in relief against the darkness of the after-time.

Is it not so with all of us? I think, the keenest pang that comes with the memory of the *tempo felice* past and gone, is the consciousness of how imperfectly we appreciated it whilst it endured. I am speaking now of the quiet and, so to speak, domestic bliss, not of the perilous ecstasies snatched betwixt storm-gusts. No doubt we thought it pleasant at the time, whilst sitting dreamily over the fire, to have soft bright hair always within reach of our caress, and to find in earnest eyes always a sympathy with our joys and sorrows—ay! though the first were no greater, than having held our own in

> The glory of the gallop,
> Forty minutes over grass,

and the last no heavier, than an error at whist suitably punished. But *how* pleasant it was, we never knew, till over all this there came a change.

Till our nerve or our purse fail, we shall probably persist in pursuing. But—saving our dear friend, Harry Copeland, who has an eye to a deal—not a living soul will care whether the good horse Esca, whose price lies heavy on our conscience, makes the utmost of a lucky start, or, after a mile of deep going, comes back to the ruck. And we frequent the 'board of green cloth' more regularly than before. But, whilst sorting our cards, it may occur to us, that, besides our saturnine partner and the rash outsider who has backed the deal against the science, none will rejoice over the rubber pulled out of the fire.

It does not much matter, of course. Only, occasionally, as we jog homewards through the twilight,

or issue forth into the grey morning, we shall find ourselves wondering, how in the old time we could ever
have been tempted to leave—were it but for an hour
—that cosy ingle-nook and that gentle company.
The hearth to which we are returning is cold and
lonely ; or there gather round it faces, familiar perchance, and not unkindly, but which can no more
fill up a certain void than Time can bridge Eternity.
The soft, bright hair has lost its sheen, if it has
not mouldered into dust; and if, in the visions of
the night, we stretch forth our hand to caress it,
when once awake we laugh the folly to scorn ; for,
to satisfy that longing, we should need to delve two
fathoms deep into the soil of God's Acre, and lift the
lid of a coffin.   And the earnest eyes—if it were possible, would they still care to sympathise with our
confessions, light or grave?

Over such a doubt, wiser heads than yours and
mine have wearied themselves in vain.   When it is
fully solved, there will be few secrets left to be
unravelled, and there will abide unbroken but one
of the Seven Seals.

# CHAPTER XVIII.

LOAMSHIRE, though a tolerably extensive county, was not large enough to contain several satraps of independent power. In the course of generations ancient families had died out or fallen into obscurity, and fresh ones had been founded; but neither from the old blood nor the new had any one arisen, rash enough to challenge the supremacy of the Dukes of Devorgoil.

Other great nobles perhaps might own estates as vast; but these were probably scattered here and there throughout the breadth of England; whereas the territory owned by this family, if not literally in a ring-fence, lay either within or immediately around the Loamshire borders: it was centralisation, not less than hereditary prestige, that made their influence overweening. Occasionally of late years, a Radical candidate, smarting under defeat, had dared to speak evil of the august name; but such a diatribe, unless non-electors formed the bulk of the audience, was seldom favourably received. The Loamshire democrats evidently thought that the line of desecration and demolishment should be drawn somewhere; much on the principle of their more advanced brethren who, furthering all ima-aginable changes in Church and State, are not pre-pared to sweep away the Crown.

The present head of the great House was not, and never could have been, personally popular; but this signified very little. People seemed to think that if such a magnate was decently affable in his public

capacity, he might almost dispense with private
courtesy. Not that there was anything rude or
repulsive about the eighth Duke of Devorgoil; his
self-assertion seldom verged on insolence, or his
arrogance on oppression: he was only a frigid
formalist, narrow of mind and shallow of brain,
more alive to the importance than to the duties of
his station, yet willing to acquit himself of these
decorously. His subscriptions to charities were
munificent; but he had never been known to bestow
the smallest mite on a beggar: he was regular in
his religious observances, and every morning in the
castle chapel at Grandmanoir, his pompous 'Amen'
drowned the voice of his domestic chaplain at family
prayers; but his creed was well-nigh as simple as
Voltaire's, and the Bible in his chamber had never
been opened since it was placed there with the rest
of the furniture. His temper was neither violent
nor particularly irritable; he was slow to take offence,
simply because he found it hard to believe that any
creature could intentionally thwart or beard him; but,
when he had once taken umbrage, his wrath would
rankle on for years, nor would atonement ever so
ample abate its venom.

There were excuses to be made for him certainly.
Even at his baptism a heavy load was laid upon his
infant shoulders. Lupus FitzRoland—these were
only two out of many names bestowed upon him
then; and how could any man be expected to walk
through life, so decorated, without either staggering
or stiffening himself under the weight of ornament?
From the time that he could stand alone, he was never
natural or child-like. At Eton some few attempts
were made 'to knock the starch out of him;' but,
as he resided there with a private tutor, he could
always take refuge from persecution under the wing
of that complacent and compassionate bear-leader.
At Oxford the college authorities, from the dean to
the cook, made obeisance to him; and fellow-com-

moners of as ancient, if not as lofty blood as his own, were not ashamed to be reckoned among his hench-men. He took the seat that had been kept warm for him in a family borough, a month after he came of age; and, before the House had decided whether his obstinate silence proceeded from choice or from incapacity, the death of his father invested him with the full purple.

There was a striking contrast betwixt sire and son.

The first—free and debonair to a fault — seemed ever equally at ease, whether the blackened rafters of a farm-kitchen or the quilted damask of a boudoir sheltered his handsome head. In both, if all tales were true, he had a habit of making himself rather too thoroughly at home; and some of these tales were told with such a circumstance, that even Loamshire loyalty could not entirely close its ears against them, and was fain to confess that " his Grace might be a little—just a little—gay." That same gaiety of his caused some bright eyes to wax dim from remorse and shame, and some honest men to curse the hour when they first made him welcome under their roof; nevertheless, when he went to his account, there was a mighty flourish of funeral trumpets in the county journals; and it would have been treason to ques-tion aloud, whether a heavy loss had befallen Loam-shire.

The eighth duke was a very different personage. From his youth upwards until now, there could not have been imputed to him the faintest lapse in morals or derogation of dignity: he walked through life with the rigid uprightness of one who has never been strongly tempted to sin. He married early and had issue—two daughters and a son; but the last died in childhood : this was the single blot on his prosperity ; and he brooded over it always with a bitter sense of personal injury. Though he treated her with due observance both in public and private, he never for-gave his wife for not replacing the dead heir ; and, though he omitted no outward religious duty, he never forgave Providence for having visited him thus. Had his chaplain ventured—the good man never did so, be sure—to preach submission to the common lot, he would have answered that the common lot was not meant to apply to ducal houses in general, much less to that of Devorgoil. And for the unlucky accident of their sex, he never forgave his daughters.

Rachel Fontenaye was very hard — Ursula very homely—of feature; and it was no wonder if neither had been sought so far by an eligible wooer; for the chance of any much below their own degree would have been hopeless, and it had somehow got noised abroad that, despite their father's princely revenues, these august damsels would not be superbly dowered.

A small spare man—with a narrow sour face, and a sharp, upturned nose, changing colour like a chameleon under extremes of heat and cold—gifted with a slow, steady flow of speech, that, aided by a pompous clearing of the throat whenever he was at a loss for a word, carried him fairly through his frequent orations—this about expresses the Duke of Devorgoil at the age of twoscore years and ten.

He was anything but a sportsman at heart; nevertheless, even here he contrived to play his part creditably. The Grandmanoir preserves had been famous for generations; but the head of game had been rather augmented than decreased under his rule, and on the bench he was a turn more severe on poachers than on sheep-stealers. To his great *battues* there were invited, almost exclusively, chiefs of his own Order—a belted earl counted rather low in the scale —and on these occasions it pleased him to walk about, followed by two giants in laced velveteen, each bearing a gun, which his Grace never discharged, save at a corner so hot that his misses were bound to pass unnoticed. The partridge-shooting he meted out to the squirearchy and certain of the clergy, in just proportion to their political influence and elec-

tioneering zeal.   In early life he was occasionally
to be seen at the covert-side, mounted on the gravest
and gentlest of cattle; but his ideas of the pursuit
probably much resembled those of a conscientious
legislator still to the fore.

Representing a constituency of which a good half
are born centaurs, Mr. Talboys considered hunting
a senatorial duty; and so maintained a costly stud;
the which, being a welter weight with impossible
hands, he generally managed to use up before the
season was through.   He never by any chance saw
anything of a run; but rode the line doggedly from
end to end, of course with countless falls; and his
rueful countenance never was known to light up save
when fate favoured him with a blank day.   On a
certain March morning he came to real grief over
stiff timber, and lay stunned for a while.   When his
senses returned, they heard him murmur softly—he
was a pious person of Low Church tendencies—
"Only a fortnight more of this, thank God,"—re-
ferring, you must understand, to the opening of the
Session, when the labours of others, and his rest,
would begin.

If in those bygone times the Duke of Devorgoil
sacrificed his inclinations to public opinion, he took
special care to sacrifice nothing more; and was never
known to risk his serene neck over anything larger
than a water-furrow; a crowd at a gate he eschewed
as if there had been pestilence in the midst thereof.
The distaste for the saddle grew on him with advanc-
ing years; and now, when a meet was honoured by
his presence, he always came in state and comfort
on the easiest of wheels.   Despite of this, throughout
his vast territory the coverts were not often drawn
blank, though by some curious fatality a straight-
goer rarely was found close to Grandmanoir.  'They
were too highly fed there,' the keepers said mourn-
fully—and keepers always know best; albeit, why a
hen-pheasant should be more harmful than a rabbit

to vulpine training, is a problem only to be solved by those faithful guardians of the game.

There were fixtures not a few on the Devorgoil domains; but, unless some royal personage or foreign potentate chanced to be his guest, the Duke never offered a lawn-meet; for this would have involved a breakfast, and anything in the shape of chance entertainment was entirely out of his line. To stately set-dinners he was fully equal, and dispensed such formal hospitality pretty liberally; but the idea of rustics, whom he scarcely knew by name, clanking in under his portals, without specific invitation; 'cutting and coming again,' under the scutcheoned roof of his banqueting-hall, and snatching refreshment on his sacred threshold, was quite too much for his nerves and sense of propriety. Absolutely discountenancing vulpicide, and subscribing largely to the hounds, he held himself *functum officio* and to spare. But the L. H., as a rule, were honest folk, caring little for the coffee-house: so long as the Duke found them foxes, they were content to trust to their modest sandwich-cases, and find their own jumping powder.

Hazlemere Cross was rather a favourite meet. Within half a league of the park-fence, it was so far removed from the inner Capua of Grandmanoir, as to make a ring not quite a certainty. If the fox sunk the hill, as generally happened when the wind lay right, he was bound to take a good line—a line, indeed, entirely after the heart of a Loamshire 'hard;' with lightish ploughs, and grass enough to satisfy any but a captious stranger, and, best of all, big, fair jumping from end to end.

Thitherwards on a murky morning that, if a breeze sprung up, looked as if it might lift towards noon, drove Lord Atherstone with his bride. With the exception of an occasional visit to Heslingford, it was the first time the pair had appeared in public since their marriage.

Said Ralph at length—

"And the nerves, Lena—are they as steady as when we started? The farm where our horses are waiting is just over yonder rise; and the meet's a short mile further on."

She smiled a little haughtily.

"The nerves are as well as can be expected. It is rather a trial to be presented to a county and a fox on the same day; but there are only two things which I am really afraid of, Monseigneur. The first is, that I shall commit some *gaucherie* of which you will be thoroughly ashamed; the second is, I shall be terribly an encumbrance if the hounds are running."

"I'll risk the *gaucherie*," he said quietly; but one of those rapid changes came over his face as he turned it towards her—"and I can't fancy you as an encumbrance yet. I am more doubtful of how I shall acquit myself. I've never played pilot before, you know; and it's a stiff country if we go over the vale. To be sure, I know every inch of it; and I've an idea there's a line of gates most of the way, though I never paid much attention to them. Still, I'm half sorry that I promised you should follow. You will remember *your* promise, though—that you would pull up the instant you felt nervous, whether it was before or after a fence. Perhaps we shall have no jumping to speak of after all, but shall be ringing round the park all day. It wouldn't break my heart if that were to happen."

"I ought to take that as a compliment," Lena answered; "but I'd rather have gone on flattering myself, that I was no great clog upon you. Could you have been so patient two months ago?"

"Certainly not. Many things are altered within the last two months, and all for the better, I believe. I shall care for hunting some time longer, I daresay; but never again as I used to care, when my life was quite lonely. I never pay compliments, as I told you once before. But this seems to me quite natural."

"We won't argue the question, at all events," she returned; "and perhaps even a 'clog' might be useful, if it cured you of rash riding. I wonder if there will be a great crowd to-day, and whether the Grandmanoir people will be out? It's rather strange that none of them have called yet. Is it their way?"

Lord Atherstone knit his brows. Plainly, his wife had touched a chord of thought that had already vibrated—not harmoniously.

"I know very little of their ways," he said. "The Duke bears me no good-will, I fancy; but we've never come into collision, and he's always been formally civil when we chanced to meet: it's impossible that he can mean to be otherwise now. It is a long, heavy drive, remember, in such weather as we've had lately, from Grandmanoir to Templestowe. He rarely misses this meet; so he will probably speak for himself before long."

There was no time for more; for just then they were turning into the little elm-avenue, that led up to the cozy farmstead where their horses had found shelter. The owner stood at the door, booted, spurred, and bareheaded, anxious to do honour to the new baroness. Unpopular to a degree amongst the gentry and peasantry of his county, Ralph was not ill-liked by the better class of yeomanry. He was a liberal, though a somewhat careless landlord; and, out hunting, often had a familiar word for a farmer, when he could scarcely spare a nod to a squire; besides, there were not a few admirers of his 'bruising' style, and amongst these was John Langlands.

So Lena met with hearty welcome; and there were pressed upon her such varied refreshments, that she was fain to compromise with a sip of home-made cherry-brandy; and then she was mounted comfortably. At this ceremony the buxom hostess assisted with intense admiration. She had hitherto not conceived it possible that any who had come to matronly estate, could get to saddle without the assistance of horse-block, or some substitute; and, when Lena seemed to spring from, rather than be lifted by, her husband's palm, Mrs. Langlands opened wide her eyes, as though she witnessed a rare *tour de gymnase.*

"My lady went up as light as a soap-bubble, I do declare," she said afterwards: "and yet, as fine a figure of a woman as you'd wish to see."

So—the groom and John Langlands following—Lord Atherstone and his wife paced slowly up the gentle ascent, on the brow of which scattered groups, growing denser fast, showed that the L. H. were like to muster strong to-day.

Will you prick forward, and see who are the earlier comers?

# CHAPTER XIX.

A PLOT of open ground, somewhat larger than an ordinary village-green — the converging-point of several roads and bridle-paths—crowning a low hill; from whence the view on one side, though not very extensive, lies open over a vale, but is hemmed in on the other three by tall plantations, and by the towering woods of Grandmanoir farther a-field. Such is Hazlemere Common. Near the centre of it stands the Cross —not a graceful spire, such as those that mark Queen Eleanor's resting-places on her long journey tombwards; but a mighty monolith, roughly hewn, doubtless, even at first, and now so maimed and worn by rough usage and weather, that, passing it carelessly, you might hardly recognise the Symbol of our faith. The date thereof, and whether it was set up in thanksgiving, or in penance, or to mark the place of blood-shedding, or to commemorate some prehistoric victory over the heathen, is not certainly known; albeit learned persons coming from afar have wrangled over it in language scarcely parliamentary, and on this stone many local antiquaries have whetted their maiden blade. There it has stood from immemorial time, keeping its own secret, if secret there be to tell; and so it will stand, after the men and manners of our century have become matter for archæologists.

Within a few rods of this same Cross, most of the personages worth your notice are grouped already. On principle, if not by choice, you will, of course, first inspect the hounds.

A level compact lot, certainly; a little low, if anything, and rather neat than airy-looking; indeed,
you might pick out several necks and shoulders too
heavily loaded for elegance, and one or two clear
cases of throatiness; but there are some rare legs
and feet, and, as a rule, no deficiency of bone.  Such
as they are, they thoroughly satisfy the Loamshire
critics, and almost satisfy their fastidious Master,
who for years past has given his whole mind to
their improvement, and is pitiless in his ' drafts.'

That is he—the silent, sedate man, sitting betwixt
his hounds and the gathering crowd, on an equally
sedate though cleverly-shaped bay.   There is rather
a workmanlike look about him, despite a precise-
ness of exterior, which even hunting-costume cannot
disguise.  When he took the Loamshire country,
purposing to be his own huntsman, his friends said
it was a rash step in many ways ; but Jasper Knowsley
did not often err on the side of rashness.  He brought
to his task great patience, a perseverance akin to
obstinacy, and no mean attainments in the Science,
acquired by sedulous study in famous schools.  He
never tries to make profit out of his office, and is
liberal enough about earth-stopping, keepers' fees,
and damages; nevertheless, he has contrived to show
sport enough to satisfy all but inveterate grumblers,
without seriously impairing his own modest revenues.
His trim chop-whiskers are thickly sprinkled with
grey, and even in his youth he was rather a neat
than a determined horseman : so, when they are running hard over a stiff country, he cannot be expected
to ride right up to his hounds; but, knowing every
gate, gap, and bridle road, he generally contrives to
be with them before they want lifting; and, should
he fail, there is always Jem Spurrell—nominally first
whip, though he never waits for the laggers in covert
—to the fore, who, for the strange tricks he plays
with his neck, might have been bred an acrobat,
and would ride at a bullfinch on fire if it came in

his line. Very mild, if not meek, of speech is our
Master, never rating even a hound violently; and
when forced to chide human ignorance or impetuo-
sity, prone rather to remonstrance than abuse. On
extreme provocation, he is capable of a certain acid
sarcasm, of the which one instance may suffice.

It was late in the afternoon; and, after a series of
disappointments, the hounds had got settled to a fox,
and pushed him steadily through a chain of small
coverts till he was bound to break over an open
country, when a youthful plunger (a squadron was
always quartered at Heslingford), determined at all
hazards to get a start, rode right down on the critical
corner; so that a chop followed, as a matter of
course. There were murmurs, as you may imagine;
but all held their peace to listen as Jasper Knowsley
approached the offender, smiling sourly.

"You're nearly a stranger in this country, sir; and
probably suppose that we met this morning expressly
for your amusement. If it has given you any pleasure to spoil the sport of a hundred or so of your
fellow-creatures, I'm sure nobody will complain.
But now—if you're *quite* satisfied, and you don't
want the hounds to run a drag, or anything of that
sort—I think, with your permission, I'll take them
home."

Then, lifting his cap courteously, he turned away.

They say that the cornet wept. Certainly, there
are men who would liefer have taken their 'month at
the mill,' than have sat there in his glistening boots;
and most of those present held the punishment equal
to the misdeed.

Perhaps our Master would be old-fashioned enough
to allow, that a certain amount of loud and strong
language is necessary to keep a field—particularly a
provincial field—in order. But this part of his duty
he shifted from his own shoulders long ago. Yonder
sits his deputy—the huge hairy man, with a face like
a full moon looming through mist, on the big, bony

brown: his hoarse voice must have reached you before you rose the crest of the hill.

This is Swinton Swarbrick's thirtieth season with the same pack; and, though it has changed hands five times at least since he first was 'blooded,' he has never wavered in his allegiance, nor strayed far from those russet tilths that, he swears, "carry a better scent than all your grazing grounds." If his means had permitted it, he would have tried his hand at the Mastership ere now; but, being free-handed to a fault, his estate, when stable-expenses and his subscription are paid, scarcely suffices his needs. Nevertheless, he is a man of great mark in the Hunt; so much so, that when he curses a culprit the anathema is supposed to descend with an official weight. Years ago, he talked himself into the idea that he was a bruising though unlucky rider; and, though Loamshire has got his measure pretty accurately, strangers often find it hard to realise, that all that laying down the law about 'lines' and 'points,' does not entail jumping one blind or big place in a week. In spite of his swagger, Swinton Swarbrick is a sportsman to the marrow of his massive bones, and a prime favourite throughout his county with high and low. Even those who have been lashed by his unsparing tongue, bear no malice. "He may bluster," they say, "but he's never nasty." And, to speak truth, one of Jasper Knowsley's slow stinging sentences is more dreaded than a string of the other's voluble blasphemies.

Look a little to the left, to the rearward of the Cross, and your glance will be apt to linger, longer than it has hitherto done, on the centre figure of the group. Did you ever see a daintier amazon, or one more happily at home in her saddle, though it is clear that the dark chestnut wants some riding?

That is no other than winsome Cissy Devereux; the pride, if you believe her friends—the pest, if you velieve her foes—of Loamshire. Polling the county through, the votes of the former would probably prevail ; for even women find it hard to hate her, or at all events to sustain the feud. Whether her life's sky be bright or lowering, her clear laugh still keeps its ring—the laugh that to some who hear it is a better tonic than ever has been devised by mediciner. Thoroughly sincere for the moment, if not always stable in her friendships ; and frank even in her small treacheries—through good or evil report bearing herself always dauntlessly—it is no wonder if many prefer shutting their eyes and believing in her, to sifting her demerits.

Her face is provokingly pretty ; and, though she is out in all weathers, the peach-bloom has not fled from her cheek, nor the sheen from her bonny brown hair. As for her figure—is it not known how shapely women, envying her habit, have sought the studio of Herr Veltermann, and abased themselves before that artist, to secure an exact fac-simile ; and how, having donned the masterpiece and compared it with the original, they have returned home despondent, and ready to rive the innocent garment to shreds?

That she will go great—very great—lengths in coquetry, her hottest partisans will allow ; whether there are any limits to her imprudence, is a question that has been discussed without, as well as within, the Loamshire border, and never, so far as society knows, been fully solved. She must assuredly more than once have strayed very near the verge of the crater ; but the lurid sulphur-fumes have never wrapped her round as yet. Besides, she changes her light loves so often that the scandal-mongers get flurried, and — like a nervous shooter, when the covey rises all round him—sometimes fail to pick their bird. Moreover, howsoever pleasant, it is not always a safe pastime to cast stones at your neigh-bour's wife, when the said neighbour is ready to catch them in the skirt of his mantle, and send them back with a will.

Now, foremost amongst the wilful beauty's adherents above mentioned, is her husband, Dick Devereux—still known amongst his intimates by his old regimental sobriquet of 'The Driver.' "There's not a woman alive fit to hold a candle to Cissy; and, if she *has* a bit of a temper, there's not an ounce of vice about her." So Dick believed when they were first engaged; and seven years of matrimony have not altered his creed. He takes his wife's bullying like a lamb; but towards the rest of the world carries a somewhat taurine temper; and, when fairly roused, is apt to run a rude tilt, without distinction of persons, or even of sexes. The fractiousness of the savage brute he is riding obliges him to keep without the circle; but you may see his heavy handsome face light up, as one of Cissy's gay impertinences requites a point-blank compliment from Sir Manners Mannering — always pompous when not coarse in his gallantries—who looks as if he had been born in those high collars and stiff throat-gear.

Besides this somewhat bloated aristocrat, the group is made up of Arthur Corbett, radiant in smiles and in attire; grave Malise Walwyn, heir to an ancient Catholic house, who, despite his fair prospects, is said to have a vocation for the priesthood; cheery Peter Assheton, the sporting parson, who, were he as powerful in the pulpit as in the pigskin, would count fewer dissenters in his parish; and a strong cavalry contingent from Heslingford, headed by Godfrey Colville—the keen-visaged man, with eyes and hair black and shining as jet. He is Cissy's latest 'love;' and will have the perilous honour of leading her to-day. Be it noted, in passing, that, though her caprices take the widest range, she has rather a leaning towards military devotion. "Dick likes them best," she says, con-

siderately; "and they're quite clever enough for me."
Indeed, it must be owned that intellectual jewels,
clumsily set, do not sparkle temptingly for this wayward lady.

And now——

There is only one poor hunting-horn available,
and such pomps are not in fashion here; but, if we
met on foreign ground, there would be a *fanfare* of
bugles; for the gorgeous barouche, drawn by four
greys, with outriders to match, sweeping down the
road, and drawing up with a jerk, brings the Duke
of Devorgoil and his daughters twain.

His Mightiness does not seem in a specially
gracious humour this morning. The sharp wind
may, perhaps, account for the vicious flush at the
tip of his nose; but the fidgety working of his thin
lips, and the frequent contraction of his brow, bode
no good. Nevertheless, he condescends to answer
the greetings of the Master and the privileged few
who venture to accost him; and acknowledges with
sufficient affability the doffing of hats and caps, till
Lord and Lady Atherstone appear on the further
verge of the little common: then the signs of discontent on the ducal visage are no longer dissembled,
and darken as the pair draw near.

Hard-featured Lady Rachel, though one would
think it difficult, waxes stiffer and stonier than her
wont; and homely Lady Ursula looks half-apprehen-
sive, half-amused; and certain of the bystanders,
more curious than their fellows, edge nearer to the
saluting-point, as if they expected something like
a scene. And as Ralph makes his way slowly
through the throng—nodding a return to divers
greetings, but never halting or turning a hair's-
breadth aside till he comes within speaking-distance
of the carriage—there is a quiet, resolute look on
his face, like that of one who, fully aware of a
danger, goes, not reluctantly, to meet it.

And a danger it is—of such a sort, moreover, as

he has never yet confronted; for, though stout heart
may help somewhat, strong hand may nothing
avail.

We needs must drop the historic present here;
for the root of these matters strikes deep into the
past

# CHAPTER XX.

THE Duke of Devorgoil was manifestly ill at ease. He sate, plucking at the sable coverlet, as though he would fain have hidden himself under its massive folds, and glancing to left and right nervously; but, shift as he would, he could no more evade the steady grey eyes than a patient can the gaze of a magnetiser. So he met them at last.

If a little formal, nothing could be more courteous than Ralph's salute—nothing more placable than his voice and manner.

"I am happy to have this opportunity, of presenting your Grace to Lady Atherstone."

Seldom has any dignitary of Church or State been plunged in direr quandary, than that in which the Lord Lieutenant of Loamshire found himself now.

That first offence of *lèse-majesté* recorded above, had never been mitigated by any after-homage on the part of the criminal. Whenever county-business brought them in contact, Lord Atherstone did not evince the smallest inclination to defer to the other's wishes or opinion. Twice or thrice when—on the occasion of a royal visit—an invitation was equivalent to a command, Ralph had partaken of a state banquet at Grandmanoir; but, of his own free will, he never had darkened those august portals; nor had he once entreated their master to honour Templestowe with his presence. Throughout all these years, the Duke had nursed a sombre resentment; waiting and watching—not over patiently—for an opportunity of slaking the same. Besides private pique, he had public grounds for enmity: he did honestly believe that Lord Atherstone was a discredit to the Order to which they both belonged, and therefore deserved, in all possible ways, to be discouraged and repressed.

Ay!—and there was something more. Lupus Fitz-Roland was far too sublime a personage to listen to gossip; to the ordinary *can-cans* of society he lent no more attention, than did the Olympians to the tittle-tattle of Troy; but he had chanced to pass through town soon after the Atherstone engagement was announced; and, as he sat conning the papers in his solitary arm-chair at the Sanctorium, certain scraps of club-talk had floated past his ear— leading him to infer that, if no grave scandal had attached to Lena Shafton, she had at least been something imprudent in her time. Now, if he had been a rigid puritan instead of a very indifferent Christian, the Duke could not have entertained a holier horror of anything in the shape of coquetry. No facilities for flirtation were provided at any of his entertainments either in town or country; and even on neutral ground, couples indulging in the most innocent of such diversions, had been known to start guiltily under his austere gaze, and fly like timid hares to the cover of the conservatory or other fastness, whither the Censor's eye could not follow.

Was not the edifice of Lord Atherstone's social sins high and broad enough already, but that he must add thereto the very corner-stone, by bringing into the county a wife, concerning whom the world's tongue had wagged lightly, if not accusingly?

All things considered, here in absolute completeness was the chance of retaliation, for which he had waited so long. It was his bounden duty—so he had told himself at least a dozen times—no less as Head of a family than as Head of a county, to assert his own position and make the Atherstones feel theirs. Yes: it should be shown, so plainly that all who rode

might read the lesson, that the House of Devorgoil
had the privilege not only of choosing their acquaintance, but of dropping the same at their pleasure.
Indeed, the Duke had rehearsed the whole scene to
his entire satisfaction : how—when the criminals
approached — he would look straight to his front,
neither frowning nor smiling, but superbly serene,
and implacably ignore their presence ; so that they
would be fain to pass on, clad in the garments of
confusion, and a warning to future misdoers.  As
for his conduct being questioned—a Lord Lieutenant
might possibly be called to account by his Sovereign ;
but, assuredly, by no other living creature.

The scheme was not ill-laid ; but, like many others
framed both by men and mice, through a slight
miscalculation it went ‘a-jee.’  The Duke had never
reckoned on his enemy coming straight at him, and
opening fire within point-blank range.

Had Hawley been told on the eve of Preston, that
on the morrow the clansmen would hurl themselves
bare-breasted on the sabres of his dragoons, he
would surely have laughed aloud.  What the result
was, we know ; and these provoking surprises will
go on happening till the end of time.

If, on the present occasion, the noble strategist
avoided total rout, he escaped not sore discomfiture.
Instead of the serene unconcern that he had intended
it should wear, his countenance was full of irritated
perplexity ; there was more of nervousness than
pomposity in the frequent clearing of his throat ;
and, evidently, something more than the right word
in the right place was a-lacking.  What he had proposed to say—or not to say—you know : what he
said, was this—

“I am—ahem—happy, to—a—make Lady—a—
Atherstone’s acquaintance.”

And, as he lifted his hat a bare inch from his
brows, his hand shook painfully.  He, also, was being
‘ executed ’ in the sight of all the people ; but he

could not, like brave old Bailly, have replied to a scoffer—'It is with the cold.'

If the baron had 'presented' his wife, it would have sounded somewhat better; but even this poor salve to the ducal dignity was wanting. Nevertheless there was now no possibility of drawing back; and, henceforward, till fresh cause of offence arose, there must be outward amity, howsoever hollow, betwixt Grandmanoir and Templestowe.

In such emergencies, it is generally a woman who shows herself most calm and cruel. Lady Rachel perhaps was made of sterner stuff than her sire; for little encouragement could be drawn from her wiry salute; and not a word, courteous or uncourteous, escaped her lips, braced like a steel trap. But Lady Ursula—*bon brin dc fille au fond*, and a degenerate Fontenaye—nearly spoilt the effect of her sister's admirable behaviour, by nodding and smiling, and putting some ridiculous question as to Lady Atherstone's sporting tastes.

Lena had not betrayed the faintest embarrassment from first to last; but she did feel very grateful towards Lady Ursula just then; and her colour rose a little as she replied "that this was almost her first essay; but that she fancied that she should grow very fond of hunting."

Jasper Knowsley had a shrewd tact of his own; and it was probably consideration for others besides his hounds, whose coats were beginning to stare under the north wind, that caused him to move off towards the covert without more delay. A glance from Ralph told his wife that the interview was over; and, after another interchange of formal salutes, the pair followed in the wake of the field.

Whether from this passage of arms—the expression is not much too strong—any of the parties concerned issued with the honours of war, is an open question; for, as to the Lord Lieutenant's intentions, or the causes that brought the same to nought, few of the spectators were deceived; and, though many admired his nerve, the extorted courtesy did not greatly improve Lord Atherstone's social credit. Perhaps Mr. Chantrey, the horse-breaker, in his homely language expressed pretty accurately the general opinion.

"The Dook, he meant to be nasty," quoth honest Will; "a blind man could see that with half an eye; but, when it come to the push, he had to drop it. It's, for all the world, like this here black colt of mine. He's got plenty of temper, but no pluck to speak of; and, if you just shake a cutting-whip at him, he'll drop his back, and lob on like a sheep. The Dook, he's had a side-binder or two from the baron in their time, I'll pound it. Old Ralph ain't by no means a pleasant sort to tackle."

It is time that we too should follow; for the rearmost hound has topped the covert-fence five minutes ago.

A promising draw certainly. There is good lying on the slope of the hill; and a perfect jungle under the alders down there in the hollow, filled, in days before drainage was known, by the ancient Mere. Hares by dozens are stealing away, and rabbits by scores scuttling about, already; and, if the air is not darkened with pheasants, as it would be within the park-fence of Grandmanoir, a whir of wings ever and anon shows that there is no danger of the foxes being starved out of this stronghold. The keeper—leaning against the gate-post yonder with an air of moody resignation—"du allow that he padded a brace at least, yester-morning." Moreover, the wind lies just right for the vale, trending away to the southward till it seems to narrow to a point in the grey distance.

A few go into covert with the hounds; but the rides must be mere quagmires after the late rains, and the body of the field keep to the sounder ground above; whilst the first whip gets forward and ensconces himself in the bend of a high bullfinch, so that, unseen himself, he can peer over the open beyond. It is not a day when, even in covert, the scent is likely to lie well; and, at the best of times, Hazlemere takes a deal of working. Very patiently the Master does work it in his own quiet fashion, seldom speaking to, much less hurrying, his hounds; so that the field—no longer overshadowed by the awful Presence, for the ducal carriage keeps to the main-road along the hill-crest— has leisure for courtesies or for chaff, as the case may be.

Arthur Corbett, visibly exulting at having stolen a march upon his fellows, presses up to salute Lady Atherstone, and lingers at her bridle-rein; and some half-dozen more are presented to Lena, including Mr. Swarbrick and the Devereux's. Though Cissy has to a certain extent got her company manners on, her cordial welcome is by far the brightest gleam of social sunshine that has crossed Lady Atherstone's path since it led her Loamshirewards. Ralph performs his part in these ceremonies creditably enough; but he is very chary of his words, and there is a grave pre-occupied look on his face, such as Lena has not seen once since their marriage.

Suddenly, from the thickest of the covert below, comes a whimper, eager, yet not quite confident; but Jasper Knowsley still sits silent and statue-like in the middle ride; for, though Mariner is the very gem of this year's entry, he is apt to be a trifle too keen: the next minute comes a sharp, joyous yelp, about which there can be no mistake; the Master smiles triumphantly—Mariner is the first produce of a famous cross—and cheers him with a will; then a deeper tongue chimes in, as Vigilant, whose speech is law, proclaims that youth may sometimes be right, though it speak before eld; and other notes swell into music —*the* music that, more than any other under heaven, maketh the ears that hear it to tingle.

Mr. Swarbrick, out on the hill-side, takes the time to a second, from a machine something larger than a travelling-clock; the which significant action causes

some of the thrusting ones to creep forward, though
Jem Spurrell, from his post of vantage, flings back
his hand warningly; but—"gently, pray gently, on
the right"—cries the mild Master, in the act of swat-
tering through a miry pool; and—"that's right, spoil
your own sport, and be d——d to you"—roars his
terrible Echo. Luckily the double-barrelled remonstrance takes effect, and the culprits draw rein before
harm is done. Soon the chorus within deepens to a
crash: from the nook of the bullfinch comes a scream,
that could no more be printed than it could be set to
notes, but which the hounds know as well as they do
the Master's horn; and, without the ceremony of taking
a run, Jem dives head-foremost into the blackthorn:
Swinton Swarbrick, with a dig of his ponderous
spurs, launches forth the bony brown, and lurches
away over the meadow, like a rock let loose, for a pet
gap which he guesses is lightly bushed up; followed
by Arthur the 'squire of dames,' and some dozen
more: Dick the Driver, who, ever since the find, has
been fighting his savage till they both are all a-foam,
with a great gasp of relief goes hurling at the spot
where the growers are thickest: Godfrey Colville—
keener for a start than he ever was from Ranks-
borough—makes, straight as a die, at the place that
he picked ten minutes ago; and Cissy Devereux,
humouring Paladin's fidgety mouth like an artist,
sails off in his wake, happier than any crowned
queen.

"Get forward to the gate, Edward" (this to his
groom); "and keep quite close to me, Lena," says
Lord Atherstone—his face lighting up at last. Those
who make for the same pass—some from awe of the
baron, more for the sake of the bonny bride—forbear
to press upon the pair, till they are fairly through.

And so the curtain is up, and the play begun.

Unluckily in many dramas, grave and gay, the
interest is apt to decline steadily from the opening
scene; and so it happened here. The first burst of a

mile or so, was quick enough to satisfy anybody; but then the hounds got bothered in some sheep-foil; and the scent, out of covert, was so miserably cold, that they never picked up their ground, or got upon good terms with their fox again. The Master of the L. H. was patient to a fault, and would potter on—as his detractors said—in almost hopeless pursuit, rather than try for a fresh one; but he was compelled to do this at last.

The second fox was a cowardly ringing brute; and, when he did break, it was only to slink over the hill along a chain of spinnies that brought him to a 'creep' through the park pales of Grandmanoir; the day, too, was lowering instead of lightening: so Lady Atherstone assented willingly to her husband's suggestion that they should turn homewards here.

The moody look had settled down on Ralph's face again, puzzling Lena not a little, and provoking her to boot; for she herself felt in unusually good spirits. She had been present at several meets before, but had never seen a covert actually drawn; and the novelty of the sights and sounds had kept her thoroughly amused. Standard Bearer had carried her admirably, and they had negotiated two or three unavoidable fences, without any difference of opinion; moreover, the L. H., as a rule, had agreeably surprised her. She liked the placid Master, who, busy as he was, had found time to be presented, exceedingly; Swinton Swarbrick, as a relic of the old Squire Western days, was inimitable; Mrs. Devereux must be charming; and Mr. Corbett—well—he smiled a little too often and too blandly, but he was pleasant to look upon, and wonderfully amusing and well-bred for a provincial banker. The Grandmanoir party did not impress her favourably; but perhaps the Duke could not help being fidgety and formal, any more than Lady Rachel could help looking acid; and, though she was glad when the interview was over, the idea of an intentional rudeness had

never crossed her mind, much less dwelt there. Perhaps there was the slightest shade of pique in her
tone, when she broke rather a long silence.

"It has been a very stupid morning for you,
Monseigneur. Indeed, I am half ashamed at having
enjoyed it so much."

Ralph started from his reverie, and his brow
cleared.

"You're quite wrong, my dear. It would have been
a very stupid morning if I had not had you to look
after, and—it's the honest truth—to admire. I don't
know whether you or Standard Bearer can claim the
most credit; but you deserve a good deal between
you. The sport has been just about what I expected
—much better than I expected, if you have been really
amused."

"But something has gone wrong," she persisted.
"I would give any reasonable sum, to know your
thoughts for the last ten minutes, unless they have
been simply wandering."

"They have not wandered far," he answered, with
his curt laugh. "I have been thinking of my own
folly and blindness—a harder word than either might
suit—which began when I first came to live in Loamshire, and have gone on ever since, from bad to
worse. I had had crosses and disappointments, of
course; but so have thousands who come out smooth
and smiling. There was nothing to make one set
one's bristles up, and keep all the world at bay.
People did try to be civil when first I came home, I
quite remember that; but all the forms and ceremonies bored me intensely, and—I showed it. There
was another opening just after Philip's marriage; but
I didn't take it, though Marian tried hard to persuade me. Of course, I've made enemies by scores.
They have never had a chance of hitting me before;
but they have got one now, and I doubt if they will
let it slip. That's what I've been thinking about, my
dear."

Lena looked up, wondering. This was not the first time she had heard of her husband's rough unsocial ways; but, as to the immediate cause which now moved him to repent them, she was still in the dark.

"Don't you overrate your unpopularity?" she said. "I thought everybody seemed good-natured enough to-day."

Ralph's keen grey eyes dwelt on her, as if he doubted whether she spoke in earnest.

"The Duke of Devorgoil, for instance? It would not have cost much trouble, to have made a friend instead of a foe of that pompous old idiot. If I had not cut him short in a congratulation speech, and if I had asked his opinion twice a year at quarter sessions, and lifted my hat an inch and a half higher whenever we met, he would have been civil enough, I dare say. Now, he would have been anything but civil three hours ago, if he had dared; but—it's a constitutional weakness, I've noticed it in him before—he always forgets what he's determined to say or do, as soon as people, not absolutely in his power, fix him with their eyes."

Lord Atherstone wished the words unsaid, as he saw the hot Shafton blood mount to his fair wife's forehead; yet he only half guessed the cause of her emotion.

That she was vexed, as well as surprised, by this new aspect of things is quite true. The old Adam is apt to rise rebelliously within the meekest and wisest of men, when they first recognise that a slight has been put upon them; especially if it be too late to resent it. Lena, being neither meek, nor wise, nor masculine, felt the full force of the sting; but she felt something more. She felt it was quite possible, that an ancient grudge, and mortified vanity, might not entirely account for the Duke of Devorgoil's demeanour; and that, if the nerve had been equal to the will, it might have been plain to Loamshire, that

Ralph Atherstone's wife, as well as Ralph Atherstone, was henceforth to be numbered amongst those whom the Lord Lieutenant did *not* delight to honour.

When Lena Shafton was first warned that, if she took not better heed, the world would make free with her name, she had smiled defiantly. If Caryl Glynne kept his promise, and came to claim her, he could never taunt her with risks incurred for him; if he came not, the gossips might talk themselves hoarse for aught she cared. But, after the early bitterness was past, and she had settled down into the weary waiting that ended as you wot of, she had, no doubt more than once, repented of her recklessness; though never so keenly as now. The better she understood her husband, the more she looked up to and trusted him; and, if it was as yet impossible to love, she found it quite easy to honour and obey. It cut her, now, to the heart, to see him taking all the blame to himself so simply and frankly, when perhaps not half of it was fairly his share; and, for a second or two, she was moved to abye the consequences of full confession. However, one glance at his face changed her purpose. Lena's courage could not be measured by the ordinary standard of womankind; but this thing she dared not do. If her voice trembled a little when she made answer, it was not with anger.

"I had not an idea of this, or I would have prayed —so hard—to be spared the introduction. Is it absolutely impossible to breathe Loamshire air, without the Duke's sanction?"

"Not at all impossible," Ralph answered more cheerily; "I've tried the experiment, you know, and I can't say that my lungs have suffered. But, if I can't amend my errors, I ought to try to prevent your paying for them; and, on the whole, I think I acted rightly to-day. The Grandmanoir folks will probably keep up to civility-mark now, and that's all that's required of them; so, I might have kept my own counsel, and not have spoilt your pleasure. I am half sorry I told you."

"You need not be," she said; "it's always best —so much best—to speak out."

Always best, of a surety; but—is it always so easy?

Had that question been put to mother Eve, she would perhaps have answered—'Nay'—before her leafen kirtle was sere.

# CHAPTER XXI.

So our first act ends; and, before the curtain rises again, you must suppose an interval of hard on a year. During this space, there was some shifting of scenes and of dresses; but in the actors or the circumstances no material change.

On that Hazlemere day, the Duke of Devorgoil had, howsoever grudgingly, entered into tacit recognisance to keep the peace towards Templestowe; and he acted up to the letter of his engagement. He drove over with his daughters to call, on a bright, balmy afternoon, when the odds against finding any healthy human creature within doors, were incalculable; and, after leaving a sheaf of cards, went his way with a sense of relief, not devoid of humiliation; such as may have been felt by the kings and kaisers of old time, who for their people's sake rather than their own, submitted to signal penance. Furthermore, after ascertaining by inquiry, careful though circuitous, that the Atherstones were absent (they had gone up to town for a fortnight), he besought the honour of their company at one of his state banquets. The visit was returned in due course, and the invitation declined with due courtesy; and so for the present the matter ended; it being understood on both sides, that, whensoever they met, all the ceremonies of distant acquaintanceship should be observed.

To a certain extent the county took its cue from the Lord Lieutenant. There was no overt case of avoidance; the Atherstones came in for their fair share of set dinner-parties, and neighbours showed themselves not averse to accept from them the like formal hospitality—Ralph had quite broken through his rule of seclusion, you will observe; and, if the effort was sometimes evident, played the host much better than might have been expected from his want of practice—but still an invisible barrier, almost resembling a line of quarantine, seemed drawn round Templestowe.

The first year of Lena's residence there was drawing to a close; and—setting Hubert Ashleigh aside whose parish duties, according to his own account, kept him much at home—she could hardly claim intimacy with more than two families—the Devereux's and the Corbetts.

That wilful Cissy was little accustomed to defer to authorities, spiritual or temporal; and was capable of quite as much audacity in her friends' quarrels, as she displayed in her own—not that there was any quarrel here; but it is certain that, had an episcopal as well as a ducal ban been actually launched against the tenants of Templestowe, Mrs. Devereux would not have cultivated their acquaintance a whit less sedulously. Now, from the first she was rather drawn towards Lady Atherstone—why, it would be difficult to say; for, though there were certain points of resemblance, their characters essentially were very different.

Both were self-willed and fearless, even to recklessness; but in Lena there was an earnestness and strength of purpose, whether for evil or for good, that, luckily for her own happiness, Mrs. Devereux lacked. Admiration was a necessity of Cissy's existence, and she would have gone out into the highways to exact it from the passers-by, rather than be stinted of the tribute; whilst Lena simply accepted homage, neither showing herself careful to seek it, nor specially grateful when it was rendered. It was not hard to guess that the one life would be

full of gay *fabliaux*, but that in the other there had
been or would be found a single grave story : here
you were looking on a bright, shallow lakelet, apt
to be stirred into mimic waves under the lightest
breeze, but never likely to be fatal in its vagaries;
there, on a deep land-locked tarn, the recesses
whereof had never yet been fully sounded, not easily
to be moved from serenity, but possibly dangerous
to the stoutest bark, if a gust should sweep down
unawares through the one gorge giving access to
the wind.

However, in the present state of civilisation,
differences of character are not a much greater
bar to friendship than differences of opinion ; and
so a kind of *camaraderie* was struck up betwixt
these two ; and, on one pretext or another, they
contrived to meet very frequently. Lord Atherstone, to speak truth, watched the growing intimacy with no great favour ; it was not that he
disliked Mrs. Devereux—indeed, personally he rather
admired her, and had often been amused by her ready
repartees and audacious sallies—but, though he never
listened to gossip, he knew that the petulant beauty
had been more than lightly spoken of, and that
there was little chance of her amending her ways.
Altogether, if he had been allowed to select a companion for his wife, his choice would scarcely have
alighted here ; but then came the question—Was
there any choice?—and Ralph rather shrank from
the answer; at any rate, he neither by word nor
deed attempted to check or thwart their arrangements. Once only, when Lena was regretting that
Hunsdon was so far from Templestowe, he smiled
coldly; and she divined, rather more easily than
if he had frowned, that here at least she need not
reckon on his sympathy.

As to the second intimacy, the expression ought
to have been limited. Mrs. Corbett's family cares
were so many and various, that, if she performed her

strict duty towards society in the visiting line, it was perhaps as much as could be expected òf her; moreover, her tastes were decidedly domestic.  For some years past her husband had been wont to appear at all sorts of entertainments, both public and private, *en garçon ;* and the arrangement seemed to suit both parties so perfectly, that it was no wonder if people in general had come to look upon it as a most natural one.   But Arthur Corbett was very often at Templestowe ; and generally he had some excuse for his presence there.

Amongst Lord Atherstone's prejudices, was an irrational dislike of the legal profession in all its branches; and for some time past divers agency matters, which usually pass through a solicitor's office, had been transacted by the Corbetts—an irregular way of doing business; but it worked well notwithstanding.  It was difficult to conceive these two men having a single idea in common; and Arthur's little weaknesses were precisely of the kind least likely to find indulgence in the eyes of the stern old *sabreur*.  Nevertheless, the baron had a high opinion of the other's shrewdness and probity; moreover, he really liked the sight of his genial face; and listened not unwillingly to his fluent prattle, especially as it always seemed to amuse Lena.

Lady Atherstone hunted pretty constantly up to the end of that season ; and, whosoever else might be in attendance, one special cavalier was safe to be found, whenever hounds were not running, not far from her bridle-rein.  This was more easily managed after her brother, carrying out his scheme of retrenchment, came down to Templestowe.  For Miles speedily struck up a great friendship with the banker; finding it exceedingly pleasant, when the meet lay beyond Heslingford, to be carted over luxuriously from the town to the covert-side, and then to have one of the 'little dinners' above mentioned to fall back upon—repasts infinitely preferable, in the dragoon's opinion, to the fare at the cavalry-barracks, where he was also made very welcome. Moreover, when they met in society, Mr. Corbett generally contrived to spend a goodly portion of the evening in Lady Atherstone's immediate vicinity. But the most captious observer could not have detected in his manner the slightest approach to philandering; without being obsequious or constrained, it was always thoroughly deferential; neither did closer acquaintance embolden him to transgress the outermost verge of familiarity.

Lena could not be said actually to encourage these assiduities—it was not her way; but that they were agreeable to her, was quite evident. Arthur certainly seemed to have the faculty, of attracting and retaining her attention to an extent not attainable by any other cavalier, whether resident or quartered in Loamshire. Before the year was out, "she had got used to him," as she confessed to Cissy Devereux. And in some women's mouths that expression means—a good deal.

Early in that same spring, Mrs. Shafton paid a long visit to Templestowe. With the state of things within doors, she had every reason to be content: she had scarcely expected to find Lena so soon and so thoroughly domesticated. If there was no absolute sympathy betwixt husband and wife, clearly there prevailed a comfortable harmony. The aspect of affairs abroad was hardly so satisfactory. Mrs. Shafton was too keen of wit, not speedily to divine that her daughter's welcome in Loamshire had been none of the warmest. For many years past she had given up the luxury of self-delusion, and was wont to look annoyances of all kinds fairly in the face; therefore, though rumours of Lord Atherstone's unpopularity had reached her ears, she never thought of imputing the coolness of the county solely to this cause. But, however far her misgivings may have travelled, she kept them to herself; and, after a few natural questions about the neighbourhood, &c., had been answered, she forbore to press Lena on the subject; neither did the latter appear inclined to pursue it. Nevertheless, you may possibly guess what prompted Mrs. Shafton, a fortnight or so after her arrival, to inquire whether there was any probability of the Ashleighs soon appearing at Templestowe.

It was unlikely that Lena could have divined the train of her mother's thoughts. Yet, she coloured a little as she looked up from her embroidery.

"I hardly know, mother. Monseigneur has never alluded to the subject; and I am sure he would have done so, if he had expected them soon."

Mrs. Shafton smiled pleasantly; as she had the knack of doing, even when her inner communings were grave.

"Perhaps he prefers that you should invite them. Men have odd scruples sometimes; and, I fancy, Lord Atherstone has more delicacy on certain points than the world gives him credit for. It would be only graceful if you were to suggest it, Lena. You liked what you saw of Lady Marian, didn't you?"

"Very much. One can't help being amused by her brisk, downright way, and quaint, original sayings; and I should think she must be honest. As for her husband, it would be almost treason, under this roof, to say exactly what I think of him; but I suppose an attractive couple is rather a rarity, and I daresay Mr. Ashleigh will never care for much of my society. Perhaps you are right, too, mother, and I wish I had spoken to Monseigneur about it sooner. I'll do so this very day."

Lady Atherstone felt much more penitent, an hour later, when she saw her husband's face light up with satisfaction at her first words. The matter must have been on his mind for some time past; or the broaching of it would not have so pleased him.

"It's very kindly thought of, my dear," he said—

"kindly for me, as well as for the children.  Marian and I have always been great friends, you know; and I'm sure you will find her improve on acquaintance : she's such a cheery creature, though a little sharp at times.  As for Philip—to do him justice, he's never much in anybody's way : he's always too much occupied with his politics and his ailments; though, I believe, both are about equally imaginary. Would you mind writing yourself to Marian ?  This address will find her."

"It's just what I should have wished to do," Lena answered; and her letter went by that day's post.

Whether Lady Marian felt specially grateful for the invitation may be doubted; but that she was ready to accept it, is certain.  Had there been no deeper motive for her so doing, a natural curiosity to see how things progressed at Templestowe, under the new *régime*, would have prevented her hesitating.

After Lord Atherstone's marriage, the Ashleighs had paid two or three visits, and then taken up their quarters at a West-end hotel.  The prices there were not extravagant; nevertheless, the thrifty couple had not yet felt such a steady draw on their purse-strings.  It so chanced that a fortnight's bill lay on the breakfast-table, side by side with Lena's note ; and Philip grumbled sorely over the items. Perhaps it was this that made him listen more readily to his wife's suggestion—"that he had really worked hard enough to earn a holiday ; and that, though the House had a good deal of business on hand before the Easter recess, it might possibly be scrambled through somehow in his absence." So the same afternoon, he paired off with another honourable invalid, whose ailments were not quite so visionary as his own ; and the end of the week found the Ashleighs once more at Templestowe.

The meeting was sufficiently cordial on all sides; and Marian quite justified her father-in-law's prediction, that she would improve on acquaintance.

Her manner towards the family-party, already assembled there, could scarcely have been improved upon : she seemed to settle into her new position without an effort, and never put on those airs of ceremony, or deference to recent authority, by which some women, under like circumstances, contrive to evince their sense of injury. She was courteous with Mrs. Shafton ; pleasantly confidential with Lena ; and so good-natured to Miles, that the dragoon, who in polite society was anything but bold, under her encouragement, waxed sometimes quite talkative. Lord Atherstone, watching her narrowly, could not detect the faintest change in her bearing towards himself ; so he, at least, was thoroughly satisfied.

Philip, too—by dint of how much private tuition will never be known—behaved himself, on the whole, very creditably. He was punctiliously, almost nervously, polite to Lena ; at proper intervals addressed a common-place remark to Mrs. Shafton ; and, if he sometimes started and shivered at Miles's sudden entrance, as though a gust of cold air had swept in, he contrived to keep his dislike of that boisterous person within decent bounds, and cursed him only to Marian—*sub sigillo.*

Without personal experience in the matter, you may conceive that the path of a stepmother—especially of a young stepmother—is beset by snares and pitfalls ; so that even Philip should have failed to catch her tripping, says not a little for Lena's tact and training.

Though all went on so smoothly in the family circle, Loamshire, as a rule, was provokingly slow to believe in the domestic happiness at Templestowe. Both at home and abroad, the Ashleighs seemed to be on the best possible terms with their stepmother ; and, perhaps, neither husband nor wife led their friends to believe, that they were dissembling with dutiful intent. But somehow, after their

visit was ended, people who knew her well began to
talk of "poor Lady Marian"—those who knew her
very slightly, of course said "poor *dear* Lady
Marian"—looking mysteriously compassionate the
while; and the prejudice against the Atherstones
was not materially abated.

It was Ralph himself who proposed that they
should spend part of the season in town; and they
had no reason to complain of their reception there.
If Lena's early imprudences were not altogether
buried, Society at least could afford to ignore them,
now that she was sheltered under a blameless name.
The baron's old comrades, several of whom had
taken family honours years ago, were very ready to
welcome him in his new character. Miss Bellingham
was one of the earliest to bring a peace-offering; and
was as affectionate, in her formal way, as if she had
never had cause to complain of her niece. Lady
Montfort, another relative, who once had found it
convenient to forget that any Shafton blood ran in
her veins, offered to be the bride's sponsoress at St.
James's. And few cared to meddle with those under
the protection of this potent and warlike dame;
whose tongue was as a two-edged sword, and who,
from the impregnable fortress of her virtue, shot
out arrows like hail at whoso presumed to flout her
pennon.

One circumstance, perhaps, smoothed the way for
Lena: even such as were gifted with disagreeably
tenacious memories, could not amuse themselves with
watching how she would bear herself towards Caryl
Glynne. Months ago he had departed on a long
yachting tour; and, since then, only vague rumours
concerning him and his fellow-wanderers had come
home.

Was Lena glad of this absence? Assuredly she
tried to persuade herself that she was so; and if,
occasionally, things around her looked strangely flat
and dull, like a picture out of which the colours

have faded, she had strength of mind enough, then,
not to admit, even to herself, that there was any
special cause.

Altogether, their sojourn in town was decidedly
a success; yet, neither the husband nor the wife was
very sorry when the time came for their moving
northwards. The grouse-disease was rather prevalent that season; so Lord Atherstone gave his Scotch
moor a jubilee: but they made a long stay at Kirkfell; and the weeks spent there were certainly the
happiest that Ralph had known since his marriage.

That the welcome was of the warmest it is needless
to say; and there was delight in the very contrast
of his present security with the doubts and hesita-
tions of last year. He never entered the cosy drawing-room, without remembering his pause on the
threshold to watch a tall white figure, and a graceful
head bowed over the flowers; and his first glimpse of
a proud beautiful face; and his first pressure of a
slender hand—all his own now—his own, as he believed, for ever. It was pleasant to listen, out on the
hill, to the banter of his jovial comrades, and to see
them afterwards vie with each other in rendering
their honest homage to his Queen; and pleasant, to
watch the complacent self-congratulation of the host;
for General Percy evidently attributed all that had
happened since to his own diplomacy and foresight.

Lena, too, was happy in a quiet fashion. The complete rest did her quite as much good as the bracing
air; and she half regretted the other engagements
which at last called them away from Kirkfell.

However, in one way or another, the autumn passed
quickly and uneventfully, till the fall of the leaf
brought the Atherstones home again once more.

# CHAPTER XXII.

"So you have condescended to come back, at last. It's a pleasant surprise, my dear. You said nothing about it in your last letter; and I began to think that you meant to shut up Templestowe, and cut Loamshire for this winter, at all events. Yes: you're improved — decidedly improved; though I almost forget how you looked when we parted. The glimpse I got of you in town don't count, you know; you were quite uncomeatable there."

Thus Mrs. Devereux—*inter oscula*—on the day following the Atherstones' return. The style of this impetuous young person, even in writing, was scarcely Johnsonian; and some of her composite words would have made a liberal lexicographer shudder.

"You put it in that way?" Lena answered. "Now, it's very odd: but *I* fancied myself neglected about that time; and forgave it, because I credited you with so many engagements."

"Engagements!" the other pouted. "As if provincials, in London for a fortnight, ever had any that mattered. Never mind; I don't want you to apologise. You can't *always* help being a great lady. But at the Devorgoil ball, for instance—a hateful crush it was, too; I spoilt the loveliest dress, and hadn't a waltz worth remembering — you were always surrounded by mightinesses. Now, I don't like mightinesses; and perhaps they don't like me. Didn't you see Lady Montfort's look of horrified curiosity, when I ventured to speak to you? I might have been Pocahontas, in native costume. It was something like—this."

O

The stony set of the pretty mobile face was irresistible; and Lena laughed outright.

"No, it escaped me; but I've good reason to recognise it. I was not always in Lady Montfort's good graces, and she remembered our cousinship rather late in the day. After all, the season tried me very much; and, if I look better, it's all owing to the northern air. Now we'll stop recrimination, if you please; and you shall open your budget of Loamshire news."

"It's a very little one," Mrs. Devereux answered meekly; "there never was such a steady humdrum old county as this. I believe everything, and everybody, is much the same as when you left. Dick's nearly a stone heavier, I'm afraid—as if a poor man, riding as he does, had any right to get stout. You needn't laugh: it's no joke to us, I assure you; he half ruins himself in horse-flesh, as it is. Some new people—a Mr. and Mrs. Malcolm—have taken Erriswell. They will be rather an acquisition, I've heard; but only the servants are there as yet. Malise Walwyn went to Rome at Easter, you know, and there's a rumour that he will come back all shaven and shorn; and they say that Sir Manners Mannering has taken to bullying his wife instead of neglecting her, and that she likes the change. Major Colville says that, if these strikes go on in the North, his detachment is certain to be moved. Perhaps it's only *pour se faire valoir*—that's so like a man—but I shall be too sorry if it's true; he leads me perfectly, and is so nice in every way, and Dick simply worships him. Poor Godfrey!"

There was much meaning in the penitent little sigh, and not a little in Lady Atherstone's smile.

"Don't be despondent," she said: "the Trades Unions have quite enough to answer for, without breaking up your family circle; and you needn't put on mourning yet for the Lost Leader. So that's all you have to tell?"

" I think so. Stop a minute, though! How stupid I am! Somebody *is* very much altered. Somebody in whom you ought to be rather interested, too. Can't you, or won't you, guess? It's Arthur Corbett."

Cissy's eyes were not her strong point—"good useful ones" she herself called them—but they were expressive enough just now, as they rested on her friend's face; however, beyond a faint curiosity, they read nothing there.

" How altered?" Lena asked, after a second's pause. " I hope nothing has gone wrong in Heslingford."

"Nothing in his bank, or in his house, that I'm aware of," Mrs. Devereux answered; "still he's decidedly changed. You remember what oppressively good spirits he was always in, and how incessantly his tongue rattled? Well: he's fallen into such an odd, absent way, and hardly does his share of conversation; and, to my certain knowledge, he has declined at least a dozen invitations in the last four months. He was never a favourite of mine—I've a vague recollection of his once having tried to establish a flirtation; but he was altogether too 'sweet;' and my tastes don't lie in that line—so I haven't troubled myself much about his secret sorrow. But he *is* a favourite of yours; and perhaps you'll be able to explain the puzzle."

Lena's brow slightly contracted.

"I particularly dislike puzzles," she said, "I suppose because I never guessed one; and I haven't the smallest intention of seeking Mr. Corbett's confidence. It will be a great pity though if he grows silent and unsociable; for the conversational capabilities of Loamshire, so far as I can judge, are rather limited; and any one, who can make talk, deserves to be encouraged. It's only a passing cloud, I daresay, at the worst; and we shall soon see Mr. Corbett as sweet and sunny as ever."

Mrs. Devereux pursed her lips demurely.

"We *shall* see," she retorted; and so changed the subject.

About the same time Lord Atherstone sat in his library, giving audience to divers dependents; and, amongst those who brought in their report, was the head keeper.

You may remember that, in the early part of this tale, allusion was made to a certain Mary Gilbert, who died within the year of Ralph Ashleigh's departure for India. John Gilbert was her brother, and the only one of the family left surviving. Born on the estate, he had always followed the same occupation; and had filled his present post nearly a quarter of a century.

A hard-featured, beetle-browed man; rather downcast of look as a rule, but whose bold clear eyes nevertheless could on occasion meet any creature's gaze unflinchingly; almost morose in his reserve; but never insolent towards his superiors, or tyrannical towards his subordinates, though he was unforgiving to a fault. People at the time said he took his sister's death greatly to heart; and, if he ruled his children strictly, none doubted that he loved them well. About his religion, too—he was a rigid Methodist—there was a gloomy tinge; and his creed evidently did not forbid a pitiless using of the arm of flesh, as the Heslingford poachers could witness. Altogether he reminded you of the old Ironsides, who, after reading out unctuously a blessing on the merciful, would go forth to smite the Malignants, hip and thigh.

As might naturally be supposed, he was a favourite with none, unless it was with his master; and, even here, the word scarcely expresses their relation. Lord Atherstone assuredly treated the head keeper with a consideration that he showed to no other retainer; for he not only allowed him to hold an opinion differing from his own, but occasionally gave up the point in dispute. Yet he did so with a certain constraint, as if the concession did not entirely spring from a regard for the other's experience and professional skill; and, though John Gilbert's manner was always perfectly respectful, if you had watched him narrowly you would perhaps have divined that a sense of duty, rather than personal attachment, was at the bottom of his proved fidelity.

The report of the game was very satisfactory, and the accounts were passed without a word of comment; but the keeper's countenance was more overcast than usual this morning; and, when all was done, he lingered as if he had not quite said his say. This did not escape Lord Atherstone.

"You've something to tell me," he said; "you'd better make a clean breast of it."

The other hesitated, shifting from foot to foot uneasily, and crushing his felt hat betwixt his horny hands.

"That's what I mean to do, my lord," he said at last. "Only, as it's altogether a matter of my own, I was loath to trouble you with it on such a busy day; but I daren't hold my peace. I'm sore troubled in my mind about Phœbe."

A touch of the Loamshire burr hung about his tongue; but the man's language was good for his station; and he spoke in a firm slow way, not slurring his words according to the fashion of the county.

"Phœbe?" the baron answered, after a moment's reflection. "That is your second daughter, isn't it? The one that went last year to her aunt, in Heslingford, to learn dressmaking? You ought to have her home if she's ailing; perhaps the town air don't suit her. I remember she looked delicate."

The keeper's face grew harder, and his eyes were still cast down.

"The air don't suit her, for certain," he said, "and she's at home this month past; but there's nought wrong with the lass's health, beyond that she's a bit drooping-like. We did it for the best, and what is ordained is ordained; but I've wished of late that she had been felled with a sore sickness—ay! if it had gone nigh to death—the day she went down yonder, so happy and hopeful."

The baron knit his brows.

"Speak out, Gilbert; I can't construe parables. You don't mean——" then he checked himself.

As Mrs. Shafton remarked, Ralph had more delicacy on some points than the world gave him credit for.

The keeper drew his breath hard, and his brown cheek flushed dusky red.

"It's a short story, my lord, and not a new one either. It's only that a—gentleman, I reckon he calls himself—has been knave enough to speak lying words to Phœbe; and that she has been fool enough to listen; and that, if God had not watched over the child, there might have happened shame as well as sorrow : with all her meek looks, she has a wicked, wilful spirit of her own, that will be broken, mayhap, before it is tamed. How do I know they were lying words? Because, for as simple as I am, I can guess whether Mr. Corbett's favourite clerk is like to mean fairly by John Gilbert's daughter."

His voice was somewhat hoarser; but it was neither raised nor quickened; and he stood now as still as a statue : yet the spirit working within the man was as evident, as if it had rent him like one possessed.

"I remember," Ralph said contemptuously;—"a good-looking, curled coxcomb, aping his master's dress and manner. I shouldn't have thought there was an ounce of harm in him. You wish me to interfere, of course; but how?"

"He wouldn't call it harm, I dare say," the other retorted. "Heslingford's a bit dull in the summer, and the evenings are long, and a gentleman must have his amusements; and, if he isn't strong enough for cricket, playing at shuttlecock with an honest girl's heart—he found it honest, I'll swear—is pretty

pastime. Yes: I do want your help, my lord. I want
Mr. Corbett told—he'll listen to *you*—that he'd better
work his clerks harder, than give them holidays to
be spent as Mr. Herbert Farland spent his but
yesterday. And I want yon gay kestrel warned that,
if he comes hanging about my place, and watching
me off on my rounds, I'll trap him as I do other
vermin, and deal with him pretty much the same. I
will, by——"

The oath did not sound like a blasphemy. It was
clear that, even in his strong passion, the speaker
had no thought of taking the Holy name in vain.

The baron pulled his huge trailing moustache, as
was his wont when perplexed or annoyed.

"It must be stopped somehow, of course," he said;
"but scarcely in that way. I don't approve of threats,
nor would I carry such a message."

John Gilbert's downcast eyes were lifted now, and
met his master's fairly.

"It's no threat," he said with a quiet sternness.
"I have sought, in much prayer, for light to guide
me in this trouble; and I think the light has come
at last. If I have God's warranty, man's judgment
is but a light thing. Mine's a rough message, my
lord, all the same; and I'd never have asked you
to carry it if I hadn't a good right so to do. You
won't disallow it either, I'll be bound, though my
poor sister has been buried over thirty year. Stop,
my lord,"—the other had risen to his feet with a
great darkness on his face—"don't think I'm casting
this up in anger. If I'd ever thought you meant
foul play, it ain't likely I'd have taken your wages.
The little she did say was said to me; and she cleared
you, that far. But it wasn't the fever that killed her.
Phœbe shan't go the same road, if I can stop it—
stop it—anyhow. I promised Mary, the very day she
died, that I'd serve you faithful during your pleasure,
and that I'd never let you guess how much I knew,
unless I was drove to it. I think I've kept that pro-

mise true. I want no thanks. I only want you to help me here, in my own way."

"No, I never meant harm," Ralph said gloomily ; "and I never guessed till now—how should I ?—that I started in life with a death lying at my door. After that, I couldn't expect to thrive. But your poor sister only did me justice ; or I couldn't look you in the face now, John Gilbert. Nevertheless, our reckoning won't be settled whilst we live : it's none the lighter for having run on all these years. I'll pay what I can though. Your message shall be delivered, word for word, before I sleep ; and you shall have the answer by this time to-morrow."

The keeper bent his head rather assentingly than gratefully, it seemed ; and so the interview ended.

# CHAPTER XXIII.

"WHAT'S good for you to know, you'll be told."

With this formula, rather terse than polite, a certain sage of my acquaintance is wont to quench feminine curiosity, issuing from whatsoever quarter. Lady Atherstone had never met with such rebuff; but she always acted on the principle notwithstanding; and, though she guessed from her husband's face that neither pleasure nor ordinary business called him into Heslingford, she let him depart without asking a single question; nor did she mention her suspicions to Mrs. Devereux.

Ralph rarely loitered when he was riding alone; but even the groom, who was used to the pace, grumbled and wondered as he led the steaming cattle to and fro before the bank-door.

"It can't be a money-mess," he ruminated; "he's as steady as old Time about sich matters, I'll pound it; though he ain't such a screw as that there blessed son of his. Somethin' wrong about the home-farm, like enough. The last oats as come in was a proper bad sample—light as fluff, wouldn't put flesh on to a pig, let alone 'art into an 'oss. P'r'aps the steward'll get the sack: not a bad job neither; I never could abear them Scotchmen."

Whilst the retainer vented his discontent, Lord Atherstone had walked straight through the counting-house into the sanctum beyond; only pausing to ascertain that the junior partner was alone.

The greeting that passed was cordial enough; but Ralph, as was his wont, came straight to the point;

and, before touching on any other matter, explained
the object of his visit. Mr. Corbett seemed much
shocked and surprised—more so, perhaps, than could
have been expected; considering his somewhat frivolous character, and that no harm had actually
happened.

"Would you—would you like to speak to Farland
yourself?" he stammered.

The other nodded his head; and, a few seconds
later, the culprit was paraded.

Herbert Farland possessed the convenient kind
of conscience which, however torpid in presence
of crime, always pricks at scent of danger. He
well remembered where and how his last free afternoon was spent, and probably guessed that the
baron's visit might bear some relation thereto; for,
as he entered, there was a decided abatement in the
jauntiness of his gait; his very curls seemed suddenly to have lost their crispness; and his ruddy
countenance was almost wan. Neither were his
tremors assuaged by the brief glance he ventured
to steal at Lord Atherstone's face; as for Mr.
Corbett's—being a strict man of business, possibly
some unlucky debtor, craving for indulgence, may
have seen such an expression there; but to his
favourite clerk it was surely strange.

"You will listen to what his lordship has to say,"
Arthur began; "and, before he speaks, you will
understand that I endorse every word."

His voice was harsh and cold: yet the words
seemed formed with a certain effort, and he sat
evidently ill at ease.

Ralph's discourse need not be recorded, for you
have heard the substance of it already; but, if brief,
it was very much to the purpose, and John Gilbert's
message was delivered faithfully.

"It's a threat, of course," he concluded, "and an
illegal one; but I don't think the Law will help you
much when you're in John Gilbert's hands, nor cure

you when you come out of them. He'll keep his word,
I know. And—mark me—whatever happens, I'll bear
him harmless, if it can be done by interest or money.
You can set us both at nought, if you please ; but I
don't think you will." And the baron smiled grimly.

Of a truth, the demeanour of no creature, standing
upright upon its feet, could be much less defiant than
was Herbert Farland's. Being neither devout nor
deeply read in Scripture, he would have subscribed
just then to every one of the Preacher's warnings
against the snares of woman's beauty ; and he vowed
that, if he ever escaped out of this net, it would
be long before he strayed again nigh the toils.
The revulsion of feeling was very natural; besides
being a man of peace by temper and profession,
he was essentially a man of the time.

It is no wonder if there be a certain calculation
in our courtships, and if a certain prudence mode-
rates our passions, when, on this side of the
Channel at least, no keener blade than the golden
sword of Justice overhangs the offender : however
his purse may suffer, his person is sure to 'scape
scot-free. Nay, even our loyal devotion must be
expressed by bloodless sacrifices. Modern knights
are not less chivalrous at heart than

> Les noirs chevaucheurs, les marcheurs dans l'ombre ;

but they seldom, very seldom, are enabled to honour
their lady at peril of life or limb : such chances only
befall the rude fisher-carle, who hopes to build a
cottage for his Janet with the silver wrung from the
wild North Sea.

The Tune of Seven Towers is far out of date. If
fair Yoland were to whisper—

> By my love go there now,
> To fetch me my coif away,
> My coif and my kirtle, with pearls arow,
> Oliver, go to-day !

the gallant would, in all likelihood, turn away to

seek a less exacting mistress before the lady had time to relent; and her bravery might lie till it rotted within the haunted moat.

But if Herbert Farland had lived in those days, it would have needed no goblin, or giant, or enchanter to turn him back; a misshapen dwarf, truculent in aspect, would have served the turn. So, on the present occasion, he poured forth a string of excuses and promises of amendment : the former, Lord Atherstone utterly disregarded; but the latter he was inclined to believe.

"I think we may trust him," he said, glancing over at Corbett.

"I think so, too," the other answered viciously. "If he would risk his bones, he'll scarcely risk his prospects, or rather, his daily bread. I only look over his misconduct, because his father died in our service—I doubt if mine would be so lenient—but he leaves at an hour's notice, if anything of the sort happens again. You hear, sir,"—this to Farland,—"you can go back to your work now. If you get into mischief for the next year to come, I'll take care it's not from having too much spare time on your hands."

The bitterness was almost beyond that of righteous anger; and it struck even Lord Atherstone—himself in no indulgent mood — as hardly proportionate to the occasion.

"Don't worry yourself about all this," he said good-naturedly, as the door closed behind the crest-fallen criminal. "I am certain this is all well ended; and no fault could possibly be charged on you. You've acted just as I expected—don't that satisfy you? We had better change the subject. I've a good deal to talk to you about, and very little time this afternoon. Will you ride over to Templestowe to-morrow? We might do some business after lunch."

"You—you are too kind," Arthur answered, still

with the same strange nervousness. "This has upset me a good deal, and I fear it would upset my father still more. I think, with your permission, in his present state of health, it had better be kept from his knowledge; we both trusted Farland so implicitly. I'll take care for the future he's more sharply looked after. To-morrow? I'm very busy just now. If the matters are not pressing, perhaps you would excuse me till the next day, or—the day after. I—I hope Lady Atherstone is quite well."

"Nothing presses. Come whenever it suits you best. I shall be shooting near home all the week, and shall be easily found. Lady Atherstone? Thanks, she's looking brilliantly after her autumn tour; but you had better judge of that for yourself. Mind; we're always glad to see you or Mrs. Corbett, or both, without any business-excuse. She and the children are flourishing, I trust? That's well. Now I'll leave you to finish your letters: I've taken up too much of your time already."

The ill plant, that was beginning to grow up in the shadow of John Gilbert's roof-tree, was cut down root and branch that autumn afternoon. It was some time before the pretty Phœbe thoroughly shook off the love-fever; but she managed to out-grow both her romance and her delicacy, and is now as comely and comfortable a yeo-woman as you would wish to see. As for Herbert Farland—married and settled long ago—Heslingford holds no soberer burgess. The junior clerks, who tremble at his frown, never dream that unruly passions could once have swelled under that stiff, spotless shirt-front; the wife of his bosom boasts of his virtues unceasingly to her less fortunate fellows; and if, in his walks abroad, his eyes linger for an instant on a fairer face or trimmer shape than common, it is only such a demure side-glance as may not misbeseem an embryo church-warden.

Indeed, the episode would not have been worth

mentioning, if it had not been for the effect it produced on one of the main characters in this story—Arthur Corbett.

Whatever caused his disquietude, it did not cease with Lord Atherstone's departure. For many minutes after he was left alone, he sat gnawing his lips, and drawing shapeless figures on the letter-paper before him. Watching him then, you would have agreed with Mrs. Devereux, that the banker was decidedly changed. Last year it would have been hard to fancy the smooth white forehead furrowed, or the gay blue eyes clouded ; yet such signs of unrest were there unmistakably now, and not for the first time.

Arthur Corbett's trouble was no worse than has befallen tens of thousands, better and stronger and wiser than he ; causing them to shrink back, as if they had come unawares on a ravening beast couched by their pathway — the consciousness of a guilty passion growing up within them, and waxing day by day more masterful—the opening of a book that, however alluring may be its first pages, must needs end with lamentations and mourning and woe.

The man's character was full of frailties and failings ; but he had never thus far knowingly harmed, or meant harm, to any fellow-creature. He had been careless and remiss, perhaps, in his family duties ; but, till within the last few months, there had not been a thought in his heart, at which his own true wife might not have smiled indulgently ; and if, in his frivolous philanderings, there was much to despise, there was nothing gravely to arraign. It was otherwise with him now. He felt that he was pursuing, in thought at least, not a delicate, stingless May-fly, but a strange, lovely creature, in whose lightest touch, for aught he knew, there might be poison. As he looked within, there came upon him a great fear, as well as great shame.

He had not been very strictly brought up ; but from youth upwards, he had been taught that respect was due to human opinion, as well as to Divine law; and the idea of scandal had been almost as contrary to his creed as that of crime. Besides, he was neither morally nor physically brave; and, out of the background of the perilously beautiful picture on which he had allowed his mind's eyes to feast for months past, there looked out a stern face and menacing eyes, warning him to come no nigher. Moreover, the sense of honour and equity, still abiding within him, made him loathe his late hypocrisy. What right had he to judge his unlucky dependent so harshly, when, if the thoughts of both had been laid bare, he ought to have stood side by side with the criminal?

Do you understand now, why Arthur Corbett was so changed? And do you need to be told that the cause was—Lena Atherstone?

At length the banker broke from his reverie, and flung away the pen with which he had been toying; muttering a few words half aloud.

"Looking brilliantly? I don't doubt it; but I won't go over to-morrow, nor the next day. I won't, I swear."

Then he betook himself to work again, with a great effort; somewhat fortified by the cordial of this virtuous resolve.

Indeed, the morrow was a busy day in Heslingford. Yet surely it was either an idle or irresolute man that, a little after noon, rode slowly through the shadows of the huge elms lining the avenue of Templestowe.

# CHAPTER XXIV.

In all counties, there are certain houses that seem fated to shelter strangers rather than their owners. Erriswell was one of these. Extravagance and unlucky speculations had made the late squire an exile whilst yet in his prime; and during his twenty years of wandering through cheap continental watering-places, though he was apt enough to boast or maunder — his tone varied according to his company or the state of his spirits—about his ancestral acres, he had not visited them thrice. The sickly youth—sole representative now of the Hornes of Erriswell—whose health required almost as much nursing as his property, had never yet set eyes upon his home; nor was it likely, even when his minority should have expired, that he would be over-eager to establish himself there. There was no difficulty in letting the Hall; the advertisements described it correctly enough, as 'a comfortable residence, suited in all respects to the requirements of a moderate family;' and changes of occupancy had not divested it of a certain old-fashioned air of dignity. It was just the place to tempt a bureaucrat, desirous of making experiment of country-life, before investing permanently in land.

Of this class indeed, had been almost invariably its tenants; and at first sight it seemed strange, that none should have chosen to abide there beyond the three or five years for which their lease was signed; but in reality this was easily accounted for. No stranger, properly introduced, had cause to complain of Loamshire hospitality; but the county-folk, as a rule, were full against the 'squatters;' and declined to accept mere length of purse as qualification for residence in the midst of them. So the merchant, manufacturer, or contractor, after a few futile attempts to be sociable, naturally waxed sullen; and, when his term had expired, if not sooner, departed grumbling, to make for himself a home amongst a less stiff-necked and gainsaying people.

However, with these Malcolms, of whom mention was lately made, the case was widely different.

There was no mystery about the husband's antecedents. Like many other cadets of old Scots families, he had received his modest portion early in life, and had sought fortune beyond the seas—with a dogged resolution as to the end, and an utter indifference as to ways and means, provided only they were honest; even as his forbears sold their swords to the highest bidder, provided only he worshipped not Mahound. He started as a sheep-farmer; but by flocks and herds alone Robert Malcolm would never have waxed wealthy so fast. He had a shrewd wit, backed by iron nerve, in business matters; and was one of those 'who,' according to his country's proverb, 'are bound either to make a spoon or spoil the horn.'

The future of the great Colony with which he had cast in his lot, was scarcely then developed. The air was alive, no doubt, with promises of wealth; but to some, if not most of these, it was ruin to give ear; and, though in the very dust of the streets there was sparkle of gold, or what looked like gold, it needed a practised assayer to discern betwixt the false metal and the true. Malcolm was equal—more than equal—to the occasion. When he first spoke of investing all the savings of four lucky years in the purchase of some building-lots near a town, then in its infancy, there was a stormy scene betwixt himself and his partner—also a Scotchman, by-the-bye

**P**

—and the latter preferred buying his mate out, to
tempting providence further in such rash company.
But douce David Anderson did not plume himself
quite so much on his prudence a twelvemonth later,
when he heard that the said lots had been resold at
a profit almost fabulous in those days; and, though
his own sheep-shearing turned out well, he looked
at the piles of fleeces with rather a jaundiced eye.
This was the foundation-stone of Archibald Malcolm's fortune; and, though the edifice built thereon
did not spring up like a magician's palace, not many
years passed before it was deep, high, and broad
enough to shelter any man, not over-weening in his
desires, luxuriously for the remainder of his days.
When Malcolm thoroughly realised this, he acted,
as was his wont, decisively, yet deliberately withal:
he did not attempt to cut the ties binding him there
at one sweep, but severed them carefully strand by
strand; gaining rather than losing in each transfer
of securities. Yet the business was done so effectually, that he sailed for England without an interest in the Colony beyond grateful memories.

So much for the husband. Of the wife little or
nothing was known, except that her maiden name
was Forrester, and that Malcolm had married her
after a month's courtship, at Florence; where her
mother, a widow, had for some time resided.

Such as they were, Loamshire was prepared to
receive the new-comers with no small kindness. In
those days, people's ideas of Australia were connected chiefly with vast sheep-farms and virgin forests;
and there was a fine healthy patriarchal smack about
money earned by the axe, the crook, or the plough,
very different from the taint of devil's dust, or the
grime of the coal-pit. Moreover, Mr. Malcolm had
left a favourable impression on those who had met
him in Heslingford, coming to and from Erriswell.

"A real good sort," said Swinton Swarbrick, "with

no d——d nonsense about him. We shall find no more three-legged ones in those coverts."

And this was only the *vox populi*, rather forcibly expressed.

On a warm October afternoon, Lady Atherstone and Mrs. Devereux paid their first visit to the Malcolms. The place was looking its best just then; for the glory of autumn was on the fine timber still standing in the park; and, evidently, not only the house, but all its belongings, had been recently set in order; though the sound of hammer and trowel, and workmen clustered here and there, showed that the stable improvements, at least, were not complete.

Mrs. Malcolm was alone in her morning-room when the visitors were announced.

A small slight woman, with no pretensions to beauty; yet with a certain attraction in her delicate face, gentle manner, and pleasant voice. They were perfect strangers; nevertheless it seemed to Lena as if she had seen that face before in a dream; and some of the cadences of the voice seemed familiar to her ears. Just so, a few chords in a melody, otherwise fresh and original, remind us of a long-forgotten tune.

There was little fear of converse languishing with Cissy Devereux to the fore; and, for half-an-hour or so, the cross-fire of conventional question and reply went on apace; though it was not without a little bitterness, that Lena listened to Mrs. Malcolm's grateful acknowledgments of the welcome she had met in Loamshire: the contrast with her own reception was somewhat striking.

"I can't imagine where my husband is," the hostess said at last. "I'm sure he cannot be very far off; for he was to drive me out later in the afternoon. He would be so very sorry to miss you: he has already had the pleasure of making Lord Atherstone's and Captain Devereux's acquaintance."

Whilst the words were on her lips the door opened, and Robert Malcolm came in.

There was nothing colonial, or even provincial, in his exterior.  His crisp, light beard was carefully trimmed; and his hale cheeks were not so deeply bronzed, as are many that had endured no fiercer sun than that which strikes on Highland corrie or Norwegian feld.  Only after looking attentively at his massive forehead, square jaw, and masterful eyes, would you divine that this man

> Was not born for luxury,
> For pleasure, nor for rest;

and that he must needs have worked hard with hand, or brain, or both, in his time.  Neither in his manner was there a tinge of the shyness or *brusquerie*, that speaks of long sojourn on the outer verge of civilisation; his demeanour was perfectly unaffected, but perhaps rather more polished than that of the average of country squires; and there was something very winning in his frank way of putting aside Lena's apology for her husband's absence.

"It's entirely my own fault, if there is any fault," he said.  "Lord Atherstone spoke very kindly about it when I met him in Heslingford; but I begged to be allowed to take the will for the deed.  Ceremonies are capital things in their place; but few men could afford to waste a whole October day, with blue skies overhead and thick turnips underfoot.  We settled it quite amicably, I assure you; and I hope to improve our acquaintance next week, shooting at Templestowe."

"I'm afraid *my* husband hadn't the grace to excuse himself," Mrs. Devereux struck in.  "His is the most hopeless case.  I used to worry him into making a round of calls with me twice a-year; but I've given that up long ago.  He used to fidget, and look at the clock till he made me feel guilty too; and his scruples about 'keeping the horses in the cold' wouldn't have deceived a child.  But he's quite enthusiastic about you, since he heard that you meant to preserve foxes. I hope that rumour is true."

"Quite true," Mr. Malcolm returned. "I want to improve the shooting here; but hunting is first in my affections: indeed I've had much more practice in saddle than with gun. The only alterations I've made are in the stables; otherwise I found this place nearly perfect. I only hope it will not prove too cold for my wife; she's far from strong."

Mrs. Malcolm laughed musically.

"He would make a tropical plant of me, if I would let him," she said; "but I'm really much stronger than I look, and not in the least an invalid. Besides, I'm certain Erriswell must be healthy. Isn't that its character, Lady Atherstone?"

"I believe so," Lena answered; "but I'm almost a stranger in Loamshire myself, you know. How thoroughly comfortable you have made the house look already! You must have quite a talent for arrangement."

"Robin has, ı believe," Mrs. Malcolm returned; "but I'm not often consulted, and have only to approve of what is done. The pictures are a great trouble to us both. We've only ventured to hang just a few of our own, you see—the walls were so very bare—and probably these will all have to be altered. That's the worst of connoisseurs; if their opinion is worth having, they're so terribly tyrannical; and my cousin is no exception to the rule. Have you ever met Caryl Glynne?"

Perhaps those vague memories, awaked within the last hour, may have unconsciously prepared Lena for the home thrust; and that there was no malice in the dealing of it was plain; nevertheless, even to such as hold with me, that on this earth of ours there breathes no creature so brave as a thoroughbred woman, her composure might have seemed marvellous.

Mrs. Devereux had accompanied her host to the window just then to give her opinion on some improvements in the flower garden; but those 'useful eyes' of hers would have detected no change in Lady Atherstone's face, unless it were the slightest possible hardening.

"I used to meet Mr. Glynne very often at one time," she said slowly—"very seldom of late years. Do you expect him here? I fancied he was still travelling."

"He's on his way home," the other answered; "and I hope his first visit in England will be here; he would be such a help to us just now, for his taste is simply perfect: he chose all the pictures that we bought in Italy. Yes: we miss Caryl dreadfully— don't we, Robin?"

Of what was said and done during the next few minutes, Lady Atherstone retained no distinct idea. She knew that Mr. Malcolm had turned from the window, answering something with a laugh; and that Cissy Devereux had taken up the thread of conversation again; but she could remember the words of neither. When her senses, so to speak, returned, she caught herself perusing the pale, delicate face before her, with an earnestness of which she was ashamed; and tracing a resemblance there line by line.

To any other eyes, perhaps, only the faintest family likeness would have been apparent; but to Lena's the curvature of the brows and the shape of the mouth, to say nothing of other features, seemed almost identical; and she wondered how this could have escaped her for an instant. With the dawn of recognition came a deepening shadow of danger, till she could have cried out in her heart, like the doomed king of Israel, "Hast thou found me, O mine enemy?"

Could friendship, pure and simple, ever subsist betwixt herself and Caryl Glynne?

When they parted she had believed it possible; and to this belief, whenever her thoughts wandered that way, she had striven hard ever since to cling. And now the conviction broke upon her that all those fair promises were a delusion, if not a snare; and that she had more cause than ever to wish him

far away. To a proud woman like Lena the bitterness of self-contempt was sufficient torture; and, for
a brief space, a faintness overcame her, like that of
sharp physical pain. This lasted a few seconds only.
However she had miscalculated her strength, she was
not weak enough to dream of submitting tamely; and
the struggle was yet distant, if struggle there must
be. But one thing she could not do—that was to sit
still there, bandying conventionalities with the innocent cause of her trouble; besides, the very atmosphere of the room seemed suddenly to have grown
hot and heavy, and she felt a nervous craving for fresh
air. In truth, they had already exceeded the usual
limits of a first call; and Mrs. Devereux, who would
willingly have tarried somewhat longer — she had
imagined a tour of the stables and gardens, under
escort of her host—could not demur when Lady Atherstone rose to depart.

Still mechanically, but without making one mistake, Lena got through the needful kind and courteous speeches; but, when she was fairly in her
carriage, the inevitable reaction possessed her; and
she leant back, with eyes half closed, scarcely hearing—certainly not understanding—her companion's
chatter; who was voluble beyond her wont in praise
of their new acquaintances.

Suddenly Mrs. Devereux checked herself.

" My dear, what *is* the matter with you? I don't
believe you've heard one word of what I've been saying; and I never saw you look so white."

Lady Atherstone half raised her heavy eye-lids;
and dropped them again, as if the light pained her.

" There's not much the matter," she said wearily—
"only, talking always tires me to death, with such a
headache as has been coming on for the last half-
hour: otherwise, I would have stayed longer, for I
saw you were amused; and I quite agree with you
about these Malcolms. I shall soon be better, if I
keep quite, quite quiet."

Were headaches known in the Age of Gold; or, when the Millennium shall prevail, will they cease to be? Certain it is that in any state, where there are secrets to conceal or pangs to dissemble, this convenient malady could no more be dispensed with, than the most necessary article of attire. How could Society possibly go on, without the trite but inexhaustible excuse that, better than any soft answer, turneth away wrath, and, for a while at least, closes the mouth of the accuser; so that the accused— whether innocent or guilty—have time to breathe and brace themselves for the question, if it must needs ensue? There are people, I believe, who discourse quite eloquently on the advantages of gout; surely as many could be found ready to cry — *Vive la migraine !*

Lady Atherstone was outwardly almost herself again before she reached home; but her 'headache' did not pass away so quickly; indeed, it kept her rather silent throughout the evening, and wakeful through most of the watches of the night. When she slept, at last, she woke with a start, fancying that some one had whispered close in her ear—"We miss him dreadfully."

" *We* miss him ?"

Well: blood is thicker than water; and, with all his faults, there was no reason why his own kindred should not regret the absence, or wish for the presence, of Caryl Glynne. But was it fitting that such words should find an echo in the heart—ay! and once almost issue from the lips—of the woman who, not a year ago, had promised loyalty at least, when Ralph Atherstone rendered to her keeping his happiness and honour?

# CHAPTER XXV

DOUBTLESS, on that October afternoon, Lena Atherstone made a disagreeable discovery; but you are
not to suppose that she thenceforth incessantly
brooded over it. She had a dauntless temper of her
own; and the mere knowledge of impending danger,
was sufficient to arouse the stubbornness inherent
in her blood. Certainly she acknowledged now,
that the links, binding her fate to Caryl Glynne's,
were not so completely severed as she had fancied;
and that he had not been far from the truth when
he "feared all was not over betwixt them." Nevertheless—supposing that this were so, and that they
met ever so often—was there any reason that she
should betray herself to others, and, most of all, to
him? Thousands of women have carried such a secret
to their graves; thousands, doubtless, still walking
blamelessly through life, are laden with the same.
Why should she be weaker than her fellows? Whilst
she mused on these things, there rose up in her,
not seldom, a spirit akin to defiance. From one
question only she shrank in fear and shame.

How would it fare with her husband, if he could
guess the truth?

It seemed impossible, utterly impossible, to take
him into her confidence now; and yet the time had
been when this had not seemed so hard. Lena was
blessed—or afflicted, if you will—with a remarkably
good memory. She could have repeated almost word
for word what had passed when she plighted her
troth to Ralph Atherstone. She knew that she had

begun a half confession then, and that only slight
encouragement was needed from him to make it
complete.  That encouragement had not been given.
"I don't wish to hear another word"—he had said.
Nevertheless, it was her duty, her bounden duty—
she recognised that only too plainly now—to have
spoken out then, though he had prayed her more
earnestly to forbear.   Even thus, the course of things
might not have been altered; but surely this ought,
then and there, to have been put to proof.  She
ought to have told him that the chasm dividing
her from Caryl Glynne, if it were wide and deep
enough to last through all eternity, had only been
opened since the rising of the sun that had barely
set; and that her hand had scarcely ceased to thrill
with the pressure of his fingers, when he bade her
good-bye.   Says the old rhyme—

> It is good to be merry and wise;
> It is good to be faithful and true;
> It is good to be off with the old love,
> Before you are on with the new.

Ay! so: but better and wiser still, at certain seasons,
to avow how the old love ended; even though the
lips should quiver, and the cheeks should burn.

When confronted with the anonymous letter, she
had borne herself more bravely; but the amends
were made something late; and the first fault was not
quite blotted out by Ralph's perfect trust and forgiveness; this she knew right well.  Once again she
might have 'freed her soul'—the day they rode homewards from Grandmanoir.

How fair these lost chances now appeared to Lena
—so fair, that she could scarcely realise how she let
them slip.  And, as often happens in these cases,
the more fully she realised that it might never be
in her power to bestow upon her husband anything
like perfect love, the more freely she confessed his
entire worthiness thereof.  It was too hard, to receive
day by day fresh proofs of his trust and tenderness;

and to feel that she could only repay these with a resolve to do him at least no wrong.

In spite of all this, it would have baffled an un-prejudiced observer, to detect any alteration in Lady Atherstone's spirits, or any constraint in her manner, either in society, or—what is much more to the purpose—when alone with her husband. Indeed, as she grew familiarised with her danger, it naturally appeared less formidable ; and, as weeks passed on bringing no word of Caryl Glynne, a feeling of half-security came over her once more ; and, when Cissy Devereux questioned her about "this famous cousin of Mrs. Malcolm's," she answered that "he was de-cidedly handsome in a peculiar style, and very agree-able, most people thought, when he exerted himself," —so unconcernedly, that the other suspected abso-lutely nothing.

As for Ralph himself, there was an increase rather than an abatement in his great content ; for the mis-giving of last year, as to his own unpopularity being visited on his fair wife, no longer galled him. Though the Duke of Devorgoil still stood on his dignity, and waxed no warmer in his courtesy, Loamshire, as a whole, began rather to repent of its unsociability. When it was bruited abroad that Lady Montfort had not only presented the bride, but constantly chaperoned her, people began to think that they had listened to vague rumours over-hastily ; and were rather disposed now to make amends for their pre-vious shortcomings. To be sure, Lady Atherstone might have chosen a safer and staider confidante than wayward Cissy Devereux ; but this could scarcely stand as an article of accusation. In fine, those in the county who were most prone to think evil of their neighbours, were content to maintain an armed neutrality towards Templestowe.

Here it is fitting that we should take up a thread of this story, that has been dropped for some time past, and see how it has fared with Caryl Glynne.

It was written, you will remember, that on the day when he said good-bye to Lena Shafton, a certain change was worked in him; and this change was more lasting than he himself would have deemed possible. It was not in his nature to fret or pine; but the feeling of loneliness that abode with him, was irksome nevertheless—so irksome that he waxed restless, and eager for any change that would divert the current of his thoughts, and prevent him from conferring with himself. Besides this, he did not care greatly, to sit still and watch the progress of Lord Atherstone's wooing. So he began to cast about for a pretext for absenting himself—not for a few days or weeks, but long enough to allow fresh interests to grow in the place of those that had been rooted up. And it was not long before such an occasion presented itself.

Perhaps Glynne was not quite so popular with his own as with the other sex, and the set in which he moved was not the most select; nevertheless, there were always plenty of men of fair position ready to welcome, if not to court, his company. The scandals attaching to his name, however dark in a moral point of view, had not hitherto touched his honour, according to the modern interpretation of the word. After spending his own patrimony, he had doubtless helped others to spend theirs in all manner of riotous living; but, so far as the world knew, had never yet acted as decoy or received jackals' wages. There was knitting of brows and shrugging of shoulders amongst usurers, Jew and Gentile, at the mere mention of his name; but none of his fellows had suffered financially through Caryl Glynne, so as to make them cry aloud in the streets; and, when he was in banishment, he could walk where he listed, without fear of meeting a more reproachful face than that of a credulous tradesman.

Nigel Lord Glenfalloch had very recently succeeded to an ancient coronet and a vast patrimony. He

was a bashful, soft-hearted creature, accustomed
from his infancy to obey rather than to command ;
for the deceased peer was fanatic as well as miserly,
and ruled his household in the good old Scots
fashion ; so that when the fetters were suddenly
broken, the heir could not at once recover the freedom of his limbs, and found it hard to walk alone.
You may easily conceive, that of friends able and
willing to guide the young Earl's tottering footsteps,
there was no lack ; but, besides being shy, he was
somewhat capricious in his likes and dislikes ; and,
though always grateful for such proffers of service,
generally shrank from them. On the mother's side
he was distantly connected with the Glynnes ; and
from the very first he took strangely to Caryl.

Indeed the latter was one of those lucky persons,
to be found in both sexes, who seem fated to
exercise over their weak brethren and sisters such
an influence and dominion as it is not given to
greater and grander natures to attain ; and they accomplish this, not by dint of arrogance of manner,
or imperiousness of will, but rather by accepting
the position in a placid, matter-of-course way, ten
times more effective than self-assertion. In Caryl's
case, perhaps, much was owing to personal prestige.
People of sterner stuff than an imaginative boy,
were apt to be powerfully impressed by beauty that
was matchless in type, if not in degree.

The mildest tale, not ballasted with a self-evident
moral, would have been deemed contraband at Eerie-
dale Castle ; but on the upper shelves of the solemn
library, barely within ladder-reach, were ensconced
certain volumes, worm-eaten, musty, and yellow,
betraying the romantic tastes of some defunct Lady
Grisel or Janet ; and in poring over these furtively,
Nigel had found a delight scarcely to be understood
by our fifth-form philosophers, for whose palate home-
made sensation-stuff is food too tame. Now, there
was set before him, in flesh and blood, the choicest

of his knightly ideals. Moreover, to the neophyte, whose pulse was always a-flutter with pleasure, admiration, or surprise, the other's unruffled self-possession, and languid *insouciance*, seemed almost sublime.

Caryl, on his part, was attracted by his innocent kinsman, irrespective of any interested views : indeed, sordid calculation was not among his vices ; and he might have thriven better, if he would have looked more often and more carefully ahead. A man of the world, not completely jaded, generally finds the Marquis Cherubin, for a while at least, pretty good company : it was diversion enough to Caryl, to watch the development of that fresh faculty of enjoyment, which with himself had vanished more rapidly than even his patrimony. Though he had no great reverence for boyhood, he had the grace to abstain from throwing Nigel into the way of grave temptation ; and—more than this—without posing as a Mentor, he contrived to keep the other clear of divers pleasant snares laid for him by others. He guessed how it would be whispered abroad, that Glynne was getting cunning in his old age, and meant to keep this pigeon for his own plucking ; but, as he had never been turned back by fear of the world's talk when he meant ill, it was scarce likely to trouble him when, for once, he meant well and honestly.

Thus things stood, when the great disappointment of his life lighted on Caryl. To his lawyer and physician he confessed himself at need ; but beyond these his confidences had never extended. So, as you may suppose, he gave no hint of his trouble to Glenfalloch ; but the latter, who was by no means so simple as he seemed, felt certain that something was amiss ; and, one morning when they were breakfasting together, he actually risked a point-blank question, as to his cousin's health. Glynne did not answer at once ; and, whilst he paused, he looked absently out of the window at the sullen mist, just beginning to settle into a slow, steady rain.

"I am not particularly well," he said at last; "but it's no case for the doctor. I haven't slept much lately, and that's safe to throw the nerves out of gear. After all, it's what any idle man ought to expect, who has lived his life, if he spends a whole winter in this infernal climate, with no hunting to keep his liver in order."

"Then, why don't you go abroad?" Nigel asked. "I would——"

Caryl gazed for a second or two at the kind, eager face over against him; and then his own lighted up, as if a sudden thought had struck him.

"You would—go anywhere, Glen? I believe you mean it, and I've half a mind to take you at your word. What do you say to a long cruise? Not a mere Mediterranean potter; but a stretch all round the Levant, taking the Morea and Thessaly on our way. You're bound to yacht, of course; and you'll be all the better for some practice, before you hoist bunting of your own. There are several good ships to be hired just now. Neale would let us have the *Selenè* as long as we liked, for a consideration; she's a safe boat, big and steady enough to carry a bishop, and she's nearly in sea-going trim. There's nothing like travel for opening the mind; and those girls' cheeks will be rather improved by a little tanning. As for the cost—not that that matters much—I really believe you'd save money by the trip, although you'll have to find me in board and lodging. Do you like the idea?"

The other sprang up, with his eyes sparkling, and his face in a glow.

"Like it?"

That was all he said; but it was enough to clench the bargain.

The Earl of Glenfalloch—being gifted with a fine constitution, a fathomless purse, and an easy temper —may still anticipate more enjoyment than usually falls to the lot of mortals; yet it is scarce likely that he will ever again feel so simply and entirely happy as he did throughout that long sea-faring.

As, from first to last, he left it absolutely to Caryl to decide where they should anchor and whither they should steer, the usual differences of opinion on these points could hardly occur; but that, during all these months, neither should have wearied of the other's society was passing strange. For, though they picked up, *en route*, several chance companions—friends of Glynne—these only took passage with them from port to port; so that the *tête-à-tête* was virtually almost unbroken. To be sure, they were both rather of a silent turn, which may partially account for the harmony. A great talker, with ever so little advantage of seniority, will sooner or later wax argumentative, possibly even didactic; and rather than sail with such an one, I at least would prefer to cast in my lot with the sages of Gotham—ay, though the weather should look lowering to windward. However, it concerns us not to follow the pair on their wanderings.

Early in the spring they began to loiter homewards by easy stages; and at Naples they chanced upon the Malcolms. Family ties sate somewhat lightly upon Glynne; but this especial cousin was rather a pet of his, and the husband, too, impressed him favourably; so he consented, readily enough, to bear them company by land so far north as Florence, meeting the *Selene* again at Leghorn.

Glenfalloch, of course, was 'agreeable'—as usual. It was all new ground to him, and he could scarcely have visited it under better auspices; for the Corso and the Cascine were as familiar to Caryl as Pall Mall or the Row; and, if too indolent himself to play *cicerone*, he could always map out the day's work for the others; neither had Nigel need to be ashamed of his enthusiasm in presence of Emily Malcolm—most inveterate and indefatigable of sight-seers.

Altogether, the quartet was nearly as successful

as the duet had been; and they were all sorry when
they parted at Leghorn.

It was fully two months later, when the *Selene*,
coasting leisurely round Spain, reached Cadiz; and
there Glynne found letters from the Malcolms, telling
him where the pictures, for which his taste was responsible, were to be hung. He was more silent
than usual all that afternoon; and sat on deck alone,
thinking and smoking, far into the night. There were
few English counties with which he was not more or
less acquainted; and he knew enough of Loamshire
to be aware, that 'a well-girt man might easily com-
pass' the space dividing Erriswell from Templestowe.

And what then? With bringing about the coincidence, lucky or unlucky, he had had nought to
do. Life was not long enough to be always com-
bating and counteracting chances: let them take their
course. Near a year of exile—so he now chose to
designate his pilgrimage—was sufficient sacrifice to
any memory, bitter or sweet. Lena Shafton had
chosen the good part, and he did not begrudge her
wisdom its reward; but was there reason in his
keeping aloof from his own kinsfolk, because the
pleasant places in which her lines had fallen lay
somewhat near? They had parted as friends; so
they might—so they *should*—meet again; and everything would go on smoothly and soberly to the
last chapter's end, though the story might be a little
dull and dreary.

But even whilst he so pondered, there swept across
him that same foreboding that he had once—more
honest with Lena than with himself—put into words.
And even whilst he muttered cynicisms, a tenderness
welled up within him, that with some would have
found vent in tears.

Alas!—rather than that one of his stamp should
soften in this wise, it were best that his heart should
abide harder than Ailsa Craig, and his eyes drier
than Sahara sand.

Q

# CHAPTER XXVI.

IT was late in the afternoon, and the cosy boudoir at Erriswell was curtained close; but it was only lighted by some oak logs burning brightly. The mistress of the mansion rested on a couch drawn up near the hearth; and, on a low chair at her feet, sat Caryl Glynne—arrived an hour ago.

Cousins, who 'behave as such,' have usually plenty to discuss on these occasions, even if they have no confidences to exchange; and, though Malcolm was never in anybody's way, it was as well, perhaps, that he had not yet returned from his hunting. Mrs. Malcolm was extolling her new home; and, as a sociable neighbourhood was not the least of its advantages, she naturally soon mentioned the tenants of Templestowe.

"I don't say they're the handsomest, Caryl; but they're certainly the most picturesque couple I ever saw. She makes such a superb *châtelaine;* and he is exactly my ideal of a Grand Master of the Temple. Don't you agree with me? You know them both by sight, at all events; indeed, I think Lady Atherstone said she had often met you."

Perhaps it was only the flicker of the firelight; but Glynne's thin lip seemed to quiver for a second, and then to curl.

"Did Lady Atherstone remember me? I almost wonder at it; for when we met often, was very long ago. I know the baron, too, well by sight; and, though I never studied his face, I dare say you're right about his type. You've rather an artistic eye,

my dear. Only one can't fancy a Grand Master
blessed with a wife. If I remember right—my history
don't go beyond Scott, to be sure—that Order were
only allowed to love *par amours*."

"I utterly forgot that part of it. No, he wouldn't
do for a Templar, after all; for you can't fancy any
one prouder and fonder of his wife. He's quite a
changed person since his marriage, I believe."

Was it only the flame, sinking just then into dull
red embers, that caused the shadows to deepen so
on Caryl's face?

"Quite a changed person," he repeated. "Ah! I
understand—has turned his spud in a croquet-mallet,
looks after the flower-garden more than the farm,
and drives my lady about in a low pony-carriage.
There's nothing like the enthusiasm of a veteran *qui
arbore le cotillon*. And is the old man's darling as
happy as the old man? If so, they must be rather a
touching pair."

Mrs. Malcolm coloured a little. Her cousin had
never yet, in her presence, ventured on any licence of
speech; but something in his manner, now, made her
feel vaguely apprehensive, especially as she could not
in the least understand it. She had lived abroad
ever since her girlhood, you must recollect; and
none of the rumours, coupling Caryl's name with Miss
Shafton's, had ever reached her ears.

"You're quite wrong," she answered rather coldly.
"I said changed, not—spoilt. I can see nothing
ridiculous in a man becoming softer and less selfish,
even late in life; and Lord Atherstone, so far, has
given no signs of dotage. He still keeps up his
credit for hard riding; and I hear it is the prettiest
sight, to see him lead his wife across country. With
the exception of Mrs. Devereux, no woman in Loamshire goes better, they say. I fancy she's thoroughly
happy; but, with these quiet, languid people, it's all
guesswork; though I like her best—just as she is."

Glynne made no immediate reply; but the rebuke,

if so it was intended, did not seem greatly to dis-
concert him; for, as he sat silent, he smiled to himself twice or thrice.

'These quiet, languid people.' Was it a quiet
heart, whose beating he had counted many a time?
Were they languid eyes, that never were unready to
answer the messages of his own? These troublesome memories! And yet, what a strong savour of
*agro-dolce* was with them all! Well: if she had
begun her training as *grande dame* betimes, it was
best so; only, you see, the contrast was rather
amusing. When he spoke again it was in quite a
different tone.

"Mrs. Devereux, too—commonly called Cissy, by
all who have the honour of her acquaintance, which
I have not as yet—I'd forgotten that other Loamshire celebrity. On the whole, you seem to have a
very lively neighbourhood—almost too lively, for such
a quiet personage as yourself, *petite cousine.*"

Emily Malcolm felt relieved, she knew not why,
at the turn in the conversation.

"Now, there's a person that would really suit you,
Caryl," she laughed; "and you would suit her, too—
so provokingly pretty, and the most unconscionable
coquette: even Robin can't help flirting with her,
under my very eyes; what he does at other times
I'm left to imagine. Listen! I do believe that is
his step. He'll be so glad to find you. He said, he
should never believe in your coming till you were
come."

The host's welcome, though not boisterous, was
abundantly cordial. He was in specially high spirits,
too, for the L. H. had had a really good run—
galloping, if not racing, all the way—and Malcolm
had kept quite in the front rank from end to end.
He had wondrous nerves; and, in point of actual
horsemanship, might have given a lesson to most
professional breakers; but an eye to hounds is not
entirely a gift of nature, and riding to them is an Art

like another. Of all this Malcolm was well aware;
and whilst he had still much to learn, he preferred
biding in the background and watching how his
betters bore themselves, to contending prematurely
for pride of place. On this principle he had acted
throughout the graver business of life, and it was
one of the secrets of his thriving; nevertheless, he
was not so modest as to let a fair chance slip, and
he was infinitely gratified by the success of to-day.
So it was all hunting-talk at first, in which Mrs.
Malcolm, too, joined not unwillingly. She sym-
pathised in all things which interested her husband;
and, besides, she liked to hear about Loamshire folk
and their doings.

Who had gone best?—Generally a difficult, as well
as an invidious question to answer; and seldom is
the vote of praise so unanimous, as when the Cheshire
bard could write—

> 'Twas a sight for us all, worth a thousand, I swear,
> To see the Black Squire how he rode the black mare:
> This meed on his merits the muse must bestow—
> First, foremost, and fleetest from old Oulton Lowe.

To-day the pace had never been so killing, as to
enable any one or two absolutely to single themselves
out and shake off the rest; but on the whole, Malcolm was inclined to assign the palm to Lord Atherstone. Mrs. Devereux and her pilot had made a
brilliant start; but, in an unlucky bend to avoid a
wet tussocky meadow, had lost ground which they
never quite regained; whereas Ralph, according to
his wont, taking the rough with the smooth, and the
fences precisely as it pleased Heaven to send them,
had cut out the work in his own line, from first to
last. On this topic, indeed, Robin was almost enthusiastic.

"You may laugh, if you like," he said; "but I call
it simply a grand sight—a man of his weight and
years, going in that fashion. There's no hurry or
flurry about it, and no larking for show; but such

straight sailing throughout; and always with the
cool, 'undeniable' look on his face, that it has worn
before this, I'll answer for it, when he had a squadron
behind him, instead of a score of jealous riders.
It's a cavalry-seat all over; but, to my mind, that's
part of the picture: I wouldn't have it altered for
the world.   And if his hands are not as light as some
people's, they're strong enough to save a fall pretty
often, and to hold the reins like a vice when he *is*
down.   However, you'll judge for yourself to-morrow,
Glynne; and many a day after, I hope.   The stable's
very full, and very fit, I'm happy to say."

Though Mrs. Malcolm did not laugh at her husband's rhapsody, she glanced aside at her cousin,
rather triumphantly, as who should say—"Was I
right or wrong a while ago?"   But Caryl answered
neither by word, nor frown, nor smile.

"I've heard the same thing before," he remarked.
"It's not for nothing, I suppose, that they christened
him the Bruising Baron.   You don't mention Lady
Atherstone, by-the-bye.   Does she ride right up to
such a lead?   If so, I think she deserves a certain
share of credit."

"She wasn't out to-day," the other replied.   "She
rides—quite wonderfully, considering that she's had
only half a season's practice.   But, though they
always go straight, I'm bound to confess that the
baron has a much keener eye for a weak place, or
a gate that will open, and never jumps timber, when
he's playing chaperon.   That's only natural, surely?"

Glynne rose up, stretching himself lazily.

"Very natural, and very proper.   Now, Robin, if
you'll show me your den, I think I'll be guilty of
one small cigar before dressing-time.   There were
two girls in my carriage, all the way down; and
though they were affable, and looked rather 'period-
ical,' I was too bashful to inquire if they minded
smoke."

# CHAPTER XXVII.

You must follow to the covert-side once more. Before you condemn the iteration, remember that to no other place in a hunting-county, during the hunting-season, are idlers so much drawn; and it is best to suit one's self to one's company, imaginary or real. This time, setting chances of sport aside, the scene itself is worth inspecting.

There might be found in England, perhaps, two or three deer-parks more extensive than Wilton; but, more ancient, scarcely one. When Grandmanoir was a bare wild, some of those gnarled oaks were already grey; and Walwyns took their pleasure there, before a Fontenaye crossed the narrow seas. Time had brought little change to this family: they were still, as they were centuries ago, essentially *de la vieille roche*—gentle and kindly to a fault in their domestic and social relations; but stiff as steel, and bitter as wormwood, when it was a question of doctrine; and, though loyalest of the loyal, never hesitating betwixt fealty to King and fealty to Church. That they should have carried out such principles so long and so unflinchingly, and yet have escaped absolute wreck in any political storm, was wonderful; and even heretics, pondering over these things, had been known to doubt whether Intercession was wholly a vague superstition, and whether some patron-saint had not really watched over them.

The house had been sacked during the Civil Wars, and its inmates driven forth to wander for a while; but their estates were never confiscated. For, when there was talk thereof amongst those who went up to divide the spoil, the Protector smote on the council-table with his brawny palm, and swore, with a lowering brow, that 'as the Lord lived, this thing should not be.' There, was growling, of course, amongst the ban-dogs balked of the toothsome morsel; but none dared to quarrel aloud with the strange clemency: only afterwards it was bruited about, that Oliver in his youth—not so sober as his manhood—had been helped by a Walwyn out of a shrewd scrape, and so paid his debt. The Round-heads kept a better memory both for friends and foes than the Cavaliers; and, after the Restoration, the Walwyns were not rewarded by augmented honours or revenue. Thenceforth they had tarried in their own place, neither molesting nor molested. They were well-read and polite folks; but in prac-tical matters, always rather behind their generation; as for making any concession to the spirit of the time—they would as soon have consented to turn their park into corn-lands. Nevertheless, they were ever popular from their exceeding courtesy, and a charity that made no distinction of creed.

That is the present head of the family—the pale, white-haired man, moving about from group to group in front of the broad stone terrace, with an evident limp in his gait. For as mild as he looks, ten years ago very few could show the way over Loamshire to Edmund Walwyn; but, since he dis-located his hip, he can only creep about on a quiet shooting-cob, and watch the find, which is a dead certainty in his coverts.

All the other personages of note you have met before at Hazlemere; and they are little, if any-thing, changed. Only the care-worn conscious look has deepened on Arthur Corbett's face, since we saw it last; and there is a restlessness in his manner, very different from the gay geniality of other days, as he strives to engage and engross Lady Atherstone's attention; whose husband stands somewhat aloof, in converse with Jasper Knowsley.

Is Lena aware of the state of things in this quarter?

A knotty question. The best of women—and she was not of the best—abide sometimes strangely deaf and blind, when, if their ears and eyes were open, it might become their duty to quench some sweet-smelling incense. At any rate, she appears to listen readily enough to Mr. Corbett's earnest talk; and there is certainly something confidential in her occasional smile. Nevertheless, she glances aside, like the rest, to see who are the new-comers, as a phaeton wheels rapidly round the sweep, and draws up on the skirts of the crowd.

There is no change in the atmosphere—not even a cloud has swept across the sun—yet in an instant everything seems to have grown dark around her; and against the blackness stands out—the face of Caryl Glynne.

With a mighty effort, and a sickening fear that the effort will be apparent, Lena turns her eyes away, and looks straight to her front. So that, when Corbett, suddenly aware that her attention is wandering, looks up appealingly, she only seems to be watching Swinton Swarbrick struggling, with frequent puffs and anathemas, to hoist himself on to the back of an elephantine beast, that keeps sidling away as though loath to receive the unconscionable load. It is rather a diverting spectacle; yet scarce sufficiently so, to account for the intentness of Lady Atherstone's gaze. Arthur is completely puzzled; but, before he can ask a question, his companion has left his side, and is walking her horse slowly towards the Erriswell carriage.

If you have at all fathomed Lena's character, you will not wonder at this impulse of hers. To certain persons passive suspense is a torture so unendurable, that, if it is in their power to end it, they will do so, no matter what the risk or cost; and, not seldom, the rashest move is the safest, after all. A casual observer would detect nothing unusual in Lady Atherstone's manner, as she ranges up to the side of the phaeton, where Mrs. Malcolm sits holding the reins, whilst her cousin stands up to doff his overcoat.

"I'm so glad to see you out at last," she begins. "I felt sure the day and the meet would tempt you; but I had no idea you would come under such escort. So you have appeared at last, Mr. Glynne. People were beginning to suppose you had pitched your tent somewhere among the Lost Tribes."

After greeting Mrs. Malcolm, she stretches her hand across to Caryl; and her fingers touch, without closing around, his.

It was admirably done; and Glynne confessed as much to himself afterwards, though he did think "she might have shown a little more feeling." However, his own demeanour was a triumph also, in its kind.

"Yes, I've been a long time away," he answers composedly;—"so long, that I feel almost like a stranger in England, and as if I ought to be introduced over again to all my acquaintances, especially if they have changed their names. It's rather late in the day to offer congratulations, Lady Atherstone; but I hope you will accept mine, even now."

She bends her head—perhaps a little haughtily.

"You don't know my husband, I think? I had better make you acquainted."

For, just then, Lord Atherstone rides up and accosts Mrs. Malcolm.

Whilst they exchange salutes, the two men scan each other; yet so warily withal that neither is conscious of the scrutiny. Lord Atherstone has often looked on that face before; but he thinks that, till now, he has never quite realised its exceeding beauty; for Levantine suns have only added to the richness of its colouring, and keen sea-breezes, added to frequent bouts of strong exercise on shore, have braced a figure apt to be effeminate in its languid *poses*. And Ralph acknowledges all this without a particle of dislike, discontent, or envy; just as he would acknowledge the perfection of any other rare master-piece of art or nature. If Glynne's appreciation is not so dispassionate, it is, after a fashion, also sincere.

'*Robin Gray!*' He wonders whether Lena, too, is remembering the nickname just now. Not a very burgess-like personage, truly, he who sits in saddle yonder, tall and square as a Doric column; not many signs of dotage in the stern straight features or of infirmity in the nervous hand, so thoroughly at home on the bridle. '*Sholto Dhu-Glas*' would have been better, if a parallel must needs be drawn from Scots story. Was not Lena right when she said, that this man was "well able to take care of his own?" Certainly, it is not without bitterness that Caryl admits this; yet with it mingles a certain satisfaction. To have yielded place to such a rival, backed by crushing odds of rank and wealth, was at least neither cowardly nor shameful. All things considered, Glynne finds it not hard to return the baron's courteous greeting in kind; so that nothing can be more satisfactory than their first interview.

After an exchange of a few more common-place sentences, the Atherstones pass on. Ralph says not a word, and Lena does not care just now to meet his eyes; nevertheless, she is conscious that they have rested on her for a second, not only trustingly, but approvingly; and, though it still throbs painfully, she carries away a lighter heart than she has known of late. She marvels a little at her own self-possession; but now, that sharp ordeal passed, she feels little fear of its failing her.

Amongst the snares laid by the Tempter, is there

one more dangerous than the confidence begotten by the first real or seeming success?

Corbett watches the colloquy with a feverish anxiety. Lena's manner, so far as he can judge, is cool and unembarrassed to a degree; yet he would give a good deal, to overhear the words that pass between her and that striking-looking stranger. That they are old acquaintances is clear; and, if it had been a question of welcoming Mrs. Malcolm only, perhaps Lady Atherstone would not have left him so abruptly. For an instant he is tempted to follow; but, though he has an excellent opinion of himself, he is rather deficient in nerve, and this keeps his curiosity in check. Whilst he yet hesitates, Malcolm rides up on his covert-hack. Arthur pushes forward at once to accost him.

"Who has driven Mrs. Malcolm over to-day?" he asks, after the usual greetings have been exchanged. "It's a new face, and a very remarkable one."

"That's my wife's cousin," the other answers, with a laugh. "Sounds like the title to a farce—doesn't it? Yes, it *is* a remarkable face; and some remarkable stories have been told about Caryl Glynne in his time—not that I believe half of them. At any rate, he's so much changed for the better now, that I consider him a safe *chaperon*. I fancy you must have heard his name before?"

Heard it? Yes. No one noting Corbett's start and change of colour would have doubted that fact. Though a polished specimen of the class, he was in the manner of his life essentially provincial; and flying visits, comprising Epsom and Ascot, crammed full with cut-and-dried engagements, had been for years past his sole uncommercial link with the metropolis. Nevertheless, that name was not strange to his ears; and at the mention of it he felt a kind of dread, such as might have stricken the dwellers in Cisalpine plains when it was rumoured that Genseric or Attila drew near. Surely, too, he had seen that face before somewhere in a crowd, and had admired it negligently.

Weak and faulty as he was—he was not such a hypocrite as to 'cry to himself peace, when there was no peace;' and, if he did not realise how far, or how fast, the current was bearing him, he knew at least that he had been swept from safe anchorage long ago, and was tossing already on a dangerous sea. Sometimes he caught himself wondering if the world was charitable or blind, so that it was evident only to himself—the guilty attraction that drew him ever to Lena Atherstone's side. But, since he set himself to win her favour, he had never seen her in company with any of her ancient familiars. In town he had only met her at two or three great entertainments, where everything was staid and stately; and in Loamshire he had only to compete with acquaintances recent as himself. Here was a familiar—with a vengeance! Was Robert Malcolm mad, to let such a wolf couch in his sheep-fold? Was Lord Atherstone mad, to countenance his wife being the first to welcome Caryl Glynne? Or was he, Arthur Corbett, mad, thus to torment himself before his time? Though it had been sorely tried of late, he did not think his own brain was wandering yet. And, in very truth, the presentiments of jealousy, irrational as they may seem, as a rule, go as little astray as any.

At this juncture, a groom brings up Malcolm's hunter; and Corbett is glad of the excuse of passing on. He draws himself clear of the crowd, on pretence of altering something in his saddle-gear; and remains there till the hounds move off, musing moodily. However, ere long, comfort, if not aid, comes from a quarter whence he has scarce expected help.

# CHAPTER XXVIII.

A FRESH arrival in a large hunting field does not create the same sensation as in a small watering-place; nevertheless, there are always people ready to take stock of any stranger of mark, especially if he be introduced by a county notable. Other eyes besides Arthur Corbett's have been levelled, you may be sure, at the Erriswell carriage; and among them are those 'useful' ones that Mrs. Devereux owns. She indulges herself in a long, leisurely survey; and, when it is concluded, these words escape her, involuntarily it would seem—

"Simply superb."

"What is superb?" Major Colville asks; who has watched with growing discontent the direction of her gaze.

Cissy glances at her cavalier, even more mutinously than is her wont.

"The scene, the weather, 'the *tout ensemble* in the corner,' the—anything you like. I am in a general-admiration frame this morning; and a very good frame too, isn't it?"

The hussar gnaws his jetty moustache, sadly marring its artistic wave.

"Nonsense: you never admired anything in your life, except a horse, a dress, or—a face. Do you suppose I don't know what you've been looking at, for the last five minutes?"

"Then, if you know so much, why do you ask questions?" she retorts coolly. "And, suppose you're right, we're not at school now, when looking to the right or left in our walks abroad cost five pages of *Télémaque*. Once for all, Godfrey, if you're going to be cross, I shall not help you out of the sulks, but——"

——"Go and talk to Mrs. Malcolm," Colville breaks in with a sneer. "That's about your mark. You see I can follow your thoughts, as well as your eyes."

There are many vulnerable points about this wilful dame; and much may be done by a well-timed appeal to her good nature, her compassion, or even her sense of justice; but attack, from whatsoever quarter, is safe to provoke defiance. She turns on her assailant —dauntless and pitiless to boot.

"That's precisely what I do intend. And—talking about following—unless you're good directly, I'll find some one else to lead me to-day. It wouldn't be hard. There's Dick would be too glad to get the chance. Wouldn't you, Dick?"

Certainly, one of the most wonderful things in nature, is the way in which finished performers in Cissy's line contrive to play off, not only one light love against the other, but their own liege lords against the lot.

The Driver coming up at this moment, and overhearing the last words, glances from one to the other rather ruefully. He has some experience in these disputes, and knows that wheresoever the right may be, there is safety for him only in espousing one side; but he is too honest to be always time-serving: on the present occasion, he strikes in at once for his brother-in-arms.

"So you've begun quarrelling already, you two? I don't wonder at it. Don't you mind her, Godfrey; she's very queer this morning: we had a bit of a breeze as we came along. Something went wrong before we started, I expect. If you let her alone, it'll blow over as the day gets on."

Mrs. Devereux laughs a little angry laugh—not altogether of vexation though. She has a keen sense of humour; and, besides, bears her husband no malice for standing by his comrade

"Of course it's my fault," she pouts. "But if you'd come up a minute sooner, Dick, and kept those great ears of yours open, you'd have heard Major Colville exceedingly rude. Now, you may keep each other company till I come back; and, if I don't see you both looking more amiable, perhaps I shan't come back at all."

Be it noted here, that amongst this lady's peculiarities, is a habit of calling an infinite number of the other sex by their Christian name. In the mouth of any other living woman it would be a vulgarism; in hers it sounds simply—unconventional. When she gives her courtiers their full title, they are for the nonce, in dire disgrace.

As Mrs. Devereux rides off, tossing her haughty little head, the two men look at each other rather blankly.

"*I* never meant to quarrel, Driver," Colville says, with something like a groan—"on this day, of all days in the year. I shouldn't wonder if I found the route come, when I get back to barracks."

The other's face lowers sympathetically.

"It's d——d hard, old man," he mutters. "If she'd known that, perhaps she wouldn't have been so short with you. Never mind; I'll put it all straight directly."

The hussar shakes his head: with every confidence in his friend's good-will, he puts no great trust in his powers of mediation. So—*les oreilles tant soit peu baisses*—they pace off slowly in Cissy's wake.

Meantime Glynne has mounted; but he still remains close to the Erriswell carriage, chatting to his cousin, and to her husband, who has just joined them. So, when Mrs. Devereux rides up and greets Mrs. Malcolm affectionately, an introduction is inevitable. Cissy would be much flattered, to say the least of it, if she could guess at the success of her first effect.

Caryl is at once attracted, not only by her tempting face and faultless figure, but by her crisp, fresh, sparkling manner; and strikes into the conversation with unusual energy. Mrs. Malcolm smiles to herself at the correctness of her prophecy; she had said, you will remember, that 'these two would be sure to suit each other.' Before five minutes are over, they are talking quite like old friends; and, when the general move towards the covert-side is made, though Malcolm drops back and mingles with the crowd, Caryl seems to think that his proper place is still close to Mrs. Devereux's rein.

Certainly things do not look more promising for Godfrey Colville, and he is not one to accept such a position meekly: indeed he has a strong, if not a violent temper; and, though throughout their intimacy he has never quite got out of Cissy's hand, she has been obliged to manage him on the give-and-take principle. Nevertheless he would die the death sooner than further bemoan himself, even to his sworn ally; and to Dick's sulky inquiry, "Who's that she's got hold of now?" he answers, with infinite coolness,—

"Haven't a notion. Staying at Erriswell, I suppose; for Malcolm has put him upon about the best in his stable. Looks as if he could ride, too."

This concession is really magnanimous; for, like many other brilliant horsemen, the Major is apt to be somewhat hypercritical and slow to admire. That Caryl's face should be strange to him is no wonder; for the former has spent more of his time abroad than in England, of late years, and Colville's regiment has but recently returned from Indian service.

"Don't you think we'd better close up?" Devereux suggests—still bent on mediation.

The hussar is hard upon his moustache once again: for himself he would like nothing better; but he rather dreads the blunders of his well-wisher's zeal.

"Not just yet," he says quietly. "We'd better

R

wait till we're wanted. It's a safe find, though it's
a chance if they don't mob their fox. If we do get
a gallop, and if I never give her a lead again, I'll
give her a good one to-day, please God!"

Despite the placidity of his tone, and the pious
turn of that last sentence, the thoughts of Colville's
heart just now are not likely to be pleasing to any
Deity delighting in mercy and loving-kindness; and
Cissy Devereux's nerve will, perchance, be put to the
proof if hounds run straight and fast.

But it is too much of a lawn-meet for real sport.
Besides the crowd in saddle and on wheels, there is a
great affluence of 'pedestrinarians;' and the weather
is too gay for scent in or out of covert.

The first fox is chopped ingloriously; and they
only potter after their second at a pace that gives no
opening for cutting down. Indeed, with the exception of a couple of jealous boys on clever ponies, and
a few breakers and farmers schooling, all are content
to take their turn at gates and gaps. Major Colville's patience—a shallow, uncertain stream at the
best—at length runs fairly dry; and having contrived,
by a succession of halts and doubles, to shake off
the honest Driver, he ranges up on Cissy's bridle-
hand. On the off-side still lounges Caryl Glynne;
with the air of one who, by prescriptive right, occu-
pies a post of honour.

To speak the truth, Caryl has been enjoying himself exceedingly. As Colville had surmised, he can
ride, and ride right well at times; but he has neither
jealousy nor ambition in this line, and thinks indifferent sport quite balanced by genial weather and
pleasant company. His companion he finds more
than pleasant: he is amused by her gay audacity,
and by the epigrammatic turn of her sketches of
Loamshire men and manners; whilst her brilliant
complexion, and lithe, quick gestures are refreshing
to his eyes, sated with the sombre, listless southern
beauty. All the while, with one of those singular

self-delusions to which men, good as well as evil, wise as well as foolish, are prone, he has been rather pluming himself on his prudence and delicacy in keeping aloof from Lena Atherstone, till the awkwardness of their first encounter shall have passed away.

With a slight hesitation, and a blush, which becomes her wonderfully, Mrs. Devereux performs the needful ceremony of introduction. Perhaps a vague suspicion of the truth crosses Caryl's mind; but it in nowise ruffles either his confidence or his composure. With the other it is very different. He has not lived so long, or so far out of the world, as not to have heard that name, and some of the tales hanging thereto, before; and the first mention of it affects him scarce more pleasantly than it did Arthur Corbett. Nevertheless, having his nerves under better control, he does not start perceptibly, and only ices his salute.

"Colville!" Glynne remarks meditatively. "You have a cousin Reginald, I think? I know him very well."

To do the Major justice, it is not often that he 'puts side on;' but when he does so, there is no mistake about it.

"Then you have the advantage of me," he retorts, with a curling lip; "it is some time since I ceased to know that person."

Caryl's is a smooth, easy temper, especially when all things march to his liking; but he was never accused of failing to take an affront on the bound. His smile is infinitely more exasperating than the other's sneer.

"Ah! family quarrels, I presume. No one is safe from them—not even such a gentle, generous creature as poor Reginald."

Insolence for insolence, the counter is more effective than the blow; and, though he scorns to break ground, the soldier feels he has the worst of the

rally.   Time and place do not serve for the recital of
the numberless grounds of offence, which have caused
the name of the unlucky *vaurien* in question to be an
ill savour in the nostrils of his most patient kinsfolk;
besides, Colville has no right to assume that the
speaker is cognisant of these.

Whilst he is casting about for a reply, Mrs. Devereux,
disquieted by the signs of hostility, intervenes.   She
has had much practice in putting high-bred cattle
together—this wayward dame—and on a few occasions has been known to manage three, and even
four abreast, with Olympian dexterity; but she has
never yet tried this especial courser in double harness,
and feels that the experiment might bring the whole
equipage to grief.   Furthermore, as has been aforesaid, she observes a certain equity in her iniquities;
and, if somewhat fickle in the transfer of her favour,
rarely changes her *cicisbeo* without decent warning.
She has found her hussar rather a cumbrance of
late, and has sometimes wished for a more complacent cavalier; if no 'fresh fere' be at hand to dry
them, her bright brown eyes will not be long tear-
blinded the morning when Colville rides away; and
that ǀthreatened route—surely it is long a-coming.
But, since the War Office will not help her out of
the difficulty, poor Godfrey has at least deserved to
be let down gently.   So pity, not less than prudence,
moves her to temporise.   As the peace - making,
evidently, cannot be conducted *à trois*, she takes her
line with her wonted promptitude.

"Mr. Glynne, I think you can be trusted alone now,
for a little while; and I want you to take a message
to your cousin.   Her carriage is in that crowd on the
cross roads, I see; but it is not likely that she will
follow much further.   I was half engaged to lunch at
Erriswell on Saturday.   Will you find out whether
this is quite settled, and let me know?"

The *congé* is unmistakable; but Caryl is not a whit
chagrined or discomfited.   He has made about the

most of the balls in his first innings, and is quite
content that others—specially others whose place he
may have usurped—should have their turn.  Moreover, it was not yesterday that he learned, and began
to act on the maxim—" *Tout vient en temps à lui qui
sait attendre ;*" and he does not fear losing much
ground by a temporary absence.  He is thoroughly
right here.  No man has wasted his time if, thus early
in an acquaintance, he can attain to be—missed.
This success he has certainly achieved.  Before he
has left her side five minutes, the fair Cissy is sensible
of a palpable, if not an aching, void.  Glynne is far
from a brilliant conversationalist; but there are men
—and women too, God wot—who contrive to say a
good deal without often unlocking their lips; and a
subdued satire in Caryl's tone gives his simplest
remarks a certain piquancy : though cut-and-thrust
repartee is more in Mrs. Devereux's style, she quite
appreciates more delicate raillery.

The Major does not shine by contrast.  To a flirtation on first principles, howsoever energetic or
prolonged, he is fully equal; and can do his share
of the talking fairly in general society; but he has
neither tact nor temper for the proper management
of a love-quarrel.

The butterfly chase is not quite so good a thing
as it looks on paper; or, at all events, is rather a
one-sided affair.  Despite the provocation, one cannot
help admiring the wily turns and lithesome wind-
ings by which the Insect-Queen manages to preserve
her freedom; but the pursuer, waxing more hot and
incensed over each disappointment, rarely contrives
to retain either grace or dignity.  And peace-making
—what heavy up-hill work it is, when the heart of one
of the parties concerned is not in it!  Notwithstanding her penitence and compassion, Mrs. Devereux finds
it so to-day; and Godfrey Colville, with all his courage
and self-confidence, finds it harder every minute to
bear up against the sense of baffling and defeat.

Surely, some of us would sympathise with him here —recalling a like occasion, when a curse seemed to lie on our tongue; when our overtures of amity seemed as clumsy, even to ourselves, as the caresses of the Æsopian ass; when, from our most innocent suggestion, shot out a sting; when the very dove, bearing our olive-branch, was by some dreadful gramarye changed into a raven, shrieking bode and giving signal of battle.

In most of these cases, the grounds of dispute are neither direct nor defined; and thus it is here. With every wish to be plaintive, the unlucky hussar cannot precisely see what he is to complain of. He himself was certainly the first to show temper, only because Cissy exercised a right that cats share with coquettes, and looked at whom she would—even if she looked somewhat long. What has happened since, is perhaps a just reprisal. So he wearies himself in beating about the bush; and Mrs. Devereux, to speak truth, does not much help him in his difficulties.

But, though she has no mind to be cornered or brought to book, she is not averse, for the nonce, to be conciliated. To all appearance, matters are soon sufficiently smooth betwixt the two, to deceive keener eyes than those of Dick the Driver; who, ranging up alongside, exults in his honest heart— not witting of the hollow truce.

# CHAPTER XXIX.

MANY who followed the fortunes of the L. H. that day found it wearisome; and rejoiced when even their patient, pertinacious master declined to persevere further and turned homewards with his hounds; but to none, certainly, did it seem so long as to Lena Atherstone.

Calm as she seemed outwardly, an inward fever consumed her. The counter-excitement of a brushing gallop might possibly have quieted the quick, the heavy, uneven throbbing of her pulse; but this relief was denied her: she was forced to pace slowly on— always more or less in a crowd, and always liable to calls on her attention, and always with a morbid consciousness that she was being watched. At first she scarcely dared to turn her head, lest she should find Caryl Glynne close by her side. Giving him credit for all possible forbearance — she could not believe that empty formalities would quite content him : he would surely seize, or make, an opportunity for one allusion to the past, even if it were to assure her once again that it was buried; and, if such were ever so gently and delicately conveyed, how could she meet it? For her confidence had drooped already; and she no longer trusted implicitly to the self-command which had borne her scatheless through their first greeting. The minutes passed on; and other voices sounded in her ears with words, almost meaningless at the moment, and impossible afterwards to remember; but not the voice she dreaded and yet hungered for. At length she grew more brave, or less patient, and ventured on one swift glance over her shoulder. This is what she saw.

On their way from covert to covert, they were crossing a broad meadow; so that the field no longer kept in column, but had opened out on either side into knots and groups. On the outermost skirts of these, a little to the rearward of Lady Atherstone, rode the couple you wot of. Lena thought she had never seen Mrs. Devereux look so charming. She was near enough to note the mischievous smile on the tempting lip, the tell-tale brilliancy of the soft complexion, and even the triumphant flash of the bright brown eyes; and on Caryl's face, waked from its languor, was a light that she knew well how to interpret — a light which perhaps she had never ceased to hope, shone for her alone.

Pride, prudence, and resolves all vanished in a spasm of fierce jealousy: her teeth tightened on her nether lip; and her cheek for an instant was colourless.

In truth, when the first sharp bitterness was past, she tried very hard to be patient and rational; she tried to persuade herself—even as Caryl had done— that he was only playing a part, and playing it for her sake. But it was all in vain. Though it helps them little in the end, women are more clear-sighted in these matters, I fancy, than we. In the earlier stages of infatuation, they are prone to invest their idol with all manner of imaginary attributes; but, when the flimsy robe of honour waxes threadbare, they will pluck it away, and thenceforth are content to worship, in its simple deformity, the clay, or iron, or brass, or stone.

Lena knew this man, perhaps, better than he knew himself. She did not hold him incapable of self-restraint or self-denial; and she had seen him, ere this, dissemble with no selfish end: but there is acting and acting; and Caryl's earnestness, just now, looked far too real to be all assumed. Ever since

that day at Erriswell, she had been schooling herself for this meeting. She might have spared her
pains, it seemed. Could he not have waited one day
—just one day—before he forced her to realise that
she was utterly forgotten—when, whilst there was
any hope, *she* had never wearied of waiting? She
never wished that they should be more than friends;
but surely something is due even to old acquaintanceship; and, when she prayed that the past might be
buried, she never reckoned on merry-making over
the scarce-closed grave. She bore Cissy no malice
for her part in all this. That gay falconer had but
swung her lure after her wont; and there was nought
to tell her, by whom the strange hawk stooping
thereto had once been reclaimed, since he bore no
broken jesses. Nay, more—if, by the magnetism of
an unuttered wish, Lena could have drawn Caryl
to her own side, she could, and would, at that moment
have forborne to frame it. Nevertheless, she did
feel very desolate and lonely; and, as she glanced
around—anywhere but to the rearward—there was a
kind of helplessness in her eyes.

Inconsistent? Of course — pitiably inconsistent.
She was far from being a perfect woman; and from
this one weakness of their sex even our exemplars
are not always free.

Lady Atherstone's glance rested first on her husband, who still rode at her side. Ralph's face, as
you know, was not an easy one to read; and assuredly,
now, it gave not the slightest indication of his having
been ruffled or annoyed. He had scarcely spoken
to Lena since they left the Erriswell carriage together;
but this was probably an accident, or attributable to
his attention having been constantly drawn off elsewhere. At this moment it was taken up by Sir
Manners Mannering, who was vaunting the unparal-
leled success of some recent experiments on his home-
farm.

Now, it so happened that the rotund baronet had

long been Lena's special aversion: she hated his pompous purse-pride, his ostentatious neglect of a wife far too good for him, and his ignoble infidelities; she absolutely loathed the insolent admiration of herself, that she had more than once detected in his savage sensual eyes. Always courteous in her coolness—she had contrived to set up a barrier betwixt them, which, so far, had baffled the other's assurance; and she was careful never to give him a chance of creeping through by the lifting of a single pale. Had the subject of their talk been more congenial to her, she would have kept silence, rather than have addressed her husband at the risk of attracting to herself Mannering's attention. So her eyes wandered off again—this time farther afield—till they lighted on Arthur Corbett.

Have you ever noticed the manœuvres of the pilot craft plying in the track of homeward-bound ships—now dropping modestly into the wake, now shooting temptingly athwart the bows of a particular vessel, but not venturing within hail without express signal? If it be plain sailing through clear weather, it is all wasted pains; for the Indiaman stands statelily on, apparently unconscious of the humble follower: but —let the weather once thicken to windward—that tacking will have served its purpose, and the patient mariner will earn his hire.

Even so, for some time past, the banker had at a decorous distance tracked Lady Atherstone; and even so, the latter did at last deign to hang out some sort of signal which, however hard to set forth on paper, was to the person for whom it was intended easy to read. They were riding, as we have said, over open ground; so, in a few seconds, without having to thrust through a throng, or any undue show of eagerness, Corbett found himself once more at Lena's side.

Perhaps he was careful not to betray the flutter of elation that he felt; for, whilst he glanced at her inquiringly, as though doubtful to what end he had

been summoned, his brows were still overcast. The
dark unquiet look, though it had been seen there
pretty often of late, was strangely out of keeping with
the somewhat insipid beauty of his comely countenance: but real passion—or even passion aptly simu-
lated—is rarely quite ridiculous, whatever be the
accessories. Macbeth, in a flowing peruke, would
doubtless try our gravity; but, if Garrick could play
the part once more, we should scarce laugh through
the closing scenes. Lena's smile was rather conciliatory than scornful.

"I want to be amused," she said; "but, perhaps,
you are hardly equal to that task. You look quite as
much bored as myself. To be sure, a day like this is
a dreadful trial of temper."

When a woman troubles herself to notice the
changes in a man's humour, it is a point scored in
the game. Corbett, though his love-making—luckily
for himself—had hitherto been mere trivial pastime,
was not such a novice in heart-lore as to be ignorant
of this; but it was his cue, now, to be sad rather
than sullen; and his brow cleared quickly.

"I don't know that I was thinking much of our
chances of sport," he said. "There are so many
worse crosses in life than a blank day—with hounds."

He had learned, of late, to throw a kind of intention
into his most innocent phrases; and the pause before
the last two syllables was cleverly put in.

"That's very true," she assented. "But when one
comes out hunting, one is supposed to leave other
cares at home."

"The old cares, perhaps," he said, with an audible
sigh; "but it is possible to find fresh ones abroad."

"Then you have heard something disagreeable.
It wouldn't be fair to ask what, and when?"

They had dropped, insensibly, some yards to the
rear of Lord Atherstone and Mannering; so that it
was scarce likely they could be overheard: nevertheless, Corbett lowered his voice almost to a whisper.

"I've heard nothing," he said; "but—I've seen."

The talk was verging on dangerous ground; but Lena was in a mood rather to court than shrink from danger.

"And what have you seen?"

"Nothing strange," he answered; "nothing but what happens every day—that new friends must give place to old."

She drew herself up haughtily at first; but the next instant her face softened.

"I suppose I ought not to understand; but I do—and I consider you very unreasonable. There's a difference between old friends and old acquaintances; also, I believe there are such things as the common courtesies of life—not that mine were in the least appreciated. Don't you think that Mrs. Devereux is doing her duty, too, in that line?"

Corbett had the wit to see that it would not profit him, any longer to decline the olive-branch.

"I think—exactly what you bid me think," he said, with one of his old gay smiles.

And so peace was re-established—ay! and something more than peace.

From what has been written down, you may augur that the intimacy betwixt these two had reached a certain point already; but, in months, it had not progressed so rapidly as it did that day. Nothing was said of which either need absolutely have been ashamed: nevertheless, if he had deigned to play the eavesdropper, it may be doubted whether there would not have been an angry tingling even in the unsuspicious ears of Ralph Atherstone.

How many women, I wonder, could trace their downfall to having stepped aside, only to avoid the sting of a jealous thought rising up, serpentwise, in their path? And how many have found poison in the draught, that was vapid enough when first they drained it as an anodyne?

# CHAPTER XXX.

ARTHUR CORBETT sat in the room where you saw him first; and the hour and his surroundings were nearly the same. He had dined, after a fashion, but with an evident lack of appetite, though he had drunk more deeply than his wont; for, convivial as he was, he had never been accused of excess. However, this last circumstance could not account for the flush on his cheek and the unsteady brightness in his eyes; for these were there before he sat down to table. When in the bosom of his family, he was usually full of prattle; but he was strangely taciturn now: his rare, jerky sentences were dropped almost at random; and, when his favourite Meta nestled up close to his knee, though he caressed her it was mechanically; there was no story ready that evening; nor, when the children's bedtime came, was any extra leave petitioned for.

Judging from a complacent, not to say fatuous, smile, which more than once flitted across his lips, the current of his musings could not have been wholly disagreeable. Nevertheless, Emma Corbett watched her husband with increasing uneasiness; and, as soon as they were quite alone, she ventured to inquire "whether he felt unwell."

Arthur looked up quickly—not smiling now.

"Unwell?" he said rather fretfully. "What on earth makes you think that? Do I look so?"

"You looked flushed when you came down to dinner, and you have eaten scarcely anything; and even Meta noticed how hot your hand was. Perhaps you have taken a chill. Dearest, indeed, if I were you, I wouldn't drink any more wine; it will only make you feverish."

Not hastily, but in a dogged, defiant fashion, most unlike himself, he drained the claret-glass to the last drop; and frowned as he filled another.

"I never felt better in my life," he said, "or in less need of doctoring. If there's a thirst on me, it's only natural after such a long tiring day. What's come to you, Emma? You're seldom subject to these fancies."

"I am not," she said in her placid way, which was yet not devoid of firmness. "It's no fancy, that something is amiss with you, Arthur—in mind, if not in body. Is there any trouble in the bank?"

"The bank?" he retorted. "No, there's nothing amiss there; our credit is good, and we're as careful of it as ever. There's nothing amiss anywhere— absolutely nothing."

His laugh was boastful, yet somewhat nervous withal; like that of one who vaunts his security to disguise a vague dread. Neither was his wife's mind quite set at ease. But, you will remember, Arthur had never given her any grave uneasiness; and, though she had abundance of common sense, she was by nature slow to suspect or think evil. After all, he might be only heated and tired: if his humour had not been quite so sweet and even of late, as heretofore, perhaps he had been working too hard: autumn was always a busy time; and, unluckily, a head clerk was absent just now on sick-leave. At any rate, she tried to smooth matters, by inquiring if he had heard any news, or seen any fresh faces, at the meet.

"No news," was the reply; "and about the usual lot were out. By-the-bye, there was one stranger—a cousin of Mrs. Malcolm, I believe—a Mr.—Glynne."

He paused before the last word, as if he were either doubtful of the name or loth to utter it. You may guess—although his wife could not—which was nearer the truth.

"Glynne," Emma said, reflectively. "I've never heard of him—have I, dear?"

In Arthur's manner towards his own womankind there was, at the best of times, a kind of indulgent superiority; but, now, the indulgence was lacking.

"I dare say you never have," he replied; "but by a good many other people he's pretty well known, and better known than trusted. He was at the bottom of that great Lester scandal, years ago; and has been mixed up with half-a-dozen similar stories since. A pleasant person to be domesticated at Erriswell!"

Emma Corbett, though no fanatic, had little sympathy with sin or sinners; but there was palpable curiosity in her next remark.

"You don't say so, Arthur! And what is he like?"

The other knit his brows; like one who has to answer either a puzzling or a distasteful question.

"It is a very peculiar face," he answered, after a while. "Handsome, I suppose, it would be called—regular features, good dark eyes, and that sort of thing—though I confess *I* was disappointed; but it has a tired, worn look; and the hair and beard are quite grey, though he can't be forty yet."

His forehead grew smooth again, as he glanced complacently at the reflection in a mirror over against him of his own comely countenance and crisp rich curls; and Mrs. Corbett smiled indulgently—she had long since learned to forgive her husband's small vanities.

"It must have a quaint effect; rather picturesque, too, I fancy. Did he seem to know any one besides the Erriswell party?"

Corbett shifted in his chair, with an evident impatience; and filled his glass again with an unsteady hand.

"How you bother about the man!" he said fretfully. "Do you suppose I was watching him all day? Well

—yes—I believe he and Lady Atherstone have met before, though it must have been a slight acquaintance."

Without a suspicion of the cause, Mrs. Corbett saw that the subject was irksome to her husband; and hastened to change it.

"Lady Atherstone? That reminds me, Arthur—when you next go to Templestowe, you must drive me over. I haven't called there since they returned."

The banker was cast into a dilemma. He had certainly thought of taking that road, and no later than the morrow; but he had meant to ride it alone; and he felt that he would rather trust to the chapter of accidents to bring about the meeting with Lena, than meet her—thus accompanied. So, after a little hesitation, he answered vaguely that "he could not say when he could get over there, as he had a good deal to do, and did not like to waste a hunting-day." Then he rose up hurriedly.

"I shall go down to Chisholm's for an hour, Emma. All the barrack-party dine there to-night. They may march at a day's notice; and I want to see Colville before he goes."

He did not wait for a reply: yet he paused on his way to the door, as if half repenting; and turned to print a conciliating kiss on his wife's forehead. She smiled once again, and let him go without a remark; but she felt, in reality, more uneasy than ever.

To leave his home after dinner, for bachelor society, was so utterly foreign to Arthur's habits, that this in itself would have disquieted her; but—speculate as she would—not a glimmer of the real truth flashed across Emma's mind. If she could not thoroughly respect her volatile consort, she did at least thoroughly trust him; and would have staked her life on his loyalty, through the warmest of his past philanderings. Moreover, perhaps the last point towards which her misgivings would have tended was Templestowe. Though she was quite content with her position, her

ideas respecting it were rather lowly than exalted;
and—setting morality altogether aside—she would
never have imputed to her husband the audacity of
aspiring to Lady Atherstone's good graces. The
quiet, almost haughty, indifference of Lena's manner
in general society would have strengthened Mrs.
Corbett's security in this quarter, had it been less
complete.

In sober, placid natures like hers, jealousy is hard
to plant, and slow of growth; but, when it has once
taken root, it is scarcely to be plucked out either by
force or cunning. After twisting it hither and thither,
Mrs. Corbett got no nearer to the solving of her puzzle;
and was fain to wait, as patiently as she might, till
time or chance should put her in the right road.

That same evening there was another conjugal
*tête-à-tête*—at Templestowe. But the serenity of this
last was not impaired by ever so light a cloud.

The one topic that might have caused embarrassment, had been got over on their way home from
hunting in a dozen words. That straight-going
*brusquerie* of Ralph Atherstone's had its advantages
sometimes; at all events, the way in which, without
any notice or preamble, he, so to speak, took the dreaded
subject by the throat, was an intense relief to Lena.

"I've known more disappointing days," he said,
in answer to a remark of hers as to their persistent
ill-luck; "for I'm not the least disappointed in—
Mr. Glynne. My dear, you don't suppose this matter
has once troubled me, since you spoke of it so frankly?
Nevertheless, I'm glad, very glad, that we've met. If
you can't guess why, I'm not clever enough to explain
it to you: but you *can* guess, I think. You behaved
so perfectly, too. I hope we shall see a good deal
more of him, if he stays long at Erriswell."

She never knew exactly what she answered; but
it was probably as much to the purpose as if she had
studied it beforehand, for Ralph looked more than
satisfied.

Lena's homœopathic remedy, as happens with many other nostrums, did, on this first time of trial, work wonders. Before the afternoon was far advanced, she had become her own indifferent self again —had interchanged a conventional sentence or two with Caryl Glynne, who loitered by her side for a few minutes on his way back to join Mrs. Devereux—had listened later, with infinite composure, to a confidential rhapsody from Cissy, the subject whereof you may guess—and had excused herself cleverly to Mrs. Malcolm, for being unable to join the proposed luncheon-party at Erriswell.

Also it was with a tranquillity, not altogether feigned, that she faced her husband at dinner. She was buoyed up, you see, by the consciousness of having said and done, as nearly as possible, the right things at the right times; and this is no bad counterfeit of an approving conscience—though it *is* a counterfeit, of course.

" Didn't you hear from your mother, this morning ?" Ralph asked, when they were alone. "When does she think of coming to us ?"

They had been rather silent of late; and, from Lena's start, it seemed that she was roused from a reverie.

" My mother ?" she said, a little vaguely. "Oh yes! I remember now. We must not expect her for six weeks at least. She has behaved so badly to her old friends in the North, that she's bound to make them some amends, now."

" I'm sorry for that," he answered. " I always like you to have a companion at this season, my dear. It's dull for you, being left so much alone. Perhaps I ought to think it would be duller yet, if it were the other way; but—I don't, you see."

" I should hope not," she said. " Indeed, it is not that. I manage very well by myself; but there's no saying when one would tire of one's own society ; and I'm so used to her, that I own I do miss my mother sometimes. I suppose it would be a mere form, to ask Philip and Marian to come to us just now : they cannot have half got through their visits?"

Lord Atherstone's lip curled, as it not seldom did at mention of his heir.

"I should think it's just possible," he said, "that their friends would be more easily contented than Mrs. Shafton's; at least, Philip's friends—for Marian, no doubt, is rather popular. You might try the experiment, though. But are you quite sure that you would like it?"

"Quite sure," she replied—with such a hearty sincerity, that it surprised as well as gratified her lord.

Cannot you comprehend the secret of her earnestness? There are dangers, not the less real because they are intangible, under the shadow of which a woman would liefer see a true woman at her side than the starkest champion that ever drew blade. But often she, who seemed sent by Heaven to succour, has proved the devil's hireling, and well worthy of her wages.

Not alone in its cruel treachery, stands the deed wrought by the mill-dams of Binnorie. And the murderess, after watching the last bubble break over the eddy in which a life has gone down, hies her home; and smooths her hair, and busks herself in brave apparel; and sits in hall among her fellows—marvelling or lamenting, with the rest, when tidings come of the disaster. And the justice, recorded in the old ballad, is too poetical frequently to recur. Yet, mayhap, some day, the tumult of many voices, each laden with its own accusation, will not smother one weak wail—

> Woe to my sister, false Helen!

As Lady Atherstone had supposed, the Ashleighs were still in the midst of their autumnal visiting-round; and the next house on their list was one of the most attractive: nevertheless, when the proposi-

tion came, it was not put aside at once, as one to
be declined as a matter of course.  Indeed, Marian
pondered over the note gravely, before she communi-
cated its contents to her husband; nor did she do
this, till she had fully made up her own mind as to
the answer.

The idea of falling back on Templestowe, when
free quarters were to be had elsewhere, seemed at
first to Philip too absurd for serious discussion; and
he was inclined to be severe on 'the convenient way
in which people freed their consciences, by sending
impossible invitations.'  Marian, as was her wont, let
him have ample line; and it was not till he stopped
and sulked, that she cautiously wound in her reel.

"Impossible—dear?  I don't quite see that."

"Don't you?" he snapped, going off again at a
tangent.  "Then you're short-sighted, for once.  Is
it likely that we're going to break half-a-dozen engagements, for no other earthly reason than because
Lady Atherstone feels dull at Templestowe?  I
wouldn't do it, if she were my own, instead of my
step-mother."

"I dare say not," she retorted.  "But—suppose
there was a reason, Philip, besides duty.  You know
very well, if it would help you with the borough,
you'd give up the pleasantest visit without a murmur.  I don't see why private interests should not be
considered sometimes, as well as parliamentary.  Now
—I can't tell you why, so don't ask me—I've an idea
that it's very much to our interest to watch how things
are going on at Templestowe, whenever we have an
opportunity.  And here *is* an opportunity, you must
own."

Could she not have told him why?  Possibly not.
Yet, by a curious coincidence, the day before, had
come a chatty letter from her trusty cousin and
counsellor.

"It would be odd," Kerneguy wrote, "if the scrap
of a *libretto*, that I copied out for you some time since,

should be worked out after all. I heard last night, that Caryl Glynne had passed through town from abroad, on his way to Erriswell, purposing 'to tarry there certain days.' Do you remember, in 'Ivanhoe,' France's message to Prince John? *A bon entendeur salut.*"

A very frank, outspoken person, Marian Ashleigh —perhaps a little too much so at times; but 'one was sure to hear the whole truth from her whether palatable or not.' So said the chorus of her kinsfolk and familiars; and they surely must have known best. Possibly, therefore, she could not, if she would, have avowed a special motive for now visiting Templestowe. As for Philip—he would as soon have suspected his wife of absolute dishonesty, as of diplomacy on her own account. He thought she was only reciting again part of the lesson that she had dinned into his ears pretty often, touching the expediency of their keeping well with the reigning powers.

"We're very good friends as it is," he grumbled; "and what use is there in watching, or what is there to watch? It's such tiresome work, too."

"Perhaps it is," she assented; "and perhaps it's not fair either that you should have tasks to do in your holiday-time. What do you say to *my* accepting the invitation? You might join me there later, after doing Westlands and two or three other pleasant places."

'A most good-natured person, Marian Ashleigh,' again chanted the chorus. No doubt. Yet, without a grain of compunction, she suggested this compromise, by which Westlands and the other 'pleasant places' were saddled with the visitation—pure and simple—of the member for Heslingford.

Philip was rather taken aback. The fact was, he had got so used to his invisible and impalpable leading-strings, that the idea of walking entirely after his own devices, for ever so brief a space, was rather startling. But he was the last person to admit this even to himself; and, if any such misgiving had crossed his mind, the mere spirit of contradiction would have made him run counter thereto. Moreover, in spite of his over-weening self-esteem, he had twice or thrice been haunted by an uneasy doubt, whether their welcome in divers places might not be attributable to his wife's popularity rather than to his own; and he was tempted to put this to the proof. Something else, too—absurd as it may sound—moved him to listen to Marian's proposal.

To the staidest and soberest of benedicts, in good bodily health—unless his shyness verge on moral helplessness — there is something alluring in the notion of temporary independence. I have no doubt that the Dean of Uttoxeter, when he comes up alone for the May meetings, treads the flags with an airier gait, and, so to speak, cocks his broad beaver more jauntily, than if there were by his side the stately and substantial form in whose company he paces to and fro under the cathedral elms.

Now this uxorious dignitary is not more incapable of misusing his freedom, than was Mr. Ashleigh. How he conducted his courtship was, as has been aforesaid, a puzzle to those who knew him well; and a flirtation, of the most ethereal nature, seemed still more out of his line. Nevertheless, he knew that at Westlands he was sure to encounter one Ellen Cadogan, for whom he had cherished a kind of weakness in days gone by; and who, if the Dalwhinnie wooing had not sped, might perchance have sate in Marian's seat. They had been very good friends since—not the less so because the lady was still unmarried; for, though in the loftiest flight of his conceit Philip never actually imputed this celibacy to himself, there was something pleasant in the idea of no other man's having been found worthy to occupy the place that he, doubtless, might have filled: whether Ellen had eagerly aspired to such an honour, he was not too careful to inquire. So there did, perchance, float be-

fore his eyes visions of confidential *causeries*, indulgent glances, and sympathetic smiles, the sweetness
of which—in all innocence, be it understood—he could
better savour alone.

Finally, in his own ungracious fashion—he always
made a fuss, if not a merit, of any concession whatsoever—he consented to let his wife have her way;
and, within a fortnight, she appeared at Templestowe.

# CHAPTER XXXI.

IT is the part of a good general to survey a likely battle-ground long before the lines are set in array, and not to hold it wasted pains even if, by force of circumstances, the issue should ultimately be tried elsewhere. Those black eyes of Marian Ashleigh's found full employment, you may be sure, when she was once established in her old quarters; neither was she in anywise disappointed, when day succeeded day without her watchfulness being rewarded. Every post brought her letters about her broken engagements, upbraiding or plaintive, according to the temper of the writers and the extent of their aggravation; and descriptions of entertainments in progress or contemplation, brought out in tantalising relief the dulness of Templestowe.

Now, country-house life, as it was understood by the friends with whom she had broken faith, being specially to Marian's taste, she was keenly alive to what she sacrificed; nevertheless, she did not for an instant repent; and tossed aside the most tempting of all these missives a little contemptuously, like one who has been offered for some valuable possession an inadequate price. Nothing, in truth, could exceed the kindness of the baron's reception; whilst Marian was almost surprised by the warmth of Lena's welcome. Indeed, she immediately began to speculate whether some special reason must not underlie this cordiality. Was it possible that domestic solitude had become intolerably irksome to Lady Atherstone? This in itself would be a notable point; but Marian felt sure this was not all; and as each night, alone in her chamber, she, so to speak, cast up the accounts of the day, more confident grew her quiet smile. That she kept her ears open, too, both at home and abroad, it is needless to say; and she had leisure to pay and receive many visits; for she herself was no horsewoman, and positively insisted on Lena's not altering on her account any hunting arrangement.

If the advent of Caryl Glynne had been comparatively unnoticed, his after-proceedings had already caused some stir in Loamshire; though the finger of rumour, thus far, pointed in a very different direction from what Lady Marian had reckoned on. Partly from indulgence, partly because they had got used to her vagaries, the county-folk were disposed to grant Mrs. Devereux large licence of action; but there are limits to any privileges whatsoever; and Cissy just now seemed to be imbued with the spirit of the daring demagogue who, to the question, " How much treason can a man write without risking the halter?" answered, "I am trying!" Even the most charitable and careless of observers guessed that the wayward dame was now playing with a much more dangerous toy than she was used to handle; and that, if she took not good heed, her dainty fingers might be seared to the bone, before all was ended.

Within forty-eight hours of that meet at Wilton, Major Colville had marched with his detachment; but, before he went, there had been time for a last interview, in which there were spoken, on one side at least, hot and bitter words. Certainly, the hussar did not aspire to be avenged in this fashion, and, possibly, he was too good-hearted to bear malice long; but, had he been more vindictive, he might have been satisfied with the retribution that seemed imminent. Mrs. Devereux's acquaintance with Glynne might almost be reckoned by hours; yet there was over her already an influence the like of which, in all her volatile life, she had never known.

> Lightly won and lightly lost,
> A fair good night to thee!

This had been the burden of her song heretofore; but she could chant that gay burden no longer. Her ingenious little arts of tormenting were useless here; it appeared impossible to make Caryl jealous, and next to impossible to make him angry: but she was more afraid of one of his cool, sarcastic glances, than of the keenest reproaches that had hitherto reached her ears. He did not woo her after any fashion to which she had been accustomed; for he seldom, if ever, made pretty speeches; neither did he appear specially thankful for any signs of her favour. But the subtle flattery of some of his careless words was harder to resist than the eloquence of his predecessors; and one of his languid smiles outweighed, as reward, all their fluent gratitude. Furthermore, there was added the new incitement—of no mean power on one of Cissy's temperament—of difficulty, not to say danger.

For the first time in their married life, Devereux took upon himself to object strongly to his fair wife's amusements; and showed it. It was only a vicarious resentment, after all, that rankled in his heart; but it was none the less stubborn for that. Colville was one of his prime favourites, and he held that the latter had been very hardly dealt with. In common kindness, when the time must needs have been so short, Cissy ought to have waited till Godfrey's back was turned before filling up his place; and, though Dick was incapable of keeping up a quarrel with his own wife, he was quite equal to cherish dislike against the second cause of her fickleness. Outwardly, as well as inwardly, the two differed so widely, that this in itself was enough to account for a certain amount of antipathy on the Driver's part; indeed, the other's voice and manner were a sufficient cause of offence to him.

"Godfrey was a bit of a don," he used to grumble;

" but he could speak out like a man, at all events, instead of mincing his words like a girl."

There was something else, too, in the background. Dick was wont to say of himself, that ' he was not quite such a fool as he looked : ' he might have denied, with perfect truth, that he was a fool at all. He was only a simple, single-minded man, who, when he trusted, trusted not by halves ; and who had let the reins of government slip through his fingers, rather from over-confidence, than from indolence or weakness. Neither did he now, for one instant, distrust his wife's power of taking excellent care of herself ; nevertheless, he did feel that she was far safer with the audacious admirers who, after a week's acquaintance, made free with her pet name, than with the quiet personage who—at least, when others were by—never waxed familiar.

It was utterly impossible that Glynne could remain blind to this state of things ; but it did not seem to disquiet or discourage him. On non-hunting days some pretext or another almost always took him over to Hunsden ; and he never, as some folks do, attempted to ignore the fact that the house had a master ; but, whether the other's temper was fair or foul, made no sort of difference in Caryl's courtesy. Only sometimes, whilst he watched the lowering face over against him, there would come upon his own a look of amused anticipation, such as a *majo* may wear, who, leaning over the barrier, looks right down into a pair of sombre red eyes, that will flash furiously by-and-by under the sting of the *banderillos.*

The Driver's displeasure had small terrors for his dauntless spouse ; and the more he sulked, the more sunnily she smiled on the object of his aversion. In truth, her past flirtations had begun to pall upon her from their very facility ; and about this one there promised to be just difficulty enough to give it a delicious tinge of romance ; for the idea of Dick's absolutely controlling or thwarting her never crossed her mind. The giddy little head was fairly turned at last: even in those few weeks, Cissy had contrived to supply a decent quantity of thread for the spindles of the scandal-mongers, and promised to furnish more.

Now, Marian Ashleigh—blameless herself on the count of coquetry—had few feelings in common with Mrs. Devereux, and they had never been thrown much together; but, on the whole, she rather liked than disliked the latter, and, in a negligent sort of way, regretted her recklessness: yet she would scarcely have stretched forth her hand to avert its consequences. Another idyll interested her much more nearly; though neither was this what she had gone forth for to see.

Before she had been a week at Templestowe, she had detected Arthur Corbett's infatuation; and had begun to speculate whither it would lead. That it was entirely one-sided, she recognised speedily. Watching Lena's face narrowly, she had never seen it light up when Arthur was announced; and more than once, after he had departed, she had sunk back wearily, like one who has somewhat overstrained her powers to play out a part—not wholly distasteful perhaps, but a part all the same. If the domestic peace of Templestowe was ever to be wrecked, it was plain the storm-wind would not blow from that quarter; nevertheless, Corbett was ere long the means of casting light on certain other of Marian's doubts —a light that made her feel sure that her vigilance was not exercised in vain.

One day the banker had ridden over to Templestowe, avowedly on business, and was apparently surprised to find that Lord Atherstone was shooting elsewhere; however, he was easily persuaded to stay luncheon; and the three sat down to that meal very amicably. He and Lady Marian were old acquaintances, of course; and it was the most natural thing in the world, that she should begin to question their visitor about Loamshire news.

" There isn't much stirring," was the reply; "though
I think people will begin to talk soon, if they haven't
begun already, about the proceedings at Hunsden.
Mrs. Devereux is a cleverish person, no doubt; but, I
fear, some day she'll go too far."

"What do you mean?" Lady Marian asked, arch-
ing her brows. " It's only one of her usual flirtations,
I suppose: surely Loamshire must have got accustomed to them by this time."

" This is an unusual one, I fancy," Arthur answered,
" or Devereux wouldn't sulk over it so. They say,
that jolly horse-laugh of his hasn't been heard for a
fortnight. You must remember, that rather a peculiar
person is now first favourite."

Lady Atherstone looked up, with a cheek certainly
paler than its wont, and a hostile light in her eyes.

"I think *you* might have remembered," she said,
" that Mrs. Devereux is my nearest friend in these
parts, and that it cannot be pleasant to me to hear
her maligned."

His countenance fell; and, though he made shift
to answer submissively, he could not force a smile.

"A thousand pardons. I ought to have remembered that; and also, perhaps, that Mr. Glynne is
an old acquaintance of yours. Indeed, I should be
very sorry to malign any one; I only repeated common report, without risking any opinion of my own."

"No, you asserted nothing," she retorted, " you
only 'feared.' They're so refreshing—these fine dis-
tinctions. If Cissy were here, I'm sure she would
appreciate your delicacy. Do let me thank you on
her behalf."

It cost him a great effort; but he did contrive to
maintain his mock humility.

"You are rather severe, Lady Atherstone. If
Mrs. Devereux were in your place, I think she
would judge me less harshly. Have you seen her
lately?"

A simple question enough—but it seemed to cover

a taunt; for Lena's colour rose, and she bit her lip as if to check a rash reply. Lady Marian glanced inquiringly from one to the other, as though not in the least understanding what was passing. And how thoroughly she understood it all!

"You're not going to quarrel?" she said, in her blunt way. "It's much ado about nothing, depend upon it. I didn't know Mr. Glynne was an old acquaintance of yours, Lena. It is rather odd that *he* hasn't found time to call, certainly. I wish he would: I own I'm curious to see him, though I don't expect to see at all a 'peculiar person.'"

The brief excitement was past already, and Lady Atherstone answered quite listlessly,

"Mr. Glynne has called"—she did not state that he was riding with Mrs. Devereux—"but we happened to be out. I believe he dines here, with the Malcolms, on Monday. You'll drive this afternoon, Marian? My ponies want exercise. But you needn't hurry away, Mr. Corbett; I want to show you the changes I've made in the north conservatory."

*Le bel* Arthur made his peace, somehow, among the flowers; and he was radiant with complacency when he took his leave. Would he have carried off so high a crest, if he could have read the meaning of Marian Ashleigh's eyes, as they followed his retreating figure, or overheard her whispered soliloquy?—

"These country coxcombs! They are almost too stupid for decoy-ducks."

# CHAPTER XXXII.

I WAS once acquainted with a wise and witty divine, who, for constructing a dialogue out of the most unpromising materials, possessed a talent probably unmatched since the days of Socrates; indeed, conversation was not a pleasure, but a necessity, of his existence; and, much as he loved the sound of his own well-tuned voice, he loved not to hear it quite alone. In the absence of another interlocutor, he would assuredly have welcomed any harmless idiot, capable of answering 'Yes' and 'No' at random. It was a great point, he was wont to say, to open a discourse with such smooth generalities as could not easily be controverted, or offend the prejudices of the most innocent stranger; and, to this end, it was proper to provide one's self with formulas suitable to every occasion. For instance—there are few civilised countries in which one would not be safe in remarking to a fellow-traveller, "There's a good deal of land about here;" or, "At this season of the year we usually have some sort of weather."

Now, the principle which this eminent man carried only into dialectics, influenced, in almost all the relations of life, the Reverend Hubert Ashleigh. He had invariably shown himself most kind and cordial towards Philip and his wife—affecting still to take a guardianly interest in the former's welfare; yet, somehow, Marian rather dreaded and distrusted the placid parson. She never could divest herself of the idea that he was playing some sort of game; but what game, or for what stakes, was a question quite

beyond her.   She scarcely thought it likely that
much useful or important information would be
gleaned in that quarter: nevertheless, on the occasion of Hubert's first visit to Templestowe (he chanced
to be absent during the earlier part of her stay) she
resolved to put this to proof; and carried him off into
the gardens, on pretext of delivering certain messages from Philip on Heslingford business.   When
these had been sufficiently discussed, Marian walked
on for awhile in silence.   Suddenly she turned on her
companion.

"Hubert, how do you think things are going on
here?"

Every one knows how difficult these quick, point-
blank questions, with nothing to lead up to them,
are to parry.   But Hubert Ashleigh was one of those
provoking people who, under the most unlikely circumstances, always seem to have anticipated the
particular form of attack.   He did not even pretend
to hesitate; but answered with his wonted deliberation
—neither less nor more.

"Most satisfactorily, I should imagine; but, really,
my opinion isn't worth much; I've seen so little of
them lately.   My work at home is doubled since
our branch-line was made, and I've just taken a
holiday, you know."

"Yes, I know," she said, with a touch of sarcasm.
"The parish must be a good deal more troublesome
than it used to be.   But I suppose you hear, Hubert,
if you don't see.   Now, I wish to learn what you do
hear.   Surely, that's only natural."

"Perfectly so; only I hear so little either.   It's
generally a case of give-and-take with the gossips;
and, as they would carry away nothing from our dull
parsonage, they bring next to nothing thither.   Besides, what would there be to gossip about here?"

"What, indeed!" she said.   "Only tattlers will
trade on slight capital sometimes.   For instance—
do people never ask, what makes Arthur Corbett

ride this road twice a week, instead of once a quarter?"

The Reverend Hubert's serene blue eyes opened somewhat wider in faint, half-reproachful surprise.

"Arthur Corbett?" he repeated. "No, I never heard that question asked ; and if I had, I should have expected to hear the same answer—business, of course. He is virtually agent to this estate, as you are aware."

"Then the estate, now, wants almost as much look-ing after as your parish. Of course, he could not possibly have any other attraction ; not, for example, *les beaux yeux de ma belle-mère ?*"

The divine drew himself up, and actually frowned.

"You're right in not putting that suggestion into decent English; and I should be sorry to think it was of your own making."

Marian laughed outright. If she stood in some dread of her politic cousin, it was not professionally that he overawed her.

"Your reverence need not look scandalised ; I didn't mean to be uncharitable. I've always thought Arthur Corbett too weak to be dangerous, and too honest to mean harm ; and I think so still : but that doesn't prevent his perpetually dangling ; and this might be only a little more serious case than common."

"Much more serious," he answered gravely. "Con-sidering Ralph's age and position, it would be an unpardonable impertinence, such as not even rumour, much less his friends, have imputed to Corbett yet. But rumour hasn't spared all our neighbours, I'm sorry to say. I can't deny, that I've heard talk about Hunsden and Erriswell."

Marian shot one of her swift side-glances at the speaker. She could not be certain that the faintest intelligence gleamed in his eyes ; yet, somehow, she fancied that Hubert Ashleigh not only had sus-picions, but that his and her own pointed towards

T

the same quarter, and that he had peered—perhaps much deeper than herself—into Lena Atherstone's past.

These instantaneous inductions are quite inexplicable, and, looking back on them, you could no more trace them, step by step, than you could count the grains of an exploding train; but it is strange how seldom they miss the mark : when they do, it is usually by over-shooting it.

Marian had great pertinacity of purpose ; and, despite the evasion—for so, no doubt, it was intended —she would have probed her cousin a little farther, had it not been for this sudden conviction. As it was, she changed her plan at once. If the parties should ever be defined in the family *imbroglio*, it would be time enough then to ascertain on which side this stubborn neutral meant to range himself; at the present juncture it might be rash to inquire, ever so cautiously, where his sympathies lay. So, composing her countenance, she shook her head.

"What a pity it is—a pity for the Malcolms, not less than for others; for I hear they're such nice people. They can scarcely be aware of what is going on ; it would be almost kind if somebody were to warn them."

"Kind, but quite impracticable. These matters are very delicate to handle, and one may do worse than merely give offence by meddling. For myself, if I held the cure of souls either at Hunsden or Erriswell, I should hardly venture to interfere. Mrs. Devereux has had great luck hitherto, better than she has deserved, I'm afraid. Let us hope it will last. Mind, I know nothing of Mr. Glynne, except by common report; but I do think he would be much better abroad; better, perhaps, anywhere than— here."

Once more their eyes met; and Marian's conviction was rather confirmed. Nevertheless, in spite of her prudent resolves, and though she was not wholly dissatisfied with the brief interview, as they were about to re-enter the conservatory, she could not refrain from firing just one parting shot.

"Then, Hubert, you think, after all, Monseigneur took a wise step last winter ?"

It may be that the parson thought his fair cousin's patience deserved some reward, or it may be that, in spite of constant practice, talking by rule somewhat wearied him ; at any rate, for once, he allowed a shade of meaning to creep into his benevolent smile.

"Wise ? Well—that is much to say ; though perhaps it can hardly be unwise, if a man, at Ralph's time of life, by any innocent and lawful means, secures a whole year of happiness, even if some sorrow should ensue. And why should there be sorrow here ? His character is wonderfully altered for the better already ; and she seems quite comfortable in her new position, and quite equal to it. And I am sure, dear Marian, the way in which you and Philip have smoothed things for her, does you both great credit. Here she comes. Lady Atherstone, if I were not a poor parish-priest, I should envy you your new gardener. I've never seen the place in such beauty, so late in the season ; and I knew it, I fear, before you were born."

Almost simultaneously, in point of time, with the colloquy just recorded, another, not much longer, but decidedly livelier, took place elsewhere.

Of the two drawing-rooms at Hunsden, the inner one was virtually a boudoir ; for within its precincts Cissy reigned absolutely paramount, — allowing neither male nor female visitors to intrude without special leave. From this interdict the master of the house himself was not exempt ; and, though he grumbled sometimes, he rarely ventured to break it : indeed, certain vivid recollections of what befell, when twice or thrice he had been unlucky enough to disturb an after-hunting siesta, sufficed to teach him caution.

It was a cheerful room, by no means luxuriously

furnished, and decorated with fewer feminine knick-knacks and more sporting appurtenances than are usually found in such apartments: indeed, even the few pictures on the walls all savoured more or less of woodcraft. Notwithstanding this, it was a thoroughly comfortable, cozy place, and evidently adapted to a two-handed chat, such as was now in progress.

Everything had gone on amicably, to say the least of it, up to a certain point, when in answer to Cissy's question, "What are you going to do on Monday?" Glynne replied—

"We don't hunt then? Anything you like till late in the afternoon. But, you know, we dine at Templestowe. You don't mean to say you're not going?"

The colour, always quick to rise, flashed up in her cheek directly.

"I do mean it; and this is the very first I've heard of your engagement. You must break it though; for I want you particularly that evening. We have some stupid people coming here, and I can't face them alone."

Glynne smiled placidly; he was too old an actor not to understand the meaning of these royal bespeaks at very short notice.

"You must face them, I'm afraid. It's a bore, of course; but, after all, it doesn't much matter, when you've once got your company-manners on. I can't possibly throw over Templestowe; it's the first time I've been formally invited there."

Even her brief experience had taught her the folly of losing her temper with Caryl; and she tried hard to master it now.

"You might surely make this sacrifice to me—if it is a sacrifice. It's the first I've ever asked of you. I daresay you had no special invitation, after all."

"Well, I had, as it happens; at least, Lord Atherstone was good enough to repeat it verbally, out hunting three days ago. Not that that makes much difference : it's a case of conscience, in the country, to keep dinner-engagements."

"Conscience!" she repeated in high disdain. "I wonder the word doesn't choke you. Conscience has about as much to do with it, as the baron had with sending out those invitations. Perhaps you will say next, that you see nothing odd in *my* having received none ?"

"On the contrary," he retorted with infinite coolness, "I do think it rather odd—nearly as odd as that you and my lady should have met so seldom lately, considering what great allies you have been by all accounts."

Her colour deepened, but this time not angrily.

"And whose fault is that ?" she said almost in a whisper. "If you don't remember how my time has been taken up for the last three weeks, I am not going to remind you. And yet I'm certain, quite certain, that Lena is not offended."

His face softened, though it was smiling still.

"That was rather an ungrateful speech of mine, I own. I daresay you're right, and that no offence has been taken. Very likely my lady thought the distance too great in this uncertain weather, or—likelier still—she never thought about it at all."

Never thought about it ? Why, Lena had lain awake for hours debating the question whether, to save herself a little more pain, it was worth while to risk the rousing of Cissy's quick temper, and, perchance, her suspicions to boot; and, with shame and contrition, had given way to the temptation at last; for it was a temptation of no mean order—the certainty of such an evening as she would thus secure. She never dreamt of deriving any special advantage from Caryl's society, or of interchanging ten words to which the whole world might not listen; but the relief would be intense of watching him for a few hours, not wholly engrossed by a comparative stranger. And it was so easily managed too ; for, doubtless,

Hunsden lay on the extremest limits of a dinner-
drive, and her husband, she knew, would be rather
pleased than vexed by the omission of these guests.
No wonder that she yielded, reviling her own cowardice
the while.

Mrs. Devereux guessed at nothing of all this : but
the common-sense, of which she had a fair share,
though it usually lay in abeyance, revolted against
the absurdity of that last excuse ; and her slender
thread of self-command snapped in twain.

" And you expect me to believe that ?" she cried
out passionately. " Why don't you bribe me to be
quiet with sugar-plums ? I've always fancied that
you and Lena knew more of each other than either
of you liked to own ; and now I am sure of it—quite
sure."

The sugar-plum suggestion was by no means an
inapt one ; for Glynne was observing her just then
with a lazy amusement, just as a man might watch
the vagaries of a pretty fractious child, for whose
good or evil training he is not responsible.

" No," he replied after a short pause. " I dropped
expectations, great and small, years ago ; or I should
have been even worse off than I am. And life's not
long enough for argument. But, as soon as you're
rational—I don't say reasonable—again, you will see
what nonsense you're talking. You're rather fond of
quoting my past misdeeds. Now—take your own
view of the question, and suppose half the stories
true—is it likely that, if things were or ever had been
as you suspect, I should have been *here* so often—or
be here now, for that matter ? The road from Erriswell to Templestowe is no longer, or harder to find,
than that which leads to Hunsden. It's a mistake,
*ma mie*, to remind me that, in common civility, I
ought to have travelled the one rather oftener ; and,
in common prudence, the other rather seldomer "

There was no menace in his steady eyes, but a
kind of authority, before which hers drooped, evi-

dently not for the first time : she cast down her arms at once.

"Don't let us quarrel," she pleaded. "Of course you're right about Monday ; and I won't bear Lena any grudge, though we *have* dined and slept at Temple-stowe before this. Only don't speak so hardly ; I'd rather you spoke harshly at any time. And—and—you're not angry, Caryl ?"

Mention has before been made of the fatal facility with which this lady glided into the Christian names of her male acquaintances, and accepted the return of the compliment ; but she seemed to pronounce this special one with a hesitation akin to shyness. And yet, how her lips lingered over it !

Too near, Cissy—much too near the crater, now. The smoke ahead curls no longer in white playful waves, but rolls lurid with the reek of the nether fires ; and the crust that your delicate feet are pressing, is scarce thick enough to cover the scalding ooze.

# CHAPTER XXXIII.

KERNEGUY had rightly presumed that his cousin's knowledge of Caryl Glynne had, till a year ago, been grounded only on flying rumours, not likely to dwell in her memory ; and, though they had talked it over since, Archie had not himself been able—perhaps he was not altogether willing—to enlighten her further on the subject; nor was it likely that she could have acquired much information elsewhere. Nevertheless, she had carefully built up her own conception of the man ; and, if no deeper motive had been at work, would doubtless have looked forward to that Monday evening with a certain eagerness.

In its main elements it was a very ordinary dinner-party ; including the usual squires and squiresses, a clerical pair besides the Hubert Ashleighs, Swinton Swarbrick, Jasper Knowsley, and a couple of the dragoons who had replaced Colville's detachment at Heslingford. Though Lady Marian was a guest now at Templestowe, she was sufficiently at home to waive her precedence ; and she followed her father-in-law into the dining-room, leaning on Mr. Malcolm's arm. She was surprised, and not ill-pleased, to find the chair on her left filled by Caryl Glynne, who had been told off to Mrs. Ashleigh.

Though they are chiefly used abroad, you have probably seen those treacherous *lorgnettes* that, by an arrangement of side-glasses, enable you to scan the boxes on either hand, at your pleasure, whilst you are supposed to be intent on the stage in front. Marian could accomplish this optical stratagem with-

out the aid of lenses; and, before she appeared to
glance in that direction, she had so perused every line
of Glynne's face, that she could easily have sketched
it afterwards from memory. Indeed, she had no
mean skill both with brush and pencil; and, purely
from an artistic point of view, there was attraction for
her in his rare perfection of feature, enhanced by its
soft silvery setting.

Born with a singularly even temperament, and, in
the seclusion of her maiden life, exposed to few
temptations,—not even a passing fancy had ever
broken Marian's rest, up to the hour when, as a
matter of policy, well-weighed and duly debated, she
accepted Philip Ashleigh. Since then, if she was not
innocent of other offences, she had not failed, even
for one second, in her loyalty towards the husband of
her choice. Such as he was, he sufficed her; and she
would no more have dreamt of instituting in her own
mind comparisons, moral or physical, to his disadvantage, than she would of confuting him before the
world, or ridiculing him when his back was turned.
Nevertheless, looking furtively on this man's face,
and listening, without checking her own converse, to
his voice—in this, too, she was agreeably disappointed
—she was fain to allow that such of her weaker
sisters as had found both dangerous to their peace,
were not wholly despicable. No slight concession
from one who, from philosophy rather than prudery,
had small indulgence for feminine frailties.

But this softening of her mood, if softening it were,
neither diverted the course of Lady Marian's speculations, nor abated her vigilance. For a while—a
very long while—there was nothing to reward it.

When Caryl greeted Lady Atherstone, both had
seemed thoroughly at their ease; and now, though he
fed in a slow, dainty, Oriental fashion, Glynne was
evidently disposed to appreciate the efforts of the
Templestowe *chef*, and did all that was required of
him in the way of conversation. To be sure, this was

not much; for Mrs. Hubert Ashleigh, being a garrulous dame, was usually quite content if she could
secure an attentive listener. And, all the while, his
eyes never once wandered towards the head of the
table, where Lady Atherstone sat, looking serenely
bored; as was no wonder, considering that she was
flanked by Jasper Knowsley and Swinton Swarbrick;
the first of whom was notoriously shy and taciturn,
whilst the last favoured his society with few remarks
till his huge appetite was appeased.

Still Marian was not discouraged. She would have
been almost disappointed if she had detected in Lena
any of the *minauderies*, or in Caryl any of the imprudences, by which underbred folk are wont to betray
themselves. Indeed, she so far accepted the position
that, finding her right-hand neighbour rather impracticable—Malcolm seemed strangely silent and
preoccupied this evening—she sought entertainment
on her left, and found it, too. For, howsoever they
might differ on other points, she and Caryl had at
least one feeling in common—a genuine love of art.
Discussing the Erriswell pictures, for most of which
he was accountable, they soon made this discovery;
and over this safe neutral ground they wandered so
pleasantly hither and thither, that Marian was almost
sorry when the signal of departure was given; and
afterwards had to sustain, to her intense amusement,
Mrs. Ashleigh's reproaches for having poached on
the latter's conversational preserves.

The men closed up, of course, round Lord Atherstone when they were left to themselves; and the
change brought Swinton Swarbrick next to the captain of heavy horse from Heslingford, whom he
tackled at once on the subject nearest to his own heart.

" May I ask what you think of our hounds, sir?"—
he began with a grim civility; for he was far from
satisfied with the keenness of the new-comers—
" though, to be sure, you've had no great opportunity
for judging as yet."

Captain Clayton was a meek specimen of the plunger; and even in his bachelor-days—he had lately made an imprudent, though most charming marriage—had never been a mighty hunter; but this he cared not to confess, and coloured rather guiltily as he murmured something about "being hardly settled yet, but he hoped as the season went on" —etc.

"Settled!" the other retorted. "It don't take long to settle a small stud; and I suppose your horses were in condition when they got here; or they ought to have been. Everybody knows what sort of station Heslingford is: I've heard some of your fellows say it's almost too good for a detachment. Major Colville said so, for one; and he always thought himself very lucky to get it. Ah! that was something like a soldier. He was a great loss, I assure you—at least to most of us, though some didn't miss him half as much as he deserved."

He glanced sourly across the table at Caryl Glynne, who at that moment was intent on selecting the plumpest out of a dish of olives.

Jovial companion as he was, Swarbrick, as his best friends allowed, was somewhat too apt to wrangle, especially over the wine-cup, and was very pertinacious in his prejudices. But more than mere prejudice was rankling now in his ample breast. He had known Devereux from childhood, and had ever been among the hottest of Cissy's partizans; and perhaps he was more at home at Hunsden than at any other place in Loamshire; though, for the last three weeks, he had not set foot within those doors. It was natural that he should look with disfavour on the man who seemed likely to bring on that cheery, if ill-ordered, household, such a sorrow as had not lighted on it yet. Finding the challenge of his angry eyes unanswered, he snorted, and broke out again.

"And how do you like our country, Mr. Glynne?

*You*'ve been out often enough to give an opinion, at all events."

If he had said—" once or twice too often "—in so many words, the speaker's meaning would not have been more apparent; but Caryl only smiled lazily, and picked out another choice specimen, as he made answer,—

" I like the country very well. I should like it rather better if the grass came a little oftener, and the fences a little seldomer. It takes some time to get used to being always in the air."

The other caught at the handle of offence, slight as it was, with an absurd eagerness.

" That's what all the swells say," he growled; " at least all except the very straightest goers, like poor Colville, for instance. Why don't they stop in their own countries, then, if they're so hard to please ?"

Jasper Knowsley shot a warning glance at his prime minister; and Lord Atherstone frowned.

" That's a curious way of arguing," he interposed; " first to press a man for his opinion, and then to quarrel with him for giving it. If strangers don't abuse our country at first, it's about as much as we can expect. There is much to be said in favour of our light ploughs; but it takes time to find out what a scent they carry. I really believe, though, we show fewer blank days than they do down in the grass. You'll please Swarbrick by allowing that much, Mr. Glynne ?"

Though Caryl's courteous reply evidently did not quite appease the irate Swinton, it paved the way for harmless general talk, which went on till coffee was brought.

Mr. Malcolm's countenance, grave throughout the evening, had grown graver yet, whilst that passage of arms was pending. To him, at least, if to no other person present, the motive of Swarbrick's churlishness was clear. His notions on these subjects were quite sufficiently civilised, and he grudged

no man or woman their amusement—in reason; but
he had honest, old-fashioned ideas as to where the
flirtation-line ought to be drawn; and he had been
tormented of late with serious doubts as to whether
the limits had not been already overstepped, and
whether Caryl's reformation was as complete as he
had believed. These doubts, it now appeared, were
not confined to his own bosom; and, whilst he recognised this, the good Robin's brow waxed more
overcast. His conceptions of hospitality were on the
grand Colonial scale; and he was disposed to allow
the largest licence to any sojourner within his gates;
nevertheless, he was not minded to aid or abet, ever
so tacitly or remotely, an act of wrong-doing. Whilst
he pondered, the general move was made; and he
was fain to defer the sifting of these things to a more
convenient season.

The great drawing-room at Templestowe was one
of those square, uncompromising apartments that
keep all their tenants more or less *en évidence;* and
Glynne, lingering for a moment as he entered, took
in the arrangement of the party assembled there at a
glance.

In a remote corner sat Lady Atherstone, apparently
deep in discourse with Mrs. Ashleigh and the other
parsoness; for she never lifted her eyes, or once
looked towards the opening door. Nevertheless, he
made two or three steps in this direction before he
checked himself, and turned towards a sofa occupied
by Lady Marian and Mrs. Malcolm. They, too, were
conversing rather earnestly; and, as Caryl drew
near, the latter beckoned with her fan, as though
impatient of his dilatory approach. It was plain
enough, from Emily's manner, that her husband had
not confided to her his misgivings, and that she had
not yet begun to look on her cousin as even a possible delinquent.

" We've been discussing the dance question, Caryl,"
she began; " and, you'll be glad to hear, Lady Marian

quite takes your view of it. She won't allow that there's any danger of our being considered 'forward,' if we confine the invitations to those we know personally. Really, people have been so very kind, that these will make up almost as many as the rooms will comfortably hold; and a crowd in the country is such a mistake."

"I *am* glad to hear it," he answered, with a courteous smile; "for I spoke with a certain amount of diffidence, you'll remember. Robin's scruples won't stand for a moment, I'm sure, before such an authority."

Lady Marian smiled, in her turn, quite cordially.

"A poor authority, I'm afraid," she said, "but it's a disinterested opinion, at all events; for I gave up round dances when I married, to please Mr. Ashleigh, and square ones are no strong temptation. But I think it a capital idea; and the Loamshire *demoiselles* owe Mrs. Malcolm a testimonial, if only for the example's sake, and the pleasant variety to the set county balls. And the time suits admirably, especially as you've been thoughtful enough to provide a moon."

"My conscience is clear," Mrs. Malcolm observed, "and I believe I can answer for Robin's, now; but before it's quite—quite settled, I ought to consult Lady Atherstone. Don't you think so, Caryl?"

He raised his brows as though the question were superfluous.

"Clearly, if you have not done so already. She seems rather busy just now; but, no doubt, she'll be at leisure before the evening's over."

"There's nothing like settling these things at once," Marian said, decisively. "Mr. Glynne, I daresay you wouldn't mind asking Lady Atherstone to spare us just five minutes. There's no fear of offence being taken over there; for Alice Ashleigh's my cousin, you know, and Mrs. Cresswell's a very old friend"

Without a trace of discomposure or reluctance, Caryl nodded assent; but, as he lounged away to fulfil his mission, Marian's gaze followed him more eagerly than ever.

Till he actually stood at her side, Lena never checked her conversation, nor seemed aware of his approach; and this was in itself full of significance to Marian. The colloquial powers of either of the other occupants of that corner were by no means sufficient to account for such rapt attention on the part of their hostess. Yet, when at last she looked up, it was with a countenance serene as Caryl's, and she answered his smile with one every whit as conventional. Scarcely three sentences could have been interchanged, when Lady Atherstone rose, evidently to comply with the message. As Caryl stood aside to give her room to pass, Marian was sure that his lips moved. Lena did not pause for an instant, or turn her head, or answer a word; but, for the first time that evening, a change swept across her face. It lasted not so long as a light breath on a mirror, yet it was enough—more than enough—for the patient watcher, and she exulted in her heart; like the fowler who, ambushed near an eyrie, waits, till limbs wax stiff and eyelids heavy, for the coming of the eagle, and, seeing afar off a dark speck in air, knows that, if he do but keep warily hidden, a very little more will bring the bold, bright-eyed quarry within rifle range.

What would she not have given, to have overheard those few muttered syllables? And yet they were strangely simple ones—too simple, one would think, to set any woman's heart-strings quivering—

"Rather hard work."

To any other ears, the words might have carried no deeper meaning than that the speaker had been unreasonably bored with the after-dinner talk, or overborne earlier in the evening by the garrulity of Mrs. Ashleigh, within the scope of which he now risked himself again. To Lena's they carried just this—

"I am growing weary of my part—that it was a part, and for whose sake it has been played, you have known, or ought to have known, all along—so weary that, if you do not aid a little, I may throw it up to-night."

That cipher-language! It is very easy to read, when one has mastered the key: only, its secrets are sometimes as costly as those of necromantic lore, and are bought at the price of an immortal soul.

If Glynne had been the Tempter incarnate, he could scarce have spoken those words more seasonably, nor would they have borne their fatal fruit more swiftly. They woke in Lena's breast an echo at once—the echo of a whisper that she had striven to silence sometimes, and sometimes listened to with a terrible eagerness—a whisper that murmured, "Despite all appearances, he has never forgotten the old days, nor me. I have only to beckon with my finger, or 'blink with my bonny brown eyes,' and he will come, to be dealt with as shall seem to me good; let who will say, 'Nay.'" She might have been braver and wiser a year—ay! or a month—ago; but the intermittent fever of the last few weeks had sadly minished her strength; and she could not shut her heart, now, against the flood of guilty happiness beating against its gates. It was wonderful, that she could manage to preserve her outward composure; for this, at least, she did achieve.

Whether, if Caryl's lips had remained quite dumb, she would have hesitated to countenance the Erriswell festivities, would be hard to say; as it was, she seconded Lady Marian's view of the case without reserve.

Malcolm must have seemed churlish if he had maintained his scruples in the face of such encouragement, especially when Lord Atherstone—laughing grimly at being consulted on such a question—cast the weight of his opinion into the same scale. So the dance—Emily entreated that it should not be called a ball—was decided upon, then and there.

Glynne soon loitered back again, and mingled with the group round the sofa. Both then and afterwards he frequently addressed Lady Atherstone, and she replied in due course ; but Marian could have sworn that, during the rest of the evening, not a sign or word of intelligence passed betwixt them.

Nevertheless, she betook herself to her well-earned rest, with the same serene satisfaction of a skilful engineer, who, after careful survey of the enemy's lines, can point to a weak place that may one day make void all other fences of the citadel.

# CHAPTER XXXIV

ERRISWELL was better adapted than many more imposing mansions for a modest entertainment, such as was now in progress. Besides the drawing-room and dining-room, devoted respectively to dancing and supper, there was available a library, opening out of Mrs. Malcolm's morning-room ; and, if these were not sufficient, those in search of coolness or seclusion might penetrate through the billiard-room into a spacious *fumoir* beyond, where two or three whist-tables were laid out.

Evidently, an artist's eye had supervised the decoration of this ground floor. There were flowers everywhere ; but not in such profusion as to load the air with perfume, or to entrap flying skirts and trailing dresses. There were sconces and lustres enough in the hall and drawing-room—the dining-room was closed, up to midnight—to bring out the sheen of silk and the glimmer of jewels, without putting complexions to a crucial test ; whilst, in the boudoir and library, the light was gradually toned down from the central brilliancy, till at the further end of the latter it faded into darkness. Indeed, in all these arrangements, Glynne had displayed a tact and energy that surprised his host, and threw his hostess into a tremor of gratitude. He only stipulated that his exertions, on their behalf, should be kept a secret from each and every one of the guests.

"You shall have all the credit, *petite cousine*," he observed ; " and, selfishly speaking, I wouldn't establish a precedent on any account. I'd rather be asked

to people's houses on my own merits, such as they
are, than professionally."

A goodly company mustered at Erriswell, including, besides all with whom you are already acquainted, some sixscore more of honourable folk, who
must perforce be nameless here. Only the Duke of
Devorgoil and his daughters, who had not settled at
Grandmanoir for the winter as yet, were absent; and
it is probable that the void did not cause the hearts of
any present seriously to ache.

The moon—perfect as the other accessories—gave
no excuse for unpunctuality; but it was very late
when the Templestowe party arrived.

Neither Lena nor Marian were apt to linger unreasonably over their toilet; however, before the
finishing touches that evening were completed,
Ralph, albeit exceeding patient in such matters,
and by no means keen about festivity, had begun to
grumble at the dilatoriness of his womankind; but
his brow cleared, as his wife entered the room in
which he was waiting, a few minutes in advance of
her step-daughter.

Though, to him at least, her beauty had always
seemed peerless, since she came to meet him through
the twilight at Kirkfell, he thought he had never
realised it till now. In very truth, Lena did look
wonderfully handsome. Perhaps, to make the picture
perfect, there might have been a slight increase of
colour; but that very pallor only seemed to enhance
the lustre of her eyes; and her toilette, without a
single meretricious detail, did ample justice to her
figure.

She wore a tunic of maize satin, over a *tulle* skirt,
of a somewhat paler shade. Amongst the soft, thick
*ruches* were scattered, rather sparsely than profusely,
small pomegranate-buds; and on her head was a
light chaplet of the same flowers, interspersed with
diamond sprays.

Lord Atherstone's eyes glittered with a loving

pride, as he stooped over his wife, and brushed her brow with his lips.

"If it is forbidden to compliment *you*, I should like to compliment Coralie," he said; "she deserves it, even if she has only carried out some one else's ideas."

"All the credit is Coralie's," Lena answered indifferently; "for, till I tried it on, I never saw the dress. She'll be glad that you approve: but she's rather in despair just now; for she never reckoned on my being so pale, and I won't allow her to correct it."

"Quite right," he answered. "Our neighbours will be very hard to please if they're not satisfied with you, as you stand. Besides, after the first waltz, the colour will come back, you'll see."

It was coming back already; for her cheek flushed a little, as she drew back and went on buttoning her glove.

"I'm not quite sure that I shall waltz at all"—she had begun, when the door opened, and Lady Marian entered.

She also was looking particularly well this evening. She was dressed very simply, according to her wont; but her grey and *cerise* were artistically blended, and harmonized better with her somewhat dark complexion than either dead white, or striking contrast of colour, could have done. She seemed in great spirits too; and did almost all the conversation during the drive to Erriswell; for, though he was ready enough to accompany his wife, the prospect of the unwonted dissipation made Lord Atherstone more taciturn than usual, and Lena only occasionally roused herself to make a necessary reply.

The last crash of a galop had just died away, when the Templestowe party made their entry; and the hall was soon half filled with couples, errant hither and thither, or availing themselves of the resting-places, of which there was no lack. Amongst these last was Mrs. Devereux. It is needless to name her cavalier.

Cissy was in the highest possible feather. She was quite conscious that her colours—white and *mazarine* blue—became her infinitely; and she was conscious too that the galop just over was a triumph; for she was a wonderful mover, when handled by an artist. Furthermore, her good opinion of herself, in both these particulars, had just been endorsed by Caryl Glynne—not very rapturously, to be sure; but she had learned to be grateful for very small mercies, and looked for no enthusiasm in this quarter.

She was a good-natured creature, in the main; and, so far as in her lay, wished to be in charity with women no less than men. When she expressed penitence for having shown temper about that Temple-stowe dinner, she really meant what she said. She had met Lady Atherstone twice since then, and on both occasions had rather gone out of her way to be amiable: now, happening to glance towards the entrance-door, she checked herself in the midst of her chatter.

"Don't you see who have just come in? I should like to go and speak to them at once."

Languidly, and, as it were, reluctantly, Caryl looked up; but, luckily for his companion's peace of mind, she did not notice the flash that, a second later, lighted up his eyes.

"Is there any hurry?" he said, without moving. "I thought we were settled here, for ten minutes, at least. What makes you so polite all of a sudden?"

"It's not exactly politeness," she answered, colouring slightly; "but, since I was—well—unjust to Lena the other day, I have been trying to make amends. She didn't know of it, to be sure; but it's on my conscience, all the same."

"If it's a case of conscience, that's another matter, and I won't balk you."

But the hall was still somewhat crowded; and, before the pair reached Lady Atherstone's side, she had been welcomed by the Malcolms, and accosted by Mr. Corbett.

A zealous dancer, as a rule, Arthur had as yet taken no active part in the festivities; but had loitered backwards and forwards from drawing-room to hall—with what purpose, looking now on his eager face, it was not difficult to divine. Almost immediately, he began to solicit the honour of the next waltz with Lady Atherstone; and it must be owned that he made the request with the confidence of one who thinks a refusal most unlikely. Indeed, that self-satisfaction, before alluded to, was more noticeable than ever to-night : there was an airiness in his tread ; and even in his attire, gorgeous beyond his wont, there was something triumphal. He looked rather blank when, instead of the ready assent on which he had reckoned, he was met by Lena's doubt about waltzing at all. However, before he could express disappointment, Mrs. Devereux and Glynne came up.

Corbett stood aside, of course, whilst greetings, rather demonstrative on Cissy's part, were exchanged ; but, as soon as he could do so decorously, he began once more to urge his claim ; for such he evidently considered it. Still Lena hesitated ; and, whilst she did so—improbable as it would seem—a swift appealing glance towards one of the bystanders escaped from under her long eyelashes ; and, almost imperceptibly, Caryl bent his head.

You may read the riddle as you will. Only remember, that, beyond those three whispered words in the Templestowe drawing-room, not a word or sign of intelligence had passed betwixt these two, since the morning when they parted—or meant to part—for ever and aye. We can no more analyse these marvels, than we can trace a message along electric wires ; but surely they are not the less wonderful because they happen hourly.

The propitious reply—more grateful, perhaps, when it came, than if it had been granted as a matter of course—made Corbett jubilant again. The banker had never quite got rid of the dread and dislike that assailed him, when he first looked on Glynne's face. Would he have liked him better, or feared him less, if he could have guessed that to this man, and none other, he owed the favour in which he exulted now? Hardly so.

"Perhaps, later in the evening, Lady Atherstone, you'll bestow one waltz on me, just for old acquaintance' sake?" Caryl said in his laziest voice; as if he was going through a necessary ceremony. "I couldn't do less," he said to Cissy, a few minutes later; and she, being still on the penitent tack, managed to believe him.

Though she had not resolved on any definite line of action, Lena had come hither to-night braced for trials of her nerve; and she was able to answer, quite as indifferently,—

"I shall be very happy. I have no other engagement; so you can write your name where you please."

He took the card she held out; and scribbled his initials at hap-hazard, as it seemed, about the middle of it—opposite to the 'Soldaten Lieder.' Then the group broke up; Lady Atherstone passing on into the dancing-room, with her husband and Lady Marian —Corbett, of course, in close attendance; the other two strolling back towards the corner they had lately left.

Lena's self-possession during the next hour or so was truly admirable. She got through her duty-talk with her friends and acquaintance, and some more confidential converse with Arthur Corbett, without once betraying that her thoughts were wandering. Nevertheless, her hand trembled exceedingly, as she laid it on Caryl's arm, when the notes floated forth of the prelude to the 'Soldaten Lieder;' and the tremor spread through every fibre of her frame, as his arm circled her waist. Even when they were all in all to each other, they had never stood as they stood now,

since those evil May days that first brought them together. Before one turn was completed, she grew
faint and dizzy : the walls seemed to swim, and the
floor to sway under her feet.

"Stop—you must stop!" she whispered—or tried
to whisper—for the words were quite inaudible, and
it was only by the working of her lips that Glynne
guessed her meaning.

They halted just opposite the doorway ; and it was
easy to escape into the hall unobserved : but the
faintness was still so strong upon her, that Lady
Atherstone hardly knew whither she had been led,
when she found herself resting on a couch at the
further end of the library, where the lights were dim.
She had so far recovered, that she had begun to think
how she could excuse her weakness, when there came
a whisper, quite close to her ear—

"My own!"

Lena started violently ; just as she had done, when
waking from one of the tormenting dreams that had
haunted her so often of late. Only this was no
dreaming, but a fatal reality. She was not tempted
now by the phantasm of Caryl Glynne, but by himself, in flesh and blood—looking down on her, with
such love in his eyes as she had never seen there
when, if in such words there was folly, there was at
least no guilt.

# CHAPTER XXXV

So the very turning-point of this woman's life had come at last.

There was no occasion for any display of wrathful virtue or offended dignity : just so much courage and coolness, and no more, as had carried Lena Shafton through that interview under Grace Moreland's roof, were needed to place Lena Atherstone safe out of harm's reach, not then alone, but probably for all coming time.

A free agent, then—at the worst, she could only have marred her own fortunes, and blighted, not for the first time, either, her mother's hopes. Now, she was fettered not only by consecrated vows, but by the knowledge of having wholly in trust the happiness of as brave and loyal a gentleman as ever drew sword. It was no question of money-troubles here ; but of a ruin, to escape from which most honest hearts would welcome penury. Yet her strength of that morning, compared to her strength of to-night, was as a giant to a sickly child.

If any good impulses yet abode in Lena's breast, that evil whisper dealt with them, as effectually as did the fratricidal poison with the royal Dane. Fears and scruples all vanished before the consciousness that Caryl had spoken truth—sinful and shameful, no doubt, but none the less the truth ; and that she was absolutely his own. Ay! and more — deride her credulity as you will—she felt sure that, in spite of appearances, no other had filled the place she left void a year ago. She meant no reproach, when she murmured—

"I have been so unhappy!"

Was that confession ample enough? Glynne, at least, thought so, as he leant over the speaker closer, yet so guardedly that it need have excited no comment even if they had not been quite alone.

"Darling, were you jealous, then, of that pretty puppet yonder? I was never so of your *amant pour rire.*"

He smiled as he spoke, but not at all cynically; indeed, all the softness left in his nature was waked just then, and a half-contrition abated the flush of victory. He knew—none better—how one-sided are these devil's bargains. What did he risk here? The dregs of a reputation, the wreck of a fortune, when all was told. As for Lena—well, she might dispose of his after-life, and he would cleave to her till death should part them: but would that make amends for what he felt she was now ready to resign?

Her answer was inaudible; and thenceforth they talked always in the lowest whispers, and hurriedly, like those who know that even seconds are precious.

Whilst the last bars of the waltz were being played, Caryl proffered his arm to his companion without speaking. She took it almost submissively, and her neck drooped a little as she rose; but her fingers did not tremble as they did a few minutes agone. Certainty—even the certainty of evil—will steady weaker nerves than hers; and for the moment she felt a strange sense of relief; like one who, weary of groping to and fro in the darkness, sees a light hard by, and is glad, though it may stream from an enemy's watch-fire.

When they whispered, no promise was asked for or given; but none the less betwixt these two a compact had just been made, such as may not easily be annulled even in this light-minded world of ours; and may, possibly, bind those who once set their hands thereto, in that other world where some cynics may find it hard to sustain their supercilious smile.

They passed quickly into the morning-room, in time to mingle unremarked with the first stragglers from the crowd without ; yet not so quickly but that, before they crossed the threshold, there vanished through the opposite door a train of silk too soft to rustle ; and the colour of it was a tender grey.

Though the 'Soldaten Lieder' was the longest waltz of that evening, many of those moving to its music held that it ceased too soon : but amongst such insatiables Corbett was not numbered.

To begin with, he was a little, just a little, over-matched. He had been guided chiefly by politic motives, in the choice of his partner. The damsel was the daughter of a good as well as an old cus-tomer, and a *débutante ;* so Arthur was bound to patronise her ; but he had not reckoned on his energies being taxed so severely. Ella Thorold meant to make the very most of her first ball ; and, during their brief intervals of rest she kept marking time pettishly, glancing reproach at her panting cavalier. Now Corbett, despite an increasing portliness, if he went his own pace, could still hold his own with the best of second-rate waltzers ; but, if he was hustled, he was sure to get into difficulties ; and the result, as in the present instance, was anything rather than a success. However, there was a heavier trouble on his mind than the mere mortification of a small vanity.

Notwithstanding the plea of old acquaintanceship, he had been inclined inwardly to dispute Glynne's claim to a 'round dance.' He had not so much as hinted at this to Lena—indeed, a feeling which he could not define made him always evade the mention of Caryl's name—but the discontent was there ; and this increased rather than abated, when, after the first turn, he missed them from among the crowd. 'Sitting out' was quite beside the bargain ; and he felt he had a right to be aggrieved. Altogether, by the time the waltz was ended, he had worked himself up into a very uncomfortable state of heat and worry.

" Poor dear old thing ! I quite pitied him. It was my fault for hurrying him so," said Ella, later in the evening to a certain cornet, as light-footed and as light-hearted as herself.

To be compassionated where he had meant to condescend, and on the score of his age—it was almost as bad as the *amant pour rire.* Though he overheard neither remark, it was a wonder that Arthur's ears were not set a-burning.

However, when he contrived to rejoin Lady Atherstone, he was not further disquieted by any signs of agitation in her face. A very close observer might have noticed that it was a shade or two paler; but, so long as the surface of things satisfied Corbett, he was not wont to look deeper; and, if he had nourished any suspicions, these would have been cured by the perfect tranquillity of Lena's tone, as she stood chatting with Mrs. Malcolm. Glynne was no longer by her side. If Arthur had wished to be querulous, opportunity would have been wanting; for, almost immediately, supper was announced; to which Lady Atherstone was escorted by the host, whilst Arthur was compelled to pair off with a squiress; and, directly afterwards, the Templestowe carriage was ordered.

In reply to Mrs. Malcolm's remonstrances, Lena pleaded that she was tired—very tired; and no one looking at her face would have thought it an idle excuse. Indeed, several people confessed to being disappointed in Lady Atherstone that evening; whilst it was allowed on all hands that her step-daughter had never looked so well. Certainly there was a strange sparkle in Lady Marian's black eyes; and the unwonted flush of her cheek—her complexion was not her strong point—was wonderfully becoming. When she assured her hostess that she had thoroughly enjoyed her evening, she spoke nothing but the truth; but if the whole truth had been laid bare, she herself might have shrunk before its baseness.

For, you who have had patience to read thus far, may guess over what she triumphed.

Lord Atherstone, too, seemed well satisfied with his entertainment; for he was a keen though indifferent whist-player, and was in vein to-night; but, at the first hint of Lena's fatigue, he was only too anxious to depart; and, in spite of Lady Marian's high spirits, it was a very silent drive homewards through the darkness.

Mrs. Devereux's recollections of that famous waltz were not much pleasanter than Mr. Corbett's. She was mated with Sir Manners Mannering, whom she detested, and only tolerated for her husband's sake, knowing that, if she once spoke her mind, Dick would have fired his last shot in the best coverts in Loamshire. It was bad enough, whilst in motion, to be trampled on and dragged out of time by her clumsy partner; worse still, whilst standing at ease, to have insolent flattery panted into her ears in his thick vinous tones; worst of all, to have to endure a double dose of the same assiduities at supper, when deep draughts had brought a coarser flush on the baronet's bloated cheeks, and a wickeder gleam into his truculent eyes. She did think Caryl might have interfered to save her this last infliction; though he had told her, at the beginning of the evening, that he really must do a certain amount of duty-work; and though he could hardly have any private motives, for ministering so sedulously to the large requirements of Mrs. Hubert Ashleigh.

She caught herself thinking half-regretfully of poor Godfrey Colville, whose 'duty-work' was entirely professional: and who would have risked a court-martial sooner than fail in his fealty to her. However, Cissy brightened up when Caryl came to claim her for the after-supper galop; and thenceforth she engrossed quite as much of his attentions as she had a right to expect—perhaps rather more. And yet it struck her at the time, though not so forcibly as when she looked back on these things afterwards, that he was more silent than usual, and that he answered occasionally in an odd, absent way—once or twice almost at random. Somehow, she had her fill of festivity rather earlier than usual; and, when Dick came up with his stereotyped question as to when she would be ready to go, she startled the honest fellow out of a yawning-fit by bidding him look for the carriage directly. The Driver was so overcome by the unlooked-for clemency, that he felt in charity even with Caryl Glynne; and—standing discreetly aside—did not seek, either by word or gesture, to hurry the protracted cloaking-process which ensued.

So the Erriswell entertainment came to an end, if not to the satisfaction of each and every one bidden thereto, very much to the satisfaction of the host and hostess.

As the last wheels rolled away, Emily Malcolm sank back on a sofa, with a sigh rather complacent than weary.

"I'm almost sorry it's over," she said; "for I don't feel the least exhausted yet, though, perhaps, I shall be a wreck to-morrow. Come here and be thanked, Caryl. I shall never call you lazy any more. I am sure quite half the success is owing to you. Well, if you won't allow that"—the shrug of Glynne's shoulders was very expressive—"at least allow that it *was* a success."

But Caryl still stood aloof, leaning his elbow on the mantel-shelf, and shading his eyes with his hands. Absurd as it may appear, it was nevertheless true that a keener thrill of remorse shot through his breast just then, than any that had visited him since he dropped that fatal whisper into Lena Atherstone's ear. There were few things—terribly few—from which he shrank; but he did shrink from accepting the gratitude of the gentle, true-hearted woman for this night's work, knowing what manner of success *he* had achieved. The feeling lasted some seconds before he could quite shake it off; and his laugh was rather forced when he answered at last.

"Be just before you're generous, *petite cousine.* Husbands seldom get credit from the best of wives, or you would have given yours his due. The whole burden of the evening was on those broad shoulders of his; and he carried it like a man. I deserve no thanks for being well amused; but, if you must pay me for settling the flowers, I'll smoke one of Robin's *Excepcionales* before we sleep, and we'll cry quits. Now you ought to be sent to bed; and, if you don't look ghost-like at luncheon to-morrow, I'll own that you've a right to be proud of your house-warming."

# CHAPTER XXXVI.

ONCE more an interval of some months must pass; but it cannot be said now, as then, that to the chief characters in this story it brought no material change.

From honour to dishonour, from innocence to guilt, from safe tranquillity to incessant peril—is the change much greater in the passage from life to death?

Yet no less an one had come over Lena Atherstone. Of the different stages thereof, or of the times or seasons of its accomplishment, it is not needful to write.

They were together, and she fell.

All the variations and *fioriture* with which you could broider it, would hardly make that sad, simple theme more expressive.

Kerneguy had not far misjudged her, when he conceived her 'wilful or reckless to any degree; but scarcely, under any provocation, cowardly, malicious, or mean. On the whole, very nearly a grand character; but of the kind which is wrecked much oftener than more ignoble ones.'

There are women who, more from triviality than utter depravity of nature, contrive to flourish, like green bay-trees, in such an atmosphere as that in which Lena was now compelled to live. They seem to find a pleasurable excitement in the very shifts and stratagems to which they are driven; the lie trips too glibly from their lissome tongue to be painful in

the utterance ; and they can furnish smiles as liberally
to the betrayed as to the betrayer. In their hearts, if
not with their lips, they could always warble the
wicked *refrain*—

> C'est le mal qui fait du bien ;
> C'est la piqûre de la rose ;
> Si on le sait c'est peu de chose,
> Si on l'ignore ce n'est rien.

But Lena could not carry her guilt so gaily. Constitutionally quite fearless, she was beset by none of
the terrors which form part of the punishment of
many in like case ; nevertheless, she did not escape
her share thereof. The passion to which she aban-
doned herself, engrossing as it was—it was the one
passion of her life, remember—still left her leisure for
prospect and retrospect. Both these might have
stings of their own ; but a trial, that came almost
hourly, was harder to endure. Familiarity with
wrong-doing, did not make it easier to her to look on
the face of the man she wronged.

Lena was not a very apt dissembler ; and any one,
less absolutely unsuspicious than Lord Atherstone,
must have guessed ere long that something was amiss :
but the quickness of perception, and straightforward
commonsense, which served Ralph well in ordinary
circumstances, seemed absolutely to fail him here.

There is a disease, much dreaded by the hunters
and trappers of the North-West, called ' night-blind-
ness.' Those who are stricken by it may be keen-
sighted as Hawkeye himself, whilst day endures ;
but, when the sun has once fairly sunk below the
horizon, there fall on them a blackness through
which pierce neither moon nor stars, and a helplessness beyond that of dotage.

Even so Ralph Atherstone, when the light that
for a brief space had brightened his home began to
fade, groped hither and thither darkling ; and there
was none to lead him by the hand.

A change in his wife's demeanour he did notice,

X

no doubt. He saw that her spirits were more than
variable, and that, instead of being languid and indifferent, she was now often restless even to irrita-
bility; but he imputed this to any save the right
cause. First, he thought that the dulness of Templestowe was beginning to tell upon her; and he strove
to provide her with more amusement both at home
and abroad: when this failed — for Lena seemed
rather to shrink from than invite society—he fell
back on another supposition, bitter, no doubt, but
still wide of the bitterer truth. She had overmuch
of his company, he thought—a rough, uncongenial
company at the best. No wonder it wearied her;
and perhaps the very effort to dissemble this weariness tried her nerves. This, too, he endeavoured to
amend. On one pretext or another, he contrived
to be abroad most days—generally alone, for Lena's
keenness for hunting seemed to have left her, and
it was only the nearest meets that she attended;
and, when he returned home, though he occasionally
looked into his wife's boudoir to tell her what the
hounds had been doing, he never lingered there as
in the old times, but retreated to the library, whence
he did not emerge till the dressing-gong sounded.

They dragged heavily, these solitary hours—more
heavily than any of those that had made up the sum
of Ralph Atherstone's stirring life. He had few
literary resources, as you may imagine; indeed, a
glance at the day's paper, or the skimming of a
magazine, was about the extent of his reading, and
he did not grow more studious now. Perhaps a book
might lie on his knees; but it was seldom, if ever,
opened, as he leaned back in his arm-chair, opposite
the fire—so motionless, that only from the gleams
shooting ever and anon from under his heavy bent
brows, could you have guessed he was not sleeping.
He never did sleep on these occasions; indeed,
though he contrived to conceal this from Lena, the
night was often far spent before his eyes were fairly

closed; and yet time was, when even a wound, when its fever had abated, would scarce have kept him wakeful. And, whilst he sat there ruminating, wander as they would, his thoughts always came back to the one starting-point. Perhaps he had made a fearful mistake, after all, and the penalty —if penalty was owing—must light not more on himself than on the woman whose happiness he had meant to secure—ay! and meant still—with all his heart, and soul, and strength. And she had seemed happy too, in a quiet fashion, during the past year. It was hard to be forced to realise—not that he put it to himself so poetically, you may be sure—that there was a worm at the root of a plant that promised fairly.

At the colour of these musings no one could have guessed—watching Lord Atherstone's bearing towards his wife, either when alone with her, or in others' presence. That he never dreamt of making a confidante of Marian Ashleigh, it is needless to say; nevertheless, her sharp eyes read the state of things, just as accurately as if every phase had been set down for her benefit in black and white. Of a truth, on a certain night that you wot of, she had learned almost as much as, for the present, she cared to know.

To one not aware of all the circumstances, she might have seemed easily contented; for not a syllable of the words whispered in the library at Erriswell had reached her ears; and, when she ventured twice or thrice to peer warily through the doorway, there was nothing in the attitude of the pair within that need reasonably have waked suspicion. Yet, I repeat, Marian Ashleigh learned then enough, and more than enough, for her purposes. That letter of Archibald Kerneguy's, every line of which she could have repeated by rote, had given her the key to it all. She had caught a glimpse— the briefest one, it is true, but still a glimpse—of Lena's face, just after the fatal confession had been murmured; and Marian could interpret its story, almost as accurately as if she had overheard the converse from first to last. Not less accurately did she interpret Lady Atherstone's sudden weariness that evening; the change in her demeanour afterwards, more marked from day to day; and the augury of the cloud that thenceforth overshadowed Templestowe.

Had this exemplary person been forced to work for her living, she would have been invaluable to any secret police; for, without any practice in that line, she had all the professional instincts of a finished detective. She knew that it was not well to be over-hasty or over-eager even in the collection of proof, much less in the production thereof; and was never likely to hinder the ends of justice through stinting the allowance of 'rope.' Having no special dislike, as you are aware, to eaves-dropping, she was not so fond of the amusement as to practise it wantonly.

On the occasion of Glynne's visits to Templestowe —they were not too frequent, but, by an odd coincidence, they always chimed in with Lord Atherstone's absence at a distant meet or shooting-party—Lady Marian displayed infinite tact and discretion. Whilst she remained in the room, she did not attempt to watch even furtively the words or looks either of hostess or guest, and did her best to keep the conversation on an easy, natural footing; and, when she left them alone—as she invariably did, by-the-bye— she had the fairest excuse for so doing. She was an exceedingly methodical person, and it was her habit to devote a certain hour to her letter-writing; after which, unless the weather was very wild, she generally took a 'constitutional.' This, her custom of an afternoon, was seldom altered, whosoever might happen to be calling at Templestowe; and there certainly was no reason for treating Caryl Glynne with more ceremony than other visitors. But she never trod a whit more slowly or softly when, on her way out, she passed the closed door of the boudoir; much less did she linger to listen. Neither did she cast a single curious glance inwards, as she paced along the terrace by its windows.

And yet it would have seemed impossible to impute to her, connivance. There was never a shade of significance in her look, or manner, or tone, either when she addressed or when she mentioned Caryl. She never bantered Lena on the subject; much less did she attempt to inveigle her into any confidences, or imply that there were any such to be made. She took just the same line with regard to purely domestic matters. Many women, under like circumstances, noticing—as of course she did notice—the growing estrangement betwixt husband and wife, would have attempted to ingratiate themselves with the former by a little extra display of duteous solicitude—not to say sympathy. Marian did nothing of the sort. When the three were together, she rattled on in her brisk, off-hand way, just as though there were no such things in this world as mysteries or misunderstandings; till Ralph was fain to smile, though in somewhat grim fashion, and Lena felt temporarily almost at ease. No wonder that both, for diverse reasons, felt loth to lose her cheery company.

When Philip, after finishing off his visits, came to fetch his wife away, he found this not so easy; indeed, Lord Atherstone had never been so near asking a favour of his son, as when he begged that Marian might be allowed to remain, at all events a little longer. Philip's nerves at any time were hardly equal to a point-blank refusal; and the novelty of the situation quite flattered him. He was in extraordinarily good humour, too, just then; for his mild platonisms at Westlands had prospered not ill, and he had visions of prolonging that innocent amusement whenever time and place should serve. So, grumbling a good deal to Marian, he assented—of course, with as bad a grace as possible; and went forth alone from the paternal roof, utterly unsuspicious of there being aught amiss there.

# CHAPTER XXXVII.

THOUGH she merely looked in, in passing, to see that things were in order at Blytheswold, Mrs. Shafton found it quite as hard, as Lena had supposed, to escape from the kindly North Country. At the worst of her struggles and trials, her *verve* and good-humour had made her a welcome, if not an honoured, guest at many houses; and, now that she had no special object in being agreeable, she was pleasanter than ever —pleasanter not only to talk with, but to look upon. Divers lines had vanished from her face; and the brightening and softening of her colour were in nowise owing to art. She moved, too, more briskly; and, altogether, seemed to draw new life from her respite from cares. For Miles, the prodigal, had grown thriftier, or luckier, of late, and now contrived to make both ends meet after a fashion: so, even in this quarter, there was peace; and, for about the first time since her maidenhood, Isabel Shafton was able to enjoy the present, without disquieting herself concerning the morrow. She did enjoy it thoroughly, and was quite sorry when she came to the last place on her list.

Here, besides several other old acquaintances, she met a certain Mrs. Mansergh, a widow like herself, and also of better birth than fortune. Though they had never been very intimate, the two had been on sufficiently amicable terms; for it happened that neither had absolutely thwarted the other's maternal tactics. Nevertheless, it was not without envy that the last-named lady contemplated the altered luck of

Blytheswold; and, doubtless, the homely parsonage,
which was all she could achieve for her handsome,
tocherless daughter, looked lowlier than ever when
contrasted with Templestowe. Though Isabel was
most temperate in her triumph, and scarcely ever
spoke of the Atherstones, unless directly questioned,
she had got a new way of smiling to herself that in-
expressibly aggravated Mrs. Mansergh; and, before
they had been two days together, she was disposed
not to let a chance slip of abating this complacency.
Such an one presented itself, in this wise.

Dinner was just over; and the womankind in the
drawing-room, left to their own devices for awhile,
were conversing languidly and discursively, as—
we are happy to believe—is their wont at such
seasons; when the hostess, by way of something
to say, inquired what sort of neighbourhood lay
round Templestowe.

"It's rather scattered," was the reply, "and not
very lively as a rule; but some new people have
just come to Erriswell, which is quite within reach;
and, from Lena's report, though she has not mentioned them lately, they sound very nice. By-the-
bye, Kate—you know everybody—can you tell me
anything about these Malcolms? The husband made
a great fortune in Australia, I understand: that
ought to help you."

Mrs. Mansergh's countenance, vague and doubtful at first, lighted up suddenly with an intelligence
by no means benign.

"Yes, that helps me," she said; "and I believe
they are rather nice, though I have not the pleasure
of *his* acquaintance. So they have settled near
Templestowe? That's rather odd; and it's rather
odd, too, my dear, that you should never have heard
who the wife is. Why, she's cousin to that handsome, wicked Caryl Glynne; and they're great allies,
too; at least, they were inseparable the winter we
were at Florence. Not that she's the least fast;

indeed, what we saw of her we liked extremely. I shouldn't wonder if *le beau cousin* were a good deal at Erriswell. In that case, the neighbourhood is likely to be much more lively. Don't you think so?"

The blackness of imminent tempest had wrapped Isabel Shafton round many a time, without causing her heart to sink as it did now, when this light cloud flecked a serene sky. But was it such a light one? Perhaps the chiefest terror and trouble of her life were linked with this name. Was it not hard that it should sound in her ears, just when she thought she had found rest, and sound more ominously than ever? For years past she honestly believed that her daughter and Caryl had never met: henceforth, it was probable they would meet not seldom. And that the former should never even have hinted in her letters at such a possibility— this was worst of all. Though the last shadow of her authority had vanished on the wedding-day, she did not, therefore, hold herself irresponsible; for, thoroughly as she trusted Lord Atherstone, she rather doubted his capability of dealing delicately with such a wilful temper as Lena's.

Despite all this, she had the courage to meet Mrs. Mansergh's malicious eyes quite steadily, and to answer quite indifferently.

"I can scarcely give an opinion; it's several years since I've seen or spoken to Mr. Glynne. I had almost forgotten his existence. Perhaps he has altered, like the rest of us: if not I should doubt his being an acquisition to any neighbourhood; and, if his cousins are wise, they won't parade him in Loamshire just yet. New-comers should never try experiments."

And then, without any violent wrench of the subject, she passed on to some county gossip.

But, before she slept that night, she had contrived a decent excuse for shortening her visit; and the end of the week found her in Loamshire.

The warmth of her welcome—and in this respect she had nothing to complain of—did not blind Mrs. Shafton to the fact that things were altered at Templestowe since she sojourned there. It was not that there were any signs of past or present disagreements : but Lord Atherstone's manner towards his wife, though kindly as ever, was tinged with a kind of reserve ; and Lena's, though still affectionate, was never playful or confidential as heretofore ; perhaps 'dutiful' would have best described it.

Much of this Mrs. Shafton noticed on the very evening of her arrival ; and the morrow only strengthened her misgivings. It was not a happy day ; for every time Lena opened her lips, when they were alone together, her mother hoped—against hope at last—that she would broach the perilous subject. It would have been such an intense relief, to see that there was no wish to avoid it. Though she believed in her to a great extent, and rejoiced to find her domiciled at Templestowe, she dared not betray uneasiness, much less put any direct questions, to Lady Marian. So she refrained herself till the party separated for the night : then she followed Lena to her dressing-room.

This was by no means an unusual proceeding ; nevertheless, Lady Atherstone knew perfectly well that not mere gossip was coming. It appeared, however, that she had no wish to avoid the interview ; for she dismissed her maid as speedily as possible ; and then, nestling herself into a *causeuse* opposite her mother, with a resigned air, awaited the opening shot. She had not to wait long.

If Mrs. Shafton's patience had been less sorely tried that day, it is probable she would have led up to the subject more delicately. As it was, she began the attack without preamble or warning.

"Have you seen nothing of the Erriswell people lately, Lena? You have hardly mentioned them, since you said that their ball was a success. You seemed to like them so much at first. Don't they improve on acquaintance?"

"They decidedly improve," Lady Atherstone answered, with much composure; "but I had no news about them likely to interest you."

Mrs. Shafton's eyes — very handsome eyes they were still—flashed scornfully.

"Not even that Caryl Glynne was staying there?" she said.

It was a random shaft; and, even whilst she loosed it, the archer prayed it might go wide of the mark.

But this was not so to be.

Lena never started, or changed colour; only her lips were slightly compressed as she replied—

"Not even that; or rather—that least of all."

Mrs. Shafton was completely taken aback, not only by the confirmation of her worst foreboding, but by an impenitence for which, with all her experience of Lena's character, she was not prepared; and it was some seconds before she found breath to murmur—

"What can you mean?"

"I will tell you," the other went on, in the same cool, even tone. "Mother dear, it is not so many years ago, but you may remember what passed when that name was spoken last by you and me. It was settled then—not by my wish surely—that it should never again be mentioned between us. I have kept my part of the agreement—that is all. I can't see what you complain of."

Mrs. Shafton was bitterly incensed; but her alarm outran her anger: what frightened her most was her daughter's resolute calmness. It seemed like that of one borne up by a strong sense of duty; and so, perchance, it was with Lena.

But duty—to whom? Alas! half the rebellions against the powers of earth and heaven have been carried on under this watchword; and in this name, almost as many crimes and cruelties have been wrought, as in the yet holier one of Faith.

"That is mere sophistry. But, if you have forgotten what you owe to your mother, you can't have
forgotten yet what you owe to your husband. You
don't suppose Lord Atherstone would ever allow that
person to darken his doors—knowing what I know?"

Lena smiled haughtily.

"He knows rather more, as it happens; and he
knew it before we were married. I even offered, if it
pleased him, to break off all acquaintance in future
with Mr. Glynne. He declined to accept that offer
then; and I believe he would be still less likely to
accept it now. If it would ease your conscience, you
can question him yourself. Only, as it is quite new
to him, it might be breaking dangerous ground.'

Dangerous? Mrs. Shafton was thoroughly aware
of this. Things must have come to a much worse—
ay, to the very worst—pass, when she should venture
on tale-bearing to Ralph Atherstone; for she felt
that, if his suspicions were once fairly roused, it would
be no easier to guide or check them than to mark out
a course and limits for a flood of fresh lava.

She pressed her kerchief to her eyes; and, when
she withdrew it, they were wet with real tears, that
sprang, perhaps, not less from vexation than sorrow;
and there were tears in her voice, too.

"I haven't deserved this."

Lena's face softened; and, crossing over from
where she sat, she bent down over her mother caressingly.

"I won't have you torment yourself, dear, and
spoil your pleasure and mine, when I've been looking
forward to your visit so long. Everything is quite
safe; and will be, if you will only think so. Won't
you trust me, as you used to do?"

A heavy sigh, only just stifled in time, nearly
belied her words. She had been insincere even in
the old time, when she let it be believed that all ties
were broken betwixt herself and Caryl Glynne; and
of late her whole life had been an acted falsehood.

Nevertheless, a direct untruth she had seldom, if ever, been forced to utter; and this one seemed to burn her lips in passing. The 'straining at the gnat,' you see, is not confined to the wearers of broad phylacteries.

Mrs. Shafton did not feel satisfied, but she felt helpless; which, for all practical purposes, comes to nearly the same thing.

"I must trust you, darling," she said piteously, "for I have no real right to call you to account now; but it would not the less break my heart if any evil befell you. Always remember that."

A kiss was Lena's answer; and with few more words they parted, with peace seemingly betwixt them; but to neither couch came ready slumber or untroubled dreams.

The next day was a very tranquil one; and the only incident worth recording, was Marian Ashleigh's announcement of her immediate departure.

"I leave Lena in very safe hands now," she said, with her cheery laugh; "and it won't do to give Philip a substantial grievance to grumble about. He has been rather cavalierly treated already."

To this resolution neither Lord Atherstone nor his wife could seriously demur. So, on the morrow, not without real reluctance, they suffered her to depart. But she herself was not loth to go.

Ill weeds, no less than stately trees, grow whilst men are sleeping; and Marian wist well that the seed sown under this roof-tree would thrive none the worse, for the present, without her tendance.

Glynne called that same afternoon. With all her prejudices in arms against him, Mrs. Shafton was bound to confess that he behaved admirably.

Neither then nor afterwards, so far as she could discern—and she watched them narrowly—did any sign of intelligence pass betwixt him and Lena; and Caryl's manner was scarcely so familiar as might have been expected in an old friend. The only approach to a confidence was bestowed on herself, when he took his leave. Lena had gone to the further end of the room, for some music that was to be returned to Erriswell.

" Will you let bygones be bygones ?" Caryl whispered.

Mrs. Shafton bent her head in silent assent; and, for some hours afterwards, she felt her cares much lightened. But on her knees, that night, she prayed earnestly that there might be some germ of truth in those fair words ; for she remembered that, when they were uttered, though the speaker held her hand, he had never looked into her eyes.

# CHAPTER XXXVIII.

BOTH Mrs. Devereux, and Arthur Corbett, were sensible of a certain change in the atmosphere. Indeed, the former's quick temper had been sorely exercised by the turn that matters had taken of late.

Glynne could not be said to have slackened in his assiduities, simply because such a word never could have applied to his listless devotion; but, somehow, it seemed to her that there was less *heart* than ever in his careless caressing words, and less pleasantness in his satire. Nevertheless, she could not complain of any absolute neglect; much less had she any pretext for jealousy. When the three met in society—which was not seldom—she failed to detect the faintest sign of intimacy between Caryl and Lena Atherstone. With all her ingenuity, she could not discover that he visited at Templestowe more frequently than mere civility demanded; and he assuredly came to Hunsden quite as often as she herself considered safe. For, strange to say, her husband began just then to cause her much trouble and uneasiness.

The quaint spirit of partisanship, of which you saw signs on that day at Wilton, was always working in the Driver's broad breast; and his animosity towards the supplanter of his comrade was in nowise abated. He was barely civil to Glynne now; and the cool *insouciance* with which the other persisted in ignoring his provocation was a further exasperation.

You may imagine Cissy's feelings one morning, when her lord abruptly announced his intention of inviting Major Colville to pay them a fortnight's visit.

"We can take in three of his horses easy enough," Dick remarked; "and I can manage him a couple of mounts. That will about see him through it."

For once Cissy was fairly disconcerted. From a dogged defiance in her husband's manner, she guessed that open contradiction was unsafe; and evasion was not much easier. At first she tried to prove, that the condition of their stable was not such as to warrant the offer of mounts to any one likely to be hard upon the cattle; but Dick only retorted sulkily, that 'this was his look-out; and that, if he were short of horses, there were plenty of Godfrey's old friends who would be glad to put him up.'

Then Cissy, growing desperate, threw away the scabbard, and gave point in earnest.

"One word's as good as fifty. I don't choose that Major Colville should be asked here, at present. We had a quarrel, just before he left; and he was exceedingly rude and unreasonable. I shall not encourage him till he thinks fit to apologise."

"Quarrelled!" the Driver retorted grimly. "I don't wonder at it—when you made such a pet, all at once, of that pied popinjay that's always fluttering about here. He'll get pinioned one of these days, if he don't mind. But *I*'m not so fond of throwing old friends over. I shall write to Godfrey by this post."

You never would have thought that Cissy's dainty lips could have set themselves so resolutely.

"Calling people names doesn't help your argument," she said. "As if you ever could argue, Dick! Well, do as you please; but, I give you fair warning, if Major Colville accepts, I shall go and pay Uncle Horace the visit I've owed him so long; and then you two 'old friends' can have the house all to yourselves. Won't that be amusing?"

Her merry, mutinous laugh rang out, till the Driver, despite his ill-humour, was fain to laugh too, though rather ruefully. He was so absurdly fond of his wife, that even in her caprice and injustice he found a charm; besides which, he had never yet drawn the curb on his 'bonny grey mare;' and had not the heart—perhaps he had not the nerve—to prove, all at once, which was master.

"Have your own way," he grumbled; "though it's hard lines all the same. But you'll make it up with poor old Godfrey, at all events? We can have him here when you're in a better mind."

To these conditions Cissy condescended, inwardly rejoicing at her escape; but her triumph was much abated, by the manner in which Glynne received her account of the passage of arms.

"It was running a great risk," he said gravely; "and I don't quite see why you didn't make the concession."

Cissy coloured high with vexation and surprise.

"You don't quite see?" she repeated. "Why, any risk was better than allowing you two to meet here. *He* really did like me; and, I daresay, likes me still."

The bitter emphasis on the pronoun did not escape Caryl; but he only lifted his brows, as if this view of the case had not struck him before.

"That would rather complicate matters, to be sure. But, though Major Colville, I fancy, has a will of his own, and is a little too apt to swagger, I give him credit for tact; and his 'likings'—that's a nice way of putting it—needn't make him forget his *savoir vivre.* As for me, I am not quarrelsome; and, if I can keep my temper with your husband, I'm not likely to lose it with your—friend. Besides——"

The angry tears sprang into her eyes.

"I don't want to hear any more sham reasons," she broke in. "The real reason is, that you never cared two straws for me, and care still less now. I suppose I'm to thank Lena Atherstone for this. I *will* thank her some day."

Caryl's countenance darkened, though he answered without a sign of irritation.

"I am rightly served for talking reason at all.

Why don't you accuse Emily too, whilst you're about
it, and threaten to make an *esclandre* at Erriswell?
That would make it quite complete. Do try and be
less childish."

"Childish!" she retorted. "Yes: you always treat
me like a child. It's the greatest misfortune to be
born good-natured. Every one thinks they can twist
you round their finger."

He laughed, more in indulgence than in irony.

"Ah! you'd like to have been a strong-minded
woman, with hard eyes, and thin lips, and thick
ankles, and an impracticable waist—wouldn't you?
Well, *mignonne*, I never should have thought meek-
ness, or long-suffering, had stood in your way. And
I fancied Queen Stork, not King Log, ruled here.
Come, that's better"—for, in spite of herself, Cissy
smiled—"now you're rational enough to listen to my
'Besides.' I was about to say that, as I must leave
Erriswell so soon, I need not stand in any one's light
—for the present, at all events."

The smile and the colour faded together from Cissy's
face.

"Going!" she whispered. "You only say that to
punish me, Caryl. Say you don't mean it, and I'll be
good—so good—directly."

"But I must mean it," he said with more tenderness than he had yet displayed. "I might outstay
even Robin Malcolm's welcome; and I have business
in town that needs looking after. But I might come
back, you know, before long."

"You *will* come back—and soon," she said, in a
lower whisper yet. Then, bowing her head, she
pressed her lips, almost timidly, upon the hand she
held.

Could this be reckless Cissy Devereux, who,
through good or evil report, for love or for fear, had
never yet been known to veil her crest before friend
or foe?

Some sense of the pitiful contrast, and of his own

Y

cruelty, forced itself on Caryl Glynne. For it was a part, and nought else, that he had been playing now for some time past. He had begun it for his amusement; and, as had happened to him a score of times before, finding in it more zest, he had thrown into it more energy than he had reckoned on exerting. It had been 'admirable good fooling' whilst it lasted; but, even if no counter influence had been at work, it may be he would have tired of it ere now: only, in that other case, he would have sought, after his custom, for fresh pastime elsewhere; instead of dissembling his weariness—with a purpose.

Such treachery, practised for a more righteous end, has a base savour. I doubt if Desgrais, in the aftertime, looked back with much pride on the cunning stratagem that lured Louise de Brinvilliers out of sanctuary; or if he easily forgot the reproach and horror of her eyes, when, instead of the loving clasp she expected, the manacles closed round her wrists.

Caryl felt no remorse; simply because, to serve or save Lena Atherstone, he would not have shrunk from torturing any other living creature: but he did feel some faint compunction just then; such as may have assailed the first Napoleon, when, to cover his retreat, a squadron or two were sent to certain death. Assuredly, he addressed himself to consoling Cissy with very unwonted earnestness—with what success you may divine. Before they parted, she was as 'reasonable' as even Caryl could desire.

Arthur Corbett, too, had his private causes of discontent; though, perhaps, they were not easier than Mrs. Devereux's to put into shape and substance.

He could not say that he was made less welcome at Templestowe than heretofore; though, somehow, it seemed harder to find excuses for his visits. Neither had Lena's manner grown cold or repellant. It was often absent and indifferent, to be sure; but then it had always been more or less so, except on a few rare occasions, such as that delicious day at Wilton.

She was still as ready to listen, if not quite so ready
to respond. But a kind of crystal curtain seemed to
have dropped betwixt them, through which, though
it hindered not sight, nor absolutely forbade speech,
all words passed faint and dull; and this barrier was
as impossible to break as if it had been built of stone
or steel. And yet the change—if change there were
—he could not, in common fairness, impute to his
having been supplanted.

That vague distrust and dislike of Glynne, alluded
to above, abode with Corbett still; but there was
not a shadow of ground for fresh suspicion. Twice
he had encountered the other at Templestowe; but,
from all that appeared on the surface, they were the
most natural of morning visits; and, on both occasions, Caryl had chosen to leave him in possession
of the field  Certainly, Arthur might have got a
salutary warning, if he had chanced to notice the
knitting of Lady Atherstone's brows when Glynne
rose to depart, and the glance—half-satirical, half-
imperative—by which that sign of discontent was
answered. But these are precisely the things that
men of the Corbett type never do notice; and the
banker missed the clue, though it lay within arm's
length. Of a truth, had he grasped it, perchance his
feet were now too weak to carry him out of the maze.

He could not possibly take Lena to task, or call
her to account; for the utmost encouragement that
he had received was not enough to warrant him in so
doing; and Arthur had the wit to see, that a false
step in this direction might be irretrievable. So he
had to content himself with vague plaintive whispers,
and glances eloquent of injury; though, for any effect
that they produced, both might as well have been
lavished on the tallest elm in the avenue. And all
the while—knowing that more boldness would have
been mere rashness—he ceased not to revile himself
as cowardly and supine; and the evil fires within him
burned more fiercely than ever.

Can you wonder that the struggle rent and wore
the man, so that, not only those near and dear to
him, but strangers, marvelled what was amiss? But
of the truth none had surmise—not even Emma Corbett, though, waking or sleeping, the fear was seldom
off her mind, that some great sorrow or disaster was
hanging over, if it had not actually stricken, her
husband. She had never directly questioned him
since the occasion you wot of; for Arthur's temper
had grown so fearfully uncertain of late that, for his
sake—not for her own—she forbore to provoke it.

A shadow, such as had probably never hung over
the staid old mansion since its foundations were laid,
began to brood there. The very children seemed to
feel the influence. Meta never asked for a story
now; and the others, instead of greeting their father
noisily, rather shrank out of his way, whispering to
each other that 'Papa wasn't well, and mustn't be
teased.' Natural affection was not yet stifled in
Arthur Corbett; and if, as was likely, he was conscious of all this, be sure he hated himself accordingly; but to amend it, he was powerless. Truly
his punishment had begun betimes; and, if it was
heavier than that which has lighted on many who
have more heavily sinned, who shall say that it was
not earned?

So, all over the tilth, the evil crop reddened and
ripened to the harvest that was near.

# CHAPTER XXXIX.

THOUGH there was little of the braggart in his nature, and he took no pride in parading his successes, Kerneguy had not been unjust in imputing to Caryl Glynne 'exceptional bad luck in compromising his female acquaintances.' It was not that he was himself specially rash, or tempted others to be so : he only seemed too indolent to take precautions, and too self-indulgent to practise restraint. But this was altered now. In his dealings with Lena Atherstone he evinced a wonderful prudence and patience ; and, so far from being exacting, often refrained from availing himself of an opportunity. And she did justice—ample justice—to his motives, and never murmured, even in her heart; though in his absence everything around her seemed so cold and dreary, that it was no wonder if she hankered for the warmth and light that his presence always brought.

Once, and once only, they came within the verge of danger.

Since Mrs. Shafton appeared at Templestowe, the *tête-à-tête* interviews had become very precarious; for, though the mother did not affect, or perhaps intend, to act duenna, she was by no means such an accommodating third as Lady Marian ; and, lacking the latter's excuses for betaking herself elsewhere, as often as not saw fit to sit the visitor out.

Caryl never betrayed a sign of annoyance ; but, on one of those occasions, after a dark, wet ride homewards, he so far yielded to a sense of injury as to write by that post to Lena, appointing an out-door meeting the following afternoon.

There was nothing picturesque in the big, ram-
bling park of Templestowe; but the ground rose
enough, in the rear of the mansion, to form something like a hanging wood. Broad belts of covert
almost entirely lined the boundary-wall; and through
these the late lord, who prided himself on his plantations, had cut glades and grass-roads, wide enough
at the narrowest for an ordinary pony-carriage.
These had long since lost their trimness, for they
were seldom traversed now; but they were kept open
for sporting purposes; and, save in very bad weather,
were always passable.

Lena had made the circuit more than once with
Marian Ashleigh, so she was not likely to miss the
place of rendezvous; and Glynne, too, found his way
thither easily, for he had been posted hard by, whilst
shooting the coverts.

It was a kind of *carrefour*, whence several rides
diverged star-wise; and evergreens grew thickly just
here, affording shelter and screen when other trees
were bare. Also, within convenient distance, was a
park-gate, seldom used now, but never locked; for
John Gilbert and his fellows kept poachers aloof,
and Lord Atherstone cared little for other intruders.

It was a good seven-mile walk from Erriswell;
and, for reasons of his own, Glynne had followed
field-paths rather than the Queen's highway. But
he looked indolence personified, as he leant back
against an oak trunk, smoking a placid cigarette.
Beyond frequent mud-flecks on his high russet boots,
he bore no signs of travel; and he might have sat for
a picture, in that soft velvet shooting dress. There
was no affectation in his habitual languor; but it
concealed an abundance of physical energy: besides
this, the effect of his Morean training had not yet
passed away.

Before he had time to grow impatient, Lena
appeared.

The manner of their interview need not be recorded; but it lasted rather longer than was prudent; for the woods were darkening into twilight when they said adieu.

They were standing close—very close — together, when they were startled by a deep voice, sounding almost in their ears, though in reality it came from a score of yards or so down a side-glade.

"Tramp! Have a care, will you? 'Ware flick!"

It was John Gilbert going his rounds, accompanied, as it happened, by a half-broken retriever. If steady old Sultan—familiar to contempt with all four-footed things—had been at his heel, the pair loitering there had been sped; for, though massive of frame, the keeper trod, from long habit, always warily, and a heavier foot would have fallen noiselessly on the soft grass and sodden leaves.

A thrill of terror—not of selfish terror, to do him justice—shot through Glynne's breast, as he drew back swiftly and silently; but one glance assured him that the holly-screen had saved them; and, when Gilbert turned the corner of the ride, for aught of discomposure or consciousness that they displayed, he and his companion might have been chatting on the Templestowe terrace.

"Yes, I don't think you could choose a better place," Caryl was saying. "Ah, Gilbert, is that you? Come here for a moment, will you?"—for, after making his rough obeisance, the keeper was passing on—"Lady Atherstone was thinking of putting up a sort of arbour somewhere about here, of heath, or anything that would be weatherproof; for it was rather too damp to be pleasant when we last lunched here. Don't you think we've found about the best spot?"

The keeper looked somewhat glum, though none but professional scruples were floating in his mind. To speak truth, he did not specially admire these mixed entertainments; and held that the presence of petticoats was, on the whole, inimical to the bag, as tending to make the afternoon shooting jealous, if not wild. However, in common with the other dependents of Templestowe, he rather favoured Lady Atherstone; and the latter had shown much kindness to his daughter, who was still ailing. So he made shift to answer with sufficient affability.

"The place is handy enough, sir, if my lady fancies such a thing. But, if I might advise, I'd shift it about ten rod backarder, pretty close to the park-wall. A stop there 'ud do more good than harm; but anything strange, set in the open here, 'ud be sure to make the birds break back. As it is, we can manage one or two fairish flushes, if you remember."

"I should be very ungrateful to forget," the other returned. "I had a real good corner—that was before luncheon, though — and I wish I'd done it more justice."

There was a charm in Caryl's manner, sometimes, which very few could resist; and, perhaps, even rugged John Gilbert was not wholly insensible to this, as he answered with a short, gruff laugh.

"You didn't do bad, sir, by no means. Anyhow, you didn't blow your birds, like yon soldier gentleman from Heslingford. He did mash 'em terrible. I think you take my meaning; and p'r'aps you'll make it clear to my lady."

Lena had so far recovered herself by this time, as to be able to take her own part in the talk; and, when Phœbe had been duly inquired after, the keeper was suffered to go on his way.

In all things pertaining to his craft, his eyes were like an Indian's on the war-trail; but, in matters like this, they were purblind. If it needed almost force to open them, when his own child was in peril, they were scarce likely to be quick-sighted concerning a comparative stranger. Moreover, though in this man there was not a touch of servility, he was not apt to think evil of dignities; neither would he lightly attaint the honour of the family whose bread

he had eaten for forty years. Had it been otherwise,
be sure that neither for fear nor favour would John
Gilbert have held his peace; and Ralph Atherstone
would have been set face to face with his dishonour
before he slept.

For Lena's sake, Glynne glossed over the peril
they had escaped so narrowly, but to himself he did
not undervalue it; and he vowed inwardly that the
like should not again be incurred. It was during
his walk homewards that he resolved on moving,
for a time at least, from his pleasant quarters; and
he broached his intention, that same evening, at
Erriswell.

Mrs. Malcolm did not venture to argue the point;
but she was evidently surprised and chagrined. Her
husband, though he expressed regret, and pressed
on Caryl a speedy return, took it much more easily.

Robin had been troubled with certain misgivings
of late, albeit they had not tended towards Templestowe. He had not failed to remark signs of growing
discontent in the master of Hunsden; and had, more
than once, reproached himself with being accessory,
in a distant degree, to the annoyance, whatsoever it
was, brooding on the jovial face. He was no ascetic,
and was willing that all around him should amuse
themselves in their own fashion; but it must be in
purity and honour, or it should not be with his good
leave. Also, he was diffident of judging the society
from which he had been severed so long; and was
well aware that many things, that to him seemed
strange and over-bold, might to others appear quite
natural and harmless. Nevertheless, his clear common-sense rarely failed to mark the boundary-line
betwixt right and wrong; and those doubts of Caryl's
real amendment waxed more frequent and troublesome. It might be only fooling, of course: but fooling, that could cause such an honest heart as Dick
Devereux's to ache, could scarcely be innocent; and
would, at all events, be the better for a check.

So, putting force on his hospitality, with many kindly words Malcolm sped the parting guest. Had he but wist of the truth, he would have thrust the other from his doors with scant leave-taking—ay! if a storm had been raging, wild enough to have uprooted the toughest oak at Erriswell.

Neither did Lena combat Caryl's resolution. When —answering her beseeching eyes, rather than her lips, which scarcely stirred—he said gently, "I must go," she pleaded no more; for she felt he had not come lightly or selfishly to such resolve.

But her whole character had changed of late. The independence and self-reliance that had once distinguished her had quite vanished; and, in all matters where Caryl could have a voice, she seemed to have surrendered free-agency, and even free-will. If the old dreams—dispelled long ago—had come true, and she had bound herself to honour and obey him in the face of God and man, she could not have performed the second more implicitly, though the first was impossible.

She promised, now, to be patient, just as she would have promised to play her part in any scheme that he judged to be expedient; and she forbore to make the parting harder by any repining.

But when he was gone——

I trust that none who read these pages—not excepting their sternest critic—will be able to fill up, from their own experience, that dreary *lacuna*. It may be a hard time, perhaps, with the men who, on sea or land, have their appointed work to do; but often it is a harder, rely on it, with 'the women that weep,' even when their tears have a right to flow. And how, think you, does it fare with them, when it is a sin to hope, and a blasphemy to pray?

Nevertheless, in point of present expediency, Glynne's departure was assuredly well-timed; for, within the same week, Miles Shafton, availing himself of a general invitation, appeared at Templestowe.

Even to him it was evident that there was a change.

not for the better ; and, had things remained *in statu,*
it is just possible he might have stumbled on the real
cause thereof—not so much from keenness of perception, as from the instincts of antipathy. If he was
sensitive anywhere, it was in regard to his sister.
Though almost all his knowledge of the matter came
from hearsay, he had never forgiven Glynne for compromising her ; and you may remember that he 'rose'
freely at the mention of this name, when he and his
comrade were discussing Lena's approaching marriage. Only—far from making no account of Caryl,
as he had then affected to do—he held the latter in
almost irrational dread ; and would not have stood
much on probabilities, in tracing the troubling of any
waters whatsoever to that fountain-head. Besides,
as you are aware, some of the best-laid ambushments
have miscarried, through the chance snapping of a
firelock, or a drunkard's blunder; and, all things considered, Miles might have proved a dangerous addition
to materials sufficiently explosive.

As it was, he decided that his relatives 'had grown
deadly dull, and wanted Lady Marian to wake
them up.' Moreover, the infection seemed to have
spread ; for Arthur Corbett was almost a nonentity
now, convivially speaking—rarely appearing at the
covert-side, and more than slack with his 'little dinners ;' Mrs. Devereux had departed, after all, to pay
that threatened visit to her uncle; whilst the Driver
—for whom Miles had always had a kind of fellow-
feeling—though he rode harder than ever, took his
pleasure sullenly and silently. The sport, too, as it
happened, was rather below the average just then.

So the hussar made his visit shorter than he had
intended ; and, casting the economy of free quarters
to the winds, sped away to the Dragon of Wantley—
the famous hostelry which, for a 'consideration,' fur-
nishes food, drink, cattle, and everything but raiment,
to 'spring captains,' and others who have no fixed
abiding-place on the grass.

# CHAPTER XL

How he excused his absence to those most interested in the question, was best known to himself; but the early and the late spring passed away, without Glynne's again appearing in Loamshire. It may be that business was not a vain pretext: his affairs were always so complicated, that, without an occasional oiling of the wheels, they were sure to come to a dead lock; and, at this time, the process necessitated a visit to Vienna.

Mrs. Devereux chafed and fretted, as a matter of course; but, when she found that frequent missives—indignant, imperative, or imploring—sent on the track of the recreant, availed nothing, a relic of prudence, backed up by a sufficiency of pride, enabled her to bide her time. However, the Driver—performing, after his wont, vicarious penance—had a very rough time of it at home; and all her other admirers were more or less hardly entreated by their imperious mistress. With a truly feminine perversity, she still deferred reconciliation with Godfrey Colville; and Dick, albeit infinitely more valorous on his friend's behalf than on his own, dared not, for the nonce, air his hospitable intentions.

Lena was patient, as she had promised—wonderfully patient; only as day succeeded day, each appearing longer than its fellow, her listlessness deepened into apathy. She seldom stirred abroad, and seemed less equal than heretofore to the effort of keeping up appearances at home.

Lord Atherstone noticed this; and his own heart waxed so heavy that twice or thrice, he was on the

verge of taking Mrs. Shafton into his counsel, and
beseeching her to confide in him, if she had guessed
at the root of Lena's melancholy. It was not pride,
but rather the delicacy of which mention has before
been made, so strangely at variance with the rest of
his character, that set a seal on his lips. It was,
doubtless, with a view to distract his wife's thoughts
at any cost, that he proposed their moving to town
immediately after Easter; not into apartments as
before, but into a house for the entire season.

Lena acceded to the plan readily, but indifferently;
yet, if the room had not chanced to be so dimly lit,
and she had not sate so far back in the shadow, even
Ralph might have marked the treacherous flush that
swept across her cheek—paler than ever of late—and
have marvelled at its cause.

Mrs. Shafton, who still stayed on at Templestowe,
was anything but pleased with the summer programme;
but it was scarcely possible for her to start any objection without treading on perilous ground, especially
after Lena had intimated that there would always be
a room at her disposal, whenever she chose to occupy
it. Indeed, the mother's misgivings had been much
less active of late, if they had not entirely slumbered,
simply from the lack of fresh matter to feed upon;
and that very elasticity of character, which had
buoyed her up through many troubles, helped to be-
guile her, now, into a false security.

Lady Atherstone did not suggest any special *locale*
for their town quarters, and her husband seemed
equally careless on the subject. This question was
settled for them by one of the convenient agents who,
at a day's notice, can purvey anything from a palace
down to a *maison de santé*, so long as they are not
stinted in terms. It was purely by accident, that Lena
found herself settled within a stone's throw of the
quiet street where the first—and last—romance of her
life began.

Though the breadth of the cycle may vary infinitely,

according to circumstances, is it not strange how often private as well as public histories repeat themselves? If the campaign has prospered, it is pleasant, doubtless, to pile arms amidst the old familiar places; but, if the battle has gone hard against them, surely the prescience of defeat will not weigh less heavily on those who have fallen back almost to the ground where, at the outset, full of strength and hope, they set their forces in array. Do you think that the hunted hare dies a whit the easier, because the last double has brought her close to her 'form?'

Had Lady Atherstone been quite innocent and heart-whole, the coincidence must needs have evoked memories that ought never to have stirred in their tombs; but, unhappily, the dry bones were clothed with flesh already, and the evil host was fit to do the bidding of the Spirit who had been permitted to call them back to life. With Lena the gulf of intervening years seemed to have vanished utterly; and old scenes stood out in as close and bold relief as if they had been enacted yesterday. More vividly than she had ever remembered it since, she recollected her first glimpse of Caryl Glynne's face—how, even then, it seemed to detach itself from the others pressing through a crowded doorway; she could have gone straight to the tree under which he waited, when, trembling despite her hardihood, she came to meet him through the fresh June morning; she could call back the very tints of the western clouds that hung over their parting, on the eve of her enforced flight northwards.

And the Tempter's whispers were more frequent than ever; and Caryl—either weary of self-denial, or waxing reckless from impunity—preached prudence no longer. Indeed, there was little of difficulty or danger to contend with, now that they were sheltered under the mantle of the Great City, which is one of refuge to worse sins than homicide.

Lord Atherstone spent all his afternoons abroad;

and his goings-out and comings-in were so regular,
that there was no chance of his appearing untime-
ously: moreover, Lena was such a favourite with
her household, that her actions were likely to be
charitably construed even by the Vigilance Committee
below stairs.

Oddly enough, perhaps the first person who conceived any serious suspicion was fair Grace Moreland. She was neither prude nor Puritan; indeed,
she was rather ingenious in inventing apologies for
the follies of her fellows, and had defended Lena
too often formerly to be apt to accuse her now.
Nevertheless, looking back on their ancient intimacy,
Grace could not but admit that it had greatly slackened; and, for awhile, bewildered herself in trying to
account for this. Now that Lena had a house of her
own, so extremely 'convenient' to Blakeney Street,
Mrs. Moreland had naturally reckoned on dropping
in, at unceremonious hours, for a confidential chat.
But, somehow, it seemed impossible to walk, straight
and unannounced, into Lena's boudoir, though, once
there, the welcome was as cordial as ever; and, twice
or thrice, Grace had actually been rebutted by a 'Not
at home,' that, she felt almost sure, was conventional.

She would have scorned espial either on friend or
foe; and it was simply by chance that, on one of
these occasions—looking back as she turned a corner
—she saw Caryl Glynne issue from the doors which
had just been closed against herself. It was a feeling
much less selfish than mortified vanity or slighted
friendship, that made Grace Moreland's light heart so
heavy that evening. With all her gentleness, she was
too proud to complain, and, though in nowise timid,
dared not play monitress here; so she let her grievance
sleep when she next met Lena. Neither till long
after did she confide her forebodings to her own husband, from whom she had seldom hitherto kept a
secret; but they did not cease to haunt her, till there
was nothing left to fear.

The Atherstones went a good deal into society; and Ralph performed late escort-duty, with a readiness and punctuality that might put many recent benedicts to shame. The opera was the only place to which Lena went alone—never quite alone, indeed; for even on these occasions she was always accompanied by her mother, Grace Moreland, or Lady Marian. The Ashleighs were in town for the season; Philip having hardened himself to the extravagance of a furnished 'flat.' But the afternoons, as has been aforesaid, the baron was fain to spend after his own devices; and, perforce, frequented his divers clubs assiduously.

One afternoon towards the end of May, he was sitting in a window of the Sanctorium, gazing out into the crowded street—intently, as it seemed, but, in reality, so vacantly that a familiar friend might have passed by unrecognised—when Sir Charles Wroughton came up, holding an open letter in his hand, and with a cloud of annoyance on his face.

"Don't you despise people who never know their own minds?" he said. "Not a fortnight ago, Tempest was too keen about Norway—slept with his fly-book under his pillow, I believe, for fear somebody should borrow his special patterns; and, now, here's a lachrymose note, regretting that he must throw me over, because his brother's coming home from India. Just as if two months would have made any difference, when they haven't met for a dozen years! So I've got to look up a second rod, at a week's notice. You don't happen to know of a decent fisherman, about my own age, and about my force at picquet—I'm full against boys and gamblers—I'd almost frank him there and back."

Lord Atherstone paused awhile; and, when he looked up to answer, there was an earnestness in his eyes utterly disproportioned to the subject.

"I only know of one man," he said; "and he's not quite up to the picquet standard, though he might

suit in other respects. Would you mind taking
me?"

Wroughton's countenance grew blank from very
surprise. "Take *you?* You must be joking; though
jokes are not in your line. I thought, when you gave
up your river, you'd given up Norway for good. Surely,
too, you've taken your house for the season; and"—
his tongue stumbled here—"and you're aware that
mine are only bachelor quarters?"

"I'm quite aware of it," Ralph replied. "Had it
been otherwise, I should never have dreamt of taking
my wife across the North Sea. But, now she's
thoroughly settled, I fancy she will manage very well
without me for a few weeks, with her mother's and
Marian's help. Anyhow, I'll consult her, and let you
have a decided answer by noon to-morrow, if you'll
hold the rod open so long."

"Of course I will," the other answered; "I'd keep
it open longer for such a chance. So don't decide
hastily; and—don't let me persuade you."

The speaker's manner was hearty, but not precisely
eager; and it was easy to divine that his inclinations
and convictions were at variance. Scandal had
hitherto spared Lady Atherstone, and not a rumour
to her disparagement had reached Wroughton's ears;
neither—being often in her company—could he himself accuse her of coquetry. Nevertheless he felt that,
if he had stood in his comrade's place, he would have
consented never to wet a salmon line again, rather
than have put some hundred leagues of sea and land
betwixt himself and so fair a wife, when the butterfly-
season was at its height. He had no exalted ideas of
marital responsibility; but there is a time for all
things, and perhaps something of the burden of the
old hunting-song was running in his head just then—

> With cheer and whoop the chase is up,
> And bachelors may fare;
> But married men should bide at home,
> From the hunting of the bear.

z

In all ages, that plea of exemption from feast or foray has generally been allowed ; and even Sparta, once only, rose to the sublime cynicism that produced the Parthenii.

But the easy-going baronet was wont to assume that every man—gentle or simple, wise or witless— was, till incapacity should be proved, the best judge of his own affairs ; and, if neither scruples nor sus- picions existed in Ralph's breast, surely it would be an ill deed to plant them there. Having forborne to bias his friend's decision either way, Wroughton felt his conscience at ease, and waited to see what the morrow would bring forth.

# CHAPTER XLI.

It was not Ralph Atherstone's way, to dally with a purpose once formed. Lena had just returned from her drive when he reached home; and he went straight to her boudoir, having ascertained that she was alone: yet, instead of broaching the object of his coming abruptly, he paved the way by inquiring about their engagements, and so forth; and, when enlightened on these points, he paused for awhile, as if meditating.

"My dear," he said at last, "do you think you could afford me a six-weeks' leave? You expect your mother almost immediately, I know; and she's a much better *chaperon* than ever I can hope to be, though a matron of your standing hardly requires one. Wroughton has offered me the second rod on his Norway river; and I've a fancy to see the old fiords once more."

A startled look came into Lena's eyes.

"Norway?" she repeated, as if doubting whether she had heard aright.

A half-smile flitted across the baron's face, which had not often been so lighted up of late.

"I suppose it sounds very far off; but, in reality, it is not so. It's straight steaming to Trondhjem; and a couple of days of kariole-work land you on the river. But, if I am wanted at home, do say so: nothing is settled yet. I wouldn't decide without consulting you."

Her fingers plucked nervously at the fringe of her mantle, and her voice faltered.

"I hardly know what to say. I should be too sorry to thwart any fancy of yours; and yet——"

Ralph was standing over against his wife, much as he had stood on that afternoon which decided their destinies; and now—even as he had done then—he drew nearer, and bent over her, less caressingly than protectingly.

"A fancy? Yes; but suppose I'd another fancy, my dear—a fancy, that you have had somewhat too much of my company of late, and that you might tire of it less hereafter, if you missed it for awhile? Don't mistake me"—he went on hurriedly; for he saw her start and shiver—"I'm not grumbling or complaining. I've no more right to wonder at your finding my society sometimes dull, than at your finding Templestowe sometimes dreary. Thirty years' difference of age must needs tell: I always reckoned on it. And I see, now, no more hindrance to our being happy, in our own way, than I did eighteen months ago. But the best of friendships—and surely ours is of the best—are none the worse for short absences; and I think we might venture to try the experiment."

The grave, cold tone suited ill with the generous words. Yet, if Lena had chanced to look up just then, she might have been saved from utter ruin, though not from guilt; for, if she had marked the quiver of the stern lip, the wistful earnestness of the deep-set eyes, and the tenderness that softened the rugged features, there surely would have been stirred within her such an agony of remorse as she had never felt yet; and, after that sharp pang, might have come slow healing.

To have avowed all—had it been possible—would have profited little; for Ralph Atherstone's love did not cast out wrath, though it could cast out fear; and, if there was no limit to his trust, there was a narrow limit to his capacity of forgiveness; nor, to save a hundred lives, dear to him as Lena's, would he have stooped to condone a crime. But she might

have cast herself on the broad breast that was still
ready to receive her; and, resting her head there,
might have vowed within herself a vow. And, if she
had kept the same thenceforth faithfully, it might
have fared with her as well as it can ever fare with
those who, if they escape from bondage, must carry
fetter-galls to their grave. But that last chance was
lost: her eyes were bent downwards still; and if,
during the next few seconds, the Tempter relaxed his
hold, he never quite unloosed it.

"You—are quite wrong," she murmured. "I never
——" The falsehood died on her lips: they could
only frame an evasion. "Could you not possibly
take me?"

He shook his head.

"Quite impossible. Women must be prepared to
rough it in the best of those lodges; and Wroughton's,
I happen to know, are literally bachelor-quarters.
Besides, even in summer, you can't depend on the
humour of the North Sea. But it was a kindly
thought, my dear; and I'm sure you meant it."

"Yes, I do mean it," she said softly.

The words need not necessarily have been quite
untrue. Obstacles, trivial as a lost horseshoe, an
unsound axle, or a lagging timepiece, have, ere this,
sufficed to arrest irreparable mischief; and, perchance,
such a faint possibility was in the background here.
It may be, that in her mind there still lingered a
vague idea—not amounting to a desire—of seeking
safety through the only means that could secure it:
though she had no strength left to fight, she might
still have found strength to fly. But the good impulse was not stable enough to persist against denial;
and, with a throb of guilty joy at her heart, Lena
yielded to what in her blindness she deemed her fate.
She never in so many words approved of the Norway
scheme; but from that moment it was tacitly settled.
And on this basis they went on to discuss, quite
tranquilly, their future plans—Ralph promising to

return home, in good time to accompany his wife to Kirkfell, where they were booked already.

Surprise does not at all express Mrs. Shafton's state of mind, when, on her arrival forty-eight hours later, she was informed of the arrangement: indeed, discontent was so plainly written on her countenance, that Lord Atherstone felt constrained to ask if the *chaperonage* of Lena would interfere with any engagements of her own.

"Not exactly that," Mrs. Shafton answered reluctantly; "but——" She came to an awkward halt here.

"But what?" Ralph inquired, after waiting patiently for the conclusion of the sentence. His brows were knit, perhaps more in perplexity than in displeasure; but Mrs. Shafton interpreted the sign in the latter wise, and her heart began to quake. Now, as ever, she made small account of any difficulty or danger that could befall herself; but she was timid where Lena was concerned; and, though she liked him well, had always held her son-in-law in some dread.

"Nothing," she faltered at last: "only — won't people think it very odd?" And she came to another check.

The frown still lingered on Lord Atherstone's brow, though his lip was curling.

"People may think what they please," he retorted, "so long as Lena and I understand each other; and I believe we do that thoroughly. When you've talked it over with her, I'm quite sure you'll be satisfied that it's a good arrangement."

The two did talk it over, in a sort of way; but Lena did not much allay her mother's scruples or misgivings. She merely observed, that the scheme was none of her suggesting; and declined to discuss its expediency, on the ground that she had already done this with Lord Atherstone. And she only assented with a careless nod to Mrs. Shafton's entreaty, that 'she would at least promise to be unusually careful.'

The leave-taking of husband and wife, though kindly on both sides, was as calm and commonplace as you can conceive; for it was rare, indeed, that the feelings of the former ever rose to the surface, and the latter's hour of grace was past. Ralph Atherstone's lips lingered no longer on the broad white brow, than the first time when they lighted there. Could he guess that, when he looked on it next, it would bear an open brand of shame?

Nevertheless, when these matters were discussed in after-time, it went hard with the baron; and people were witty or severe, according to their temper, on the slackness of his guardianship; and some there were who, when his back was turned, scrupled not to cry, 'wittol,' 'dullard,' and harder names yet, if such there be—wearing, of course, to his face, looks of demurest sympathy. Perchance, many who read this story will be prone to range themselves in the same seat of the scornful; yet, there is something to be said on the other side.

If manners are altered, men and women are much the same as when they, in Camelot, lived, and sinned, and suffered. After all, did Arthur's perfect trust impair his perfect honour? If any made mock thereat, they were not knights loyal as Gareth, or dames innocent as Enid; but rather traitors like to him who,

> ever like a subtle beast,
> Lay couchant with his eyes upon the throne,
> Ready to spring;

or wantons like to her who triumphed in the woods of Broceliande. Remember, it was Vivien's gibe that stirred the wizard's cold blood to such loathing, as almost saved him from the snare. Least of all, be sure, did Launcelot and Guenevere despise the 'blameless king.' And yet the crime, never noted by his clear pure eyes, was one

> clamour'd by the child,
> Not whisper'd in the corner.

I do not purpose to carry the parallel beyond a certain point. Besides courage, generosity, and uprightness, few elements of a hero of chivalry existed in Ralph Atherstone; neither could any specially lofty aspirations, or affairs of momentous import, excuse his thoughts for wandering from what concerned him more nearly. His folly, if you choose to call it so, was after the manner of his generation and the measure of his capacity; yet it was of such a sort as not even those who profited by it could deride. From first to last, Glynne never spoke slightingly to Lena of her husband, or felt thoroughly at his ease in the other's presence.

As for her—Well, even in this life, and even by womankind, 'varying and mutable,' there is sometimes dealt justice, more even-handed than we suppose, to Gawain and Pelleas.

Are you aweary of Lyonnesse? Perhaps not, if you think with me, that it is scarce possible to read the Idylls so often, as to find nothing to learn or to admire; even though the story—more's the pity— like Cambuscans', is thus far 'left half-told.' Profit, surely, as well as pleasure, may be drawn from almost every page; nor will I admit that true and wise words have less power when wedded to sweet, solemn rhythm, than when conveyed in doggrel, grating like a handsaw. *Missa est apologia.*

# CHAPTER LXII.

MARIAN ASHLEIGH was scarcely less astonished than Mrs. Shafton had been, when she was informed of her father-in-law's intentions; though she took the news much more tranquilly. The pursing of her lips, and the lifting of her brows, might signify disapproval; yet covert triumph sparkled in her eyes.

Unless I have wholly failed in sketching her character, these signs will not seem to you strange; but —lest any should be at a loss to interpret them—let us speak plainly at last.

From the moment that she heard of Lena Shafton as the future mistress of Templestowe, Marian had never ceased to regard her as an enemy, against whom all offensive measures were fair; and had never faltered in her purpose of lowering the usurper from her pride of place. She formed, at first, no set plan of action; but gradually developed it—moulding each chance and circumstance as it arose, and never holding her hand for pity, remorse, or shame. When she came to know Lena personally, her animosity neither increased nor diminished : it was the wife, not the woman, that she hated, and was prepared to sacrifice on grounds of purely political expediency. She would, doubtless, have attempted, sooner or later, in some fashion or other, to sow seeds of dissension at Templestowe, if her natural shrewdness, working out those hints of Kerneguy's, had not whispered that, in all probability, swifter and surer means would present themselves. After she heard of Caryl Glynne's appearance in Loamshire, she had never doubted as to the result; and the only fault in her calculations was the setting it at too long a date.

Had she been forced to give an account of her actions, she would have alleged that she had done nothing to hurry or change the course of events; but had simply let it flow on. And, it may be, in strict human justice, the plea would have held good. In these cases there is no 'misprision of felony;' and no formal penalty attaches to those who—themselves on firm ground—seeing one of their fellows sink, inch by inch, into the deadly quicksand, stir neither tongue nor finger. However, construed by another code, certain flaws might be found in such neutrality as Marian's.

Grant, that she was not bound to take action on suspicion and probability. But remember, after that night when she played the spy at Erriswell, it would have been mere prevarication to question whether Ralph Atherstone's honour was imperilled; and, thenceforth, in holding her peace—to say nothing of furnishing opportunity — she wilfully connived at crime. Rather a liberal reading of neutrality, this.

Now, if any man had presumed to whisper into Marian Ashleigh's ear an unseemly word, she would have requited the offence with a cool contempt, more effective than loud indignation; and would have passed on, shaking, so to speak, the dust from her spotless stole. Nevertheless, such a part as she had been playing for some months past, it might not be safe to propose to certain of the *togatæ*. Rank has its privileges—save the mark! 'So, *sessa*, and let the world slide.'

This being premised, you will understand why Marian's eyes flashed gleefully, when she heard of the baron's resolution, and why she forebore either to encourage or dissuade him. But, in spite of policy and philosophy, she did experience a slight pang of compunction when he came to bid her good-bye— she knew so well what his welcome home again was like to be—and it so far influenced her, that she could not answer, audibly, Ralph's last injunction, "You'll be sure to take care of Lena." For this weakness, she may perhaps be forgiven.

Lord Atherstone had not been gone a week, when the effects of his absence became manifest. As Mrs. Shafton had presaged, people did think it 'very odd,' and scrupled not to say so; and vague rumours began to take form and substance, rapidly as the smoke curling out of the Afreet's prison. Perhaps some of Marian Ashleigh's parlour-magic was at work; at any rate, it was wonderful how suddenly the world's memory became refreshed with regard to divers old stories, and how quickly divers hatchets were disinterred. Lady Atherstone and Glynne very rarely were seen together in public; and, on these occasions, there was nothing to blame, or even to comment upon, in their demeanour; nevertheless, their names were coupled constantly and significantly, now; and those who professed to see below the surface of things, waited for the scandal that was bound to ensue; just as those who listen to the rumbling geyser, look for the outburst of scalding spray.

Certain of these whispers reached the august ears of his Grace of Devorgoil, causing them to tingle not ungratefully. Feeling himself beyond ken of Ralph Atherstone's masterful eyes, he swelled with righteous indignation and valour. One afternoon the two carriages came side by side in the lock at the head of the Mile; and, then and there, the Duke redeemed his slackness at Hazlemere. Lady Rachel Fontenaye ably seconded her sire; whilst Lady Ursula, blushing guiltily, was fain to 'let pass the justice of the king.' Before nightfall it was known to all whom it might concern, and to many whom it concerned not a whit, that Grandmanoir had inflicted on Templestowe the cut direct.

Amongst the spectators there were several not inclined to favour Lady Atherstone; but even these were fain to own that she bore herself superbly. She had no companion to keep her in countenance—her mother was too unwell to drive that day—but she neither shrank nor changed colour under the insult: indeed, the slightest curl of her lip was the only token that she noticed it.

Hard by stood the Master of the Loamshire Hunt, almost hidden by the burly form of Swinton Swarbrick. Both saw what happened; and Jasper Knowsley's brow contracted, whilst the other's face crimsoned angrily.

"Did you see that?" he growled. "I wonder what old Clear-Starch's game is."

Swinton guessed pretty well what was amiss; but he was loath to think or speak evil, especially of those for whom he had a liking; and Lena was popular enough amongst the male folk in Loamshire, if she had not been able to conciliate the womankind.

The Master answered never a word; but he glided forward through the throng, and the next instant he stood at Lady Atherstone's carriage-door. Swarbrick followed eagerly, shouldering aside the crowd with scant ceremony; and, if the converse of the pair was not very intellectual or interesting, it certainly helped to relieve an awkward situation.

Down in their own country, their partisanship might have availed somewhat in stemming the tide of public opinion; here, they were but straws in the stream: nevertheless the good intention was the same. For many a long day afterwards, the Master and his co-adjutor were in disfavour at Grandmanoir; indeed, but for official considerations, his Grace would certainly have withdrawn his support from the hounds. However, neither has withered perceptibly under the ducal frown—perhaps because neither has forgotten the sad smile with which Lena Atherstone requited their timely courtesy.

Not from this quarter, you may be sure, came the

tale-bearing ; yet the incident just recorded was discussed, throughout Loamshire, before it was many
hours old.

On the third morning, Lady Marian was sitting
alone, when Hubert Ashleigh was announced.

The brow of the placid divine was unusually overcast. He put curtly aside Marian's questions as to
local news, and did not even stop to inquire after
Philip before breaking ground.

"It is a very unpleasant business that has brought
me here ; and, though you may throw some light on
it, Marian, I can scarcely hope that you will alter its
complexion. Is it possible that I have been misin-
formed as to the Duke's behaviour to Lady Atherstone ?"

She shook her head with a sympathetic sigh.

"It is too true, I'm afraid. I can't tell you how
shocked and surprised I was, when I heard of it the
same evening. We all know his pride and prejudice ;
but——"

"Yes," he interrupted, "and we all know, too, that,
even in Ralph's absence, he never would have dared
to be insolent, unless on safe grounds. Now, I have
come to ask you what these grounds are. You can
answer me, I feel certain, Marian. When you said
'surprised,' a minute ago, I think you could scarcely
have meant it."

She did not like his tone, it was so perfectly different from any she had heard him use ; and, to gain
time, she tried evasion.

"Surely, you had better ask Philip."

"Philip!" he sneered. "I should prefer sounding
the first chance acquaintance I met. I've no doubt
he's fussing away, at this moment, on committee,
just as if no cloud were hanging over his house.
There is such a cloud : it is useless to deny it. You'd
best be frank and open with me."

"I've no reason for being otherwise," she retorted,
"except that it is painful to speak of such things,

even amongst relations. It is said that Lena has seen a great deal too much lately of Caryl Glynne— Mrs. Malcolm's cousin, you'll remember. They were very intimate once—indeed, I fancy, almost engaged —and ill-natured people will draw their own conclusions."

Hubert Ashleigh, though time-serving and worldly-wise, was devoid neither of honour nor religion; under all his tinsel and varnish, sound metal showed itself, when proved by fire. He could make small sacrifices to expediency; but would no more have countenanced or connived at actual wrong-doing, than he would openly have violated his ordination vow. He had never approved of the second marriage; but coquetry was the worst he had imputed to Lena; and, in their interview at Templestowe, Marian had overshot the mark, in supposing that Hubert's suspicions kept pace with her own. If the recent rumours affecting his family had floated down into Loamshire, they had not reached his quiet parsonage; and he felt something, now, of the horror of one who, suddenly turning his head, finds a spectre in his track. Moreover, his sluggish blood was stirred, at hearing such shame hinted at coolly, if not flippantly. He had ever thought more highly of Marian Ashleigh's prudence than of her principles; yet, when a certain suspicion crossed his mind, he drove it back at first indignantly; and the very idea that he had nearly done her injustice, helped to keep his wrath in check. Nevertheless, there was some harshness in his tone.

"Ill-natured people! And what have the others said or done? Was it in good-nature that they let poor Ralph go a thousand miles away, when his name was to be dragged through the mire? Marian, if you had the faintest surmise of all this, it was your bounden duty to keep him here, at any risk or cost. How far has it gone? I *will* be answered."

The woman who had never been overawed by Ralph Atherstone, was not likely to be intimidated

by Hubert Ashleigh. His manner, too, chafed not
less than it puzzled her; and her temper began to
rise.

"The privileges of relationship may be carried a
little too far. If you *will* be answered, you had better
apply to Lady Atherstone's mother, or to herself. I
was never appointed her conscience-keeper. I'm
neither brave enough to go tale-bearing to Monseigneur; nor strong enough to hold him in leading-
strings; nor"—she paused, and went on with a malign
laugh—"fool enough to crush my fingers betwixt bark
and wood."

The other gazed at her, as if doubting whether he
had heard aright; and, as he so gazed, the dreadful
suspicion that he had repulsed five minutes ago thrust
itself forward again, and would not be exorcised.
When he spoke, it was in the subdued tone that, with
some people, betokens the presence of great fear.

"Has any word been sent to Norway of what has
happened?"

"Not by me," she answered, in the same cool,
defiant way. "Once for all, I wish you to understand
that I wash my hands of the whole affair."

The resolute look on the parson's face, as he rose
to his feet silently, made Marian Ashleigh uneasy at
last. There was anxiety in her eyes, and the slightest
tremor in her voice, as she asked hurriedly—

"Where are you going? What do you intend to
do?"

"I am going to write to Ralph Atherstone," Hubert answered. "You do not choose to give me any
information, it seems, and I do not choose to hunt up
evidence; but I shall write to him something of what
I fear—all that I know. It is not much; but it is
more than enough to bring him home without an
hour's delay; and I pray God it may bring him in
time!"

'In time'—The two syllables struck unpleasantly
on Marian's ear. Was it possible that, though bitter

misery might ensue, the complete ruin on which she had reckoned might yet be averted? Remember, beyond the unsupported testimony of her own eyes and ears, there was, so far as she knew, no substantial proof to convict the criminals; some overt act of theirs was needed to complete the case. In her eagerness, she started up and laid her hand on Ashleigh's arm.

"Have you reflected? Will you give him such fearful pain, when, perhaps——"

He shook himself roughly loose.

"There is no 'perhaps,' and you know it. As for the pain, I no more shrink from inflicting it than I would from searing a mad dog's bite. Let me go—I am wasting time here."

He spoke with a vehemence that actually cowed her; but, a moment afterwards, the parson's somewhat commonplace features settled into a stern earnestness, such as they had never worn when, from his appointed place, he launched forth anathema or warning.

"Marian," he said, "if I wrong you in my thoughts, I need to ask pardon from Heaven, as well as from you. If I have not wronged you, it is too late to preach. Listen, nevertheless. You spoke of washing your hands of this matter. If they have had art or part therein, I believe they will not be cleansed throughout eternity; and, as there is a Judge above us, I believe your sin is past forgiveness."

Then Hubert Ashleigh went out.

# CHAPTER XLIII.

IF Lady Marian's nerves were somewhat shaken by the curious phenomenon she had just witnessed, they did not, you may be sure, remain long a-fluttering. Before her reverend cousin had been gone half an hour, she could afford to smile at her late impressions, and was taking cool counsel with herself as to future measures; possibly, the recollection of having been rather foiled in the passage of words, may have added a little extra viciousness to her resolve. Turning matters over thus leisurely, she came to the conclusion that, if other strings were properly worked, Hubert Ashleigh's interference, instead of averting, might hasten a catastrophe. Her meditations carried her on to luncheon-time; and, after partaking of that meal with a remarkably good appetite, she ordered her carriage, and drove straight to Gaunt Street, where the Atherstones resided. She knew enough of the habits of the house to be sure of finding its mistress at home at that hour, and probably alone. She was right in both calculations; for Mrs. Shafton was still too unwell to leave her room.

If Lady Atherstone's thoughts had not been so much engrossed of late, she would assuredly have noticed, not only the comparative rarity of her step-daughter's visits, but also a decided coolness in the other's manner. The jests and quips, that used to fall so readily from Marian, were never heard now; and her remarks, when not formal and commonplace, were decidedly sub-acid. But one of the worst symptoms of these moral maladies, is that utter indifference to the sayings and doings either of friend or foe. Lady

A A

Atherstone had winced perhaps—though she never showed it—under the first sting of the Duke of Devorgoil's insult: but even this did not rankle as it would have done a year ago; and the little pain it caused her she was careful to smother, for Caryl's sake—any woman will tell you why.

Though she liked her downright ways, and had often been amused by her brisk sallies, she had never conceived any deep attachment for Marian; and, though she believed her to be passably honest, some instinct, backed by a suspicion of which we will speak anon, kept Lena from trusting her step-daughter implicitly. So long as the other chose to be amiable and amicable, it was well; if it pleased her to take another line, it would be a pity—that was all—and they would only have to see less of each other. Since that incident in the Park, the two had not met; and, if Lady Atherstone bestowed a thought on the subject, she perhaps fancied that this might partly account for the hard look on her visitor's face. However, Marian opened the trenches in a closer parallel.

"Have you seen anything of Hubert Ashleigh?"

Lena's eyes opened in languid surprise.

"Hubert Ashleigh? I hadn't a notion he was in town. What brought him up, I wonder?"

"Very unpleasant business—to use his own words. He came to ask me, whether he had heard a true report of the Duke of Devorgoil's behaviour the other day."

"And what did you answer?"

The long lashes had drooped again; and there was not a shade of eagerness in the question.

"What *could* I answer? There was nothing to contradict, and—well—not much to explain. I could only leave him to form his own conclusions."

"*Et puis?*" Lena inquired listlessly.

The apathy, real or assumed, began to exasperate Marian. She pressed her lips tightly together—a sure token that her temper was rising.

"Rather difficult to answer either in French or English," she replied; "unless one had the gift of prophecy. Testing the patience of society, is an exciting amusement, I daresay; but it is apt to be expensive. I suppose you have counted the cost, Lady Atherstone."

As often happens where there is nearly equality of age, the two had always called each other by their Christian names; and, besides the significant formality, there was a sardonic emphasis on the last words. There was no change in Lena's indolent attitude; but her thin nostrils dilated.

"Don't you think you had better speak a little more plainly? It saves so much trouble."

Marian's black eyes gleamed rancorously.

"That's what I came here for—for that, and one other purpose; and I'm not likely to trouble you much hereafter. You know perfectly well why the Duke acted as he did, and whether his example is likely to be followed. I, for one, cannot blame him. I've no right to call you to account; but I have a right to be careful of my own good name—if only for Philip's sake; and I should risk it, if I came often—or ever again, after what has passed—to a house where Caryl Glynne is made so welcome."

Then, for the first time, Lena looked the other steadfastly in the face, and smiled.

"Thanks," she said—"that is plain-speaking, at all events. Yes, you're very right to be cautious, especially 'for Philip's sake.' Poor Philip! I'm afraid you did not think quite enough of him, during that month at Templestowe. You had no scruples about my visitors, then. Is it not rather late in the day to lift up your testimony?"

Lady Marian's colour rose. Though she did not dream that the secret of her supineness had been fathomed, the very allusion to it angered her.

"Not a bit too late," she retorted sharply. "I had no sort of reason for suspecting even imprudence, then; now, I have reason for suspecting worse—the very worst."

'No reason!' Was it chance, then, that night at Erriswell, that brought Marian Ashleigh so close to a curtained door; and, whilst she lurked there, were her ears deadened that they should not hear, and her eyes blinded that they should not see? 'Yet,' said her friends, 'she carried sincerity to a fault:' and—once more—they must have known best. Lady Atherstone shrugged her shoulders.

"Certainly the past matters little; and it is not worth while to discuss the present or future, when we are sure not to agree. You have told me what line you mean to take. Is there much more to say?"

During the last few seconds, Marian's cheek had paled again; and the gleaming of her eyes was changed for a cold, cruel glitter.

"Not much," she answered—"only this, indeed. My second purpose in coming here, was to tell you that, by this post, Hubert Ashleigh has written to Norway—I use his own words again—'something of what he fears, all that he knows;' and that he counts on Lord Atherstone's returning without an hour's delay."

Eagerly and hungrily she watched how the stab would tell; but Lena neither blenched nor started. The hands, that lay clasped on her lap, were locked a little more tightly perhaps—that was all.

"Are you quite sure of this?" she asked, after a pause.

"Absolutely sure," Marian answered viciously—more and more irritated by the glinting of that last home-thrust.

"Then I ought to thank you for your warning," the other went on, with the same serenity.

Now, to any nature not quite senseless or servile, long dissimulation, even with a righteous end in view, must needs be galling. I fancy that, in all his austere life, Junius Brutus never savoured such a delight, as

when he cast off the fool's mask beside dead Lucretia.
Marian Ashleigh was neither humble nor submissive;
and her resentments were not less keen than abiding :
judge, if she had found the duteous step-daughter
easy to play.   She was not even now ashamed of her
treachery; nevertheless, the memory of the kindly
words she had lavished on her enemy, stung her like
a shame.   At any cost, she would for once enjoy the
luxury of speaking her mind—specially, as the need
of temporising seemed past.

"You wouldn't thank me," she said in a bitter
whisper, "if you knew all.   But you do know—you
must have known throughout, if you were not wilfully
blind—what sort of friendship ours was likely to be.
Did you expect me to take you to my heart, for sitting
down in a place that, even whilst Lord Atherstone
lived, ought to have been mine—only mine?   It was
scarcely worth while scheming for that place, to lose
it again so soon—for you *will* lose it.   If I had not
been quite sure of this, perhaps I should not have
warned you of Hubert's proceedings.   It is your last
chance, however; so make the best or the worst of it."

Frank, certainly—almost unfemininely so ; yet only
half frank, after all.   The warning was just as much
part of a plan, as any other one of Marian's sayings
and doings since she began to contrive.

There was, once upon a time, a prisoner kept in
ward, whose life was a sore hindrance to the King;
but with whom, for state-reasons, it was not safe to
deal by foul means, howsoever covert.   On a certain
night, there were flung through the cell-window, a file
and a rope.   The steel was sharp, and the cord seemed
trustworthy ; and, very soon, the captive swung in
free air.   Joyfully he descended, knot by knot, till he
reached the last ; and then—well, the rope, unluckily,
was some ten fathoms too short ; and, when the dawn
broke, the sentinels saw on the jagged rocks beneath,
a crushed human wreck.   The good governor was very
wroth ; but there was none on whom to charge the

blame : they could only take up the corpse, and bury it with due rite and dole.

A true story, I believe ; and one that, mayhap, has been repeated often enough since, with variations, and without such fatal ending. The illustration, probably, did not suggest itself to Lena Atherstone ; but, as she watched the malign mouth and cruel eyes, a certain suspicion ripened into assurance.

You may not have forgotten that, after discussing with Lord Atherstone the anonymous letter, she put it carefully away. Months later, happening to glance at the cover of one of Marian's notes, she felt sure that there was a similarity in the addresses ; and, on comparing them, she was still more struck by this ; but, at the moment, she decided that the resemblance, which did not extend to the body of the handwriting, must be fortuitous. However, she locked up the two envelopes together ; and, thenceforth, whenever the idea recurred to her, she always strove to banish it. Now, however, the conviction flashed upon her, that she had never done Marian an injustice : the latter had simply been consistent, it seemed, from first to last. Nevertheless—unlikely as it may appear—with her indignation mingled a kind of compassionate wonder.

Not long ago, an acquaintance of mine discovered that he had been persistently robbed by a friend who had been all the time living, if not under his roof, at least chiefly on his bounty. When the first shock of annoyance was past, this good fellow was heard to remark—" Poor devil ! I'd no notion he was so hard driven ; it must have been awfully up-hill work, sometimes, for his father's son."

Perhaps some such notion crossed Lena's mind ; for she answered rather thoughtfully than angrily.

" And I never did you any wilful harm ! It all sounds very strange. Well,"—here her face hardened a little—" as we are not likely to meet again often, I should like to give you back something that belongs to you."

Crossing the room, she opened a writing-case with a key hanging from her watch-chain. The next minute she had laid the anonymous letter and the other envelope, side by side, before Marian Ashleigh.

"One need not be an expert to trace the resemblance," Lena said quietly. " You seem rather fond of 'warnings.' Perhaps the first was as 'kindly meant' as the last. If you have forgotten that sentence, you had better refresh your memory. At any rate, take back these papers : if they fall into other hands, they might still be dangerous—to you."

The strongest, not less than the weakest, minds, are liable occasionally to be thrown off their balance; and, though in one case the disabling may be but temporary, whilst it lasts, both are about on a par. Marian was so completely taken back, that she could not frame a denial, much less answer sarcasm in kind. The fierce eagerness with which she clutched at the letter, and crushed it betwixt her fingers, was in itself an avowal. She rose up hastily, meaning to end the interview; but, before she could determine how best to do so, Lena had glided away ; and the other, glancing round, found herself alone.

The triumph of virtue and the discomfiture of vice, were surely very near. Yet the woman did not look much like a conqueror, who stood there, with brows knit and downcast, and sullen eyes riveted on the scrap of crumpled paper, peering out of her clenched hand.

Nevertheless I trust that the victress retains your sympathies to the last; and that you will neither withhold your laurel-wreath, nor refuse to cry, with me—*Ave, Imperatrix !*

# CHAPTER XLIV.

You have not been required to assist at many such; but of another interview, that happened that same evening, you must needs take cognizance.

Lena Atherstone and Caryl Glynne sat alone together; and the latter had just been made aware of the situation. He did not affect to make light of it; and, as he mused silently for a while, his trouble and doubt were plain to discern.

It is with this as with other less dangerous games: so long as a single card remains to be drawn, those who are playing for their last stake generally refuse to believe that some freak of fortune may not yet save them; only when the last, the very last, is turned, are they fain to acknowledge that there is nothing left but to pay the ruinous score.

Nevertheless, there was small leaven of selfishness in Glynne's anxieties. It must be owned, that this was not the first time he had found himself in a like perilous position, and he had comparatively little to lose; but, had the consequences been thrice as harmful to himself, I do believe that he would have thought solely of the consequences to Lena. He had not loved her well enough to abstain from tempting her to sin—knowing well whither the temptation would surely lead—perhaps because it was not in his nature so to love. But, though she was more precious to him than ever since she had become part and parcel of his existence, he loved her well enough, now, to have severed the link, if that would have saved her. Ay!—more than this—if he could have borne her harmless at the cost of his own life, he would scarcely have begrudged the sacrifice. But it was too late : they were bound to stand or fall together ; and he shrank from the prospect of her future.

Some day-dreams are almost as rapid in their changes as any visions of the night. During that brief pause, in the midst of many other memories— vividly as if they had been uttered yesterday—his own words came back to Caryl Glynne.

" Whenever I do go down, I'll think of the chance I have had ; but—I'll sink alone."

Was it all a false form of speech ? Hardly so ; though since it had been bitterly belied. For his chances of keeping afloat—were they brighter now than then ? As he answered the question to himself, he hardly smothered a curse.

I may have erred in portraying it at all ; but I can honestly affirm that I have not purposed to cast a rosy halo of romance round a black, ugly crime. Therefore I do not shrink from setting forth things in a plain, practical light, at the risk of making baseness seem more base.

Some time ago there appeared a curious story—the title has utterly escaped me—not very polished or coherent in construction, but full of a quaint philosophy, and paradoxes less expressed than implied : with an undercurrent of cynicisms throughout, moral sentiments in profusion floated on the surface ; and the rewards and punishments were distributed with the most rigid propriety. One of the main incidents in the tale is an elopement ; and the sufferings of the criminals are photographed with a painful minuteness : only these appear to have been caused, not so much by remorse, as by the extreme scantiness of their resources ; and the author concludes with the deduction, that, ' setting right and wrong aside, and having regard solely to temporal welfare, no man ought to covet his neighbour's wife who—has not a competence.'

After all, when we consider how few joys may not be moderated, how few sorrows may not be embittered, by that wretched *cura peculi*, it may not seem wonderful if financial anxieties formed part of Glynne's trouble.  As for himself, of late years, at all events, he had lived from hand to mouth, on the simple principle of taking no thought for the morrow, and trusting to the chapter of accidents to pull him through— stinting himself, meanwhile, in no fancy whatsoever. Now Lena, before her marriage, had known little of luxury, and the economies to which she had been accustomed, Caryl, perhaps, would have called privations ; but, at the worst, there was always a solid roof, if a rude one, over her head ; and her daily bread, if neither sweet nor soft, was sure.

The woodlands of Bohemia look tempting enough when the sun shimmers through wealth of green leaves, and when the breeze just wafts aside the smoke of the camp-fire; but, when the black north-wind sends the snow-flakes flying through the bare branches, the Nut-Brown Maid herself may be apt to envy the sober housewives sitting cosily in ' biggit land.'

If Caryl was not absolutely free of the forest, he had seen enough of it not to fear trusting himself there ; but he did shrink from bringing Lena amongst the shifts and perils of social outlawry.  Wheresoever he went, he would find comrades, such as they were ; but as for her—thenceforth, could she hope to clasp the hand of any woman whose touch was not dishonour ?  Nay—how sore soever her strait—was it certain that even the mother that bore her would not pass by on the other side ?

And yet—what help for it ?

When he first heard of the Duke of Devorgoil's insolence—it had chafed him far more than he betrayed to Lena—he knew it was the beginning of the end : only, till the end came, he had not fairly faced it. His reverie was broken at last by a low whisper.

" Are you so surprised then, Caryl ?"

He had dealt very gently with her since she had passed wholly into his power; and, when they were alone together, a cynicism, or even an irony, seldom escaped him. He drew her closer to him now, as he answered—

"Not surprised, darling; but very, very sorry: for I fear there is but one way."

"Yes, only one," she murmured—"and we must make haste. Don't you think *hc* will make haste, when he reads that letter?"

She shivered like an aspen where she sat.

Glynne bit his lip: lack of courage was not among his failings; and it was no dread of the consequences that made him loath—if loath he was—to meet the man he had so wronged. The sight of Lena's terror was very galling—it implied a doubt of his power or will to protect her; and there came a touch of the old sarcasm into his tone.

"Don't tremble so. We shall be far enough away before the avenger comes; but I'd rather have fancied that we did not fly for fear."

She drew backward a little, lifting her head almost haughtily.

"For fear? No: even *I* am not afraid; at least, not in that way. If the proofs against me were a thousand times stronger—if my own mother accused me —I need only look into his face, and say—'It is not true'—and he would believe, in spite of all. But I cannot do it—I cannot say it. Caryl, you will not ask it of me? I would rather be trampled under his feet, than forgiven—so."

Amidst the turmoil of his thoughts, Glynne found time to draw a certain comparison. For many years he had held Lena's heart — of late he had held her whole soul—in his keeping; yet she would never have said of him, what she had just said of the loyal gentleman whom she had never learned to love, and whose home she had not scrupled to desolate.

"I understand," he answered with some bitterness;

"and I ought to have understood at first. No, I ask you to do nothing, except to trust in me always; though trusting has brought you to this pass. My poor darling!"—his voice shook a little here—"you have a rough road before you, though I'll do my best to smooth it."

She nestled close to his shoulder; looking up at him with eyes full of a rapt devotion, such as may scarce be justified by any earthly love howsoever lawful, and of a triumph withal, like that of one who, after long toil and pain, sees the victory sure; and, even to him who was familiar with its every cadence, her voice sounded strangely sweet.

"Caryl, was it very long ago when we parted at Grace Moreland's? It seems so: yet I remember, if you have forgotten, some words of mine—'If you say to me, "Come," I will come, and never repent it afterwards.' I have not grown a coward since; and, though you would not then, you will—you must—dare to say it now."

He did say it—perhaps not very intelligibly. Through the long anxious talk which ensued, we need not follow.

When Glynne reached home, several letters lay on his table, that had arrived by the second post. All, save one, he flung aside after a rapid glance at their contents: this superscription was in a firm, bold handwriting, though unmistakably feminine. Caryl held it in his hand for several seconds, unopened, as if irresolute: then he crossed the room, and held the letter over the flame of a spirit-lamp, till it was reduced to ashes; and, as he dropped the last blackened fragment, he smiled rather scornfully.

It was not a great sacrifice: nevertheless it was a sign that he intended to keep the guilty compact, signed that afternoon, fully and faithfully; for the letter, as you may have divined, came from Hunsden, and brought a slighted woman's final appeal.

It had cost the writer much time and study, and

tears not a few; for sweet Cissy Devereux had never before set her hand to an elegiac, though she had, doubtless, received a sufficiency. She had a right to reckon on her maiden effort being perused, if not appreciated. But the luck has not changed since the *Heroides* were penned; and the deserted loves of our day fare not much better than Phyllis or Œnone.

However, with this light-minded matron we cannot condole. Let us only hope that the sharp lesson to her vanity, to say nothing of her heart, may be of profit; and that, in after-time, memory may whisper, seasonably,—*Neu crede colori.*

# CHAPTER XLV

On a bench, under the broad eaves of his fishing lodge, sat Sir Charles Wroughton; watching, with a lazy appreciation, the play of the purple light through the hanging pine-wood; and, though his arms ached with the day's work—it was all honest casting, not trailing, on that river—jubilant over the landing of nine fair fish out of eleven hooked, including one that might possibly rank 'King' of the season. Moreover, certain savoury steams issuing from within were anything but an offence to his nostrils; and perhaps his chiefest anxiety at the moment was—lest he should be obliged to wait dinner for his comrade, or feed alone.

He was neither disquieted nor excited by the appearance of the post-kariole; for the Miller of the Dee himself was not freer of cares and ties than this jovial old bachelor. Club-gossip was about all his letters were likely to contain; and the papers could scarcely bring heavier tidings than that the tenner, invested on a friend's promising two-year-old, had gone the way of other 'certainties.' The news, good or bad, would keep perfectly till after dinner; so, after a careless glance at the contents of the packet, he was putting them aside *en masse*, when a thought seemed to strike him; and he sorted the letters over again carefully.

"It's devilish odd," he grumbled—"only one for him, and that not in my lady's hand. He won't half like that; and—*I* don't half like it."

Somehow, the keen edge was suddenly taken off

his appetite ; and when, lifting his eyes, he saw Ralph Atherstone crossing the meadow betwixt the house and the river, with the long, sweeping stride that he himself, though hale and active for his years, had often envied, Charles Wroughton frowned, instead of smiling as he would have done a few seconds ago. Cheerily, however, he hailed his friend with the regular question—

"Well, what luck ?"

"Nothing to complain of, and not much to boast of either," Ralph answered. ·"Seven fish but not a twenty-pounder amongst them. I see the post has come in."

And, with an eagerness contrasting strongly with the other's apathy, he turned· over the letters, one by one.

A misgiving that he did not care to define, made Wroughton betake himself within doors, without casting a glance over his shoulder; and it might have been ten minutes or so before he emerged again.

On that same bench Lord Atherstone sat, his head bent and partially averted ; so that, till the other came quite close, his visage remained unseen. The first glimpse of it made Wroughton start a pace backward.

Men have been wounded, even unto death, and have suffered torture worse than any that wounds can bring, without their faces changing as Ralph's had changed. The steady light had gone out of the deep eyes ; the healthy brown cheeks looked grey and wan ; and the firm lips seemed rather tense than set.

"What has happened ?"

Wroughton spoke eagerly, but in a hushed voice. as men do who stand in presence of some great calamity.

The other did not answer for a while. Though there breathed few prouder creatures than Ralph Atherstone, it was not selfish pride that made him loath to confide in that trusty comrade. However, he took his part at last, and held out the open letter, saying—

"You—may—read."

His lips were parched and stiff, as from long drought; and he was forced to moisten them, before he could form the three syllables separately.

With a lowering brow, the other did as he was desired; but, as he reached the end of the letter, his countenance somewhat cleared. After all, Hubert Ashleigh brought no direct charge: he only stated the Duke of Devorgoil's conduct, and how it must be accounted for; and prayed his cousin to hasten back, to look after his own honour. So Wroughton—fighting hard against his own impressions—strove to persuade himself, that Lena's imprudence might have stopped short of guilt; and said as much. The baron plucked his comrade by the sleeve; and drew him nearer, till the other's ear was almost on a level with his own lips: his voice, though hoarse and low, was quite distinct now.

"I think nothing of this," he answered, taking the letter back. "I promised her, long ago, that, if all the world accused her, I would never doubt till she herself told me it was time. She *has* told me; for, since we parted, she has not written one word."

Against the terrible conviction of his manner, it was impossible to argue; and in Wroughton's simple pharmacy there was no salve for a grief like this

A long heavy silence ensued. At last—

"God help her!" quoth Ralph Atherstone.

Now, this intercession came not from an anointed priest, or devout Levite, or pious elder, but from a hard, heathenish old Philistine, with knees unpliable to prayer. But would the meekest of them have found it easy, whilst reeling under the bitter blow, to plead for the woman who dealt it?

Moreover, in those simple words there was an utter hopelessness, which stirred chords in Charles Wroughton's heart, that had been still for many a day: he turned on his heel; and, for a second or two, meadow, wood, and river, swam before him somewhat mistily.

When he looked round again, Ralph had risen to his feet: the wanness had gone out of his face, and the cloud out of his eyes; and his lip was firm as ever.

"I've no time to spare," he said; "for, of course, I start to-night. There's always the chance of a steamer at Trondhjem."

Within the last few minutes, Wroughton had found time to reproach himself, for having tempted his friend out of England when such a crisis was imminent; though afterwards he came to believe that the catastrophe could only have been deferred.

"I'll go with you," he said hastily; and he meant it, be sure.

The baron laid his hand on his old comrade's shoulder, thanking him with a dreary smile.

"You may follow, if you will; for I fear you'll have little heart for the fishing after this. But—try and understand why I'd rather go alone."

The other did understand, or, at least, he made no further remonstrance; and the two went into the house together.

An hour later, Lord Atherstone—having eaten and drunk sparingly—was ready for the road.

"Do you think you'll be in time?" Wroughton asked, as he wrung his friend's hand at parting.

It may sound a cruel question; but both these men were wont, in face of a certain disaster, to grapple with, rather than ignore it.

"I've small hope," Ralph answered; "yet, if I come ever so late, there will be work for me to do."

He spoke with marvellous calmness; but the deadly glitter of his eyes was not hard to interpret. The listener guessed at once what manner of work was like, ere long, to occupy the hand he still held; and what manner of stain was like to rest upon it before all was done. But he, too, was Philistine enough to maintain that the punishment of certain wrongs should not be left to Time or any other avenger. Despite of conventional difficulties, and the 'divine voice of the people,' there are still places where a desperate man may set himself foot to foot with his enemy, in the bad old fashion ; and—beyond the narrow seas, at least— there is sometimes a grave as well as a comic side to that ordeal. Wroughton knew that, within the last hour, a doom had gone forth against a guilty life, almost as sure as if it had been pronounced from a judgment-seat; and he would no more have averted it, than have withstood the hangman in his office. At any rate, to the crime, if crime it were, by his hearty farewell g₁ip, he was made accessory.

It is useless to describe Ralph Atherstone's journey. To those who have never been forced to undertake such an one, the picture would seem over-wrought : such as have had the dreadful experience, will need no limner ; for few memories are darker and deeper in grain than these.

Years, happy and peaceful, may pass before we forget how, as we sped along, whether sun or moon was shining, whether the skies were clear or murky, the face of nature wore always the same veil—how every hindrance by the way seemed to mock at our misery ; albeit we were ever haunted by the thought, that the sands, dropping so slowly through our glass, might be running out with awful swiftness in a dark- ened chamber far away—how, at last, despite that feverish impatience, the sick fluttering of the heart waxed so intolerable, that we would fain have had a hundred more of the weary miles to travel rather than be so near our journey's end—how, when we drew quite near, our hot, tired eyes were strained to catch the first sign of good or ill—how the heavy lids drooped, as if they would never lift again, when we recognised that there was nothing left to hope or fear.

Yet, when at our dreariest, we had cause to thank Heaven, if the horror awaiting us was nothing worse than death.

Ralph at least was spared the torture of inactive

delay. A Hull steamer started within a few hours of his reaching Trondhjem; and, though heavily laden for the coarse weather she encountered, the good ship ploughed sturdily through the angry North Sea. But those five days scored on his face deeper lines than the last five lustres had left. It was not that he seemed aged or broken; and his features were of the type that, under sore sickness, hardly change: nevertheless, they *were* changed; and a gaunt, savage look possessed them, such as they had never worn when his mood was at the angriest.

No wonder that, when Lord Atherstone reached home, he found none bold enough to set before him the bitter truth; and that only from the white, frightened faces around he guessed that he had, indeed, come—too late.

# CHAPTER XLVI.

A CLEVER and influential backer of horses, when asked if he was going to Newmarket, answered gravely—"It entirely depends on whether I can raise enough for my railway-ticket." Having once surmounted this difficulty, he started full of confidence, and had a remarkably good week; on the proceeds whereof he wintered in much luxury.

Some such large trust in Providence—or whatever other power the 'plungers' believe in—probably induced Miles Shafton to travel down to try a promising five-year-old near Heslingford. Prompt payment was, of course, out of the question; but he thought a three-shilling stamp, with the promise of a share in future winnings, might possibly tempt the sporting farmer. At any rate, 'looking over the brute could do no harm.'

However, the owner did not quite see things in this light: so Miles sat in the ante-room of the barracks, where he had found quarters; brooding, with a sense of injury, over his fruitless journey; and striving to stimulate a moderate appetite with much embittered sherry.

An accommodating train, that reached Heslingford just in time for ·dinner, not unfrequently brought a visitor; but Frank Dacre's appearance was a surprise to every one there present.

The new comer seemed rather embarrassed than gratified by his noisy welcome; and, as soon as he could extricate himself, he walked straight up to Shafton, and touched him on the shoulder.

"Look here, Buster," he said, "come outside for a
minute; I've something to say to you."

Miles tossed off the remainder of his bitters, with
a sound betwixt a growl and a groan.

"What is it?" he asked, as he went out. "Bad news,
of course? The Czar's broken down, I suppose."

The other did not answer till the door was shut
behind them.

"It's worse than that—pretty near the worst that
can be, I'm afraid. Your sister went off last night
with Caryl Glynne."

Miles staggered backward as if he had been struck,
half lifting his clenched hand.

"It's a —— lie!" he said huskily; and then stood
panting.

Dacre shook his head.

"Hard words won't mend it, old man," he said.
"I shouldn't have brought a bit of idle scandal all
this way. Black as it is, it's the truth, and you'd better face it; though, after all, it's no fault of yours, and
I don't see what you can do."

Looking into Shafton's blood-shot eyes, and remembering of what race he came, you might have
guessed why so many dark pages were to be found
in the annals of Blytheswold.

"Don't you?" he asked, in a fierce whisper.
"They've got a long start; but that doesn't matter.
Never mind me, just now. I'll tell you what you can
do, though. Go in there, and make what excuse you
like for my bolting—so long as it isn't the right one;
and meet me at the station, if you don't mean stop-
ping here. I've something to do before the train
starts; but I shan't miss it."

Under ordinary difficulties his brain was apt to get
muddled; but the shock, and that first gust of passion,
seemed to have cleared it; for, as he strode away, he
looked far more cool and collected than Dacre, whose
face, as he stood there, was quite a study of perplexity.

Perhaps you would never guess whither Miles

Shafton's steps were bent. The leading idea in his mind was, of course, pursuit of the fugitives; for, knowing nothing of Hubert Ashleigh's letter, he could not tell how soon Lord Atherstone would be able to take his own part. But before the resolve had been five seconds formed, he bethought himself that his feet would be tied, unless he provided himself with the sinews of war. Looking at his own immediate resources, a fifty-pound note seemed to Miles utterly unattainable; though, with a week's notice, and through the usual 'channels,' he might possibly have secured ten times the sum. He doubted whether his mother could help him thus far; and, besides, though not often troubled by scruples, he loathed the notion of taxing her at such a time. Even if the will of his hosts had been good, he misdoubted their power to oblige him; and, besides, he had no mind that his family affairs should be discussed that night in the ante-room. He thought he saw a better way out of his difficulty than any of these; and, as he walked straight and swiftly towards Corbett's house, he was troubled by none of the qualms that usually beset a borrower. He remembered certain good-natured hints thrown out in old times; and, somehow, if it were necessary, he thought it would be easier to confide in Arthur than in his light-minded comrades.

Miles was shown into the library, for the master of the house was in his dressing-room; from which, however, he presently emerged—as usual, in gorgeous array. If this man had been going to the scaffold, I believe he would still have donned his purple, and fine linen, and jewels. There was a shade of surprise in his welcome; for the visit was, to say the least, unseasonable, especially as the two had met before that day; but the other did not leave him long in suspense.

"I've no time for beating about the bush," he said. "I've come to ask you to lend me fifty pounds; or a little more, if you can manage it."

Corbett was considerably taken aback: he had no idea of refusing; but at the word 'lend' his professional instincts awoke, and he answered with professional hesitation.

"Well—I hardly know. Do you want the money to-night?"

"I want it within the hour," the other retorted. "You'll guess why, when I tell you what I want it for. Here—I may as well make a clean breast of it —there's a real bad business about Lena."

Arthur's face crimsoned, and his lips worked convulsively.

"About Lena?"

The familiarity was quite unintentional: he was only repeating the words mechanically.

"Yes," the other went on through his teeth. "All the world will know to-morrow—if they don't know it already — that she bolted last night with Caryl Glynne. Now, I mean to have his blood; and I want money to hunt him down."

Corbett dropped into a chair, covering his face with his hands: all at once he broke out into shrill hysteric laughter.

There are few drearier sounds than that of a grown man's weeping; yet such merriment is worse to listen to.

"Gone—with Caryl Glynne?" Arthur panted after a while, catching his breath betwixt each syllable; "and—you come to *me* for help? It's too—absurd; " and he laughed again.

Shafton strode forwards; and, gripping the other's shoulder, thrust him back in the chair.

"You had best stop that," he said savagely. "What are you drivelling about? Why shouldn't I——"

'Come to you?' he would have said. But, just then, there flashed across the speaker's mind a shameful conviction; and it became plain to him, why, in his present strait, he ought to have sought aid from almost any living creature, rather than from him who sat cowering there. There was no place for pity in Miles's heart, just then; it was because he dared not trust himself near Arthur Corbett, that he drew a pace backward; and as he stood there, with arms tightly folded, his eyes gleamed more felly than they had done when he first heard the ill tidings.

"So that's it," he said, low and bitterly. "She fooled *you*, too, did she? There—you needn't babble —I know, somehow, it was no worse; or my hands would be nearer your throat now. But I wish I had guessed it sooner; I wouldn't have wasted this half-hour."

The banker started up, striving hard to compose his voice and face.

"You won't leave me so? You'll let me——"

As he turned the door-handle, Shafton faced about.

"Let you help me?" he snarled—"Not whilst there's a purse to be stolen elsewhere." Then he went out.

Corbett had the sense to lock himself in; but, for many minutes afterwards, he remembered nothing. He had a vague impression of Emma's knocking at the door, and pleading piteously for admittance, and of his having muttered some excuse; but what words passed he never knew.

The suddenness made the blow more stunning; yet, of itself, it was sufficiently heavy. In some characters, self-esteem is almost a ruling passion; and with Corbett, now, even the sting of baffled desire was less keen than the consciousness of having been made the stalking-horse of Caryl Glynne's designs, and of having been not only deceived but derided. No wonder, that his wits—never of the stablest— went a-wandering. With so black a care peering over their shoulder, stouter horsemen than he have scarce sat saddle-fast.

Nevertheless he had not locked out his better angel. Few of us can afford to be judged after our intentions; and Arthur, remember—whether of his own free will or no—had been kept from actual crime;

and for his sin, whatsoever it was, he did then make
sharp if short atonement.  Moreover, it may be—for
these things are mysteries—that for the sake of those
innocents whose welfare was knit up in his, he met
with mercy ampler than he deserved.  Certain it is,
that he came forth from the chamber of his penance,
both better and wiser—so much wiser, that before
he slept, he found strength to confess himself to
Emma, neither concealing nor extenuating aught of
the miserable past; and she—when love and pity had
mastered jealous shame—found strength to absolve
him.

It was long before the old genial light came back
to Arthur Corbett's face, and perchance a kind of
cloud thenceforth always tempered its sunshine; but
not again, I think, till death shall divide them, will
he wring from his true wife's eyes, tears bitter as
those she shed that night when there was none to
watch her weeping.

Manna distilling from a flintstone, or a fountain
of milk in the desert, would scarcely seem more curious phenomena than spare cash in certain purses.
However, miracles will sometimes happen; and when
Miles, on their journey townwards, revealed his financial difficulty, to his intense astonishment he found
his comrade able and willing to assist him.  How
those five crisp notes came into Frank Dacre's possession, is entirely beside the question; it is sufficient
to say that he 'parted' without a pang.

So, with one worry the less on his mind, Shafton
betook himself to Gaunt Street.  But little information was to be gathered there.  Lady Atherstone's
own maid—tearfully incoherent — could only testify
to her mistress's having taken away absolutely nothing in the way of jewels or apparel; even the
travelling-bag that always accompanied her, stood
locked in its place.  The other servants could contri-
bute no facts whatever; and Miles was in no mood to
listen to their previous suspicions or presentiments.

Mrs. Shafton, it appeared, though scarcely able to quit her room, had moved to an hotel hard by; and thither, despite the lateness of the hour, her son repaired.

But neither here did he obtain any furtherance of his quest. Mrs. Shafton seemed utterly prostrated, both in mind and body; and it was hard to believe that she was the same woman who, all her life long, had shewn so brave a front to trouble.

That old one of 'the last straw,' is amongst the truest of proverbs. The weary journey may be very near its end, and the added load may seem absurdly trifling; but when the patient beast once sinks down, with despair in its big bright eyes, despite of threats or caresses, it is like to lie there till the desert-wind comes to bleach its bones.

At Miles's angry question—"Didn't you suspect anything?"—his mother's wan cheek flushed guiltily.

"Not since I left Templestowe," she murmured. "I had misgivings at first; but lately—I can't tell why—I had begun to feel safe; and yet I ought to have guessed that something was wrong, that last evening. She was so loath to leave me; and there were tears in her eyes when she kissed me—poor darling!"

The other ground his strong white teeth audibly.

"Poor darling! Then, in spite of all, she's your favourite still?"

Isabel Shafton looked up with a flash of her old spirit; but the next instant her weary head drooped.

"That taunt would hurt, if I deserved it," she said; "but you know best, Miles, which of my children I spoiled, and how I have been punished. I think I never can forgive Lena; but I can't help pitying, or —God forgive me, if it's wrong—loving her still."

He felt he had been unjust; but wrath and shame made him cruel.

"Be as charitable as you like," he muttered—"only one saint in a family's enough, and *I* don't mean to

forgive. I suppose you can't help me to track them,
mother; and perhaps you wouldn't, if you could.
Never mind, I'll manage it my own way."

She put out her weak, trembling hand, and caught
him by the arm as he rose. Alas! before her wed-
ding-wreath was faded, she had learned to read the
augury of a certain look in a Shafton's eyes. For
generations past, it had been known throughout the
country-side, that, howsoever slack in other matters,
they of Blytheswold were seldom laggards in their
vengeance. Despite the faintness that nearly mastered her, her great fear enabled Isabel Shafton to
speak calmly.

"Miles, it's useless arguing with you; but, before
you act rashly, will you remember Lord Atherstone
may be expected home almost hourly? Hubert Ashleigh, it seems, wrote to warn him at least a week
ago. I heard this from Marian only to-day."

Shafton started, and drew himself as it were together; like a bull who, whilst lowering his horns to
charge, is dazzled by the glitter of the matador's blade.
Something quite distinct from the differences of age
and station, had imbued Miles with an awe of the
man whose name he had just heard; and, even in the
heat of his passion, he felt loath to take Ralph Atherstone's quarrel out of Ralph Atherstone's hand. As
he stood gnawing his nether lip, it was plain he
wavered.

"A creditable thing, too," he grumbled—"that the
warning should have come from a country parson,
with all of us to the fore. But it makes a difference.
I'll hold on a day or so, anyhow; and only set the
wires to work: that can do no harm, and may save
*him* trouble." He paused here; and a shade of contrition came over his sullen face, as he stooped to
bestow a rough caress. "Poor mother! I've been
a bit hard on you, I'm afraid; but, with one worry
and another, I'm half wild. I won't keep you up
any longer; you look half dead, as it is. Now try

and sleep; you shall hear all that there is to hear to-morrow."

That scant amends, though it could not stop the aching of Isabel Shafton's heart, assuredly helped to smooth her pillow.

Early the next day, after obtaining renewal of leave, Miles began to track the fugitives; and it soon appeared that the trail was plain enough to be followed up even by a detective. If you remember certain scruples of Glynne's, you will perhaps understand why he took such slight precautions to mask his flight. He had used no disguise; and a double passage, from Southampton to the Channel Islands, was secured in his own name.

These travellers were scarcely of the common tourist-type; so they were easily traced from Jersey to St. Malo, and thence across country to Porhaix, a small coast-town in Finisterre.

Thus spoke the telegraph; for the tracker chose to remain in ambush, whence he could watch the 'harboured' game till the huntsman should appear; and of all this, within an hour of his reaching home, Lord Atherstone was made aware.

The baron received the news—broken to him in Miles Shafton's rough, blundering way—with a singular composure; nor did he forget to thank the latter for his zeal, though he decisively declined his company to Brittany.

It was impossible to pursue his journey before evening. How that long, lonely day passed with Ralph Atherstone, will never be known; for his doors were locked till he descended to make a hasty meal before starting. It may be —for have not men drowsed at the torture-post?—that he slept. At any rate, when he came forth, though the gaunt, haggard look was always there, his face was comparatively calm; there was not a sign of weariness in his firm, elastic gait; and he carried his grey head as erectly as if he had never known sorrow or shame.

# CHAPTER XLVII.

A DULL, slumbering place is Porhaix, and never likely to wax much livelier; for there is no reason why the rail should stretch out a side-feeler through a sterile country, poor in minerals; nor is there aught to tempt tourist or antiquarian to turn aside: even the fisher-errant gives the place a wide berth; for the river—wayward and rapid enough a few leagues higher up—has forgot to ripple before it reaches Porhaix; and none would think of casting fly in the sluggish, turbid flow.

To be sure, few are aware that, in the cellars of an uncouth-looking hostel, there are still stored certain cobwebbed flasks, the like of which it would have puzzled Voisin in his palmiest days to produce; ay, or even poor Pascal, with whom be peace! For the ancient hostess, steeped to the lips in the prejudices of *la vieille roche*, would lay the dust of her court-yard with that rare liquor, rather than moisten there-with the clay of the *commis voyageur;* though she grudges it not to any traveller able to discourse with her concerning the decadence of *La Bretagne Bre-tonnante*, or the glories of La Vendée.

It is not a healthy place either; for it nestles too close against the shoulder of the hill for free circula-tion of air; and, though it lies so near the sea that the rising tide laps languidly against the flood-gates of the little basin, the landward breeze, sweeping over ooze and marish, loses much of the crispness it caught up from the brine. If you meet a ruddy or bronzed face in the narrow, noisome streets, it is almost sure to be owned by a peasant or sailor : fevers and agues visit Porhaix not rarely, and are apt to linger there.

Late on a sultry afternoon, a *calèche* dragged heavily up the long ascent leading to the town. It held two travellers : one of whom was Ralph Atherstone ; the other—a short, sharp-visaged man—was Askew, the detective, who, warned by telegraph, had met his employer at the last stage. When they reached the first straggling houses of Porhaix, Askew stopped the carriage.

"We'll get out here, my lord, if you please," he said, "and let the trap go on to the Lion."

The detective had found time, as they drove along, to give an account of his proceedings. Since he harboured the fugitives, he had practically never lost sight of the Fleur-de-Lis—the second best of the three hostels of which Porhaix could boast—where they had taken up their quarters. For, whenever he himself went off duty, he had had the house watched by a stolid native, not likely to risk his hire by babbling. One circumstance had rather puzzled Askew : for the last forty-eight hours, he was certain that neither Glynne nor his companion had left the inn ; and, during such sultry weather, it seemed passing strange, that they should have refrained from taking the air after nightfall, even if they feared to go abroad by day.

"It ain't likely they could have winded us," the detective observed ; "I have taken good care of that. I half suspect there's illness there. There's a nasty fever hanging hereabouts, though the townsfolk won't allow it. For the last few days I've noticed that custom is uncommon slack at the Floordeliss ; and there are no loafers about the gateway."

Lord Atherstone's brow contracted, and his lip quivered slightly. He could scarcely endure to hear the woman he had so loved and honoured spoken of in a hard, matter-of-fact way like any other criminal : furthermore—does it sound like the folly of dotage ?

—the impulse that had caused him to cry, "God help
her!" was plucking at his heart once again, and he
shrank from the thought of Lena in suffering; for, if
punishment had so soon overtaken either sinner, he
did not doubt where it had lighted. But this pang,
like the others, he bore silently; and the two men
walked on, winding through by-streets, till they emerged into the little *Place* at an angle of which stood
the Fleur-de-Lis.

As Askew had observed, the house had a desolate
look: not a solitary *calèche* stood in the court-yard;
the cloth was not even laid in the empty *salle*, the
door of which stood ajar; and it was some time before
a slatternly handmaid answered the summons of the
gate-bell. At Lord Atherstone's question—"Are any
English travellers staying in the house?" she stood
sulkily helpless, and at last disappeared, muttering
something about 'seeking *madame.*' After a while
she returned, to say that an English couple were indeed lodging there; but that they could receive no
visit, inasmuch as '*ce monsieur souffrait toujours.*'

The dark flush, of which mention has before been
made, rose to the baron's cheek and abode there. So
it was not Lena who had been stricken down; but that
other, whose life he had thought, in his blindness,
belonged to him, Ralph Atherstone, as much as if he
had bought it with a price. What—if it were, after
all, to be taken out of his hand?

He did not notice how Askew shrank backwards
into the open air; but, thrusting aside the grumbling
Josille, strode quickly up the stairs. No need to ask
his way; for, as he set foot in the corridor above, a
low moan from a chamber over against him, told
Ralph that his search was ended.

You may wonder what brought the fugitives to
Porhaix. It happened in this wise. Glynne had
never deceived himself as to the probable consequences of the step he had taken; and guessed how
unlikely it was that Ralph Atherstone would leave

the avenging of his wrong to law, human or divine.
Now, men of this stamp have very quaint notions of
honour; and Caryl, though he had little right to stand
on his dignity, could not bring himself to fly far from
the face of his enemy. Nevertheless, he chose to
enjoy some brief breathing-space before the storm
should break; and, if his sin was to cost him his life,
he would have just one week of quasi-domestic happiness Long ago, in his wanderings, he had come
across the odd, out-of-the-way old town; and it struck
him as being exactly suited for his present purpose.

But the Dead-Sea fruit turned to ashes, almost before he had savoured it. On the evening of the second
day after their arrival Glynne felt a strange lassi-
tude, followed by a dizziness and burning heat; before
morning broke the fever had mastered him, and his
brain was wandering. So it had gone on, from bad
to worse, till the Porhaix doctors owned that they had
exhausted their simple skill, and Lena was fain to
realise that she might soon have to 'dree her weird'
—alone.

She deserved it all, of course; and, if justice were
always done so swiftly and sternly, many, standing
on the verge of as in like hers, might be saved
through fear; yet even Marian Ashleigh might have
pitied the woman, crouching there beside the miserable wreck of her love, and waiting for the end. It
was she that had moaned; for during the last two
hours only a slow, laboured breathing, and an occasional twitch of pain, had told that Caryl's stupor
was not yet death.

In pure weariness—this was the third day of incessant watching—Lena had dropped her aching head
on the coverlet; and, when the door opened, she did
not stir: she thought it was only the doctor, returning to quench her last faint ray of hope. But, when
no one entered, she did look up; and the next instant
she had sprung to her feet, with a fresh terror in her
hot, tearless eyes.

Surely, no errand of mercy or healing had brought *him* thither, who stood on the threshold—tall, grim, and motionless—like a statue of Retribution. And, as the gaze of husband and wife met, from a church hard by, the *Angelus* began to sound.

It must have been the merest chance; but, as Ralph strode a pace forward, a shudder ran through the prostrate figure; and the seal of the heavy lids was broken; and the glazing eyes opened wide. But Caryl Glynne had done with love or hate, with shame or remorse, with submission or defiance; his ears were shut against pleading and menace, against fond and angry words alike. He looked—or seemed to look—now, upon the woman whose beauty he had so lusted after, and the man whose grey hairs he had so dishonoured; and yet his cheek never flushed, and his fingers never stirred.

A Presence darkened that chamber, of which none were aware—a Shape that, pressing one hand on the damp brow, with the other waved off the human avenger; whispering—"Stand back, he is mine!" And, on the hither side of the grave, the adulterer could not be arraigned. A criminal may be dragged from sanctuary, or slain betwixt the horns of the altar; but, though his sin be as scarlet, he is safe under the mantle of Azrael.

Lena, half-distraught already in her despair, forgot all this: with a low, piteous cry, she flung herself forward; holding her paramour half-embraced, as though she would have shielded him from a blow.

Alas! for the true, generous heart—misconstrued even to the bitter end. The memory of his great wrong, the thirst for vengeance, and the sense of shame, were all swept away by the flood of pity that welled up in Ralph Atherstone's breast just then; and the stern soldier stood there—innocent of malice as any ' chrisom child.' Nay, he found time, even then, to accuse himself of having been unwittingly accessory to all this misery. If he had not set at

nought his own presentiments, to say nothing of
Lena's warning, it might have fared better with the
three ; but, lest his life should remain lonely, he
risked its being made desolate. Perhaps he was
rightly punished. After all, that other had loved
Lena *first ;* and to love her once, was to love her
always. Was it so certain that he himself would
have withstood a like temptation in his hot youth
—ay! or even on the morning when he woke, at
Kirkfell, from those troubled dreams?

A long silence followed, broken only by Lena's
frightened sobbing; for the sick man had relapsed
into stupor. Then Ralph Atherstone's voice was
heard—muffled and hollow, like that of one speaking
through a barred helmet.

"You have nothing to fear."

And he went out, closing the door very softly.

Do the words seem to you few and meagre, for such
a meeting? Well—on the stage there is a good deal
of talking or singing, as the case may be, at the
climax of the drama ; but, in real life, as a rule, the
strongest 'situation' does not entail the longest
speeches.

> Brief were the words of stern debate,
> That spoke the foemen's deadly hate—

wrote no mean judge of human nature ; and the principle holds, be sure, in love not less than in war.
Though he was as good a soldier as Christian, it
is beyond a doubt, that Havelock's fluent oratory
rather lessened his credit with his soldiery.

# CHAPTER XLVIII

LORD ATHERSTONE found the detective loitering in the *Place*, at a respectful distance from the door. This intrepid officer would have boarded a plague-ship in the discharge of his duty; but he had a great aversion to needless risks; and, amongst his professional perils, the pestilence that walketh in darkness was perhaps the one he liked the least. So, with manifest satisfaction, he received a liberal largess, and permission to depart.

"A rare good-plucked one," Askew muttered to himself as he walked away. "One of the sort that never flinch till they drop. But he *will* drop before long, if I'm not mistaken. He looks as if he had got a touch of the fever already."

Nevertheless, Ralph Atherstone was, in reality, calmer than he had felt since his great sorrow lighted on him. He took pains to ascertain from the inn-folk, that the sick chamber lacked not needful tendance; and keener wits than theirs would have seen nothing suspicious in his manner. Indeed, when he reached the other hotel, where his baggage had been sent, he actually forced himself to partake of food and drink; for he knew there might be still work for him, though not of such a sort as he had come to do. Then he walked forth into the air again; and sat down on a stone bench in the *Place* aforesaid, opposite, though not near, the door of the Fleur-de-Lis.

Night came on apace; and the mist, rolling up from seaward, hid meadow and marsh, and climbed half-way up the hill-side; and the idlers, who had

gathered round to inspect and comment on the
stranger, dropped off one by one; and lights twinkled
in the windows for a while; and then—they keep
early hours in those parts—the town grew dark and
quiet; and the faint, late moon struggled through
the sullen clouds at last; and still Ralph Atherstone
sat there, only lifting his head from time to time to
watch the house over-against him.

Late in the evening, a stout, fussy-looking person
—evidently the chief mediciner of Porhaix—had entered the Fleur-de-Lis, and had not since emerged.
The windows of the sick chamber looked towards the
court-yard; so it was impossible to guess how things
were going there. The dawn was just breaking, when
the inn-door opened; and the doctor appeared on
the threshold, speaking to some one behind him.
Ralph could not catch the words; but the shrug of
the shoulders, and the spreading forth of the palms,
were significant enough: he knew at once that all
was quite, quite over. An impulse, that he could not
himself have defined, made him rise to his feet; but
he checked himself when he had taken one pace forward; and, sitting down again, resumed his watch.

Perhaps half an hour might have passed—time at
such seasons is hard to reckon—when the door was
pushed open again, very slowly, and a woman came
out.  Ralph Atherstone's pulse gave a great leap,
and then seemed to stand still. If the light had been
thrice as dim, would he not have known that figure,
and its stately grace, among a thousand? Yet he
never stirred; though his crossed arms tightened
themselves athwart his breast, as if he would have
held himself down by main force.

Doubtingly and waveringly, feeling each step as
sleep-walkers do, Lena advanced ten paces or so into
the *Place ;* then she stopped, smoothing the hair on
her forehead with both her palms, and gazing all
round her in a strange, bewildered way. Her face
was very white—white, not with the clearness of wax,

but the dulness of ashes—only the lips were crimson-purple. And her great brown eyes, brighter even than their wont, glittered with some nameless fear.

It was full morning now; and Ralph—near enough to note all this—refrained himself no longer. Lena did not seem to notice his approach at first; but. when he came quite close, she turned towards him —smiling. Better if she had cried aloud in her agony, or cast herself writhing at his feet, than have smiled in such wise.

"So you have come back, Monseigneur," she said in that wonderful *mezza voce* of hers, which even yet kept its music. "I'm so sorry we quarrelled; for you were in the right. It is much best that we two should not meet. But I may write, and tell him so? We are such old, old friends."

And her fingers plucked nervously at the waist-cord of her dressing-robe; just as they had done at the fringe of her mantle, when she first heard of the Norway plan.

The baron had looked on some ghastly sights in his time; but never a one of these sent such a chill through his marrow, as froze it now. Yet there was nothing strange or unnatural here. The brain-chord, strained by watching and misery, to say nothing of remorse, had snapped in twain; and the fever-fire, smouldering perhaps for many hours past, had broken out—that was all. Any physician in fair practice could quote a score of such cases, no doubt. But it cost Ralph such an effort to speak, that his voice sounded harshly.

"You must go in again at once; you are very ill."

Perhaps the stern tone jarred on her ear; or perhaps—the phases of these disorders are very sudden —a flash of light darted through the clouds of her brain; for she started violently, and the terror of her eyes became dreadfully defined.

"Go in?" she repeated in a shuddering whisper— "In there—where *that* is lying?"

And then the colour faded out of her lips, too; and
she sank slowly down, till she crouched at her husband's feet—white and cold.

Never before had this woman looked on death; and
it may be that some strange horror attended the passing of a most guilty soul—the Porhaix doctor, when
questioned by his fellows, only shrugged his shoulders;
muttering, "*C'était bien dur. Allez!*"—and into these
matters it is not well to pry. But it is certain that,
to Lena's other tortures on that night, there was added
physical fear.

However, now, the tormentors held their hand, and
there was granted to her some respite; for it was a
senseless body that Ralph Atherstone gathered up,
and carried indoors, so tenderly. And the long, long
swoon was followed by delirium, that lasted for days.

Whilst she lay swaying betwixt life and death,
Lena never guessed that

> Hands used to grip the sword-hilt hard,

had learned to be light and gentle as a girl's as they
bathed her throbbing forehead, or smoothed her pillow. But even the sullen inn-folk, who looked upon
sickness under their roof as a personal injury, were
moved to wonder and pity. They settled the whole
story to their own satisfaction: *la moustache grise* was
a stern uncle, or guardian at the least, who had been
very wroth at an imprudent marriage; and then, repenting himself, had brought forgiveness too late.

Amidst his watching, Lord Atherstone found time
to do the last kindness to his enemy. It was he who
by rich largess—to be spent in charity or masses, as
the *curé* should will—smoothed away certain clerical
scruples; and, though he shrank back with a muttered excuse, when the hostess prayed him to look
once more on the corpse's face—"*Il est beau comme
un ange,*" *madame* whispered persuasively — Ralph
stood by bare-headed, whilst, with such maimed rite

as that Church allows to such as die without her
Unction, the earth was heaped over Caryl Glynne.

But the cross set up there bears not even an initial.
And, surely, it is best that this should be a nameless
grave.

Of something else, too, the baron took care. When
Lena opened her eyes, after her first convalescent
sleep, they rested upon a figure that they recognised,
though they were swimming mistily; and though it
was bowed and broken since she saw it last. She
was too weak to wonder, how her mother came to
be sitting there.

Now, I am not at all prepared to defend Mrs. Shafton. It was perhaps her bounden duty, to wait at
least a decent interval, before stretching forth her
hand to such a sinner; even though it was over her
own child's head that the deep waters were rolling.
But this unregenerate matron would not look at things
in the right light. Though she was still ailing, she
hasted to obey Lord Atherstone's summons; and, for
the first time in her life, set her son's anger utterly at
nought. The tidings of Glynne's death seemed rather
to exasperate than pacify Miles.

"It would be very convenient that she should die,
of course"—the mother said, with a strange bitterness—"but there is no reason why she should die
alone; and, if she lives, she shall never be alone
whilst I can help it. You may cast us *both* off, if you
choose."

Miles, who really was not so hard of heart as he
seemed, grumbled a sort of apology; but Mrs. Shafton scarcely listened to this, in her eagerness to depart.

During her journey to Porhaix—she travelled much
faster than the trusty Julie thought safe—though her
unselfish fears were far the strongest, one dread came
uppermost, not seldom, in Isabel Shafton's mind—the
dread of meeting Ralph Atherstone. But, when she
did meet him, she wondered how she could ever have

been afraid. She never remembered his manner so gentle: he seemed only too grateful to her for coming; and never alluded to the past.

"I am assured all danger is over," he said; "and I leave here to-night. But I shall see Miles as soon as I get home; and you will be well taken care of. You would like to go up-stairs now"—it was in the court-yard that they were standing—"Good-bye."

Isabel Shafton was not given to hero-worship; but a reverence, such as she had never felt for any living creature, filled her heart as she looked into the worn, furrowed face—terribly changed and aged —and saw that, even in its sorrow, it was not hardened against her. She wrung his hand in her trembling fingers, whilst her tears flowed fast.

"God in heaven bless you!" she murmured.

"May God forgive us all!" said Ralph Atherstone.

Each understood the other's meaning right well. With no more words, they parted; and met never again.

# CHAPTER XLIX.

THOUGH the ill news concerning Templestowe came home to no other Loamshire dwelling, as it did to that one house in Heslingford, it created a passable excitement throughout the county: notably, on Erriswell it came like a thunder-clap.

Malcolm's life, though busy and stirring, had been so far uneventful, that his nerves had scarcely been tried by any purely uncommercial disaster; and it may fairly be said, that this was their rudest shock. His notions of morality, as has been aforesaid, though not austere, were inflexible; and, besides this, he highly respected Lord Atherstone: even the asperities of the other's character contrasted favourably, in Robin's eyes, with the polished inanity of certain gilded youths. He felt, now, as if he could scarcely look any honest man in the face; though he had only been accessory to the crime by innocently harbouring the criminal; and though his suspicions, such as they were, had pointed to a widely different quarter. He could not trust himself to speak on the subject even to his wife.

Emily Malcolm's indignation, at first, was to the full as keen; and perhaps her conscience pricked her more sharply. She had been blind, quite blind, it is true; but that very blindness was culpable; and, now that it was too late, she bethought herself of more than one incident that ought to have opened her eyes.

Altogether, a great gloom fell upon the cheery house, and a shadow like that of shame.

At Hunsden, the intelligence did not create as

much commotion as one might have reckoned on.
The fair falconer, regnant there, had for some time
past despaired of reclaiming her 'haggard;' and,
though the sense of injury was still hot, she had tried
hard to persuade herself, that now she cared little
where the truant sought perch or prey. However,
the blow was sharp, if not altogether unexpected;
and furthermore, it was a sore trial to her patience,
to detect covert gleams of exultation in the Driver's
eyes, when he brought the news.

Dick was really sorry for Lord Atherstone; but he
could not refrain from triumphing a little, inwardly,
over the justification of his antipathy and the avenging of his supplanted comrade.

Nevertheless, Mrs. Devereux's first words were—
"Poor Lena!" They were quite honestly spoken,
and of the impulse prompting them, a better woman
might have been proud. The wayward, wilful little
heart was not yet so hard, but that, even when most
angered, it could pity any creature doomed, thenceforward, to trust only to the tender mercies of Caryl
Glynne.

Hubert Ashleigh was much grieved and shocked
by the catastrophe. To be sure, it might have been
stretching his duty, to have interfered sooner; and,
when he did interfere, he had both spoken and acted
with unwonted energy. Nevertheless, he did not feel
altogether conscience-free; and he was further tormented by a dread lest the dark drama should not
be quite played out.

In these last misgivings the parson was not alone.
After the first babble of surprise had subsided, there
came in Loamshire and elsewhere a kind of hush of
expectation; and people began to wonder, in what
guise Ralph Atherstone's vengeance would descend:
that he would seek it not slackly, none doubted, who
knew the man. Ere long a rumour of the truth oozed
out—none could tell whence it came; for Miles Shafton, who alone could have spoken with certainty,

kept a dogged silence—and soon it was known that a mightier Avenger had taken one of the criminals into his charge, and had laid upon the other a hand, heavy well-nigh unto death.

Then a reaction ensued; and the world—often as unjust in indulgence as in cruelty—spoke far more gently than he had deserved, of the seducer; and, strange to say, spared some compassion to his victim.

'They had had great temptations; for they had been lovers, long ago; and only money-troubles had kept them apart. The marriage was a forced one, no doubt; and the least that Mrs. Shafton could have done, after getting her way, was to look after her daughter; especially as Lord Atherstone seemed to have lacked both common sense and common prudence. Credulity was all very well in its way; but they could scarcely pity a crabbed old man, who left so fair a wife always to her own devices, and absolutely alone at a most critical time. He was almost rightly served.'

And then—timid at first, but swelling presently into an audible antiphony—certain voices, chiefly of course *soprani*, began to chant Caryl Glynne's dirge; making moan, as they could not bewail his worth, over the beauty he had misused, the talents he had wasted, and the promise he had belied. Finally, perhaps, there was more moistening of filmy kerchiefs, than usually follows the announcement of 'a great man fallen in Israel.'

Of such weakness, one puissant personage was assuredly clear. The Duke of Devorgoil, carrying his nose at an acuter upward angle than ever snuffed the air triumphantly, as became the champion of virtue and of his order. Perchance, in coming time, if the offender were properly humbled by his chastisement, the finger of clemency might be extended to Ralph Atherstone: at any rate, Grandmanoir was even with Templestowe at last.

The member for Heslingford, for a fortnight or so,

fussed and fidgeted beyond his wont; but he did not seem entirely crushed by the family misfortune: though, save when grumbling to two or three special cronies, he had the grace to give the subject a wide berth; and, till the days of wondering had expired, rarely showed in public, except in his place at St. Stephen's.

Marian was even more reserved and reticent. She took no living creature into her counsel, and altogether shrank from society; but the few who were admitted into her presence, reported her as looking very anxious and worn; and everybody agreed that 'of course she took it very much to heart, and that it was very hard upon her'—not specifying the hardship. Altogether, this exemplary matron's behaviour, on this trying occasion, added perhaps another leaf to her ample chaplet.

However, Archibald Kerneguy, pondering over these things, one afternoon when work was slack, thus expressed himself to his habitual confidants, the whispering elms of the Mall:—

"A clever woman, that cousin of mine—devilish clever, I may say. She won that game, with the odds dead against her; though, to the end of time, we shall never know what cards she held, or how she played them. Quite a credit to the family. But,"—here Archie smiled sourly—"the Lord deliver us from falling into her hand!"

The town-bred gossips soon fastened on a fresh scandal; but it was long before Loamshire folk ceased to discourse on the tragedy, the earlier scenes of which had been enacted in the midst of them. The blackness of the crime was somewhat toned down by the suddenness of the retribution; and many went so far as to pity Lena, whilst few spoke even of the dead despiteously.

Robin Malcolm, though he said in his own heart, that 'nothing in his life became Caryl Glynne like the leaving it,' could not bring himself to chide, when

he saw his wife's tears a-flowing : only, by tacit consent, that name thenceforth was never uttered by
either, and the place of a certain portrait was made
void on the wall

Neither in Dick Devereux's eyes was there a spark
of triumph, when he brought this news home ; and,
with more tact than the world gave him credit for, so
soon as he had delivered it, he left Cissy alone. His
suspicions had never advanced beyond vague misgiving, you will remember ; but, had they been
stronger, he would not, specially at such a season,
have stooped to espial.

How do you think she took the catastrophe ? It
seems to me, no *man* can answer that question.

There are recesses in the woman-heart, which the
luckiest of us have never seen illumined, and wind-
ings, that the most adventurous have never pene-
trated. Once or twice there was a flash of light, or
perhaps we thought we held the clue : but it was only
a flash ; and, when the thread snapped suddenly, for a
while we felt more helplessly at fault than before.

Remember the words of one who had studied the
sex, as schoolmen study palimpsests, and who, if he
had kept a record of his evil victories from boyhood
upwards, might have boasted—' *Nulla dies sine lineá.*'

"I know now," quoth the wicked, witty old noble,
" how little I have known."

He was very near his end then ; and mock modesty
was not among his failings.

Cissy Devereux was by no means vindictive : though
easily moved to anger, she was almost incapable of
lasting malice ; and, when her resentment was at the
bitterest, had such a chance presented itself, she would
probably have shrunk from deeply injuring either her
rival or the man who, for his own purposes, had trifled
with her so cruelly. Nevertheless, when her first horror had subsided, it may be that she found a dreary
satisfaction in the thought that all was over, quite
over, now ; that even pride need not hinder her from

forgiving her enemies; and that, if she could settle matters with her own conscience, the last year might lie buried in the Breton graveyard. In almost all powerful medicines, there is a germ of poison; and, perchance, the draught that this woman had been forced to drink—so perilously sweet at first, at last so bitter—was wholesome in the end.

She never will be quoted as a domestic model; but no new scandal has since been linked to her name; and, though she never stands on her dignity, none of her old 'loves' have been reinstated. Even Godfrey Colville, to whom she certainly owed some amends, found her hopelessly friendly; and, though he still gives her a lead whenever he is in that country, his privileges extend no further. At all other times, the Driver, to his great pride and contentment, is allowed to play *chaperon :* indeed, in many ways, at home as well as abroad, Dick has much benefited by the change. Though still wilful and outspoken as ever, Cissy has gained much ground in the county since she ceased to shock its proprieties; and, when Swinton Swarbrick avers defiantly that 'there never was a grain of harm in her, and he knew it all along,' very few think it their duty to argue the point, or by raking up the past, incense that truculent partisan.

We read of people who in their sleep, or otherwise unwittingly, walk carelessly along the very edge of an abyss; but, on being made aware of the peril they have barely escaped, wax sick and mazed with fear. Just such a terror and trembling fell upon Arthur Corbett, when he heard of what had happened beyond sea. Luckily for himself and for others, there never was in this man the making of a great criminal: if temptation had quite mastered him, he would still have striven to temporise, and to make terms with the world, if not with his own conscience—after the fashion of the old *abbés,* who, in their midnight prowlings, seldom forgot cloak or mask, and handled sin, as it were, with perfumed gloves. It seemed to him as if he had actually, albeit unconsciously, stood within the shadow of death ; and he felt like one who, having against all likelihood come scathless out of a plague-stricken city, for a while breathes not freely even in untainted air.

However, soon ensued an agreeable sense of security. Natures like Corbett's are incapable of enduring self-reproach ; and, whilst he congratulated himself on his escape, the fount of his domestic affections, that had trickled but slowly of late, gushed forth plenteously. The voices of his children had never sounded so pleasantly in his ears ; his wife's homely face was to him more attractive than when he first wooed her ; and the shade of the trees in his plaisance had never seemed to him so grateful, as when he remembered how often, with a fluttering or aching heart, he had passed under the elms of Templestowe.

Probably, under any circumstances, Arthur's virtuous resolutions would have endured ; but this rude shock, doubtless, braced their vigour. And so, perchance here, too, there sprang up a good crop, where there had been sown worse than tares.

# CHAPTER L.

ONLY his lawyer, Miles Shafton, and Sir Charles Wroughton, were made aware of Lord Atherstone's return; and none of these interviews—they were of the briefest—deserve to be recorded. He made no attempt to see either Philip or Marian; indeed, they did not know he was in England, till they heard, casually, that he was at Templestowe.

Marian had not expected to find her father-in-law very tractable under the circumstances; but his strange conduct puzzled her uncomfortably; and, after waiting a decent time, she composed, with infinite care and pains, a cautious little note, wherein she expressed her own and Philip's anxiety to be of service; hazarding, moreover, a hope that she at least, ere long, might be wanted in Loamshire. By return of post came the following:—

"DEAR MARIAN,

"I know your motives are kind; but the only good service I will ask from either you or Philip, is absolute silence as to the past. For a very long time I shall prefer being quite alone: indeed, in all your future arrangements, you must leave Templestowe out of the question. It is not likely you will see it again, before it becomes your own.

"Affectionately yours,

"A."

As she read, Marian bit her lip till the blood started; and the same malign lowering came over

her face, as had possessed it when she first heard of
the betrothal; but there was added to it, now, a more
marked despondency.

Was it worth while to have schemed, and plotted,
and connived—to have trampled under foot all self-
esteem—to have been subjected to Hubert Ashleigh's
shameful suspicions—worst of all, to have lain detected at her enemy's mercy, and to have owed her
safety to the other's scorn—only to find herself farther
than ever from reinstatement in the coveted place?
There was no scope for her talents, now; for she
knew that pleading or argument would not be more
wasted on a granite block, than on Ralph Atherstone when his purpose was set. So long as the
baron lived—and he was still in the vigour, if not
in the prime, of his strength—for any benefit that
she or Philip was like to derive from it, Templestowe
might as well be owned by a stranger. For years to
come, she would probably not rule a larger household
than they at present owned; and, instead of dis-
pensing, liberally though justly, the goods of another,
she would have to practise petty economies, partly on
her own account, partly to pacify Philip's avarice.
Of course, he would fret and grumble more than ever;
and, now that its doors were closed against him —
utterly ignoring his former prejudices—would hanker
after Templestowe, like a lost Eden.

Furthermore, she was tormented by a doubt whether Ralph would so absolutely have rejected her
sympathy, if he had merely desired to be alone. Beyond the death of one of the fugitives, and the sore
sickness of the other, Marian knew literally nothing
of what had happened in Brittany. Was it possible
that Lena, either repenting of her clemency, or waxing malicious in her despair, or, perchance, wandering in her speech, had after all brought up the anonymous letter? Though all material proof had been
destroyed long ago, Marian wist right well what
manner of fruit the bare suspicion, once planted in

the baron's mind, was likely to produce. Supposing things were so, in all probability she would never be put on her defence ; and, even if she were, she sorely mistrusted the effect of special pleading : she pictured to herself the look that would come into Ralph's eyes, when she should allege that 'she had done everything for the best.'

Altogether, this virtuous lady's frame of mind was by no means enviable ; especially as upon these worries came the necessity of sooner or later explaining to her husband, that Templestowe must thenceforth be struck out of their visiting-list.

Philip was completely taken aback. It was plain that he, too, had reckoned on resuming his old quarters, and, now that the evil spirits had gone forth, on finding the house ready swept and garnished. Once installed there, he would doubtless have cavilled and grumbled, not less persistently than heretofore ; but, conversing with him now, a stranger might have fancied that, for Philip, no other 'angle of earth' had real attraction ; and might have been tempted to condole with the victim of paternal tyranny.

But Marian was no stranger ; and there could not be a stronger proof of her depression, than the fact, that she listened without a smile to these querulous outbreaks, and without a frown to the frequent taunts as to the result of all her waitings and watchings.

You can guess, perhaps, what made her so silent and submissive. Under the rosy sunset of success, the roughest places on the road behind look smooth, and a soft haze broods over the morass that wellnigh engulfed us ; but, under the cold grey sky of failure, it is not pleasant to look back : nor in truth is there need. Do not the slough-stains on our garments, and the thorn-marks on our flesh, witness by what manner of paths we have come hither?

Now, Marian had failed, if not in the achieving of her immediate purposes, assuredly in the attainment of her final desire ; and, to the consciousness of this,

there was added something more. Perhaps in few
rational bipeds could there be found less of manly
dignity and sterling rectitude than in Philip Ashleigh; his moral like his physical organization had
to a certain extent gone awry. Nevertheless, had he
guessed at the work to which she had set her hand,
I think, for a long time to come, he would have been
afraid, if not ashamed, to lay his head on the same
pillow with Marian's. Because she neither deeply
loved nor venerated her husband, the consciousness
of this stung her not less keenly.

So, even in these early days, she, too, began to
pay off some portion of the heavy accompt written,
elsewhere, against her name.

Nevertheless, you who are behind the scenes will
have divined that the baron's seeming churlishness
arose from no suspicion, however distant, of the truth.
The hankering after solitude whilst a grievous wound
rankles, which the meekest of men share with the
fiercest brutes, may have had much to do with it.
The softer sex sometimes wax more sociable under
their pain; but few males are exempt from this instinct, though they comport themselves very dif-
ferently when once *in eremo*. The big round tears of
the stricken hart may mingle with the water-brooks;
but the dry eyes of the old 'tusker' gleam dangerously, as he couches stiff and sore in his lair. Besides this, Ralph was not minded to endure any sight
or sound likely to remind him of the recent past. He
could not have looked upon Marian's face, or listened
to her voice, without remembering how often that
cheery presence had dispelled the first light clouds
of the gathering storm. It was the more ungracious
now to reject her sympathy; but it could not be otherwise, even though she should think him ungrateful to
boot.

That he should have shut himself up in Templestowe will not appear strange, if you remember what
manner of life Ralph had led there, from his return

from India up to Philip's marriage. If he could but
fancy the last few years a blank, it was only falling
back on his hermit habits again.

But, unhappily, it is easier to wake the dead than
to command certain 'fancies.'  We may lock the
door fast of a certain chamber, or wall it up for ever;
but none the less shall we be haunted by the rustling
of silks in the desolate corridors —none the less out
of a vacant mirror will peer

The face that was fatally fair—

none the less a gush of fragrance from the flowers,
neglected now, will bring back the subtle, nameless
perfume that was wont to set our senses tingling.

However, local influences made things neither better nor worse for Ralph Atherstone.  If he had travelled on, never sleeping twice under the same roof,
till he broke down from sheer weariness, through all
those months his waking and, very often, his sleeping
thoughts would still have centred on one object—his
false, lost wife. The idea of reconciliation did not once
cross his mind.  Though she would have been unconscious of the caress, his lips never brushed her brow
when he left her at Porhaix; neither would they have
done so, if on those heavy eyelids had lain an eternal
seal.  Ay, and if—being very near his own end—he
had heard Lena's voice without, pleading for admis-
sion, he would have barred the door against her with
the last effort of his strength and will.  Their paths
in this world must thenceforth be as though they had
never blended; and even in another world — if his
speculation ranged so far — they were like to be
divided.

But the generosity—or whatever else stood him in
the stead of Christian charity—that had made Ralph
Atherstone accuse himself instead of others, abode
with him still.  In the old happy time he was not
more anxious to fulfil her lightest fancy, than he was
now to spare Lena all needless shame.  The scandal-

mongers smacked their lips in anticipation of a *cause célèbre*: but the savoury meat was not served; and, after waiting till they were weary, they were fain to fill themselves with less dainty food. Lord Atherstone never asked from the Law even such scanty redress as a 'separation' can afford. He intimated as much to Miles Shafton in their first and only interview; and his chief business with his lawyer, was the securing to Lady Atherstone a more than sufficient alimony.

When this was noised abroad, Society considered itself decidedly ill-used, and murmured accordingly; for, though an enfranchised husband cannot too soon exult in his liberty, there are certain bondmen who can scarcely walk the streets without contempt of the Divorce Court. Some few were of a different opinion; and Sir Charles Wroughton, in converse with one or two intimates—in public he utterly declined to discuss the subject—maintained that his friend had done wisely and well.

"They say a good horse is never dear," the baronet remarked allegorically; "but nothing's a bargain to a man who can't ride; and, if it cost him ever so little, what use is freedom now to Ralph Atherstone?"

What use, indeed? The speaker could better himself have answered the question when, somewhat later —almost forcing the *consigne*—he gained entrance to Templestowe. After the first evening—when, in a dry, matter-of-fact way he made his comrade aware of what had happened since they parted, and of his own intentions with regard to Lena—the baron made no allusion to the past, and, evidently, looked for neither advice nor condolence. But it was a dreary visit for good-natured Charles Wroughton; and it told well for his unselfishness that he should have proposed, at his departure, returning in October.

"I shall be too glad—if you can stand it," Ralph replied.

But there was no gladness in his face; and, though

it was no longer so drawn and haggard, it seemed as if no emotion, either for weal or woe, was likely thenceforth to ruffle its rigid quietude.

The lease of his Scottish moor expired, as it chanced, that year; and he was, of course, a defaulter at Kirkfell. The party assembled there was not nearly so cheery as usual; for there was not one of the guests that did not sympathise in the sorrow that had lighted on their old comrade, though the matter was seldom broached amongst them—General Percy himself studiously avoiding it.

How during the next three months it fared with the baron, it would be hard to say; for he saw none but his own immediate dependents, and these only on business. But, when Wroughton returned in October, it seemed to him that his friend was outwardly much the same as he had been before his marriage. Ralph's bodily vigour, at any rate, was unimpaired; for his pace over rough or deep ground once more moved the pursy baronet to envy.

The head keeper watched his master with an admiring wonder. Men of his stamp, however ignorant, can always appreciate hardihood; and—remembering his own anxieties—John Gilbert guessed how much hardihood was needed here. Perchance, too, he sometimes reproached himself for having been so easily hoodwinked on a certain afternoon; and the change in his demeanour was quite as expressive, as if he had put sympathy into words.

On the whole, Wroughton's second sojourn at Templestowe was much more satisfactory; and he was greatly encouraged by noticing that Ralph, if he took little interest in other matters, had begun to look carefully after the condition of his stable. Nevertheless, he was not a little surprised, when a month later—shooting a hundred miles away—he heard that the 'bruising baron' had gone, quite in the old form, through the first really fast thing of the season with Knowsley's hounds.

But if one of the Crusaders, who lie carven in stone in Heslingford Minster, had appeared at the coverside in full panoply, bestriding a barded *destrier*, Loamshire could not have been much more astonished. With such a tragedy as had lately passed under their eyes, these honest folks had hitherto been acquainted only by hearsay ; and that one of the principal actors therein — albeit he was rather sinned against than sinning—should venture so soon to front the public ken, seemed to many a violent breach of decorum ; and the sympathy, which had been entirely on the side of the injured husband, was checked, if not changed in its channel.

"He was just the same as ever," people said; " though, for a while, he had seemed to soften on the surface, his heart was always like the nether millstone. Perhaps, after all, there were more excuses for the wife than she had got credit for. She might have been sharply provoked, as well as strongly tempted."

Not a few, no doubt, were kinder and juster in their judgment; but delicacy kept these aloof as much as dislike did the others. And so, on that day, and for many days after, the crowd shrank back a little as Ralph passed through the midst of them ; and, though all saluted him with studied courtesy, never a one gave him outspoken welcome or wrung his hand.

But the man, with whom his trustiest comrade had not ventured to condole, was not likely to wince under lack of sympathy from his neighbours. It is doubtful if the baron even noticed the fashion of his reception. That it did not in anywise gall him is certain. It suited his purpose to seek the only distraction against thought that lay in his power ; and from his purpose he never again turned aside to please a friend or appease a foe. Whilst his pulse was quickened with strong exercise, or the occasional excitement of peril, his phantoms left him in peace. They were waiting for him at home, he knew : but what mat-

tered that ?  He had got used to them—so used, that
he would have been almost sorry had they been exorcised for ever.

Thenceforth, the tenor of Ralph Atherstone's life
did not vary.  Society—in the general sense of the
word—knew him no more.  But when he paid his
rare, brief visits to London, he did not affect to avoid
his acquaintances at his clubs or elsewhere ; nor was
he much more reserved, or taciturn, than usual.  He
seldom neglected to call on the Ashleighs, who had
established themselves in a modest house on the
Belgravian frontier; and, at these times, his manner
was sufficiently kind, if not precisely cordial.  But he
never hinted that their presence would be even tolerated at home ; and Marian—though she more than
once determined to risk it—never quite ventured to
broach the subject.  Twice or thrice in each autumn
and winter, Wroughton, and a few intimates of the
same standing, came to stay at Templestowe; but,
with the exception of Hubert Ashleigh, the doors
were open to no other visitor.  Ralph always rode
into Heslingford when he had occasion to confer with
Corbett; and the latter much preferred this method
of transacting their business.  Nothing short of
absolute necessity would have induced Arthur to
trust himself again under the shadow of those fatal
elms.

Also the baron was occasionally seen at purely
bachelor shooting parties, without as well as within
the borders of Loamshire ; but one thing was noticeable — he never set his foot north of the Humber.
How —living utterly alone, with no ostensible distraction — Ralph managed to get through the late
spring and summer, was a puzzle to all who troubled
themselves to consider the matter.  He had always
been a negligent, though not a hard landlord; and
he did not seem to take more interest than heretofore in his estates.  Indeed, at this season, except
when he went out for his daily ride—he never omitted

this, however foul the weather—he was seldom seen out of doors.

Once, when the Chairmanship of the Quarter Sessions was to be decided, Lord Atherstone appeared in the magistrates' room at Heslingford. There he met the Duke of Devorgoil. The intentions of this potentate were pacific, not to say conciliatory. He came prepared to condone by-gone offences, and never doubted but that he would be met half way; for he considered that by his conduct in the Park he had rather espoused the husband's cause. So, when Ralph came near, his Grace leant forward in his seat with a formal smile, stretching forth a half-reluctant hand.

With no more ceremony than the Duke himself would have shown to a vagrant craving for alms, the other passed on; but the fell gleam of the grey eyes sent a shiver through the marrow of Lupus Fitz-Roland's bones. He had not often erred on the side of charity towards his fellow-men; and, whilst he lived, did not again so compromise himself.

Only He, to whom all hearts are open, knows whether Ralph Atherstone's was as tough as the world believed it; and whether length of pain brought numbness at last. This much is certain : his sorrow, however deep and enduring, left few outward traces. That journey homewards from Norway had aged his face, as you know; but succeeding years brought few, if any, more ravages. He never looked bent or broken; and his marvellous bodily energy continued unabated.

A gusty morning had been followed by a wilder noon: but, in spite of wind and sleet, the hounds and their patient master had stuck resolutely to their fox, till they killed him barely within the limits of their country. The baron had never gone more bruisingly; and more than one Loamshire 'hard' — none other saw the finish—looked after him admiringly as he rode away, alone as usual, through the twilight.

That same evening Lord Atherstone, having done fair justice to his meal, sat in his favourite place—a

deep arm-chair drawn up in front of the hearth. His
attitude did not betoken weariness; and his eyes
looked rather wakeful than drowsy as they peered
into the blaze. It was blowing more than a half-
gale outside; and the great avenue-elms creaked and
groaned, much as they had done on that luckless
evening when the bride was brought home. Did
Ralph remember this? Possibly: for, as he pondered, his brow grew more furrowed and his cheeks
perceptibly paler. At last his breathing waxed
laboured and heavy, till there came a sound like
a quick gasping sob; and then—silence.

And the fire sank lower and lower, till the big logs
smouldered into heaps of ashes—dusky red at first,
grey-white at last—and the lamp flickered and went
out. But Ralph Atherstone sat there, still as a statue; and so they found him sitting, just after the
break of dawn.

He had been dead some hours—of heart disease,
the doctors averred. His countenance showed no
signs of pain: indeed, it looked gentler and softer
than it had often looked in life.

If this were so, can you not divine what was the
latest vision he saw in the fire?

# CHAPTER LI.

Now, it behoves us to go back and take up one more thread, before we roll up warp and woof.

Though Lord Atherstone had rightly believed all danger to be past when he departed from Porhaix, Lena's recovery was very slow; and it was weeks before her strength sufficed for travel. If she did not mend quicker, it was not for lack of tender nursing.

It is possible that, in her heart, the mother never quite forgave; but not a single taunt or reproach, then or afterwards, passed her lips; and, outwardly, they seemed drawn closer together than they had been in the old times. In the spirit, not less than in the letter, she carried out her promise that—"While she lived, Lena should not be alone." But she never, thenceforth, attempted to thwart or control her. When Lena went out by herself, on the day preceding their departure from Porhaix, Mrs. Shafton did not remonstrate against the imprudence or offer her company, though she guessed—as you perchance may guess—whither her daughter was going.

Slowly, but travelling always by the least-frequented ways, the two crept back to Blytheswold. Though the light of early autumn was upon them, the fells had never looked more desolate, or the house more dreary: yet both felt a certain respite and relief. It was home, at all events; and from that refuge neither again was likely to emerge.

Troubles, ere long, beside those of their own making—Isabel never quite absolved herself as to the past—came upon them there. For Miles's downward career, which had seemed checked for awhile, was renewed with terrible rapidity. The sale of his commission, which was soon forced upon him, scarcely stayed for a moment the baying of the ravenous lawhounds; and, to avert more family dishonour, the mother was called on for fresh sacrifices. She had no spirit left for anger, and she was too weary to complain. She knew that the world made excuses for the prodigal, saying, 'that he had never been utterly reckless till after his sister's shame.' There might be a grain of truth in this; but if not—what mattered it? She had tried hard to do the best for both her children; and, if everything had gone bitterly wrong, it could never now be mended. In her own weak—perhaps you may call it wicked—way she loved them both to the very last; and, when she bade them good-bye, you would never have guessed that she had anything to forgive.

For Isabel Shafton's troubles, though they ended not speedily, are ended now; and, if no high praise or reward awaited her beyond the Dark River, let us hope, in charity, that she at least found—rest.

And Lena?

Many may think that it would have been more merciful if, in Porhaix graveyard, there had been laid another coffin. But wiser and holier folk, than any who are like to scan these pages, have held that it is well with those who are permitted to balance some part—however small—of their debt to Divine Justice, before they pass hence to be no more seen. If such tenets be true, this woman was, perhaps, dealt with more graciously than she deserved; for her remorse, if unavailing, was after the measure of her guilt and the strength of her nature.

She was none of those comfortable penitents who scourge themselves with silken cords, and fast on dainty loaves and fishes; and who, after they deem they have made sufficing atonement, count themselves among the Elect; and, finally, almost exult in

past guilt, contrasting it with present sanctity. If
the doctrine of Penance had entered into her creed,
she would, probably, have wrought it out to the uttermost; and, because it had no such outlet, her repentance was not the less poignant. It was keen enough
to overbear other sorrows—ay, and even the evil love
that had drawn all her life awry.

Her thoughts travelled towards Templestowe to the
full as often as towards Porhaix; and though in her
dreams she still sometimes saw Caryl Glynne's face
—not as she had seen it last, but dangerously beautiful as of yore—she saw more frequently yet another
face, out of which the deep grey eyes looked rather
sadly than wrathfully. Her loneliness after her
mother's death it would be hard to exaggerate. For
letters were almost as rare as visitors at Blytheswold: even Grace Moreland, who still clung stealthily
to the old allegiance, wrote only twice or thrice a
year. Yet what was this loneliness to that which
had fallen on the generous heart that had trusted her
to the very end, and, after the end had come, had
pitied and forborne? When in the fulness of time
the news of her widowhood arrived, her tears flowed
faster than on that afternoon, when she printed a
farewell kiss on the scarce-knit turf of Caryl Glynne's
grave.

It is impossible that, amidst the ceaseless troubles
and privations of her life, Lena should not have sometimes remembered the home, where her caprices were
law, and were often divined before they were outspoken. But, though she might have secured affluence by one stroke of her pen, she never used that
power. Neither before nor after Lord Atherstone's
death—though his lawyers pressed the point urgently
and repeatedly — could she be induced to touch a
penny of the liberal alimony left to her, beyond the
interest of her own scanty portion.

Strange as this may seem, it was stranger yet that
Miles should have taken the same view of the case.

At the very hardest of their straits, it probably never occurred to him to look for relief in that quarter : certainly the suggestion never passed his lips. He did but follow the fashion of his race. From cruelty, or tyranny, or rapine, the Shaftons of Blytheswold had seldom withheld their hand; but small meannesses were not in the blood. However, his scruples began and ended here. It would be difficult to conceive greater mortifying of the flesh and spirit, than that which must have been laid on any woman doomed to live under the same roof with that unlucky spendthrift.

There were excuses for him, to be sure. Throughout all time disbanded soldiers have been proverbially prone to discontent, especially when, like our poor ex-hussar, they have neither amusement, occupation, nor resources. Though he had never followed it up with much zeal or diligence, Miles was really fond of his profession. It had its small hardships, of course ; but, on the whole, barrack-life suited him wonderfully well: his appetite was always better at mess than elsewhere; and the ante-room chaff was quite intellectual enough for him. As he sat drinking moodily, he would recall some of those roystering guest-nights, and fancy how the old set were 'carrying on' just now, until he ground his teeth with rage. The shooting and hunting within reach were both indifferent; and he could not afford to follow up either satisfactorily. Also, if he had had the inclination, he would have lacked the means to mingle with such of the neighbours as would have made him welcome; and a remnant of pride made him shrink from carouses in a tavern or by a farmhouse ingle.

Perhaps it was only natural that his temper, always unamiable, should wax savage in solitude. He generally refrained, in Lena's presence, from violence of word or gesture ; but his sullenness was almost harder to bear ; and, as he sat glowering from under his bent

brows, she could easily guess that he was adding up,
over and over again, the sum of rack and ruin, for
which he held her chiefly accountable.  Sometimes,
when his mood was at the worst, he was tempted
to bid her seek shelter elsewhere; but, though bro-
therly affection had been slain within him, he could
not quite bring himself to turn Lena adrift; and, besides, he was haunted by certain words spoken by
their mother when very near her end.  She, at least,
had never done him wrong; and for her sake Miles
practised forbearance.

But such forbearance as it was!  To any that had
known Lena in the old times, her patience and self-
restraint would have seemed incredible.  She was
never provoked to retort; her great brown eyes—
her sole remnant of beauty now—if sometimes pleading, were never reproachful; and, though she never
got a word of thanks, she did not weary in her efforts
to smooth matters both within and without doors.
On one point only she would have her own way.
Despite his grumbling, she persisted in devoting to
charity what Miles considered an utterly unreasonable proportion of her pittance.  The poor were very
poor in those parts; and, at certain seasons, there
was much distress, albeit little murmuring.  Such
help as Lena could give was really valuable; and
scarcely any weather kept her from carrying food and
raiment where they were most wanted.  These errands
were her sole distraction; perhaps she was selfish in
clinging to it.

Nevertheless, if such an institution as a Sisterhood
had been known there, Lena would not have enrolled
herself therein; for one of its chief duties she could
not have performed.  Howsoever sore the need, she
has never yet ventured to read a prayer to the sick
or dying.  A sense of her own unworthiness may
partly account for this; but, truth to speak, she is
still no devotee.  Despite the sincerity of her repentance, it is tinged with a kind of heathenism; and

it may be doubted whether it has, thus far, brought her nearer to heaven.

A dreary picture—is it not? Yet it must stand so.

As we walk through the great forest, beyond which lies the Silent Land, our path is lined with the flourishing bay-trees that have sprung from evil germs; but, deeper in the thicket, there stand, or lie prone, trunks so withered, warped, and broken, that it is hard to fancy they once burgeoned no less freshly than their fellows.

The lips of Sin are as tempting, her cheek as rosy, her locks as golden, as they were before Paradise was lost. But under her glistening robes may still be discerned the loathly snake-coils; and she has never shaken off the comrade who shared her watch at the gate of Hell.

It may, perhaps, be a refreshing contrast to turn to Templestowe.

No remorse, you may be sure, troubles the complacency of the exemplary dame regnant there. Yet is her triumph not quite complete. The happiness, even of great and good people, is marred sometimes by absurd trifles. Endowed with the universal respect of all Loamshire—why should Marian Atherstone fret over the consciousness, that by one of her neighbours she is heartily despised? One would think that the *châtelaine* of Templestowe might afford to ignore the fact, that even in society Hubert Ashleigh has always contrived to evade touching her hand, and that, beyond the necessary forms of courtesy, he has never addressed to her a word. Besides this, Philip has grown so much more fretful and unreasonable of late, that it can only be accounted for by his failing health; and Marian cannot always repel a disagreeable misgiving that her tenure of dignity may be brief after all. It will be a poor return for all her pains and skill, if she is doomed to subside into early dowagerhood.

However, a sere leaf or two does not much impair

the splendour of such a garland as binds her brows; and her sense of self-approval, at all events, will remain unabated to the end.   And yet, perhaps, not to the very end.   For, I suppose, she will have to appear, like the rest of us, in a certain Court where there will be no pleading of privilege; and it remains to be seen how she will then fare.

That day will witness some strange surprises, no doubt; but on these does it become us to speculate, to whom even the written Apocalypse is an un fathomed mystery?

Yet this much I do believe.

When, amongst those who have sinned open-eyed, Lena is arraigned, there will be sorrow, rather than triumph, on one spirit's face; and, if his voice may not be heard on her behalf, Ralph Atherstone will keep silence, there—as here.

THE END.

PRINTED BY VIRTUE AND CO., CITY ROAD, LONDON.